FINAL EXTINCTION

BY

RICK A. MULLINS

DEDICATION

This sci-fi adventure is dedicated to my sister, Melissa, who continuously crafts wonderful covers from images I give her. Thanks sis! Without you and your additional computer assistance, my sci-fi/fantasy adventures in the multiverse would be nothing more than lonely files on my laptop.

TABLE OF CONTENTS

[1] A dangerous start.

Hermes Alexander stood at the edge of the cliff gazing across the lake's windswept surface, small whitecaps blinking in the morning sun. He'd been away from their family's island refuge many times before today, but always in a protected environment and knowing when he would return. Today was different.

He felt a familiar presence behind him and smiled. "Are you coming little brother, or have you decided to stay home where it's safe?"

"No Tina," he used the shorted version of her name that was the best he could do when he first started talking at nine months. "Just memorizing this morning's sky over the lake. It'll be a while before we see it this way again."

She put her hand on his shoulder. "Only a couple of months, less if we keep our heads."

"I'm all for keeping our heads," he replied with a smile as he turned toward her.

"C'mon Xan, we don't want to make Gar hold the boat too long." She used the shortened version of his best friend's name's that was also all he could say when he first started talking.

Without another word, she turned and walked away, her long legs eating up the ground. Being five centimeters taller at a hundred eighty-eight, it only took him a few steps to catch her.

"I thought he wasn't going," he said when he drew even and measured his steps to her pace.

She gave a knowing smile. "He wasn't

because he was kind of hot for that new teacher, then he found out she's married and has two kids. *Then* he found out she's over forty and he can't drink legally for another few days. He spent all last night while *we* were getting a proper night's sleep packing and closing his affairs."

"Well, he and I have gone without sleep one night enough times to know what to expect. You going to leave him off guard duty the first night?"

She hesitated a moment and he gave her a sideways look.

"About that." She didn't have to go any further as they came around the forest crowding the edge of the cliff and could see their boat tied up.

Standing at the end of the dock and without much success, Hagar was trying to get his two hellhound puppies in the boat. They were the last survivors of a mixed-gene litter that was newly established and proven. The last two had learned the dangers that lurked in water by watching their two packmates be consumed. The breed was smart enough the two pups also knew boats traveled over that same dangerous water.

Xan was surprised he'd gotten them close to the shore since the last one of their packmates had been lost on this same pier.

"Ah, Hermes and Athena! Here you are!" the giant's voice boomed, then he leaned down from his nearly three-meter height and spoke at a reduced, but still loud volume. "Tina my friend, could you see if you can get Fred and Ginger on the boat, please. They're a little nervous."

Tina smiled and patted her large friend on

the forearm. "Sure, Gar. Hey there you two, come over here."

The pups, each nearly their full hundred-fifty plus kilo adult weight at eleven months, smothered Tina in slobbery kisses as she *calmed* them. In seconds, they were walking at her side over the gangplank that led to the deck of the ferry.

"Kind of nervous around water what with losing two packmates to monsters, but they'll make good camp guards."

Xan looked at the two hellhound pups, and they still were gangly pups at eleven months. Gene-hacked and bred through several generations, they would be the perfect companion to the new breed of giants.

"Your grandfather's people brought your bags and I loaded them while Tina was reminding you what time we were supposed to leave."

Xan nodded. They had packed everything the night before so they could leave shortly after sunrise when the bigger lake mosa and kraken were less active.

As soon as Xan and Gar stepped aboard the crew lifted the gangplank and the dock crew loosened lines and played them out as the captain engaged the electric jets. In moments, they were away from Kelley's Island on their grand adventure.

"What's up with them?" Xan asked his sister after Gar went inside the cabin where Fred and Ginger were hiding from lake monsters.

She glanced at two of their old friends also making the trip to the mainland with them, a pair of giants, like Gar, as much family as any they knew.

"They're on a mission to the east but I couldn't get what or where out of them."

"Ha! Neither of us ever could get through their mind blocks. Did you check our gear?"

"Yes. Each of us has an extra bag, a big one, which means we'll need pack beasts instead of walking like we intended," she said with a half shrug. "You want to get pack runners to carry the bags or ride?"

"Pack runners need a firm hand on a leash more often than not," he replied. "If we have to hang onto them anyway, may as well ride."

She nodded once and the subject was decided.

They were silent the rest of the trip across the lake to the Huron village docks. Their ferry slowed as it came to the stone and steel safety barrier that allowed the village access to the shoreline and lake waters without fear of being eaten. Permanent spotters watched for genetically made monsters whenever the gates were opened for boat traffic.

Alarms and horns sounded between the shore and ferry, and the gate was opened just in time for them to slip through, then closed before any of the larger carnivores could dart within the protected waters. Crew onboard walked the rails looking downward to see if anything tried to sneak through beneath their hull. Each wielded a clear shield to protect themselves from the belligerent mega archer fish that fed on the fist-sized bugs inhabiting the shoreline.

After taking its turn passing through the

single gate the ferry made its way through the congested port to its dock. The two giants followed when they made their way to the stables but declined to help them carry the extra bags.

Gar did that with minimal grumbling while Tina kept the pups from reveling in being away from the water and running off to sniff everything in sight. When they finally got to the stables, they found their grandfather had already arranged for mounts.

"Well, at least he didn't try to make his own," Xan grumbled. "These are about the best for wilderness camping and travel. But I'm not sure if even one of these would make a good mount for Gar."

"Oh *please*," the giant sneered. "I can run at twenty kay-pee-aitch five hours straight, rest an hour and do it again before bedtime. That's what I do when I leave the island every couple of weeks, meet up with some friends and run a day or two to someplace new, check it out, then run back home. Well, their home here in Huron. I usually spend another night here because nobody's stupid enough to take a small boat out on the lake at night."

His face fell. "That's why I lost two pups before Tina and you started helping me with training." As usual his face lit up again with his new thought. "Good thing is I still have a breeding pair and they *really* do what I say now because their packmates were lost doing something I told them not to do."

"But to get back to riding that tiny little thing," he pointed at the burly, genetically altered warhorse, "ain't happening. It can carry my gear, but it better keep up with me."

Xan smiled. He and his sister could easily keep up with their friend on any daylong run, but Tina and he had talked about making this more of a leisurely jog. The three altered horses could easily carry the two of them and their extra gear and run almost as fast and far while Gar ran.

Xan examined the animals while his sister spoke with the stablemaster about whatever she always argued about when bartering. He smiled, knowing it wouldn't take much effort to *influence* the man to smooth over whatever financial problem there was, but neither of them would actually *act* on their abilities to do so.

The horses were still horses, genetically, but like he and his sister, there had been several modifications to make them more capable of functioning in the new world.

The specimen Xan examined was a little larger than a riding horse of the beginning of the millennium but had a narrower chest. Two ribs had been added and the barrel narrowed to make a thinner ride for human legs to compensate for the larger body. The longer, thinner lungs gave the new horse increased endurance while providing a more comfortable saddle width. The heavier spine more than carried the weight of a rider and supplies and would carry Gar just as easily as Xan. The beasts were tall enough that even a giant's feet wouldn't drag the ground.

The legs were also more muscular and the single hoof was altered to form three splayed toes that gave support in sand or shallow water while giving the horse better defenses against the creatures that now populated the wilds.

Thick hair around the legs and lower regions helped protect the sturdy beasts from the unwanted attentions of smaller carnivores. A scattering of bony plates on the rump and neck added to the huge teeth the altered species needed for defense and to crop small bushes and leafy branches as well as grass.

Xan was sure he and his sister could instill sufficient training habits in the next couple of days to make them perfect for their needs. Without hesitation, he began moving their gear around to pack the three horses.

He knew Gar would run instead of ride and put more weight on the third horse so all three carried the same amount. The two giants watched silently as they packed their gear and prepared to leave, waiting till they led the horses out of the stables before stepping forward.

"Well hello, Uncle Frick, Aunt Frack, no, thanks for the offer, but we'll load everything ourselves."

"Heh-heh, you would have anyway young Xan, and whined the entire time about some imagined failure on our part," Frick said. "It was best for all to simply allow you unencumbered incompetence on our part."

Xan one-eyed one of the few people in the world he truly trusted. "I can never be sure if you're serious or not."

Frick, Frederick to anyone other than the

siblings, smiled. "That is as it should be, young Xan, especially with your abilities."

Frack, Francine to any who didn't want a cracked skull, approached and held out two packages. "We couldn't let you go without gifts. There is also something from your grandfather in there as well."

"Be safe and we will see you soon," Frick said, then the two giants retrieved the cart they had brought on the ferry and headed toward the east gate.

"Well, I guess that means we're on our own, hunh sis?"

She snorted and one-eyed her gift their grampa had *apparently* left something in. "What is he up to now?"

"What do you mean, now?" Xan chuckled. "Don't you mean *this time*?"

She shrugged her agreement. "What have you got?"

"Really nice vestpack with a hydration vine and lots of pockets." He looked in one and sighed. "They're full of packets of that stuff he made us with, the *nanocellus sapien immortallus* he gave mom when we were in the oven."

He dug into the back of the vestpack. "Looks like two full packs in each of four pockets around the hydration vine. There are a few dozen nanite vials in the kidney belt's medpack, too, but only the eight prenatal packets."

He looked her in the eye. "Looks like we get to offer the relatives a chance to have kids like us. If they want."

"If *we* want," she insisted. "There are some Family I wouldn't want to have what we have. They'd corrupt it."

"Are you sure?" he wondered aloud. "The recipients might see what their parents are and want to be the opposite."

"That works both ways," his sister reminded him. "Look at our parents, and our grandfather. Both of our parents died…"

"Supposedly," he interjected.

"Okay, both of our parents *supposedly* died. No bodies were ever recovered or identified from remains but that was over ten years ago and neither of them have been heard from since."

He glared at her for her lack of faith but let it go as she continued, "It looks like grampa is ready to enlarge our Elvish family tree. Each of us has the means to start eight separate lines of those like us."

He didn't mention the fact the two of them were looked at as freaks by the majority of humanity. Their oddly long and tufted ears were bad enough, but their overlarge lavender eyes and empathic abilities instilled fear in a growing number of people.

"Do we need more like us?"

"If there were more like us, we wouldn't be so different," she reminded him yet again, then added what they both suspected. "And you know we're not the only ones. People somewhat like us were one of the favorites of the gene cosmetics at the beginning of the Fall. Lots of Elves running around the world."

"Besides us, there's no shortage of giants, dwarves, were-folk, and even mer-folk, so we're not the only ones with genetic modifications. And that doesn't include all the treatments that were standard for several years in several states and all government medical facilities."

"I'd bet a five-gram gold coin we're not the only ones with this newest batch." She gestured toward the pockets holding the NSI packets. "I bet Frick and Frack have more in that cart they went off with, just like the ones we carry." She lifted her vest pack as she ranted.

Xan shrugged his agreement. "He's been doing that since before we were born. You want to help him make more freaks like us? I wouldn't mind so much if he'd have done it when he made us."

She had no response to that and he made himself busy checking his chosen horse while he got himself back together. "Sorry sis. I should be over that."

They were both quiet for several minutes as they busied themselves with their horses. Gar was oblivious to their quandary as he checked the supplies a third time.

Fred and Ginger frolicked around them and the horses as they prepared to leave, having the best day of their lives since the day before.

It was almost an hour after midday before they set out for the southern gate along with a small convoy of supply trucks going the same direction. Their journey started with sharing the security of those heavy trucks plus a half-dozen other riders like themselves and a pair of sauro carrying wicker cabins and cargo bags.

Similar in body style to what bones of sauropods looked, most sauro designs were actually made from a combination of elephant, camel, alpaca, and horse DNA. There was considerable tinkering and the addition of some of the newly created sequences required to get the final design and temperament right for a multipurpose mount.

With their muscular bodies, hair and bone armor, as well as larger hooves and teeth, they were naturally, or *unnaturally* protected from the dangers of a world where genetic experimentation had produced known horrors from past epochs and newly imagined monsters.

Like their horses, the many variations of sauro and cera were a common means of transport outside the walls of a reduced civilization.

Xan smiled inwardly as a passing thought crossed his mind. Before the fall of the world it was terrorism, plague, and zombies that were forecast as the source of Armageddon. Nobody expected it to be the genetic equivalent of an arms race. History had shown how it happened, but history isn't written by those in the process of living it, not till the final chapters anyway.

There were those who tried to regulate genetic research after CRISPR opened the field and new techniques improved on that first major breakthrough, but they were hampered by political realities.

Sure, laws were passed, but most people didn't understand the truth to the tired old joke that *'we have to pass this law so we can see what's in it'*. Most people didn't understand that was how *all* laws worked. First a law is passed, then it goes to a rules committee to make the individual *rules* a new law worked under.

As was the case with every other law, when the rules committees met for laws passed to regulate genetic research, it was the gene corporations who sent most of the lobbyists to meet with the committee. Consequently, it was the people most likely to benefit from a porous law who made the rules under which they would operate.

Those same corporations began creating whatever creature or plant their customers paid for, and it didn't take long for dangerous fauna and flora to escape controlled conditions, or to be released on purpose. The ultimate invasive species because they were *designed* to be, they took over everywhere they found themselves.

Behind them, the gate, like that of every city, village, or farm compound in the world now, closed to protect the huddling masses from the monsters created to stimulate an increasingly bored population.

Xan had been to several cities along the lake coast in his eighteen years, and out west by air, but only outside in an armed and armored truck like the ones in their convoy. As the gate closed behind them, he felt exposed and put a hand to the carbine that rode within easy reach in the saddle holster in front of him and the shotgun on the other side.

He may not have been exposed like this before but he knew what kind of monsters inhabited the lands he and his sister and best friend were going to travel through.

He looked at his sister as they rode and could tell through their link she was just as nervous.

"You don't have to worry till after the Burbs," a voice called out and Xan looked at the truck beside him where a grizzled and bearded face protruded above a gun turret on the roof. "Anything that came into that," he waved at the dozens of individual towers that lined the road leading to the south gate, "would have already been killed and the carcass cleaned this late in the day."

"I'd say you can mostly relax till nightfall," the man said as he grinned a toothy smile. "Of course, that don't mean you can sleep in the saddle."

Xan smiled in response as his *gift* told him the man was being friendly. "If you see me doze off just throw something at me."

"A pastry would work best," Tina joined in and the burly man laughed.

"If I had a pastry it would already be gone. You kids and that giant I saw with those two pups traveling far?"

"Across the Ohio to visit relatives we've only met a couple times outside a video screen," he replied since *that* part of their journey wasn't secret.

"Long way through some nasty country with worse on the other side of the river."

"Yeah," he agreed. "We're prepared and know where we can get inside at night."

"Hah! End of the world and still have cell phones and hotel reserva..." his eyes grew wide and he spun his guns around. "Raptors! Raptors on the right!"

[2] Raptors behind and ahead.

Xan wasn't the most experienced in life outside the protections of a city wall or an island, but he had spent the majority of his eighteen years in competitions involving dozens of skills. His shotgun was in his hand and the safety off as soon as he felt the emotional reaction of the man in the truck.

Another of the *gifts* his grandfather had given him in the womb told him the attacker was there before he turned and training allowed him to dodge and shoot at the same time. Throwing himself backwards in the saddle he fired a round upward as the raptor sailed over him in its missed attack.

He felt the raptor's mind for just a second before the shot took its head off and didn't waste time for a follow-up as his horse spun to face the next danger. Gunfire sounded all around as the convoy dealt with the unexpected so close to the main gate and still among the stone and steel towers that had replaced the stick homes of a half century earlier.

His aim was automatic as he homed in on the closest raptor minds and fired without conscious thought as they focused on him. The heavy shotgun rounds knocked raptors down or stopped them in mid jump as he sprayed death on any that came within his mental *sight*.

To the side he saw Gar swinging the small tree he called a staff, his two hellhound pups ripping the throats out of the raptors he knocked down while guarding his flanks.

He moved Xanthos next to Tina's Thoth as they put the truck at their back. Their horses' training held and they were able to present a less tempting target long enough for Xan to assess the situation better.

Off to their left a scream drew their attention as a raptor succeeded in dragging a rider from his horse. Xan put a round through the back of the raptor's skull just before it ripped the man's throat out, throwing the creature away from him.

Another raptor got between Xanthos and the truck and he shot it knowing the truck's armor would stop any pellets that missed. Another raptor got through but Tina's Thoth kicked it so hard it took a couple of tries to shake the body loose from a three-toed hoof and a couple more stomps to stop the raptor's screaming.

Turning at a scream, Xan saw another of their attackers with its head lunging through the window of the truck behind the one they were backed against. He turned Xanthos that way and pumped his last round into the raptor's neck, severing the head from the body.

As fast as it started, the attack was over and the last of the raptors were fleeing as he switched the empty shotgun for his carbine. A few last shots took down a couple more before they were gone, then another scream drew his attention back to the truck with the raptor's head in the window.

Xanthos' training held in a stressful situation a second time in moments and Xan was able to not be mistaken for another enemy when he leapt from the saddle and dragged the horse the few steps to the truck's door.

He started to stick his head up to look inside when his gift surged and he ducked just as a shotgun went off through the window, the breeze of the pellets as they wafted by his cheek showing how close they'd come. "Hey! Hey! It's over, I'm on your side!"

A moan sounded then a frantic voice yelled. "Help! Help! It bit him!" Xan tried the door but it was locked. "Unlock the door! I have medical training."

"I can't reach it."

"I'm going to put my hand through the window," he yelled. "Don't shoot me."

Hoping it wouldn't be shot off, he waved a hand then followed it by quickly raising up and looking inside. An older woman sat behind the wheel with a shotgun in one hand and trying to push a younger man off her where he had recoiled out of his seat from the raptor's attack.

The raptor's jaws were locked around the moaning man's right arm and there was a lot of blood.

He reached through the window and unlocked the door. He was quickly half inside the truck and prying the raptor's jaws open with his long knife and throwing the head aside. He cut what was left of the sleeve away, reached to his side and disconnected the kidney belt med kit and pulled it around in front of him.

With years of experience in putting together the kits he quickly found the vial he needed. Ignoring the man's increased agitation as his moans grew and he tried to pull away from the rough handling, Xan popped a vial and poured the contents over the worst wound.

The medical nanites soaked into the wound and the pumping blood stopped as he dug out another vial. Taking more time now the first nanites were working their tech magic, he squirted a portion into each of the smaller bites.

He was still applying medical nanites when someone ran up behind him and yanked the door wider. Xan had felt the man's emotions as he approached and spoke quickly, "He's okay, he's okay. I got to him in time."

"What? What?" The man they'd been joking with only minutes ago looked frantic for a moment when he saw the raptor's head and the amount of blood. "Oh god, my boy."

Xan turned and used his gift to project calm. "There's a lot of damage but I got to him in time with medical nanites. He won't lose the arm and in a couple of weeks all he'll have will be a few scars."

"Medical nanites. I ... we can't..."

Xan put a calming hand on the man's arm and lied, "I wasn't watching where I should have and your warning saved my life. All I got to save was an arm, so I still owe you."

The burly man smiled through his beard as the emotions of the situation calmed. "How about we just call it even." He held out his hand. "Thanks for saving my son's arm."

Xan shook the man's hand then moved out of the way. "He still needs to have the arm looked at and a better job of cleaning and closing it up to limit scarring. I'll give you another nanite vial for the follow-up treatment, but he should be okay by the time he wakes up."

"He didn't put the window up when he was reloading," the woman in the driver's seat said.

"Yeah, been trying to get him to do that for years, mom," the bearded man said then looked around. "There's no reason that many raptors should have gotten so close to the gate without alarms going off. Something's wrong here."

They turned as Tina rode up to join them and pointed. "They were inside that compound there. Looks like they got in through a weak spot in the wall late in the night and caught the family by surprise. If they hadn't had to go through the same single hole to come back out at us a little at a time instead of all at once, we'd have been in trouble."

"There were two panic rooms, with two adult survivors in the basement, and two adults and three children in the top floor, but no access to communications. Five confirmed dead."

"No backup comm in their panic rooms," the bearded man shook his head disgustedly. "*Stupid*!"

"How about ours?" Xan asked.

She pursed her lips. "One dead horse and rider, and a couple other wounds like this one."

The convoy had a schedule to keep and were on their way again before the authorities from inside the city walls came out to investigate. The brother of the man killed stayed behind and would return to the city after recovering what was left of his kin. Delayed by the ambush and battle they had to move faster to get to the first village on their route.

"Day one and only forty klicks," Gar grumbled as he plodded along beside his packhorse. "Could run back to Huron, sleep at a friend's house, and be back here before you leave."

Xan smiled as they passed through Norwalk's northern gate. "But, my impatient friend, this way we get to spend a night in a new town every night and meet actual *people*. And instead of roughing it we also get a shower and two hot meals on either side of a soft bed inside monster-proof walls."

"Monster-proof walls didn't help those people back there," the big man jerked a finger behind them.

"Different situation," he replied when the caravan began to splinter as each group went their own way. "We're in a good place one block from downtown. Family history says we used to stop there every time we came back from Aunt Sue's. Well, not *we*, that was before Tina and I were born, before every home had to be monster proofed."

They rode on through town, shedding delivery trucks and riders on the way till it was just the three of them and the heavily armed and armored Postal truck.

"Here we are," Xan said moments after the Postal truck swerved to the side to deliver its load of mail to the Post Office before continuing its route.

They dismounted and walked their horses into the stables next to a stone tower.

"I hear it used to be three stories before the walls went up," Xan told his large friend as they found the four stalls they had reserved together.

"I'll be fine here," Gar insisted as he threw his bedroll down on the fresh straw. "I'll be able to watch the horses and nobody allows hellhounds in their rooms."

The puppies in question were busy sniffing every centimeter of their stall, those of the three horses they now considered part of their pack, and anywhere else they could get a nose into despite the nervousness of the stable's other tenants.

"Besides, the beds are always too short and flimsy. Let me get Fred and Ginger settled, change out of road clothes, and I'll meet you two wherever you tell me we're eating."

"Heh, okay my friend." Xan turned to point over the high wall. "See the top of the building there on the other side of the street? Restaurant *and* bar so we don't have to go far. It's close enough we won't get lost and Tina and I are in that hotel on the other corner."

Xan and Tina removed saddles, wiped down their horses while they munched on fresh feed, then grabbed their personal saddlebags and left their giant friend to find their reserved rooms.

The unexpected raptor ambush had delayed them, but there were no other confrontations where they usually happened so they were not as late as they thought they would be. With separate rooms, they were able to take showers, change into clean clothes, and meet Gar in a little more than a half hour.

"Oh wow," the big man whispered loudly when they entered the building together.

They were shown to a large table with several large pillows thrown down to replace the chair at Gar's position. The adjustment wasn't something those with giant friends weren't used to. Being too big for normal tables and chairs, giants simply sat cross-legged on a thick pad next to tables to be at the same level as their smaller tablemates. The three were ushered to a table and within moments their orders taken and first drinks served.

"Pups are good?" Xan wondered after his first drink of ale.

"Oh yes," Gar replied, then plopped an entire cored apple into his mouth, chewed thrice and swallowed before taking his first drink.

"After you left the night shift guard came by and sat with them while I cleaned up. By the time I was ready to join you they'd been fed and watered and were sleeping where they can watch our horses. They are content."

"These are good," he popped another whole apple in his mouth then drained his pint mug and gave it a skeptical look. "Good finger food, tiny mugs."

Tina ran her finger alongside her nose and smiled. He was still a day away from his eighteenth birthday, the youngest of the three of them, and it would not do to draw the wrong sort of attention.

Gar got the message and didn't complain when the curvy waitress brought him another pint mug instead of a giant-sized pitcher-mug.

"Oh look, they have cera-steaks and sauro-burgers," Tina exclaimed as they looked over the menu.

"I want a dozen dino-wings in dante sauce," Gar declared as he scanned the menu. "A double order of tater wedges, a dozen large garlic bread sticks with salsa, and another pint of ale, please."

He smiled widely, took a tiny sip of the ale she'd just brought him, then winked at her.

At nearly three times his age she simply snorted, wrote on her pad, and looked at Tina. "And you miss?"

They quickly ordered and began to enjoy the evening, eating more than enough of dishes they couldn't normally get on their island home to make up for their lack, and drinking more than they were used to. Eventually they left the comfort of the restaurant bar and began to roam Main Street.

Eventually they found themselves by a vendor's cart that provided several different kinds of meat and fresh vegetable kabobs seasoned with herbs genetically designed to absorb alcohol. They were just beginning to come out of the most enjoyable effects of their revelry when the first alarm sounded.

"Okay folks, that's the signal for anybody with any sense to get inside strong walls," the vendor said as he started to close up his cart.

"Wait, just like that?" Gar complained. He drained his mug and handed it to the vendor, then came alert when the alarm changed. "Is that something to be worried about?"

"Not if you hurry and don't have far to go to safety," the vendor replied as he ran while his cart was still unsecured.

"Which way?" Gar asked, despite already knowing.

"We're on the furthest end of West Main Street," Xan said what they all knew. "Six blocks east and one south and we're home."

They started to move as he spoke and hadn't gone two blocks when they caught up with the vendor. His cart had caught in a slot in a drain grate around one of the street trees. They pulled it free in seconds but the alarm changed again and the vendor stopped trying to free his cart and pulled out a very large, double-barreled staff-like weapon.

Before Xan or the others could ask what the vendor was thinking, he pressed some buttons and an arc of controlled lightning played between the two points at the end.

"Raptors have been getting brave and inventive lately," the vendor said as he looked for danger. "I sure hope you people didn't let a little partying keep you from carrying some sort of defense."

Gar didn't hesitate to reach over his shoulder and grab one of the electric batons strapped to his back while Xan reached into his vest holster for his backup pistol. Tina pulled her own pistol, both of them wishing they had more than what their vest packs contained to face whatever it was the alarms warned of. Both decided in the future they wouldn't be as complacent inside city walls as they'd been this time.

"So, what's up?" Gar asked as they continued to move in the direction the vendor had been going.

"That's the alarm for the wall being breached by raptors. They've been breeding faster than usual lately and breaking into all kinds of places not normally at risk." The vendor dragged his cart a few steps, stopped and waved his double-pronged lightning rods around as he inspected nearby shadows before dragging his cart another few steps.

"Last I heard there was a new strain that thinks tactically. Gene hackers just can't stop tinkering. Frackers are gonna extinct us yet!"

Xan smiled at the young man's use of the eco-curse as they moved as quickly as possible. He and his friends could easily abandon the vendor and his cart and be back inside secure walls in minutes, but that would leave the vendor to whatever had caused full alarms to be sounded within the town's walls.

As they fast-walked the streets toward wherever the vendor was going, weapons ready and senses probing the darkness, they could hear the scrabbling of clawed feet running toward them.

"Frack!" the vendor exclaimed. "It sounds like the wall fell and there's a million of them. Here we are, quick, everybody inside."

The vendor opened a rollup door in the wall between two buildings and they pushed the cart inside then squeezed in around it to the alley behind as the vendor rolled the door closed behind them.

"That door won't last long if they want

through," the man said as he slung his stunner over his shoulder then spritzed chlorine through the visor/gun port, then more at their feet. "Best I can do, you three run ahead, all the way to the end, let's go."

He grabbed the handles to his cart, and followed them the length of the alley, passing doors on both sides till it dead-ended at a ladder to the roof of the next building. "Up, up, all the way to the top, hurry."

The vendor quickly attached two hanging cables to the roof of his cart when they heard a loud scrabbling at the door on the other end of the alley. "Go, go, quickly now."

They didn't need further encouragement as they holstered their pistols and baton. Tina led her brother, then Gar physically grabbed the vendor and lifted him up the first couple meters before going last. They climbed the five-story wall quickly, Gar needing a little help over the edge when the top rung threatened to come loose.

"Been meaning to fix that but I'm less than half your weight so it never wiggled that much before," the vendor said as they gathered around him. "Here, help me with this."

He moved a heavy framework connected to the cables the vendor had hooked to the roof of his cart, to the edge of the building. "Lock that wheel, would you? Just push, yes, that's it."

After locking the wheel, Xan leaned over to see the cables tighten and begin lifting the cart when the man engaged an electric motor. He looked at the other end of the dark alley and noticed the door and wall still intact before he moved away from the edge.

"It'll take a few minutes and stop automatically when it gets to the top," the vendor explained, then pointed toward a bench seat nearby. "I switch between the rickshaw seat and the food cart. But where are my manners? My name is Rick, Rick Shaw... no *really*."

"And this is my wife, Amanda," he said as a tall young woman approached. "We just found out today we're pregnant."

As the winch slowly pulled the cart up, they made introductions all around.

"We have the entire roof of this building to ourselves," Amanda explained. "I tend the garden and Rick hauls people around during the day and serves hot food in the evening."

"Amanda does computer stuff for the tenants of the rest of our building and I do handyman stuff for our rooftop rent," Rick explained. "Ah, here we go, unlock that wheel please and help me pull it in."

Xan did so and began to pull when there was a screech and a raptor leapt from where it had been hanging onto the front of the cart.

[3] Bridge confrontation.

The raptor leapt at Amanda but Gar was close enough he could reach across and punch it in the side of the head. It went down but recovered quickly.

Xan and Tina both drew their pistols but they were too close to everybody else to fire safely. They didn't have a chance to act as Rick snatched up the twin barreled weapon he'd displayed earlier, and stabbed the gene hacked carny.

The raptor screamed for a second then went limp but Rick kept the end against it and the trigger depressed. "Come into my home and threaten mine," he growled.

He kept the stunner against the raptor till its bowels released and its lungs deflated. He quickly retrieved an ax and chopped the raptor's head off in a single swing. "There! Now I'm sure you're not faking it."

Almost as one they all moved to the edge of the building and looked down the five stories to the alley.

Even without his heightened night vision Xan could see three more raptors milling around trying each of the ground floor doors. It only took a few seconds for them to notice the watchers.

"Don't worry about those doors," Rick said. "They were all dino-proofed before we put up the wall at the end of the alley. I'm more concerned with how they got in. The door and wall above it both look intact."

"Could they have jumped?" Gar wondered. "I know they can leap six or seven meters, but straight up?"

"No, they're not jumping, Gar," Xan said as they watched two raptors form a base for a third to climb up to investigate a small window.

A gunshot from inside the second story window sent the raptor to the ground. Seconds later the remaining two ran to the end of the alley and began tearing at the more exposed framework. Before they could break through, people leaned out from windows in the buildings on either side of the alley and seconds later all the raptors were dead.

"Well, looks like Amanda and I get a whole raptor to ourselves," Rick said, then gave Gar a calculating look. "Unless the big fella here wants to take a third of a share for giving me a chance to stick him with my stunner."

"Nah, you can have the whole thing, 'cept maybe all the teeth I loosened and few feathers."

"Done!" Rick exclaimed and held out a hand.

Gar engulfed it in his massive paw, they shook and sealed the deal.

"The wall around the stables isn't much higher than the one at the end of the alley," Xan observed. "How do we get there quickest?"

"Across the roofs, then the ladder down from the last building."

"How do we get across?" Gar was looking anxious. "My pups are there. They need me."

"All the rooftops are connected," Rick explained as he led them to the next one, a four-story building topped by another green garden. "Go across here and down to Main Street. The Library is on one corner and there's a little park on the other corner."

Rick escorted them across, quickly introducing them to other rooftop residents as they went. "That's the Library and the park across the corner. You can climb back to the roofs and cross to the Smith Stables or go around the back side at ground level behind Main Street and hope the raptors don't see you. With all the alarms going off I don't expect you to have any trouble getting their attention to open the back gate."

"What do you think?" Xan asked his sister as Gar hovered over both of them worrying about his puppies.

"If we take the roofs, we have to deal with each rooftop resident," Tina observed. "But if we just run at ground level around the back a couple blocks, we'll be at the stable doors."

Rick shrugged his acceptance of their decision. "Just make sure you signal the stable snipers so they don't shoot you. This is something we haven't had to deal with too often and some people might be trigger nervous."

"Thanks," Xan said, then caught the eyes of his sister and best friend. "You ready to run at ground level?"

"We can be there before we could climb the next building." Gar contributed. "I vote a ground level run."

"Sounds good to me. Thank you, my friend," he shook Rick's hand. "We have to leave now, but my sister and I have a proposition to present to you tomorrow, before we leave Norwalk."

With that they hurried down the ladder to street level, Gar glad he didn't damage any of the ladder rungs embedded in the side of the building.

There were no raptors in sight when they reached the ground and drew weapons. They hurried across the street, through the small park, and between the genetically altered maple trees that gave the town its totem name.

Moving swiftly, they were at the west gate of the stables in moments without encountering any living raptors. Gar poked one dead raptor with the end of a baton as they waited patiently for the guards to open the door. Almost immediately Gar was covered in slobbery kisses from Fred and Ginger

"Our snipers were out as soon as the alarm for the wall breach sounded," the elder Smith informed them as soon as they were inside.

Xan and Tina took the report as Gar was busy greeting his puppies.

"The horses…" Xan started.

"Are fine," the stablemaster cut him off. "We've practiced for these types of drills for years despite the city telling us it wasn't needed. You won't see anything but dead raptors near our walls. We've noticed they learn quickly, so the rest seemed to have decided to stay away from our immediate area. They're still out there, just not near us."

His smile was wide. "When this is all over,

we'll go out and claim our trophies."

Gar was so happy to see his pups safe, he was oblivious to their conversation as the stablemaster continued. "Your friend's pups alerted us to that group sneaking up from the dark side of our wall while several more made obvious mock attacks on the lit side. Before you leave tomorrow, we'll give you a few teeth and a claw or two for that help."

The alarm changed again, then the bell on the Courthouse tower sounded three times. "That's the signal the breach has been sealed but there are still raptors inside the wall. Well, I'm assuming you've had enough excitement for one night and will return to your rooms?"

"Yes, it's late and we have a long ride tomorrow," Xan said, taking the stablemaster's hint.

"This way please to the door closest to the hotel's back entrance."

Xan and Tina said good night to Gar and the pups, then waited for the sentry to give the all clear to exit the stables and walk across the street to the hotel. The gunfire that occasionally sounded didn't disturb their sleep.

The next morning, they were saddling the horses after a big breakfast while Gar recounted his night. "Pups woke me up once when an armored police van chased a half-dozen raptors down the street. That was late enough I just stayed up and had breakfast with the stable hands and helped them do their morning chores."

"I found out there've been rumors of a local gene hacker group trying to mix up a smarter raptor.

Rumor is they claim that once the raptors are sentient, they'll mellow out and recognize humans as people instead of food. The local authorities couldn't confirm it was anything more than a rumor to shut them down. The stablemaster says this breach and the reports of the pack we encountered up by Huron and a couple other places in just two days pretty much confirm the rumor."

"Any reports of more attacks south of here?" Xan asked as he cinched the last strap.

"No, the two we know about and two really big incursions east of here almost to Cleveland. The sheriff thinks that's where the hackers are based and the two groups we encountered are splinters from the main pack looking for their own territory."

"Okay, everybody ready?" Xan asked.

"I thought you were going to talk to the Shaws," Gar reminded them.

"Already did. Treated them to breakfast and it cost less than feeding you."

Gar ignored the dig but could only wait a moment before his curiosity got the better of him. "So? Anything you'd like to share with your best friend."

Xan smiled as he mounted Xanthos. "They accepted two packs of the prenatal NSI vials. One for the baby they just found out about and another for the next."

"They're good with having their kids be freaks like us?"

Tina snorted from atop Thoth as Xan replied. "Another couple of generations and us freaks will outnumber purebloods. They said they wanted their kids to have the best chance of living through the rest of the end of the world but couldn't afford the price and didn't want to be some unknown gene hacker's test subject. Grampa is well known and normally commands a price only governments can afford so they jumped on the free offer."

The three of them and their animals were soon on the main road out of town and through the south gate, joining a stream of people coming and going. Like all towns and cities, the size enclosed depended on the willingness of the population to fund and defend their outer wall.

Some had a compact footprint for the main town while others went bigger, ringing an area that was sometimes five or six kilometers or more in diameter. No matter the size of the central village or city, there were dozens of smaller compounds ranging in size from single family towers, to castles with interior courts, to individual gated communities that were almost self-contained villages in their own right.

They joined the traffic line and kept a steady pace as carts and riders and armored trucks exited or merged onto the main road. By midday traffic had thinned to the point there was only a single sauro with a wicker cabin, a pair of cera towing wagons, and four heavy cargo trucks.

They knew they were away from home when mostly clear pavement was replaced by marked roads covered in an accumulated layer of dirt and grass. They made their next camp at a truck stop east of Mansfield where the grassway that used to be Rt30 crossed the one at the old I-71.

"I hear the government's thinking about repairing the Eisenhower Interstate system," Gar said as they sat at the back of the large restaurant lounge inside the truck stop.

"I think by now it would be re*build*, not repair," Xan said before taking a drink of his ale.

"What are they going to do about all the grazers that have claimed the medians and borders?" Tina wondered.

"Nobody knows. From what the stablehands back in Norwalk told me, it hasn't gone much further than politicians making promises everybody knows they can't keep. Thin out the wild dino herds, reconnect the towns and cities after cleaning up the grassways, and move back to heavy vehicles and faster speeds on the repaved highways."

"Air and water are cleaner and most people have already adjusted to the slower pace using gene altered livestock," Xan said, gesturing toward a line of sauro and cera, and something that somewhat resembled a cross between a hump-backed bison and a steroid laced brahma bull with a rhino's horn.

The beasts were almost as large as an Indian elephant with a single nose horn at least four meters long. Two of them pulled an armored cargo wagon with a sturdy cabin on the roof.

"Going to have to kill a lot of dinos," Tina said.

They all knew what she meant since the word *dino* now meant almost all gene-altered animals no matter where or when the DNA came from. The only exceptions were the human variants with whatever mythical resemblance they displayed.

When Xan and his sister weren't being called freaks, they were defined as elves while Gar was obviously a giant. There were other variants that groups of humans decided fit their personalities, then condemned their children to live with those body styles. Dwarves, elves, giants, mer-folk, and were-folk like wolfen and pantha were the most popular.

Then there were those in the orbital stations. Adapted to micro-gravity, the newer generation had changed their legs to a second set of arms and toughened their skin and bodies to withstand higher levels of radiation. One group was trying to develop vacuum tolerances, but all of those so far had died.

Their second night was uneventful and the next day they joined most of the occupants of the truck stop in leaving and heading in their various directions.

Xan led the way around the rest area's wall to the grassy on-ramp and by evening they reached the wide bypass around Columbus. The entire surface was covered in grazing wildlife of so many variations it was near impossible to identify them all.

"So, this is the quickest way and best road?" Gar laughed. "You have a different meaning for quick than me, my friend."

"Yes," Xan replied tolerantly as travelers moved on and off the grass highway all around them. "Either that or go straight through Columbus to where I-70 crosses. Not much change in distance, but the traffic will be thicker since it's inside their wall."

"From what I heard one man tell another, this herd circles Columbus all year round. The city has a short hunting season to keep the numbers manageable. Their numbers will thin out in a few klicks at the most and if we go behind the herd the road will also be stripped of any growth a predator could hide behind."

"Of course," he added, "there won't be many predators because the city has gun towers along the wall to keep them away."

"Let's follow behind those trucks," Tina suggested as she nudged her horse forward. "They're wide enough to have to go our speed to find a way through and will take some attention away from Fred and Ginger."

Xan and Gar didn't reply as they followed the rest of the traffic heading east on the old by-pass around Columbus.

Before the time of rampant gene manipulation, the interstate system was well maintained and forbidden to pedestrian or animal traffic. Not long after the first villages began building walls that restriction was enforced less.

Governments found it hard to allocate money to protect citizens and maintain an expansive road infrastructure after another round of tax cuts. Before long wild dinos began grazing the medians and borders of the highways and they brought mud and debris to begin covering the paved surfaces.

It started slow on the least traveled roads, then the outer lanes of wider, multilane highways, but within a decade of the first recorded accidental release of a new dino line, isolated less-traveled pavements were covered with enough dirt to support grass roots. Now, decades later, it was rare to find exposed pavement for any distance on any road outside a community's wall.

They followed the truck through the grazing dinos for almost three kilometers before the herd thinned enough the wheeled vehicle was able to go faster and pull away. Luckily none of the more belligerent species of dino took exception to them or the hellhounds, who were surprisingly restrained in their sniffing range.

They moved quickly and made it all the way around the wall to the I-70 intersection and headed east. They passed several smaller walled compounds alongside the highway and stayed in one that had stable space for their horses with a loft above to sleep.

"We're making pretty good time," Gar commented as they prepared to set out southeast on the I-77 grassway the third morning.

"Thanks, big guy," Xan laughed. "Now you've done it."

"What?"

"Travel tips, there's no better way to frack up our journey than to point out we haven't been fracked yet."

Gar gave him a skeptical look but didn't dispute the Murphyism.

"We should be to the river by nightfall," Tina observed with a smile as she mounted Thoth. "We already knew it was going to get rougher on the other side of the bridge, so maybe Gar's karma hit won't get us till then."

The young giant scowled at her, then took up the reins to their packhorse, Phobos, and led their group with a steady lope that Xanthos and Thoth easily maintained. Fred and Ginger ran twice as far because they had to investigate every interesting scent on their trail, enjoying the best day of their lives since the day before.

They ran through the morning, stopped at noon at one of the old rest areas converted into twin castles flanking the interstate grassway. There was another large herd of grazers at one point that slowed them enough it was nearing sunset when they got to the bridge across the Ohio River.

"See," Gar gloated, "no karma hit. We going to camp on this side or the other?"

Xan looked at the setting sun and the crowds around the bridge. "Looks like a celebration going on. Maybe we should get something on this side and go across tomorrow."

They entered the gate through the wall around the north side of the bridge, then tried three places to stable their horses and all were overfilled to the point customers were complaining about crowded conditions.

"Looks like we cross now," Xan said as he led Xanthos toward the bridge.

They joined the lines heading in that direction and when they got to the bridge itself were greeted by a man in a garishly colored jacket and pants that covered the meter-long stilts he walked on.

"Welcome! Welcome to the twentieth

annual Ohio River Salmon Spawn. Get your license to fish the entire run for only ten silver dollars or five from midnight to midnight. You sir, do you intend to fish?"

"Hadn't considered it, but might," Gar replied as he looked the normal human on stilts in the eyes. "Got to get a place for our horses before we do anything."

The stilt-man nodded, told them to have a nice day, and quickly tried for a different customer.

They were halfway across the bridge when a voice called out angrily. "Hey, look at da freaks! Hey freak, who let ya outta yer cage?"

Xan turned to see several unaltered humans wearing dino leather jackets embossed with the symbol of the Pure Human Society.

Xan ignored them and started to turn when one of the men grabbed a spring tomato from a vendor's cart and threw it at them, hitting Gar in the back with a wet *slap*.

[4] Dog and Pony.

Gar was able to restrain Fred and Ginger but two of the bigots raised large-bore weapons and their vocal leader sneered. "Ya better curb yer filthy animals freak or I'll have me a coupl'a new rugs."

"Is there a problem here?" a stern voice asked and Xan turned to see a pair of uniformed police approaching.

"No problem yet, Depady," the belligerent man sneered. "Freak over there threatened ta sick his freak animals on me and ma friends. We was just about ta teach 'em some manners."

"Seems I saw somebody throw an unpaid for tomato first," the female deputy observed, glaring at the leader of the group.

"Now there ya go again little sister, takin' sides against yer own kind. Pa would be ashamed of ya."

"Probably big brother," the lady deputy replied as the older deputy let her take charge. "But he got himself killed trying to lynch a man for *looking wrong* at a woman you don't even like."

"May not like her cuz she didn't pick tha right god, but at least *she's* a real human, not some freak like he was."

"Don't matter big brother. You were told to behave and you promised you would. Now I'm going to have to ask you to leave Bridgetown."

"What! Me an' ma boys paid fer our fishin' tickets! That's ten silver dollars *each*! Hain't even started fishin' yet an' can't get refunds."

"Should have thought about that before you broke your promise. Now leave, or do I have to arrest you, again."

"Oughta be ashamed o' yerself baby sister, treatin' kin like this fer freaks. Prolly teach dat whelp yer carryin' ta be a freak lover too."

"No Rufus," she said sadly. "What I'll teach *all* my kids will be not to hate like pa tried to teach me. Unlike you, I'm going to break the cycle."

Rufus spat, but not so close as to spit *at* his sister, then glared at Gar. "Ain't done wit' ya freak. Ya cost me an' ma friends fitty dollars. I don't fergit things like dat."

"That's enough Rufus!" the deputy growled through gritted teeth. "One more word and I'll arrest you for creating a nuisance, stealing produce, assault, and inciting a riot... *again*. You and your friends are banned from Bridgetown for the entire River Spawn Festival. Now leave!"

By this time several other law enforcement uniforms had gathered and Rufus saw that his group was outnumbered. "Fine! Let's go boys." He glared at the three friends again but knew better than to push his luck by saying anything more.

Xan was glad when the rowdy bigots went toward the Ohio side of the bridge instead of the same direction they were traveling.

"Sorry about that folks," the young woman said. "My pa was an angry man who didn't know who to blame, so he took it out on those changed by new science because it was easy. I'm doing my best to break the cycle, but it's a hard swim against a strong current. I'm always fighting to keep Rufus from poisoning his own kids but arresting him once or twice a month isn't helping any."

"But you folks don't need to hear my sob story," she said with a smile. "It's late and you need to get your horses stabled for the night and relax after a day on the road."

"Here, let me make a call." She pulled out her phone as several officers escorted Rufus and his friends off the north side of the bridge. "Okay, there's enough room at the Dog and Pony. It's a hotel and tavern with a good kitchen and stables in the back. It's outside the Bridgetown wall, but they have a wall of their own and cheaper prices. Do you want me to make a reservation?"

Xan looked at his friends, then smiled at the deputy. "Yes, please."

"Okay," she said into her phone, "that's three people, one of them a big guy, with three big horses and two hellhounds. Okay, thanks." She put her phone in a pocket and smiled. "They confirmed the reservations. I've been there and they have giant sized beds, so that's covered, too."

"Thank you so much," Tina said as she shook the deputy's hand.

"Don't mention it. I live nearby and will probably stop by for a drink or three after I get off duty, so I'll probably see you later."

They said their good-byes and went their separate ways, Gar stopping at the center of the bridge to watch the fishermen and women.

"This time of year, the nessies follow the new salmon up the river to spawn, then they lay their own eggs on the riverbanks," a burly dwarf with massive arms explained as he dropped a line into the water.

Almost immediately he began reeling a catch in. "Whoo-ie, got me a big'un!"

Xan leaned over the rail to the bridge to see a silvery shape as long as the dwarf was tall flipping its tail back and forth as if it could swim away.

"Grab that net there big fella and get ready to scoop her up before she spills her eggs."

Gar was quick enough to get the net under the new breed of Ohio Salmon before she expelled her eggs. "Good job big fella! Oh, she's a beauty, too, and we got her before she voided."

He dipped a cup into the bottom of the special net and pulled it out full of roe. "A mug of Ohio Caviar for your help."

Hagar accepted the offer, knowing doing so absolved the fisher of any other compensation. He downed the entire mug in a single gulp and handed back the empty. "Nothing much better than fresh salmon roe. Thank you, sir."

Before they'd gone more than a dozen steps the man was pulling in another catch and Gar leaned over to watch him reel it in. "Either a male or he got it up before it voided."

They reached the other end of the bridge without further incident and were approached by a uniformed pair. "Welcome to our half of the Ohio River Salmon Spawn, folks. Bridge unit called and asked us to watch out for a vengeful relative. We've had to detain him before and know what to look for."

He pointed. "That road will take you to the

east gate. Go three blocks south and the Dog and Pony is on the far-right corner. Have a safe evening."

They thanked the officers and took the indicated road as darkness settled in. Wide and tall enough to encompass a two-lane highway it was open to the steady traffic of the salmon spawn celebration. They greeted the large presence of smiling police officers at the gate and passed through the wall of the West Virginia half of Bridgetown.

Just outside the doors a double lane bordered the physical wall to left and right. Several smaller man doors could be seen along its length as well as a few walking bridges between the wall and taller buildings outside the city proper. Each block they passed was an enclosed fortress with individual towers sticking up at the corners.

The southwest corner of the third block was no different, except in design. As they approached the front corner presented a cut stone face flanked by twin towers standing five stories high. A wide patio balcony stretched between the towers at the third floor.

A large triangular plaza fronted the impressive castle's front. A large wooden plaque with an engraved hellhound and warhorse similar to the ones they rode adorned the stone of the balcony above the open oak doors.

"This must be our stop," Gar said as they crossed from the road to the triangular plaza in front of the impressive castle. "Looks like our kind of place."

"Welcome, friends," a well-armed sentry said with a smile as his partner remained alert to any danger. Another pair of guards stood underneath the balcony and a trio of armed civilians gathered near a wheeled vendor's cart. "The check-in desk is on your right."

"Thank you," Xan said as he dismounted and led Xanthos into the high tunnel behind the doorway.

On the right were two windows with a smiling receptionist behind each and he approached the nearest. "Three rooms with one large bed, three horses, and two hellhounds for one night please. A reservation was called ahead a little earlier."

He signed the registration papers slid through the slot, paid with gold and silver coins, and the attendant gave him his instructions with accompanying hand gestures. "The tavern is in and between the towers above us, the guest rooms are inside the walls to either side of the front walls. The stables are on the other side of the interior park on the rear walls. Go straight along the central path to the back to stable your animals. Enjoy yourselves."

Xan led the rest through the tunnel into the interior plaza. The front two-thirds just inside the angled walls of the Dog and Pony contained benches and gaming tables surrounded by decorative shrubs and flower mounds. The back third held a sandy exercise paddock in front of a row of dozens of large stalls against the rear two walls.

"We have stalls one, two, and three," Xan said as he aimed for the numbers written above the stalls.

"What about Fred and Ginger?"

"All three of you in the ground floor room on the end of the south wing right next to the horses." He gave a small laugh. "Seems like everybody else's idea of the worst spots. Tina and I have the rooms above yours, we'll all be close to our animals and furthest away from people partying all night."

"Wish I could thank that officer," Tina said as they walked their horses to the left side of the paddock. "She got us out of some needless delays and found us the perfect accommodations."

"She said something about coming here after her shift," he said as he removed Xanthos' saddle and put it in the rack. He had just started to brush his horse down when a stablehand came by with a cart piled high and emptied bags into feed troughs.

When they were finished grooming their horses and ensuring feed bins were full and water fresh and circulated, they headed inside to check out their rooms.

"I have a bed that actually fits," Gar said later as he lifted his first legal drink. "As far as I could stretch I couldn't touch my toes and head at the same time. I can't even do that in my bed at home."

"And Fred and Ginger are thrilled with their den, it even has a door out to the paddock. I called down to the office and they said they could enclose all three of our stalls with an extension and open the stall doors. I went ahead and paid for it myself and checked it out before I came up here to join you."

"Front office called and let us know while we were getting cleaned up," Tina said. "From my window, the horses looked just as happy to see the pups as the pups did them."

Gar smiled and took a sip of his giant-sized mug instead of a gulp. "Your training is already bonding them into a team."

"And us into a team with them," Xan said. "Or, them with us, whatever."

"I will say, in only a few days we're all beginning to work together quite well," Tina said as the server approached. "Hello Eve, we've decided to try the Challenger for three."

The server smiled. "Giants are counted as two, so if you wish to Challenge, it will be as four."

Xan took a moment to catch each of his tablemates' eyes before looking at the server. "Yes, we *Challenge* at level four."

Before the first course was delivered, they made sure to identify their Adnaq, their Altered DNA Quotient, and the manager formally accepted their Challenge. They were hungry and their bodies were designed to process calories quickly and efficiently, so they didn't hold back.

A few minutes later the first plates of ribs arrived with their second drinks and they dug in. They didn't hesitate to keep ordering after the first plates of ribs were followed by struthy fingers and tater wedges, then by river crab leg logs dipped in butter.

The surf courses were followed by more turf, with the more recent versions of bison and ostrich in both steak and roast with side vegetables.

Then there were the drinks. It was part of the Challenge when one was genetically augmented. Certain drinks were required as a part of a certain number of courses and it was Gar's birthday and he was officially an adult.

Whenever it looked like they were about to have too many plates on their table they cleared space enough to take a short breather. At nine courses, they finally called it quits and dumped their unfinished plates into a doggie bag for Fred and Ginger.

"We could have won, you know," Gar said later as they watched Fred and Ginger playing with the horses in the extended paddock.

"Yeah, but we decided to lose before we started. It does two things," Xan said as he held up a finger. "One, it makes people underestimate us. And two, we can afford to lose and show we honor the results of our Challenge *if* we lose. It's actually in the budget over and above our personal purses."

"Grampa Alexander the Great *planned and funded* a throwaway night of spending, just for good will in a place he would never visit."

"Yes, through us," Xan said as he laughed with his large friend. "Without fanfare, spread our good name to counteract anything negative spoken by people like the ones we met on the bridge. Now, I'm going to bed so I'm ready for the most dangerous part of our journey."

[5] Strangler vines.

"I'm definitely going to time any trip I take back this way to pass through here," Xan said as they led their horses toward the front gate.

"A filling meal and comfortable night's sleep with well cared-for mounts and a hearty breakfast," Tina said. "I would give the Dog and Pony a five-star ranking."

They walked their horses through the park area and the tunnel, mounted, and joined the morning traffic. They were several kilometers outside the suburbs before traffic thinned and they shared the grassway with only two others. One was the regular mail being carried by a triceratops carrying a wicker wagon. The other was a man riding a two-legged runner.

"He's a form of struthymimus with some raptor genes. I named him Spot, for the obvious reason," Sesco Silverstone said after introducing himself. The two-legged beast's only marking was a large circular spot of white in the middle of his forehead. The rest of the body was a mottled forest green.

"Just traveling," he continued as the small caravan continued south. "I'm not going anywhere planned. Mind if I ride with you? I'm pretty good with these," he put a hand to the carbine and shotgun in saddle sheaths in front of his legs, "and Spot can kick the guts out of one of those big raptors in the middle of its killing leap."

"I can't guarantee a place to stay out of the

weather, but you're more than welcome to join us," Xan said.

Sesco patted the large bundle in the cargo harness behind his saddle. "Got a sleeping bag tent but I should be able to get something better if there's anything to be got. I've slept under the stars more often than not this time of year. What brings you out this way?"

"Going to Madison to meet with relatives. Place just outside of town called Blackrock Mountain. It'd be a hard run to make in one day but we've got a sunset stop planned."

"Probably the same place near where the mail wagon stops. It's very cleverly called Midway and the prices are larger than the quality of accommodations and drink would warrant. I would also advise against eating the food."

"Been there before?" Xan asked as their small caravan followed the grassy path that had been a paved highway a few decades earlier.

Sesco smiled with past memories. "Couple of times on the way further south and back. Madison is a lot better, nicer people and more options. Really nice library. I think I know a couple of folks from Blackrock. The rest mostly keep to themselves, something about a recent swarm of revenuers."

Xan smiled as Xanthos and Spot matched their pace even with their different physiques. "Yeah, that was about fifty years ago when the government tried to blackmail my grandfather into doing some genetic work."

"From what I've been able to piece together

from all the stories I've been told," Sesco said, "this one rogue agency decided to take hostages. Problem was, they took children whose parents' ancestors had been defending their mountain for longer than the country existed."

"Probably the same incident. My grandfather moved north after the entire invading government contingent disappeared. Their bodies were never found, but the government can't force them to allow a search without admitting they were an illegal black ops unit."

"Fifty years isn't that long when it's your own government invading your home, the same government *you* supported. I'm surprised you know a couple of them."

"You'd be surprised who you might meet in a library," Sesco laughed a second before Spot made an excited sideways hop. "Beware! There's something on our right side."

In a practiced motion, Gar wrapped the pack horse's lead to the back of Thoth's saddle and pulled his heavy staff from its sheath. Tina moved into a defensive position on the other side of the mail wagon while Sesco and Gar ranged further out to their right side.

As Gar approached a thick bush, a shape rushed out and directly at him. The giant moved faster than it seemed possible and he whacked the massive boar in the head with the end of his staff. The mutated animal staggered backward a few steps and slowly sank to its knees unconscious.

"There's a den under the bush," the giant reported as he inspected the mother's reason for attacking. "I can hear the piglets inside. She'll come around in less than a minute so we might want to hurry past this spot."

The mail wagon's triceratops was the slowest, but it had been stimulated by the boar's attack enough to be able to be coaxed into a steady fast-walk for almost a minute. That was enough to get them out of the mother boar's sight when she came out of her stunned state.

After another minute, the cera slowed to its species' normal walking speed just as they came to a forest with vines hanging from high limbs. The strangler vines away from the road reached almost to the ground while the ends of those above the road were higher.

Every time one of them passed beneath a strangler, a knife swung to keep the road clear. Traffic in both people and grazers kept the grassway through the forest cleared curb to curb up to five meters high till the strip down the center where limbs weren't strong enough to hold the parasitic vines. Off the road and into the forest, stranglers hung like hair with barely enough room for a careful human or raptor to pass. Unresponsive to slow movement and a light touch, if jostled too much the vine convulsed in the direction of the contact. Curling around and grasping, small needles in the adult wood numbed the victim and slowly drank body fluids.

The area on both sides of the cleared road was covered with the remains of animals that had calmly walked into the kill zone to graze. Eventually they made too much contact with a hanging tentacle and panicked when it wrapped them in a coiling grip, contacting another and another strangler in the process. The bigger the animal the more vines it triggered and several large rotting or mummified carcasses hung from dozens of vines on either side of the road. Skeletons and scattered bones littered the ground below the stranglers.

"What the frack is that?"

Xan looked back at the wagon's driver, then in the direction he was pointing just as Sesco answered, "An executioner's cage. The current occupant has only been there a few days and is probably still alive."

They heard a moan from the cage as they came closer, then passed by as Sesco continued, "The venom from the adult vine numbs the victim then when its sack's reservoir is empty the needle begins to dissolve the tissue and drink the nutrients. By that time there are usually so many needles injecting their venom into the victim, it has died of venom overdose or strangulation."

The moans grew louder as the occupant of the cage woke enough to realize people were nearby. Through his empathic abilities Xan could feel the man's internal screams as he pleaded with the voices to end his pain. It took an effort to close off the connection as Sesco continued.

"The cage is designed to allow minimal points of contact for the strangler while also protecting the convicted from constriction. The points where the vine can reach become focal points of severe pain once the flesh dissolving venom follows the numbing injection."

"What would warrant such a vile punishment?" Tina wondered as she pulled her carbine to end the man's suffering.

"He was caught kidnapping, raping, then butchering alive and eating children under five years old. Recorded each one, three before he was caught."

Tina returned the carbine to its saddle holster and turned her back on the moaning coming from the hanging cage as they continued along the grassway.

"He claimed he gained their life essences, adding their full measure of life to his own. Said he needed ten to make sure he lived a thousand years to become a god."

They ignored the moaning as they rode on.

The rest of the ride through the forest was made in silence and when they exited the woods, they could see Midway in the distance. The halfway compound wasn't a safe refuge. It was a tower with four open stalls surrounding the base. The three-story tower itself couldn't hold more than a single private residence with a bunk slot above each stall. The stalls around the base didn't even have doors to close them off from hunting animals.

"Might as well sleep out in the open," Gar grumbled as they neared the building.

"Ha!" Sesco slapped his leg as he enjoyed the looks on their faces. "Nobody stays here! It's named Midway because that's where it is. There's another place a couple ridges over where everybody stays. We'll get there early enough in the day it won't be full. Big enough stables for plenty of animals and a couple dozen guest rooms with good food and drink in their tavern, too."

The hill in question was an hour's ride through a smaller forest with a thick hair of strangler vines when they reached the top and looked to the hilltop on the other side where the larger castle stood. A slowly moving mass of animals of every size and shape carpeted the open pasture down the hill they topped, across the low valley, and back up the other side to that refuge.

"Well, that changes things," Sesco said. "I've only seen it like this a couple times and explains why we haven't seen any riders going the other way. Making it across by nightfall just got a little chancier."

"Can't we just form into a tight pack and let the cera lead us through?" Xan said as he stood in his stirrups to gain a higher viewpoint.

Sesco pointed. "We can't go anywhere near that herd of triceratops or one of the young bulls will challenge our mail wagon to a fight. The wagon wouldn't survive that or we'd have to shoot the challenger. These animals are well aware of the sound of human weapons and the noise followed by the young bull's collapse would most likely start a local stampede that could spread."

He pointed in another direction. "Over that way is a bull oliphant everybody else is avoiding and the ring around him is thicker than other parts of the migration."

"The oliphant is moving toward the cera," Gar said as he studied the moving mass of animals grazing the three-kilometer wide valley. If we aim for where he is now it should be clear by the time we get there."

"What if he clears space we can move through, then agitates the cera and starts a stampede that comes back at us?" Xan plotted the path in his mind as the grazing animals moved in response to each other.

"How long till they move on their own?" the mailman called out.

"They'll most likely be gone by morning," Sesco replied as he scanned the open area left and right. "I don't see a thinning in either direction, so not before midnight at the earliest. We can chance going across, go back to Midway since it's not that far, or find a spot nearby to camp for the night."

"Not a lot of good choices," Xan said as he looked closer at the tree line and pointed his chin. "Those four trees right at the corner of the grassway at the edge of the forest behind us would be almost ideal. We could back the mail wagon inside and cut off the stranglers that can reach us."

"There was a nice stone outcrop inside the trees that could provide extra protection. Can't be any worse than what Midway had and we have to go through the forest again to get back there. No telling what hunters are behind us."

"Good point, sis," Xan said. "What do you think, Gar?"

"I'm for going straight through. If anything happens and critters started panicking, we can stop and form up with our point into the tide, just like we always train to do."

"Actually," the wagon driver said as he turned his cera toward the spotted grouping of trees, "I choose the rocky, enclosed space at the tree line."

Xan shrugged at Sesco and followed the wagon as it moved away from the sod covered road.

"That's some root crumbling rock," Gar commented as they inspected the small enclosure. "Easy to move and the stone will make a good wall."

Fred and Gracie sniffed at every corner and seemed to know to stay away from the nearest stranglers, growling at them when they came close. The horses and cera also refused to approach the stranglers.

"Back the wagon right in here and we'll clear out this loose stone to make room," Xan said as he dismounted and began moving boulders at his upper physical level.

In moments, everybody but the mail wagon driver was helping. It took almost an hour to clear enough space to get the wagon backed in far enough the triceratops' horns were all that projected from between the two outer trees.

"Drain the vines about three, four hours then seal the fluid in a bottle or small cask with various amounts of water and it'll ferment on its own," Sesco said. "Doesn't matter who puts their name on the label, it's always called Stranglewine."

"Is that how the needles are harvested for med kits?" Tina had read how to collect them but wanted another source.

"Yes," Sesco smiled at his new elven friend. "Once the vine has been drained you can cut the needles and their venom sacs out." He patted the bag behind his saddle. "I always carry freshly harvested needles in my med kit and can't wait to get some extra to sell."

"What's making those over there twitch and reach?" Gar asked as he dragged a newly cut vine to the bucket behind the wagon.

"Some of them are from the same parent plant up there," Sesco pointed to the treetops around them. "The parts we're cutting off are connected, but in the long run that's better because those outer vines will become increasingly defensive and hungry."

"Still don't get why the mailman won't help," Gar grumbled as he dropped another huge boulder on the pile between the two outer and inner trees.

"He can't help and this spot remain public," Sesco explained. "If he helps then this location becomes property of the Postal Service and will most likely become a branch office by next year. Since he's not helping, he can call some friends or relatives and they can be out here sometime tomorrow to claim the spot first."

"So, what are our options?" Gar stacked another large boulder in the pile between two of the trees.

"Claim a portion of the enclosure or offer it to another for a percentage or an outright price. I usually contribute some of mine to the local library."

The mailman watched them work from his perch atop the wagon. "I've called my family and they're preparing the resources to establish the second phase of a private settlement."

Xan looked at his sister and signaled through their mental connections, then directed his abilities at his best friend and received a smiling nod. "We three agree to reserve declaration of claim for twenty-four hours. Till then we'll do our best to ensure this is a secure position."

Sesco smiled, bowed, and went to explain things to the mailman. The sun was nearing the horizon and Xan was piling the last of the wood he'd gathered when the seemingly always useful traveler returned.

"The mailman accepts our offer of refuge in the stall we've cleared. Do you guarantee safety within the defined perimeter?"

"Yes," Tina replied. "We ensure his safety as long as we're present."

They spent the next hour cutting strangler vines a safe distance back from the enclosure and digging rock away from the split outcrop. The cera wagon slowly moved backwards into the niche being excavated into the edge of the forest, every meter giving the triceratops more protection. By the time the sun touched the horizon, only the tips of the draft animal's horns projected between the two flanking trees on the outer perimeter.

On the sides, the stone was stacked and piled in the beginnings of walls that would protect the cargo garage from any natural assault. With three sides protected by ground reaching stranglers, they were better protected than what they would have had at Midway.

The shape of the stone outcrop was high in the back between the two wider spaced trees, giving them enough room for their mounts as well as space for a large fire. The top was even with the roof of the cabin atop the cera and gave them an excellent view of the valley in the bright moonlight.

"This looks like a good place for a chimney, JJ," Gar said as he fed a log to the fire.

The mailman, Jarod Jackson, smiled and nodded. "That's exactly what I thought while you were clearing the loose stone. There's enough room for a good-sized kitchen, and a living area over the wagon bay."

"Might need taller turret towers outside of the trees," Xan said just as the triceratops rose from his resting position.

The movement raised the flat roof of the wicker cabin and Xan was beside JJ as they pulled weapons to face what the cera had sensed. He sent a mental probe outward and touched the mind of a hunter.

A second later the largest carnisaur he'd ever seen stuck its enormous head around the tree on their left and roared a challenge.

[6] Plant versus animal.

The roof deck of the mail carrier wagon pitched as the triceratops made a jab forward with his upper horns and JJ almost fell.

There were always gene hackers who wanted things bigger and badder than anybody else's creation. Although there was a limit to which a living body could eat enough to maintain health, or even function, that upper limit was considerable with enough genetic tinkering.

There were also other ways to make something badder without making it bigger. Somebody had figured out how to do that and Xan gaped at something only a twisted mind could design.

It most likely came from a rex, or whatever combination of genes had resulted in what looked most like a rex. Only this rex would make nature's version look like an adolescent, and it had arms that weren't those of a normal rex. The face was shorter and wider than a normal rex, with four protruding fangs as long as Xan was tall.

"Holy frack… it *does* exist," JJ whispered as the rex roared again and looked for a way to get at a meal.

Then a second, even larger rex came around the first and added her hunting scream to her mate's while the cera backed up a couple of steps, then lunged forward three. The move caught the first rex by surprise and he got stabbed in the inner thigh as his longer arm raked down the cera's shield.

The shield was bone, but it was also a mating device and was covered in brightly colored skin full of blood vessels. The rex's claws left ragged red gashes in trade for the deep gouge in his thigh. Blood streamed into the cera's face and down the rex's leg.

All of this had taken mere seconds and as the rex backed up in response to the wound, four heavy weapons barked at the massive beasts. The gene hackers showed their level of both genius and viciousness as the heavy rounds made dull thuds in thickly armored hide.

The female lunged forward and managed to grab the cera's two upper horns with a strong grip and lunge at the people firing shotguns and carbines point blank into her head. She clamped her jaws on the cera's shield and began dragging him out of his protective enclosure. The genetic designers had expanded the rex's head with bone shields covering its eyes and at the angle it had on the cera they couldn't blind it with a shot.

The cera was strong and had benefitted from its own design improvements, larger size and longer horns being two, and it was a lot stronger than nature's own, but it was not as strong as the rex. The hellhounds bit and harassed the rex from below while trying to avoid a deadly kick from feet with meter long claws, but the rex was slowly dragging the cera outward.

Gar lunged with his staff, a carbon composite interwoven around several tech devices, including powerful illuminators on the end. He stretched forward and with his longer reach added to the length of the staff was able to get the tip under the female rex's eye shields.

Nature couldn't fix a reaction that burned the eyes and the rex released her grip on the cera's frill when she was startled by the intense light. Everybody was ready when she roared at the puny snacks that were denying her a meal, and weapons rained buckshot and armor piercing rounds into her open mouth.

Gene hackers could do a lot, but they couldn't make their creations totally invulnerable. Too much armor inside the thighs and it couldn't walk, run, or move sideways quickly in battle. There had to be a tradeoff in the head or it would be too big to carry and the inside of the mouth was a weak point in an animal that used its roar to intimidate.

The rex gurgled another scream that shook the trees around them and backed out of the enclosure. She lashed her tail in anger and the bone spurs that lined it gouged into the trunk of the tree on the left, then the one on the right as she moved away from the tree line and roared at the valley.

The male moved in to take her place as the sound of thousands of pounding feet came from nearby.

"Stampede!" JJ yelled.

"Pretty sure they're going every which way but *this* one," Sesco laughed as he put a couple of ineffective rounds into the male rex's armored face. "Hey, wait, where you going, Xan?"

Gar laughed and slapped the young man on the shoulder hard enough to make him stumble.

"Something stupid, no doubt."

"Tell me they're not…"

"Oh yeah, that would be stupid enough. Get your cameras out!"

"Hey, hey, hey you big dummy!" Xan yelled as he ran. "Bet you can't catch me!"

On the other side of the wagon enclosure Xan could sense his sister as she copied his actions luring the other rex the opposite direction. With night vision equal to his own the male noticed him and abandoned the cera to stalk him along the tree line.

Xan ran further away from the nascent wagon bay and past the trimmed stranglers then out toward the cautious rex. He waggled his carbine's flashlight back and forth to get the hunter's attention as he yelled then picked up a rock, ran several steps forward, and threw it at the angry beast. He ran a couple more steps forward and put a couple of rounds into the rex's belly, then turned and ran.

The rex had been taunted and insulted by his inability to get to his prey and knew the danger within the forest, but he was wired as a hunter. When prey ran, you chased.

Xan dodged the first few stranglers he passed but slapped at others as he ran by. Those he slapped were beginning their initial curling reflex just as the rex hit them. He dove between two vines, kicking out with his feet just as he flew by and rolled below the reach of the vines in the next rank as the rex began to fight the ones grabbing him.

The captured rex's roars were drowned out

by the ones coming from the other side of the wagon as his sister's mind assured him she was safe and successful as well with the larger female. He crawled toward the stone outcropping as the roars began to turn into screams of desperation.

When he reached the line where they'd trimmed the stranglers he rose to his feet and looked back at the results of his efforts. His augmented night vision allowed him to see the struggling rex as dozens of strangler vines curled in an unbreakable grip.

The rex thrashed and roared and screamed, the echoes of his and his mate's voices scaring everything within hearing range into a blind panic. In the brief silences between the two rexes' screams the sound of the stampede grew more distant as every creature in the valley ahead of them fled the sounds of battle.

"Bet we could cross the valley now, no problem," Gar called down from the edge of their camp as he recorded the male's capture.

"Bet we're safer here no matter how empty the valley gets," Xan called back. "Rent's already paid, too."

He climbed up the side of the spine of stone and joined the others just as Tina came up the other side. "Good job, sis."

"You too, and that was good thinking, Gar. She remembered the light and followed mine faster than I expected. I could smell her breath just before the vines finally stopped her, but no matter how strong you are you can't do anything if your feet aren't on the ground."

The two rexes became more and more entangled as the vines continued to coil and grasp their prey. New vines coiled and grabbed, adding to those already grasping the rexes.

"Shame their skins are so thick," Tina said. "Probably end up like that execution cage, only getting a few access points."

"Won't matter," Xan said, pointing. "Looks like both of them will be strangled before the dissolving starts."

The vines were not static and continued to move and coil to get more and more surface area covered. In the process, they eventually wrung the necks of their captives and even though it would take a while, they would continue to move and curl to find all the soft places to inject their flesh-eating solvents.

They watched for nearly an hour before they heard the male's neck snap but both rexes had died within fifteen minutes of their feet leaving the ground.

"I'm thinking you'll have a couple of fine heads to mount when you get this place built," Gar opined. "I'd put 'em on the two towers you put up front. And the lower legs could be made into bar stools, gotta have bar stools."

"That big momma's legs might even make a stool strong enough to hold you," Tina teased.

"Proper stool and a mug of Stranglewine with a view of the valley from a safe balcony sounds pretty good to me," the big man replied with a smile.

"Well, any time you're back this way and

we can offer that, we will," JJ said. "In fact, that goes for all of you. You too Sesco even though all you did was talk while the others worked and watched when they killed the rexes."

"I was imparting valuable information and expert supervision for your first example," he held up his phone, "plus, I got video."

"Two Dragons, no, *Twin* Dragons! That's what I'll name it. Yes, Twin Dragons."

"How about Hanging Dragons," Gar suggested.

"Or Strangled Dragons," Sesco added with a sly smile.

A loud crack from the side sounded as the female's neck broke and they all laughed nervously after reflexively reaching for weapons.

"Snap Dragons," Xan said and it took several seconds before the laughter died down, then he pointed. "Looks like somebody's crossing the valley."

"That would be my family and friends," JJ said as his teeth gleamed brightly from within the ebon darkness of his face. "Just got the text, they have cement mix and enough heavy equipment to complete the first level and roof. As soon as they get here, we'll post the 'Papers of Intent' and claim the spot."

He looked at the rest. "That's when you declare your intent as shareholders."

"You already know my wishes," Sesco said. "My share is to go to a library that can double as a classroom for your children. I'll see to any discrepancies I find in the stocking of books and children's crafting materials next time I'm this way."

"Done," JJ replied and turned to Xan and Tina. "In addition to a one quarter share in the current camp, you each are the sole owners of the rexes you succeeded in defeating in battle."

"Wait a minute," Gar objected. "If I hadn't blinded that big mother fracking mother, she would be eating your cera and the other one would have chased us out of our fancy camp or be eating us."

"That's right," Xan said with a laugh. "You get the legs."

"I get the legs and for my additional share I want you to build a balcony tavern high enough the tallest monsters can't reach, with stools sturdy enough for me to not have to be careful sitting."

"Done!" JJ laughed. "And you two?"

There was a brief flash of signals, both physical and mental before Xan spoke. "Mount the two skulls to either side of the tavern balcony and add two tables, each large enough for Gar and a guest."

"Plus," Tina added, "add a kitchen to the tavern and serve an ale in addition to stranglewine. I prefer a stout ale with a decent meal at the end of a day of travel."

"Done and done!" JJ exclaimed with a smile. "And tables large enough for Gar will easily hold four smaller people."

Gar smiled at the mailman saying *smaller* instead of *normal*. "That's just for the dragons. For my other share, I want a night's lodging and a meal fit for a giant on either side of that night's lodging, for two."

JJ gave a mock scowl at Gar remembering the other share, then gave a theatrical performance to bely the graciousness of the offer. "Very well, room for a night for two in a proper bed for a giant with supper and breakfast for two on either side. Done, my friend."

Gar's hand engulfed that of the smaller, but large mailman. "Done."

Tina put her hands over those of her friend and the mailman. "My brother and I add our pledge to those of the others and make the same request. We *each* declare our ownership shares to be paid in full with a night's lodging at giant levels with a giant's portion supper and breakfast for two on either side."

"Ha! Well played! Done and done," JJ laughed after Xan placed his hands over all the others and said 'agree'.

A moment later Sesco added his hands. "Dragon Slayer Library. The kids could do plays re-enacting how the two skulls and four stools were obtained by the three heroes."

"Oh gods," Gar moaned. "You wouldn't." The second part came out as more of a threat than a question.

Sesco smiled and spread his hands. "It's what I do. I travel around and just happen to find myself in situations of benefit, then I pass the fruits of my adventures to ensuring education doesn't fail along with most of the formerly dominant species of this world."

"He cons people out of money and uses it to

build schools and, apparently, single room libraries in isolated homes," JJ joked while stating a sincere respect for the scholar that both Xan and Tina could feel empathically.

They also felt Sesco's embarrassment, that was quickly overshadowed by the satisfaction of something good done. The moment was broken up by the first of the vehicles containing JJ's family and friends making the best of a once-in-a-lifetime opportunity.

Introductions were done in passing and time had to be taken to get the first arrivals to stop playing with the pups or gawking at the strangled monsters. With the two giant rexes trussed up and keeping the border strangler vines busy feeding, new workers could travel further to collect valuable stone boulders for the walls of the new castle.

"Going wider than I thought you would," Xan commented as he set another stone in place.

"Once everybody saw what it looked like we decided to build the wall outside the nearest trees to give us a protected courtyard," JJ explained. "We're still over solid stone over the entire back end and the extra room will give us space for horse stalls once we cut more of the stone away."

The sound of the power saws cutting bocks of stone for the castle sounded in the night, adding to the imagined echoes of the dying mega rexes, the true dragons that some evil genius gene hacker had constructed. Invulnerable hunter dragons defeated by patiently waiting plants.

"Pups are having fun but we're not getting any sleep. Are we going to travel tired or stay another day?" the question in Gar's voice was evident.

"Deals have already been made and any extra effort is voluntary as far as I'm concerned," Xan said with a chuckle. "I'm going to sell my labor for a ride to the other side of the valley for me and Xanthos on one of those trucks shedding its load of concrete bags."

"Sounds good to me," Gar replied, then got a nod from Tina, who made Sesco nervous when she turned her gaze on him.

"Me too," the traveling scholar chimed in as a pair of armored trucks drove by the construction and headed for the other side of the valley.

The night went faster than expected as additional trucks arrived while a pair of muddy trucks raced by the other way, toward the next village. They were kept busy till someone constructed a buffet breakfast held on makeshift tables. Work stopped as the sun lit the morning sky and started burning off the night's fog.

"Sure are a lot of people for one little family castle," Gar observed as he gazed at a plate of pancakes covered in syrup and pieces of fruit.

"Heh-heh," JJ's eyes sparkled. "People have been itching to do something with this hilltop for years but the stranglers and the lack of start-up help just never came about. We're getting a little help now but these people are going to use us as a safe refuge and starting point to look for their own claims along the grassway through the trees of this hilltop."

"Do you know how strangler fields are

harvested? A log is wrapped with a fresh hide and presented to the vine. The vine is marked at the highest point of the coil and when it finishes consuming the nutrients and uncoils it's severed and harvested at that high point. The cellulose of the log is a nutrient they usually don't get and makes a different kind of wine that goes better with fish and poultry than the redder meats."

"In another decade, this mountaintop will be a commercial strangler field instead of a wild one. My family will own only what we can manage of that area but the addition of the skulls and feet of two of the fabled mountain dragons will give us a story telling of glorious battle with monsters. That and our corner position on the grassway will combine to draw patrons to our future tavern."

After their breakfast, they loaded their mounts on trucks, the mail cerawagon getting its own truck, and drove away as the workers continued to build a base level around the rocky outcrop they'd chosen as an emergency camp the night before.

The ride through the next village past the main castle they could see from the other side of the valley contained a scattering of single-family towers wrapped in vertical gardens. They were on the other side of the mountaintop village and halfway down the dip in the next valley when flashing lights flagged them down.

"Seems this group of angry people arrived in a pair of muddy, armored trucks late last night looking for a troll and two pointy-eared freaks they had a grudge against," JJ explained after talking to the police officers. "Got all rowdy and drunk and thrown in jail when they started a fight in a tavern. Sesco and I assured the officers we didn't associate with freaks and neither did our giant and elven friends. They thanked us and went back to make their reports."

Xan snorted a laugh and shook his head as he looked at his sister. "Looks like we got that crosswind grampa always warned us about."

"Yes, it does. I'm more concerned with his sister," Tina said as she got her phone out and began tapping at the screen, then read the texted reply. "She's okay and her and her husband have announced their pregnancy."

Xan caught the thought they hadn't announced the use of his and his sister's gift of prenatal NSI injections when the deputy visited the Dog and Pony the night they stayed there. The police woman had kept it a secret or had decided to not use the injections past the first one Tina had administered herself to show how.

Of course, being the initial dosage, it was also the most powerful. The resulting birth would definitely be elven, but some of the more refined attributes Xan and Tina displayed might be muted or absent if they didn't use the monthly follow-up injections.

The ride was uneventful and they passed the point where they could have expected to be if they'd have made their best time. It was still midafternoon when they reached the point where they'd requested to be let off.

"Thank you," Xan said to the driver as he

shook his hand. "This is more than enough. We won't draw as much attention this way."

The driver knew that wasn't true since Gar and Sesco's videos of the battle with the dragon rex were already being broadcast. But it would look less flamboyantly extravagant.

The mail wagon had already stayed behind to continue its route and all four of their mounts fit on a single tractor trailer. They offloaded north of Madison at a spot out of sight of the main road's grassway and the truck was on its way back without another vehicle driving by.

After a short break to get themselves together they exited the small side hollow back to the main grassway into Madison. Three kilometers further they encountered their first residents and word spread the grandchildren of the black sheep of Blackrock Mountain had returned.

[7] A deadly game of tag.

"I really like short visits," Gar said as they hurried out of town. "Makes people miss you more."

"As long as they miss when they're shooting," Sesco said as he looked over his shoulder. "Your family reunions always this exciting, Xan?"

"Actually, no, not till this time anyway. Maybe it was the new batch of grampa's satanic elixir that tripped the trigger." He looked at his cousin Lilac and her husband Stone riding the same breed of struthie Sesco rode.

They had a six-year old son who bravely managed to hold the reins to the cerapig that towed the small wagon containing everything the small family owned. With one of the struthies riding beside the cerapig the child was able to build confidence under controlled conditions. The grassway was open and they made good time escaping their bad reception.

"Frack them!" Lilac stormed as her struthy caught her mood and pranced excitedly. "What did they expect me to do after being born like this? Wait till one of them has another kid like me. It's going to happen because grampa spread his bugs before he escaped and it's just a matter of time before it shows in everybody's kids."

Everyone looked at her husband who was born to another purist family but showed augmented features. Their second child was yet to show but Lilac already knew she was pregnant and had accepted the prenatal NSI gift.

"You say they'll also work on Eaglewing?" Lilac asked as she rode on the other side of the cerapig from Tina.

"Yes, just not as much because of his age. Actually, from what grampa explained, at his age and already showing elvish signs, considerably more than the side effects on you from the treatments for your child. Heightened senses will be one, and resistance to disease is another. That last one will also result in better physical shape which only helps if you train your body to respond to excess stress."

"Which means you're going to have Gar beat on me and my husband," Lilac grumbled.

"Not at first," Tina laughed. "My brother and I will toughen you up before we give him a chance to knock you around. But not till after the baby's born."

"Gee thanks, cousin," the young mother smiled as she genuinely relaxed for the first time since her pointy eared son had been born. "So, what's the plan?"

Tina laughed. "Sorry. We drag you out of your home with a tiny wagon with all you own and no place to call home then just ride off like it's nothing."

"Don't you worry about that Athena. Stone and I were about ready to leave before we found out you were coming. In fact, you helped us plan better."

She laughed gaily and her struthy mirrored her emotions and strutted. "Stone and I began trading favors and selling assets and buying what we needed to travel the road. These mounts are a mated pair and are at their prime, and the cerapig was inseminated and confirmed pregnant when we got her papers earlier this week. The rest of what we have is maximized for worth and travel weight."

"By the time the rest of the family realized what we were doing we had the wagon packed with the last of what we owned or needed for the road and were just waiting for you to get here. That's why we were there to meet you first when you got into town."

"Good thing too," Sesco said. "Makes a quick turnaround easier if you're not settled in comfortably."

"You sound like you're used to rushing out of a village you just got to," Tina joked as they rode the open grassway in the late evening.

Sesco blushed despite himself. "It's happened on occasion. Usually for the *controversial* books I stock or my asked opinion. At least they haven't burned down one of my libraries yet. Hey Eaglewing, you glad to be out from under disapproving eyes?"

"Yes sir!" the young child replied loudly, grateful to be included in the adult talk. "Air smells free!"

"Yes, it does, son," Stone said, smiling warmly at his son. "And among those who judge by character instead of appearance."

Eaglewing took a more confident grasp of the reins to the wagon even though a mutant struthy on one side and a genetically augmented warhorse on the other directed the passive cerapig along the grassway where the highway used to be.

They topped the last hill before the village they'd bypassed the night before and were just starting down the long grade of their last downhill leg when two large trucks pulled up and JJ stuck his head out of the first one's cab. "Hey folks, want a ride to a nice place I heard about?"

There was a lot of back-slapping and hand shaking as they loaded their wagon, six mounts, and two hellhounds onto the two trailers and headed to the growing castle on the edge of Dragontop Woods.

"I take it your family reunion didn't go like planned," JJ said as they rode through the village they never visited.

"Kind of a bust," Xan said as he held Xanthos' halter inside the open trailer, the breeze of their travel welcome in the late evening. "Got away with the only family brave enough to face some stubborn folks already lost to gene hackers."

"Yeah, world always changes too fast for some hide-bound folk to keep up," JJ said with a shake of the head.

"Maybe keeping some pure bloodlines isn't such a bad idea," Xan said. "What if they last longer than us?"

"What ifs don't matter," Tina declared. "As long as we don't separate ourselves again. Grampa's NSI works on everybody. Yes, it has more elvish adaptations than any other but other strains work just as well on giants or were-folk."

"Yeah, gives us pointy ears and better

eyesight in the dark," Gar joked theatrically. "Fred and Ginger have that."

They laughed and talked to calm themselves and their mounts, then unloaded when they got back to the growing castle between the two strangled dragon rexes.

A half circle of trucks and trailers arced in front of the four trees and the stone outcrop they embraced. Dozens of people and pieces of heavy equipment swarmed over the area as construction to secure the space continued.

"You have a big family," Gar deadpanned as they walked their mounts behind JJ, between the two trailers, and into the empty wagon bay.

"Heh-heh," JJ looked around at the construction. "Most of these people will be gone about the same time you leave in the morning. We're just trading a bit of strangler training for some grunt work hauling stone or bags of concrete mix to build our wall. Even got to show some folks how quick you need to cut down a careless person caught by a strangler and how long it takes the venom to wear off and a nearly strangled person be able to walk again. Nothing like an inattentive fool to give people a visual lessen."

Their future pledges of accommodation didn't count against them as they had to sleep under the limbs and stars, but by surprise the next morning there was a food tent on the other side of the grassway.

"That's what it's for," Lilac insisted as she shared some of her family's supplies.

"You planned this?' Tina was surprised.

"Yes, no, not me, Stone. He knew what we were doing, how it would be seen when you showed up and we declared our intentions and how the family would react. He said we would need a large meal the first morning, and it had to be of the kinds of favored foods we would miss from home the most to show we could have the same pleasures on the road. Then the people building the castle at Dragontop Woods were preparing their tent and instead of having a small breakfast for just our group we added our fresh eggs, cerapig bacon, and fresh fruit pies to theirs so everybody could have more."

"Don't happen often but I definitely had my fill and I thank you for the half peach cobbler I had for dessert, Lilac," Gar said as he walked beside the pack horse with Fred and Ginger frolicking nearby, having the best day of their lives since yesterday.

They left Dragontop Woods, passed Midway, and into the larger strangler infested forest without incident. Halfway through the main forest they came upon several people butchering the rear half of a sauro that was being dragged into the forest by strangler vines.

"Wild sauro got his head too far inside the border where the grass was taller and knocked against a vine a bit too hard," Sesco said after talking to one of the butchers. "They were in time to get the whole tenderloin, some ribs, and both rear quarters before the vines dragged the rest into the forest. I got a two-kilo roast in payment for information so we have fresh meat for our supper coals."

The migration had stopped traffic north, but with the valley again open the road was more crowded than usual. A couple hundred meters further there was another large animal being dragged into the forest after getting too close but it wasn't giving up easily.

Standing easily four meters at the top of its massive and maned shoulders, it sported a single horn that was as long as the beast was tall. The stranglers had hold of the horn only and were pulling hard but their numbing venom wasn't working.

The mutant bull, twice the size of the domesticated one they'd seen a few days ago, jerked backwards and one of the three vines moving toward the face tore free. The bull threw his head down and lurched back as the other two vines slipped away. With a bellow of rage, the bull stepped forward and tilted his head, then began slashing at the hanging vines, shredding them in a meters-wide swath.

Xan signaled his sister and friend and they picked up their speed as they passed the enraged beast, then called out to Sesco. "See if we can get by while he's busy showing those plants who's boss."

Sesco nodded and went to get the wagon moving a little faster while he spoke to the group that had joined them from behind.

"Might want to do more than just hurry," one man said as the others began to pass the wagon on the side opposite the one-horned bull. "Wild unitaur are ornery in the best of times and don't tolerate much of anything."

"Unitaur?"

"Yeah, half unicorn and half minotaur, unitaur. Don't walk fast, run," he said the last over his shoulder after urging his mount to do just that.

Xan looked at the unitaur as it turned another circle, slashing strangler vines but disturbing more when he backed into them. He almost got caught once more but powerful muscles twisted and his horn shredded the offending vines.

"Head to the other side at an angle," he called out as he moved Xanthos next to Stone. "If he comes this way I want as much distance as possible between us."

"Got it," his cousin's husband said, then began to nudge the wagon to the left.

The unitaur was on their right and habit had caused travelers to travel on the right in the direction they were going. Going against traffic was considered rude and was known to start fights in crowded situations, but the grassway was relatively open at this point and with four lanes, Xan hoped they would be far enough away from the angry beast to avoid attention. The level of danger was more than enough to buck tradition.

The five riders that had ridden with them most of the way were over a hundred meters further when Sesco rode up next to him. "Unitaur is out of the vines and attacking the ground. He's not a happy monster."

He dropped back as the others gained distance and turned Xanthos toward the angry monster as Gar trotted over, Fred and Ginger locking their eyes on the unitaur. "Looks like we might have to play tag with him."

Gar smiled and the hellhounds whined with anticipation. "Ready when you are."

"Tag?"

"Yeah, Sesco," Xan said. "It's a fun game when you're rested and have help. Sucks if you lose."

"What do we do?"

"We're going north, so we want him to go the other way. If he does it on his own, we're good, but if he decides to go our way, we discourage him by pissing him off enough to chase us the other direction."

"Sounds like fun," Sesco eyed the huge beast still bellowing and looking for something to smash. "Wagon and everybody else are almost out of sight against the forest on the other side."

"Too late," Gar said. "Beastie is looking around and yes, we've been spotted."

"Tag! Unitaur's it!" Xan yelled then gave Xanthos the signal and the genetically augmented horse he'd begun to be empathically linked with leaped forward.

He and Gar ran at an angle that kept close enough to draw the bull's attention while turning it around to head south. Fred and Ginger were the first to score coup on the enraged beast, nipping at his flanks as he turned and twisted while Gar and Xan taunted him from either side.

They couldn't get the unitaur to go the way they wanted till Sesco ran up on his struthy, spun, and the two-legged runner lifted its tail and squirted urine into the monster's face. Luckily, he knew enough to immediately run and the three of them shot away toward the south as fast as they could go, whooping and hollering all the way.

It only took a second for the unitaur to bellow enough to make the nearest strangler vines coil, then he burst after his newest tormentors. The two mounts, a giant, and two hellhounds had a head start but the unitaur's designers had anticipated the dangers their creations might face.

Gar looked over his shoulder. "He's gaining! Hundred meters."

They waited till the big man called out fifty meters before they picked up their speed to keep the same distance.

"Good stamina," Xan laughed. "The strongest don't usually last this long. End of the forest coming up. We'll split when we're clear."

"I have straight ahead," Sesco said as Gar and Xan maneuvered to go left and right.

They passed another group of travelers who screamed and scattered but the unitaur ignored them even though he almost trampled one horse and rider. He did body slam a hadro that panicked, sending the rider and saddle one way and the hadro another.

When they burst out of the forest Gar swerved to the left and around the Midway tower while Xan headed west into the open grasslands. The unitaur ignored both and followed the smell of the one that had given the most insult.

Xan and Gar tried several times to lure the enraged beast to the side but its focus on Sesco's struthy was unbreakable.

Instead Xan raced ahead and screamed a warning as they entered the gap where the road went through Dragontop Woods. Newly arrived settlers and other travelers scattered but the unitaur ignored all but those directly in his path.

"Starting to tire," Gar's voice bounced with his pounding boots.

"You or the monster," Xan laughed. "Hanging Dragons coming up. Looks like somebody called ahead."

"Gutting spikes!" Sesco yelled. "Head for the gap between those trucks!"

He urged his struthy on with Xan and Gar close behind. They slowed enough to avoid the metal contraptions spiked into the ground in the gap between the line of armored vehicles. The enraged unitaur didn't slow down as it followed through the gap after its prey.

As soon as the pursued were through, each line of gutting spikes sprang up at an angle toward the oncoming monster. Running full speed, the unitaur impaled itself on one line and kept running.

The beast's designers were efficient and ensured a thick mane to protect their creation's head and shoulders, but just like the dragon rex, they had to make their monsters capable of functioning. Unitaur depended on their thick mane where other designs used bone for armor, but there were gaps in the junctures of legs and body.

The tallest of the angled spikes entered the unitaur under the left front shoulder at the same time the two shortest entered the belly. The blades on either side of the spikes weren't razor sharp, but the massive bodied unitaur was moving over fifty kph.

Xan and Gar followed Sesco's lead when he didn't slow down and were glad they did.

The line of gutting spikes split the unitaur down the middle, eviscerating it on the run but the enraged monster continued chasing them. Blood and guts flowed out of the body cavity for another fifty yards before the behemoth grunted and fell face first into the ground.

Gar laughed and approached the downed beast and slapped the horn standing taller than him.

"Tag," he said just as Sesco yelled, "*NO!*"

Not dead yet, the unitaur slashed with its horn in one last act of defiance.

[8] The ultimate mobile home.

Gar ducked faster than it seemed possible, grabbed the horn from underneath, and his momentum swung him around and up just as the unitaur slashed the other way.

"Hang on Gar," Sesco yelled. "He's not completely dead yet!"

People came running from every direction but none approached any closer than the swing of the giant's head as Gar hung on to the bucking and slashing horn

"How long does it take," Xan asked as the mighty beast refused to admit it was dead.

Sesco scratched his head as Fred and Ginger watched Gar being thrown back and forth. "Don't really know. Never seen one actually in the process, only those already dead and mostly eaten."

"Hang on tight Gar," he yelled, "shouldn't be long now."

"Brought us another monster, eh?"

"Hi JJ. Yeah, thought you might want another trophy."

"Going to run out of places to hang 'em pretty soon. Hey Gar," the former mailman called out, "I think you've almost won!"

The unitaur finally exhaled its death rattle despite half its lungs along with the rest of its inner organs dragged in a line behind it but Gar hung on for a moment longer to make sure. He didn't release his firm grip till Fred and Ginger began sniffing around the massive head and biting the lips.

"I want my money back," Gar laughed. "Damned ride stopped just when it got to be fun. Hey JJ, those your spikes saved Sesco from being road kill?"

"Hey, Gar. He would have come after you two next. Yeah, the spikes are for the front patio as a passive deterrent. Already mounted two of them when we got word what was chasing you fellas. Got the other two in place just in time. So, what half do you want?"

"Heh-heh, Xan, what do you think?"

"I was the one it was chasing," Sesco said. "Put my share into a bigger library and mount the head in the tavern."

"Done!" JJ said and they shook.

"Make the legs into stools for the tavern," Xan said. "Plus, a free night's stay and giant-sized meal for two with appropriate drinks on either side, and we'll take as much of the tenderloin and rib rolls we can carry."

"Agree," Gar said.

"Done and done!" JJ said.

He didn't waste any time and teams were cleaning up the offal while another group started peeling the hide away from the carcass. They were tending their mounts when the newly retired mailman joined them.

"The rest of your people sent word they found a tower to hole up for the night. You can join them if you don't mind pushing sunset or you can stay the night here." He smiled wide. "Since we don't have any rooms available yet, you won't be obliged to use up owed favors."

"Probably talk us into hauling stone again, then have to sleep on rocks while noisy construction goes on all night," Gar said with a laugh. "It's not that far and this time we won't be running for our lives."

"Agreed. You ready, Sesco?"

"Yeah, Spot is rested and fed and should be able to make a good pace."

"We'll leave as soon as we can get our tenderloin roasts and rib rolls," Xan said.

"They were being packed when I came to find you, and here they are. We cut the loins in meter lengths and each one is in a sealed tube. There are two of each in each saddlebag. I'm freezing the rest and I'll send a car with them tomorrow to catch up with you so they'll last another day."

Xan glanced at the other two. "No, go ahead and keep the rest. We said what we could carry and the deal was done."

JJ nodded and spoke to one of the many people coming up to talk with him. When they walked their mounts out of the growing stables two more tubes and a bacon slab were being crammed into each saddlebag.

"Everything's sealed and strong so you won't smell too much like lunch. Thank you again my friends and at least *act* like you're making an attempt at being safe."

"Why start now?" Gar asked as one of the men butchering the unitaur threw chunks of raw scrap meat to Fred and Ginger. The pups looked at him first then grabbed the offerings when Gar signaled. He thanked the butchers when they gave him a couple of bagged bloody joints that would provide hours of puppy gnawing and hurried to catch the two riders.

They started out at an easy pace and when their mounts were limbered up, increased their speed till they were at a comfortable lope. Gar and the pups had no trouble keeping up with the horse and struthy, and the ground flowed beneath their feet. The run was uneventful and they made it through the larger forest without mishap.

Tina waited beside the grassway in front of a solid looking tower above a dirt-covered dome. "It'll be a little tight, but there's room for the wagon and animals. We have to share with another cerapig and two draft animals."

He could feel the smile she didn't let slip as he followed her into the large stables below the living quarters. His sister's horse and the two struthies were on the right beside a cage with two cerapigs and the wagon was parked between them and two immense… somethings.

"That's an interesting body shape," Gar deadpanned as he entered behind Xan.

"They look like a cross between a bathtub and a six-legged turtle," Xan said as he stared. "The spikes are a nice touch."

"See the wicker carriers hanging from the rafters?" Tina pointed. "There are two each of two designs, one for cargo and minimal passengers, and the other for passengers only. The owners hit a nonhuman gene lottery back before we were born and this is what they came up with as the best defense against monsters gone wild."

"Pretty good forward thinking," Sesco said as he tended to Spot. "Plenty of room and enough spikes to discourage all but the worst monsters."

"Like dragon rexes and unitaurs," Gar said as he signaled caution to the pups investigating the enormous living cargo trucks. "Well, maybe not belligerent fracking unitaurs... or hungry dragon rexes."

"And probably basilisk and assuredly mosasaurs if they swim the oceans," the traveling scholar said.

"Not going to catch me in something that small crossing any ocean, maybe the lake back home in daylight, but even that better be armed and armored."

Xan laughed at his friend, who foolishly swam in that lake many times when their lake mosa was nearby. There was even a fuzzy video of him riding her back on a foggy night, but he always insisted the person in the video wasn't him.

"How about a river voyage down the Ohio, my friend?"

Gar laughed and began brushing the packhorse. "Depends on whether or not there's anything not widely advertised, like dragon rex and unitaurs."

"And basilisk," Sesco reminded them. "And about a hundred other things imagined by some crazy gene hacker."

It didn't take long to finish feeding and

grooming their animals and become acquainted with their hosts. Herb West was a gene hacker and not ashamed of his learned craft.

"I won that lottery thing back thirty-six or seven years ago and even though I was only twenty-four, I saw where things were headed. I designed the best living defense for a world gone mad I could think of and made sure I was the lead assistant for every step of the way of its design. By the time the winnings were gone I not only had the first-generation model but all the equipment to continue and the basic learning. I spent the last couple decades perfecting the design and finally hit the sweet spot with the latest clutch."

Xan watched as several miniature versions of the bus sized turtle wagons scampered around as only the young can do. The parents were settled onto their belly armor and ignored the babies crawling over them and chewing on their extremities.

"But now I have a major problem."

"Uh-oh, grab your purses everybody," Sesco said as their host smiled.

"Nothing so drastic, my young vagabond."

Several sets of eyebrows rose, including those of the gene doctor's wife Rhiannon as the elderly gene hacker continued, "I have a whole clutch of newborns without the minor glitches the two parents have."

"The young will grow fast and I'll dissect three or four of the original twelve eggs to get a look at their make-up. They'll need room to grow and if I don't sell the parents, I'll have to butcher them. It would be much better if I were able to sell them to people traveling with meager possessions and outdoor protections."

Sesco snorted as the old man's maneuvering became clear. "What could such a destitute family offer, or their traveling companions, that would equal what you could get for that much meat?"

Doctor West smiled. "Let's go down to the stables and take a look at what I'm selling, then we'll talk about what they might be worth alive."

He led them back down from the open living area of the tower to where the two massive turtles rested while babies played around them. "The cargo carrier has all the comforts of home for a family or small crew forward and still carry four horses or struthies with room to spare for a pregnant cerapig in the back."

"You're trying hard to get us to find your cargo turtles desirable over what we already possess, but you still haven't said what you would want in payment."

"You may be the one doing all the talking, but you aren't the one with the payment I want." The gene doctor turned away from Sesco and locked eyes with Xan. "And please don't insult my intelligence by claiming to not know what I'm talking about."

Xan looked at his sister, then back at their host. "It's true the two hybrids would be useful, but we don't know their capabilities. If they've spent their lives within the confines of your property, they may not last walking twenty klicks and we'd be right back where we started, but with two massive, half-dead, turtle-bus gene-hacked failures."

"Here we go," Rhiannon complained. "Tina, Lilac, let's go up to the kitchen and start jerking some of that meat you're carrying while it's still fresh. If I know Herbert, he'll be bartering and dealing with your boys till I start turning lights off."

They gathered the saddlebags of tenderloin, rib roast tubes, and bacon, and were gone in minutes, but the others didn't notice as the doctor showed them the turtles.

"We take them out *running* every third day and *walking* twenty klicks out and back the other two unless something happens. In the last nine months, we've only missed three days of our exercise schedule and those were all due to extreme weather events."

"Running how far and how fast every third day?" Xan probed.

"Two, ten klick stretches of grassway at a run out then a fast lope on the way back without a rest. 25kph out and fifteen to seventeen on the way back. Doesn't sound like much, but that's with one or the other carriers and a kiloton of weight. Normal steady-walking speed the other two training days is also with a full load at ten to twelve kph for twenty klicks out and back nonstop, and it's a smooth ride."

His smile was wide and full of pride. "Wouldn't do to have the premier mobile home one could imagine and not give it the best endurance I could."

"They swim far enough above the water the inside of the carriers stays dry even with meter high waves. I know because I've crossed the Ohio several times and come out ahead in a number of confrontations with river beasties. There aren't many of today's dangers that could get through my babies' other defenses.

"The spikes are one of my favorite. They're not that long because long breaks. They're shorter and sturdier and inject a venom that burns and causes severe muscle pain but doesn't kill. Get enough and even something the size of the monsters you folks have already defeated would be too incapacitated to defend itself much less continue attacking. They grow back in about two months if they're broken off at the base, quicker the higher up they break."

"See that skirt of quills around the lower rim of the shell? Anything comes up from below is going to get a face or tentacle full of quills loaded with knockout juice. I can tell you from experience they work in deterring aggression from below while crossing rivers. They work pretty efficiently for raptors, snipes, and other ground level annoyances too," he added with a wide smile.

"Break them off and notch the base and they make great crossbow pistol darts. Each quill has a venom that will paralyze somebody Gar's size in about three seconds for about ten minutes. He would be wide awake and can breathe and blink, but that's about it. There are a couple thousand recessed growth pores and they regrow long enough to extend outside the pore in about a week if the turtle gets regular feed, which can be just about anything, including meat."

"You still haven't said what you're asking price is," Xan couldn't help but know, but any deal required two open offerings.

"Look at this," West said instead. "See the way the feet spread? They can swim almost as fast as they can slow walk and if anything tries to take a bite those claws can do some damage. Made them strong enough to gouge steel and the skin is the best gene designed armor. They can pull them in so only the armored knuckles and claws protrude and they can kick out to four meters. And check this out."

He released a rope and began lowering one of the carriers. "They're made of living wicker and I've woven in several different kinds of edible plants."

"That's strawberry," Stone said. "And those look like potato and peanut. You got them to grow aboveground."

"Yes, good eye, my friend. There are also green bean and cherry tomato vines, bell and jalapeno peppers, plus canibud. One corner post is apple," he pointed, "one avocado, and the back two are almond and peach. The leaves are edible and everything is tweaked enough to give all the vitamins and nutrients a body needs."

"The roots are in the bottom of the floor and the turtle *sweats* the nutrients through the bottom of the body cavity to support the wicker cabin. Combine the turtle and carrier and you have the ultimate, self-sufficient mobile home."

"And you've field tested everything?" Xan probed the gene hacker as he asked and was satisfied with the sincerity of the reply as Doctor

West eagerly explained every aspect of his genetic marvel.

"Oh yes, young man. I could do no less if I was to construct the ideal mobile home for the end of civilization as we know it. The turtles are fully capable of traveling at much faster than their namesake and for extended durations, their bodies provide defensive weaponry in the form of poisoned darts and shell spines."

"They're also designed with the body cavity to hold these lightweight carriers with a source of perpetually replenishing foods woven into their walls. Oh, and a luminescent moss grows on the interior of the roof."

Xan smiled as the eccentric gene hacker showed the prize of a lifetime of work. "And what, may I ask, is the price one would want for one of these wonders of the apocalypse?"

"One? Oh no young man, they are a mated pair and I would never dream of splitting them. No, they go together or not at all. Oh, and I mentioned they are a mated pair. Well, it seems while I was taking samples and doing lab work and such, after the female laid her last clutch of eggs and I took them away, she and her mate did what comes naturally."

He grimaced. "Well, as naturally as two creatures designed for utility instead of sexual mobility can. I'm not even sure how they did what they did, but one day I found all of Honey's rear spikes broken off and scattered about a disheveled paddock. Soon after I discovered that she was pregnant and will lay her eggs in about three months. I'm not even sure how the young will turn out since I did all insemination medically every prior generation and additional work on the eggs after they were lain."

"How much?"

The gene hacker, Doctor Herbert West, smiled. "If you insist on no further bartering, I have an opening offer. I would trade both turtles and your choice of wicker cabins for two of those prenatal packs of your grandfather's new invention, nanocellus sapien immortallus I believe it is called."

[9] River Basilisk.

"You have to admit, it was a good trade," Tina said as they rode in front of the lead turtle.

Xan shrugged. It had been a better than good trade, especially since their relatives had refused to even meet them much less accept the offer of genetically augmented elven children. "There's no telling what he'll do with it, maybe even make a virus that kills it."

"Doubt that since the whole purpose of asking for two prenatal packets was because he and his wife were going to test it on themselves. No, it was a good trade but I can't help but wonder what he'll do."

"Probably figure out how to get the stuff to bring back the dead," he muttered.

She laughed. "Century is almost over and no zombie plague yet."

"That's what somebody always says in those old movies just before somebody else does just what was said hadn't happened yet."

"Great bit of pretzel logic there, little brother." She looked back at the steadily plodding turtle with a smiling Eaglewing sitting in the driver's saddle fixed to the shell niche above the turtle's mobile head. His mother sat at his side in the second saddle, ready to take the reins but letting her son gain confidence and experience as well as having the turtle learn his *hand* at the controls. Her husband drove the second turtle with their cerapig and struthies, while the lead turtle carried Gar's packhorse, Phobos.

"Good choice for carriers."

He nodded his head in agreement. "I'm surprised how much the old doctor crammed into such a tiny space. Freezer, fridge, smart stovetop and oven, and all of it run on batteries powered by rooftop solar vine."

She smiled and gestured behind them. "Two armed and armored, walking vegetable gardens with all electric kitchens and enough room to carry everything we need, including our horses, across grasslands, swamplands, or rivers. No oceans, maybe a small lake or two in daylight, but no oceans."

"Agreed," he laughed. "No ocean crossings. Strangler infested forests are out too."

"Yes, no oceans or strangler forests. Anything else?"

"We'll probably add to the list before we get home but that's a start," he said with a smile.

"Home, have you noticed the daily reports are looking kind of…"

"…repetitive," he finished her thought. "Yeah. I sent a deep query with my security passcode and got back a hold pattern. It's like there's nobody home."

With that thought in their minds they rode in silence for a while, getting more stares for their unique transportation as they got closer to Bridgetown.

"Almost didn't get through the front gate," Gar said not long after as they sat at a balcony table looking out over the interior of the Dog and Pony that evening.

"Had almost a meter on each side and roof," Xan said, then took a drink of ale before choosing a grilling unitaur cube and spearing it. He ate the cube then speared a mushroom cap and ate it.

"Doc had another good idea with those sheaths for the spikes and the skirt for the quills," Sesco commented as he speared the last of their fresh selections on the hot side of the grill.

"Yeah, a lot of curious people putting hands and faces where they shouldn't," Stone said, then smiled. "Probably find a bunch of them full of quills lying in a ring around each turtle come sunrise."

"There are bets on how many get jabbed," Xan said. "I put a silver dollar on six and two on eleven."

"I think you threw the one dollar bet away," Sesco said. "I hear it's already up to three with one of those getting hit twice, and the liquor hasn't even begun to flow steady yet."

"Oh, and thanks for..." Xan started when Sesco waved him off.

"Not a problem. Gives me a room all to myself and I get to test the carrier's lighting at the same time I check out those books I bought. Besides, why waste gold on fancy rooms with hard walls when I can have something all to myself that breathes with the wind?"

Tina and Xan exchanged looks, smiled, and took a sip from their mugs at the same time before Xan spoke while she speared a cube of unitaur tenderloin. "Our own funds were planned for the length of our trip south then back home and are close to exhausted. After tonight we may have the opportunity to see how crowded it gets."

"There's plenty of room," the traveling scholar said as he waved a speared sliver of grilled bell pepper. "And since the lights are on till about two in the morning, I won't be bothering anybody when I stay up late reading."

"What was that one book," Tina waved a speared pineapple wedge with a meat cube, "the big one?"

"Picture book of some of the monsters that have been sighted. Some are actual pictures and others are different levels of rough sketches on up to realistic art. Both our trophies are in there with pictures and artwork for each, including descriptions and recommendations for staying alive."

"Paper looked weird when you showed me the picture of the unitaur," Gar said.

"It's made from that new type of hemp, similar to the canibud vines in the carrier," the scholar replied. "Ink and paper are both supposed to last for a thousand years and there are a couple dozen blank pages scattered through the different sections for additional entries. I also purchased the special ink colors that are genetically designed for that paper so I can sketch new ones."

"Going to draw stick figures of what you see?" Gar teased as he waved a grilled kabob.

Sesco smiled and dug into the large shoulder bag he had begun to carry once he was able to obtain new reading material and pulled out the book in question. Turning to one of the early pages he presented it to the giant. "That's one of mine."

Tina stretched across the table and he turned it toward her. She raised an eyebrow. "You drew that."

"Yes, from a safe vantage point and hidden while that particular crab monster daintily dissected and ate the mega bison in the picture. Got the video if you want to see the live version. There're three other pages of mine inside and I plan on adding several more on the blank pages."

He closed the book, put it back in the bag, and pulled out another that was larger. "Got this before I met you folks. It's full of blank pages or was when I got it over a year ago. It's about half full now but most of it is recreations of other things I've done and a lifetime of memories."

He grew pensive a moment as Tina casually relieved him of the weight. "Didn't know there was so much till I started putting it down."

Tina started laughing and turned the book so the others could see. The last picture showed Gar hanging onto the unitaur's horn when he first grabbed it, with his feet almost horizontal and a huge grin splitting his face. Fred and Ginger were also in the picture, each sitting and watching the show. The caption read: The best day of Gar's life.

"Well it was," Gar deadpanned, then lifted his mug. "Each is always better than the one before and the next better still."

They dutifully did the clink-and-drink to seal the toast, finished their table grill assortment, moved to the outer wall's balcony, and found a table overlooking the street corner. After getting another round, they watched the evening traffic in silence for several minutes as people traveled into and out of the twin village straddling the old interstate bridge.

"Eaglewing is asleep and the pups are on guard," Lilac said when she found them. "Thank you, Gar, nights out are precious, even if it's just an hour or two."

Gar nodded and smiled. "You're welcome, but you're not the only one needs to get the occasional break from youthful exuberance."

The day wore on as they relaxed from an early start and a quicker trip than expected, talking and watching the busy corner. Both manmade and biological vehicles of varying sizes rolled or walked by the crossroads, the numbers peaking an hour before sunset.

When the amount of vehicles began to diminish, with some of them heading for the night to safe compounds, they ordered their evening meal. Plates began arriving at their and several other tables just before the noise level in the tavern below them rose.

"Seems a bit rowdier than usual," the server said as she flipped the centerpiece rod with the green side down and the blue side up. "If you folks need anything just turn this back the other way. Looks like it's going to be a busy night and it'll be easier than one of you trying to wave us down. Blue signal stick is *we're okay* and green is a polite *hey you*. Polite gets served quicker than rude yelling when it gets crazy busy like this." Then she was gone.

It didn't matter for several minutes because their food was hot and they'd worked up an appetite watching traffic for over an hour. The server brought another round at the same time she collected the first round of plates, then traded empties for more plates a few minutes later. Her last appearance traded a fresh round for empty mugs and plates as she cleared their table.

The traffic continued to thin and dropped to almost nothing when the last sunlight fled while the noise level below rose and the remaining tables on the high balcony filled. Just as the corner streetlights began to glow brighter than the fading day, a last cerawagon approached.

Tina sat up straighter as the wagon left the road and headed for the Dog and Pony. Looking at Xan she nodded and sat back. "Okay, we'll wait for them to come up here."

Sesco looked from one to the other and rose from his chair. "You know, I don't think I've sat in one spot for so long in a while. Think I'll wander around and socialize a bit, maybe show off my etchings." Before anyone could react, he darted between busy staff and around tables and disappeared.

"Apparently, it's what he does," Xan said when Stone and Lilac traded a look.

Lilac nodded. "Should we be armed?"

Xan gave a small laugh. "I would hope it doesn't come to that but I'm pretty sure each of us has our Second Amendment protection on hand despite being inside secure walls."

They continued to relax above the plaza overlooking the corner as the night grew darker and the streetlights of every corner dotting the night grew brighter. Between each island of light fewer and fewer bobbing lanterns showed where the last of the traffic was heading home or trying to get inside the village wall before night monsters prowled.

Gar was in the process of turning the signal stick green side up when Sgt. Bekka Cloverfield and her husband Tanner found them. The server appeared before they could get seated and they ordered another round of drinks and snacks while returning the color stick to blue side up.

"My brother found out what we were doing and threatened to cut any freak baby out of me and burn it," Bekka informed them with fire in her eyes. "My own brother! Had to throw him in jail again, but for some reason he got more people stirred up and when he got bailed, they got together. They stopped openly agitating, but they're still meeting privately."

"Tanner has been a detective as long as I've been a sergeant and we both think they're planning something big and just laying low till they strike. Those big tanks you're driving are kind of hard to miss and people are watching. You couldn't have known, but that gene hacker you got them from is a sort of local celebrity of the *in*famous kind in these parts and that got another kind of agitator stirred up."

"The cerawagon we came in is a dummy," Tanner took up the story after the server arrived, swarmed around them briefly trading full plates and mugs for empties, then disappeared. "Our real rig is parked on the other side of the river, all packed with everything we own of importance and ready to drive… wherever."

"You'll be riding with us till then, of course," Tina said, putting a comforting hand over Bekka's.

"Going to be hard to sneak a pair of turtles the size of houses across the bridge and there are protest crowds already gathering from one end to the other. That's why so many people are leaving town. If we hadn't called ahead when you were first sighted, we wouldn't have a stall here at the Dog and Pony for the diversion wagon."

Xan and Tina traded a look, then nodded and Tina explained. "Why don't we act like everything is normal and tell everybody we're crossing the bridge tomorrow and going home. Then we return to our rooms and wait till the halls are clear to go to the turtles and sneak out the back door."

"Still have to cross the bridge," Tanner reminded them.

"They're turtles, they swim," Xan said. "And we have verification they easily survive what the depths of the Ohio can dish out. We'll head for the nearest place we can cross and be on the Ohio side just about the time the main bunch of agitators arrive on the bridge to spew their particular brand of bigoted hatred at sunrise."

"Then we meet up with the people guarding your wagon and head north." Everybody but Gar missed the look Tina gave Xan before she hid her worry with a deep-fried river salmon nugget.

Xan gave a short shake of his head when his friend looked his way, before continuing, "Luckily we saved stable fees by putting all our animals aboard the turtles for the night. When we go, we won't have to create any additional commotion, just walk the turtles out the back door. Anybody not passed out will still be at the tavern and the streets should be empty."

"Somebody should find Sesco and tell him," Tanner said.

Xan gave a small chuckle. "You met him already?"

"Yes, introduced himself and told us where to find you. He was vouched for by Chief McCoy, so we knew we could trust him. Said he was with you. He is, isn't he?"

"Oh yes," Tina said, adding with a mischievous smile. "More and more every day."

"Well, if we're going to make a silent exit, Lilac and I should make sure our half of the escape wagons are ready to run."

Several minutes later Sesco swung by and they got a final round of drinks. "I was able to arrange a little diversion to keep attention on the bridge at sunrise."

"Already? That was fast," Gar said as he gave the scholar the stinkeye.

Sesco shrugged. "Couple of drinks bought, some questions asked and answered, then a few coins given and suggestions of fun entertainment made. Simple really and only a twenty percent chance of it not happening."

At several raised eyebrows, he explained. "A lot of folks around here like to poke a stick in the eye of the high and mighty purists every now and then. Trouble is those high and mighty sometimes react violently when they're laughed at and there are supposed to be more of that ilk than normal on the bridge tomorrow."

He shrugged. "Harmless pokes in fun can quickly become less enjoyable when the fearfully belligerent overreact when they're on the less positive side of public attention and bullets fly."

The thought of that level of violence was enough to squelch any enjoyment they might have had the rest of the night. Their evening ended early and they managed to be back at the turtles long before the rowdiness of the night began to shed casualties.

The solution to crowded stables and interior court came when several drunks started a fight in the plaza in front of the Dog and Pony. As spectators rushed to the other side of the compound to watch the brawl, they casually walked their turtles through the back gate and across to the unlit fourth road out from the wall.

The cheering and groans from the drunken spectators were loud behind them as their turtles trotted westward. They crossed the spoke road to the west gate and a couple klicks past where the wall curved around to form a high pier out into the river.

"I was told there was a park here *back in the day*," Sesco made one-handed air quotes, "which I took to mean before genetic monsters began making the wilderness bigger. There," he pointed, "those three close hardwood trees on one side and twin evergreens in line on the right. The old boat ramp is between them so we should be able to just walk in."

Xan gave his new friend a skeptical look. "You know all this how?"

"When I was socializing back at the Dog and Pony, this one fella showed me a mural in a back room that showed both sides of Bridgetown and the shoreline for several miles. It was so old it marked distances in miles instead of kilometers. Right about where we are now there's a picture that looks just like that," the scholar pointed again at the scene in front of them.

"There should be another ramp on the other side about a kilometer downstream. According to my source there's an old road from the park on that side to the main grassway that's in use and regularly cleared of predator concealment."

He shrugged. "That's the only part I couldn't find out about except from one source. Everybody else I talked to said he was crazy but he claims to know there's a way for our turtles to get through. Everybody else says there's another spot another two klicks downstream that leads right to the main grassway, but that's a scattered village with a handful of private compounds in sight at any one time."

"Your choice, but we need to hurry if we want to be across before sunrise. Go in here and head to the park on the other side, or go downstream further before we head across for that tower community and dozens of sets of bored, gossipy eyes."

"Cross now," Xan said and Gar engaged the levers that nudged the turtle to tell it what to do instead of reins and knee pressure.

"Whoa!" the big man laughed as Honey surged ahead and waded right in.

"Bear almost ran us over coming after," Sesco said after looking over their mounts' heads and out the back of the carrier. "I guess turtles like swimming."

Xan left Gar and his sister to their driving and followed the scholar between the animals to the aft rail and sniffed. "Honey's sweat just changed, she's working different muscles swimming."

"Amazing how Doctor West got the sweat stuff needed to fertilize the plants to smell like honeysuckle," the scholar said as he memorized the scene through the rear of the immense, designed and manufactured animal. "And Bear is a better name than Straw, or Barry, more like a warrior's name despite how good he smells when he gets sweaty."

When Sesco returned forward, Xan stayed at the rear for a few moments watching as the sky to the east began to be less black, the moon setting to the west lighting Bear's shape as he swam mere meters behind and upstream from his mate.

To Xan's genetically augmented eyes, the soft moonlight was more than enough for him to clearly see Stone and Tanner sitting at the control saddles. The ride was surprisingly smooth and he felt every stroke of the six powerful legs as they propelled the turtle across the river. Smiling at the two in the front of the other turtle he saw their faces change when Bear lurched in the water and began to fall back.

"Hey," he yelled to the front of the carrier, "something's happening to the other turtle."

Then his eyes went wide as the head of a snake big enough to swallow a ten-meter alligator appeared over the top of Bear's wicker carrier.

[10] Basilisk, oliphants, and raptors, oh my.

The giant river snake seemed to pause then a coil that was as thick as he was tall appeared then sank out of sight while the basilisk's head slowly drooped till it rested on the roof of the carrier. Xan was surprised the carrier didn't collapse from the weight.

Tina and Sesco rushed back with weapons ready to see the basilisk struggling to move and Bear soldiering on, his head just high enough for him to see his mate slowing to stay with him.

"I showed Gar where we need to land," Sesco said. "We might need to swim against the current a bit if we need to block for Bear."

Tina was giving hand signals and Stone waved as Tanner pushed hard on the heavy levers that told Bear what to do. By pushing his head to the right, Bear turned just enough to compensate for the extra weight and fight the current more.

By the time they reached the northern shore they were downstream from their target and moved into a small inlet. Honey went in first with Bear dragging the paralyzed river serpent as far out of the water as he could. They were trying to figure out how to remove the massive snake when a figure came out of the forest.

"Well hello," Sesco said when he noticed Xan's change of focus. "Hey everybody, this is the fella told me about this spot, goes by the name

Rocky River. Rocky, you seem to not have had any problem getting here before us."

"Didn't have to stay out late to sneak off or worry about being stopped on the bridge by fools protesting an inevitable future. Was already here and watching when your mutant turtles went swimming."

He walked over to where he could get a look at the paralyzed snake. "Looks like you reeled in ol' Betsy. She's been getting a little too big for her own good lately and folks were 'bout ready to show her how vicious humans can be."

"Met that crazy doctor once and he told me about his turtles. You might want to put Betsy out again pretty soon or start cutting her head off now, and I do mean *now*," Rocky said as he began to back up.

Sesco seemed to have been thinking first and quickly ran into the back of Honey's rear stable and returned with a pair of the special 'quill whackers' they'd made. He ran at the slowly recovering snake, tossing one of the rods to Xan as he passed.

Xan caught the shaft, leaped using one of the lower spikes as a jump point to gain altitude, and jabbed the enormous snake in the throat just as the tongue appeared to *taste* her surroundings. The whackers were two meters long and covered in turtle quills for the top half meter with a tight pack attached to the tip.

He pulled away, leaving the bundle of quills deeply embedded in the soft flesh of the basilisk's throat, and dropped to the ankle-deep water.

Swinging the rod, he jammed more quills into the serpent's belly as Sesco climbed up on Betsy's back and whacked her repeatedly around the base of the head and neck.

Behind Bear, the rest of the snake began to undulate in the water as the turtle moved a couple of steps further onto land behind Honey.

Xan and Sesco continued whacking the snake over the forward four or five meters till all their quills were expended. The rear end of the lengthy monster continued to wave in the shallow water, but at a slower and slower pace.

"That gives us maybe ten or twelve minutes to finish whatever we're going to do," Xan said as everybody looked at the snake still partially wrapped around Bear's shell and carrier.

"Do you want the snake or not," Rocky was quickly impatient.

Gar snorted a laugh. "What would we want a hundred-foot river serpent for? Give me a few teeth and a patch of skin and you can have the rest of my share."

The rest quickly agreed and Rocky gave a measured whistle. The nearby foliage rustled and shook and an enormous oliphant emerged from the woods. Her twin trunks were flanked by tusks that were sheathed in bladed harnesses. Her trunk-like tail waved a broadsword longer and more robust than that of the general oliphant.

"This is Elly, I know, not real inventive, but there was a time when she was small enough to sleep in my lap. Well, put her head in my lap anyways. You folks want most of the teeth, some hide, and anything surprising we find, so we'll do the head first."

"Elly, honey, could you pull ol' Betsy off that big turtle, please? Don't bump the spines or those quills around the bottom edge, they're stingers worse than strangler vines. As soon as you get her clear, cut her head off, please."

Without hesitation Elly reached up with a pair of trunks twice as long as the normal African bull elephant before CRISPR and poorly regulated genetic research changed the creatures of Earth. Almost daintily considering she was at the upper limit of physical size capable even with genetically reinforced muscle and bone, the brobdingnagian behemoth lifted the serpent's head away from Bear's back. She carefully pulled the body off the three spikes it was impaled on, and pulled back at the best angle to stretch the head out over the ground at the water's edge.

Ol' Betsy gave out a slow hiss and her tongue began to emerge as she awakened quicker than her first paralyzing injections. Unconcerned, Elly held the head down, lifted her tail sword high, then spun with impressive speed and chopped through the full diameter of one side of the neck.

Ol' Betsy hissed again, but the sound also came in a bubbling gurgle on the nearer half. Elly was unconcerned as the rear end of the snake began to thrash in the water, turning and holding the snake's head steady as she raised her sword high again.

She waited till she felt the snake relax, then spun and chopped through the spine. Another quick chop and the head came free, and Elly calmly carried it away from the river's edge. Not finished yet, she found a large log and jammed it into the back of the serpent's gaping jaws.

"There you go folks," Rocky said as Elly walked back to the snake and pulled the rest of the carcass out of the river. "Take what you want, but you might want to do it fast. Blood in the water is going to draw hungry critters of all shapes and sizes."

"I'd appreciate it if you'd move your turtles so Elly can get more of Ol' Betsy far enough so's I can see what she's got in her first stomach." He pointed. "The quickest way to the grassway is that way. Elly keeps it clear so you can't miss it."

"Gar, Stone, and Tanner, could you help me dig these teeth out while the others move the turtles?" Xan said as he used the heavy hatchet he'd gotten from Honey's tool bin to start on an upper canine. He had the eight largest loose or out when Gar disconnected the entire lower jaw and dragged it toward Bear's cargo bay.

He was back and finishing cutting the skin from the face to get at the soft meat for the pups when Rocky approached and threw down a pile of mucous covered objects. "Said a share of any surprises. Not really a surprise to me, but the first stomach was full of stuff. Might want to throw a few buckets of water over that and you'll still need gloves." He waggled his leather clad fingers. "Probably should throw the gloves away afterwards, too, instead of putting them with other stuff."

Gar ran down to the water's edge for a

couple buckets of water while the turtles walked into the woods. When the mess was cleaned, they had several silver, gold, and platinum necklaces, and a couple dozen highly polished stones and nuggets.

"Smart enough to keep all the coins for himself," Sesco commented as they tossed gloves already starting to dissolve over the aft rail. "How much time did we lose?"

"About an hour from the very best we could have hoped for," Xan estimated.

He cocked his head as he felt his sister's mind in the front turtle. "Even better. The grassway is in sight."

Sesco looked at the old sat-phone he carried. "Looks like there's a big confrontation at the bridge. Seems some jokesters made big paper turtles and tried to carry them across, but they didn't get far. All the agitators are blocking everything on the Ohio side and the partiers are gathered on the West Virginia side with all the cops in the middle keeping both sides apart."

He smiled. "There's one report about ol' Betsy attacking a yacht at sunrise and eating everybody on board, but the disturbance on the Bridgetown bridge is clogging all the regional newsfeeds."

Minutes later they were walking at a steady pace along a grassway that was devoid of human traffic but had several small herds of wild sauro, hadro, and cera with a few furred and shelled specimens scattered among the prevailing dinosaur variants.

"Sure wish I could have gotten some snake skin," Sesco said. "Would have made a good book cover. I'd trade my share of the stomach booty for some if I could."

Gar one-eyed his new friend. "Seeing as how you were the one quick enough to get the whackers and did more than your share in keeping ol' Betsy pacified while Elly cut her head off, you can have the hide from the lower jaw. As is, of course. You'll have to cure it yourself."

"Done!" Sesco laughed and wasted no time to find the rolled hide and begin checking it out. In minutes, he had both Gar and Tanner helping by holding it out for him while he measured.

After a while he scowled. "You know, we're far enough ahead of schedule we could stop for a bit to assess things."

Xan laughed and slapped the scholar on the shoulder. "Good idea my friend." He hopped over the rear rail instead of opening it and from there, and jumped off the angled tailbone to the ground.

The massive living cargo carriers moved at a turtle's pace, but their legs were much longer than nature's own design. Even though they moved at a relatively slow and steady pace, they covered considerable distance with each tripedal step.

But that was still only a fraction of what Xan could sprint and he was even with the drivers' saddles in seconds. "Hey sis, we're ahead of what we expected and the party is still going strong at the bridge. Let's make a quick stop to take stock and see how things look."

For answer Tina stood on her saddle, a hand

on the edge of Honey's upper shell as she scanned the grassway ahead. "We've passed several places that looked good. I'm sure we'll see another soon, in fact, that spot there looks big enough for both turtles."

Xan ran ahead seventy meters and to the edge of the grazer-manicured grassway. It was rocky enough in this area there were several gaps in the strangler infested trees. The trees on either side were large but far enough from the ridges it provided a wide trail for animals to get deeper into the forest where stranglers were less predominant.

Tina saw the design of the landscape as Lilac steered that way and directed their cousin as Xan led the way inside. Honey kicked at the scree and detritus within the wide split in the rocky ledge with every step as she climbed into the shelter of the woods. She was above the rock and into the fold between the two hills when Xan signaled and they stopped her. He got back to the edge of the grassway just as Bekka got Bear turned around and started backing him into the game trail.

When they were inside the cleft between the two hills the only thing that showed was the front third of Bear's body and most of that was camouflaged by the living weave of the carrier.

"We can stay as long as we want," Xan said as they gathered in the space between the two resting turtles, most of them sitting on the aft rails.

"The more klicks we put between us and Bridgetown, the better," Bekka said. "And we still need to get our own cerawagon. We're not even logging onto our media site or sending emails just in case my brother is looking for clues to where we are. In fact, both our phones are off and the batteries out till we put another night behind us."

"We're with you, hon," Lilac said as she patted the young woman's hand. "Got enough of the same kind of family to know what you're going through."

Bekka smiled as she leaned into Stone for additional comfort.

Before anyone else could speak they heard the unmistakable sound of emergency sirens coming from the village and scattered compounds of the river community downstream from Elly's park. They were concealed enough to not be seen as first one, then another heavy emergency truck roared by on eight huge off-road monster tires.

The newest design for armed and armored emergency vehicles consisted of an ambulance compartment and a main mobile home cabin and crew seats sitting atop four flat, water tanks. Both of the ones that raced by also had the tracks at top and bottom that allowed a special working pod to get to any position around the truck. Robotic arms on the pod could access several kinds of tool or weapon for fighting fires or monsters.

They waited a few minutes and several smaller emergency and law enforcement trucks followed, sirens blaring and grazing animals scattering again at this second disturbance.

Sesco was on his sat-phone again and several heads crowded his as they watched over his shoulders. The screen showed a live feed from a helicopter view of the riot on the Bridgetown bridge.

"How does one get a sat-phone with a live news feed?" Detective Cloverfield gave Sesco his *authority* glare.

Sesco waved a hand negligently. "Helped someone once with an extra and traded legally for a couple of software additions in the years since. The company that made this model went out of business because they made their product so good they never broke. Other manufacturers are buying up all the old ones to smash so people start buying their cheap knockoffs that need replacing every few years."

"According to the news, Bekka, it was the other group, the ones that have some sort of personal problem with our Doctor West, that started it. One group stayed on the West Virginia side and were waiting to kill the abominations. When the real turtles didn't show up, they decided setting fire to the half-sized paper and cloth effigies would suffice. There was a lot of glued layers and the paper sculptures weren't as big as we are, but were still big and they burned hot enough to set the vender stalls and contents afire."

"Most of the police were in the middle of the bridge keeping the two groups apart. There weren't enough on the West Virginia side to catch the perpetrators but dozens of people got pictures and video of them with their phones."

"How many were hurt?" Bekka's glare was fierce. She had warned them to not put too many on a separation line in the middle of a closed bridge. She had advocated for leaving the bridge open and putting all efforts at either end.

"Surprisingly few," Sesco said as he read the crawler below the video with the talking head speaking to a witness. "Oh wait, seems there were several severe injuries. I guess a few of the torchers chose a high river wall to escape and fell into the river. Only two of the five were pulled out alive and they were missing both legs."

"Most of the injuries are broken bones from falls and smoke inhalation but the evacuation stayed ahead of the hottest fire. A lot of fire damage but extra units from surrounding communities are keeping the worst of it restricted to south end of the bridge."

"There are the two trucks that just passed us. Heh-heh, they're driving right up onto the bridge and hosing down everything on both sides of the south end, including rioters."

"Wait, here's an interview with the Captain of the two trucks that passed us." The heads crowding around his pressed closer.

The uniformed man said the grassway he'd driven on to get to the scene was completely clear of *any* human traffic on horse or wagon, especially any giant turtles.

"We need to go," Xan said. "They just confirmed we aren't in one of the few places we could be. We're going to see people anyway, but the first reports are from the most credible witnesses and on every news feed."

"They'll recycle those clips every hour till they're all quoting each other," Sesco said as he put his sat-phone away. "Any new reports will be ignored till the first picture shows up and if I know a few pranksters as well as I think I do, fake news pictures of us in all kinds of places will start showing up soon anyway."

They moved fast and Xan ran out into the open grassway to see if any vehicles were in sight. A fast-moving truck would be best as it would give one more witness to them not being where they were.

"Pull up a step to give me room to get Xanthos out, then wait till after the two trucks I saw coming go by."

"Okay," Stone said as he settled onto the left-hand saddle.

Xan ran back alongside the mutant turtle as Bear stood and moved forward three meters then settled back down to rest on his belly shell. He explained what was happening as he finished readying his horse and led him out of the rear. They could see around and over Bear's carrier as the two, large armed and armored trucks roared by.

Xan was just about to mount as Bear stood up to leave their hiding place when a fierce roar sounded from in front of Honey, followed by a second and a third.

Xan swung into the saddle and pulled his carbine as Xanthos turned toward the challenge just as a pack of raptors came through the woods where the stranglers were thinnest.

[11] Puzzle pieces.

He had the weapon up and aiming at the nearest raptor when it staggered and fell. As he turned, he saw a hand extend from inside the wicker cabin with one of the pistol crossbows and another raptor staggered.

Since those at the front of the carrier had the better targets and less noisy weapons the occupants of the trucks that had just passed might hear, he held his fire. Holstering his carbine, he urged Xanthos to follow Bear out of the narrow stone path between the grassway and the strangler forest. Tina and Sesco were quickly mounted and they followed Gar as he ran out after Bear with Fred and Ginger guarding their rear.

Honey backed out of the narrow canyon and the raptors cautiously followed, nudging and sniffing at their packmates that had fallen to paralyzing darts. Some of the smaller raptors stayed with their stricken packmates while a team of five began to stalk the horse and struthy that were more their size.

Gar had his staff and stood his ground with Fred and Ginger on either side as two of the raptors moved one way and two others the other while the fifth bobbed and weaved to distract them.

Without waiting Gar took three quick steps forward and whacked the raptor in the side of the head with one end of the staff, then swept its feet out from under it on the return swing. Fred and Ginger were ready and rushed in to maul the raptor while it was down, one crushing its skull with massive jaws while the other ripped its throat out.

The three of them were in a protective position again before the flanking raptors could react.

The turtles had continued on at their steady pace and Xan came up on one side of his friends while his sister guarded their other side. Both horses reared and kicked out with genetically altered hooves, each catching a stalking raptor in the head.

When Xanthos spun to kick back, Xan swung the sword he'd pulled and slashed at the other raptor, chopping off one of the grasping hands with their wickedly clawed fingers. Xanthos kicked the second raptor solidly, throwing it several meters back and into the nearest strangler. The vine grabbed the unlucky hunter, but it was dead before the grasping vine caught it.

Another raptor fell to the paralyzing darts and the others began to get nervous and no longer pressed the retreating prey.

"That would be another good place to build a homestead," Tina said as they rode behind the turtles so they could keep an eye on the raptors.

"Lots of good places," Sesco said on her other side as they rode three abreast. Gar and the pups roamed from border to border so the hellhounds could sniff everything. "Problem isn't the number of good places to settle away from walled cities. Problem is resources to get secure before you move in. The major part of those resources is security and sometimes they're more dangerous than the gene hacked monsters."

"No, there are plenty of good places a resourceful family or group could homestead, but most would be killed before they could build a base structure sturdy enough to resist monsters designed to kill and destroy. Like Dragontop Hill before we got there. Looks like we're coming up on walled towers."

"On it," Tina said and urged Thoth to a gallop to catch up to the turtle carrying Bekka and Tanner.

"Raptors never left the parking spot," Gar said as they continued to scan their perimeter for danger. "You realize it's not even lunch yet, don't you?"

Sesco snorted a laugh as they came up to the first tower. "I've gotten into more trouble in the few days I've known you people than six months before. Of course, part of that was holed up in a library through winter, but even so, libraries aren't always safe."

"What," Xan asked, "you owe somebody money and they knew just where to find you if you weren't in a tavern?" Sesco didn't react in a way anyone else would notice, but Xan was becoming close enough to him he *felt* when his teasing barb hit home. "Really? Heh, you're going to have to change some of your habits if common thugs don't have trouble finding you."

Sesco gave him the stinkeye and he laughed again. "You might as well get used to it, my friend, especially if you keep on giving my sister goo-goo eyes."

"I do not!"

Xan snorted. "Even Fred and Ginger notice and watch you when you're doing it."

Sesco gave him an openmouthed gape and he laughed again. "Yes, and my sister is about ready to chase you off if you don't stop, or speak your intentions."

"My *intentions*?"

"Yeah, something like, hey lady, want to see my etchings?"

"Did he see something?" Tina asked when she returned to the back of the convoy as Sesco quickly rode away, then immediately read him. "You didn't! Hermes Alexander! Now he'll bolt next chance he gets."

"Heh-heh, wait, what, you mean? But he's, he's…"

"A *Librarian*? Yes, and probably has a girl in every village, little brother. Wouldn't surprise me, but so what? He's smart, he's considerate of others to a fault, and he's pulled his own and more in every situation we've found ourselves in. And let me tell you little brother, we've been through considerably more than what I was led to believe we would encounter. Our little trip is suspiciously looking more and more like one of grampa's training scenarios."

Xan's analytical mind hadn't considered that as worth adding to the equations surrounding their journey. As pieces of information jelled, he added them together in a rush. "He knew the situation on Blackrock Mountain, probably the attitudes brewing at Bridgetown, too. Most smaller giants could easily be big purebreds, most dwarves are just short, stocky people, and most elves either don't have the size of our ears or cover them with hats."

"Hunh, two obvious elves and the biggest giant in the state with horses that don't look anything like horses, plus a pair of unleashed hellhounds, and he sent us through one of the concentrations of social disruption on horseback instead of armored trucks."

Tina nodded. "I was talking to Rhiannon and she all but said grampa and the doctor used to be friends, but just drifted apart because they were each so engrossed in their own work. She said she didn't actually know how he knew about the NSI we were carrying."

"Rocky mentioned knowing the doctor and now I think about it, he had the doc in mind when he talked to Elly. I bet the doc built her and Rocky paid with that riverboat he said he won twenty years ago."

"Doc West was waiting at the end of the road back to his tower when we came out of the strangler forest," Tina continued. "Rhiannon came out with cold drinks while we were talking and offered a fresh meal and safe stabling while we waited for the rest of you."

"The whole trip was a set-up," he snorted. "But why? And is the blackout from home part of it or," he stopped, then tilted his head and his sister waited as one of his attributes kicked in. His mind raced in several directions as Xanthos walked without direction till he came out of his mentat trance with a sigh.

"Either the blackout is part of some test that

includes the amount of NSI we were given, or the test was to prepare us for something that has the blackout as part of what is going on at home."

"Basically, a test or training for an imminent danger that may have already happened at home."

"Yeah, sis, looks like. I'm still trying to figure out how the others fit in, though. Oh." His eyes went vacant a few seconds. "We're recruiting families all carrying or will carry elven children of an improved line. But are we collecting them to bring home and how does the blackout come in?"

"What about Frick and Frack, or should I say, Frederic and Francine."

"There's a giant enclave a couple hundred klicks southeast of Buffalo that keeps getting harassed by their neighbors. I remember Francine telling me about it a couple days before we left but it didn't click till just now."

"So, we're collecting elves and Gar's preceding generation is doing the same with a giant version of NSI. And now I think about it, grampa said something about visiting that dwarf family that lives on the Canadian side of the lake after we were gone."

"Three of the five or six most numerous of the human variants given a new genetic elixir and… what?" He was still fuming when they came to a group of towers in a scattered cluster that didn't come close enough to create a village.

Bekka and Tanner dropped away from the turtle they were riding and darted into one of the compounds. Minutes later a pair of riders dressed with the local version of floppy hat and cloak left the compound and rode past them at speed. They rode on, Gar and Sesco moving to the front to lead the caravan of genetic mutants through the more populated area. When they came to the crossroad north of Bridgetown, they fell in behind a large cerawagon among several other travelers heading north.

They joined several dozen wagons and mechanical trucks and armored vans in one of the former roadside rests on the old interstate and reunited with Bekka and Tanner at their cerawagon.

"We were thinking of a saurowagon for the size and utility for later," Bekka explained as she gave them a tour, "but decided to go with smaller with more speed. We got her at a discount because the seller was in the middle of a family emergency and needed to get home."

"He said she was younger, but she can't be and be as big as she already is," Tanner said. "If she's only one-year old then she's going to be a huge cera when she gets her full growth."

"I noticed a few things I don't normally see on cera species," Sesco said. "The legs are kind of gangly and the feet are oversized for the rest of the body, just like a juvenile not fully grown into its body. Could very easily be a yearling, especially with that smaller frill. Sure, she has some impressive horns but they only look big because of the size and shape of the head and longer neck."

"I'm willing to bet, in a year this little lady will be able to keep up with any of our horses and struthies. Maybe not in a racing sprint, but in a long hard lope. This is a cowboy's cera."

Xan sighed inwardly and gave his sister a smile. "You say you got her from some fella needing to sell fast at a loss, and your inspection of the animal's pedigree was confirmed by two reputable vets, one of them a personal friend."

"Yes, why?" Tanner was becoming suspicious but not knowing why.

"Oh, just a theory my sister and I have been playing with. That's a really nice cabin, did it come with the cera?"

"Yes," Tanner's voice dropped and he scowled.

"Oh, don't worry. In fact, if what Tina and I suspect is true then you were given a valuable gift you may need in the future and charged only enough to keep you from becoming suspicious. How long ago was it you first decided to shop for a wagon?"

"The day after you left the Dog and Pony was the first time we looked at the ones being advertised for sale. We checked on two when this fella came up and made his offer. Since he had to have cash we sold as much as we couldn't carry and called in the last of our favors to stock on staples and extra ammo."

"I hope you don' think I'm prying, but did this fella mention a secret safe?"

"Yes," Bekka growled. "It's in a hard to get to spot in a corner under the fold-down table and chairs. We didn't have anything to put in it, so haven't looked at it yet."

Xan didn't say anything else, and after a few moments Bekka and Tanner stalked away and climbed into the cabin resting on its extended legs. Several minutes later they returned, each carrying a metal box.

"It's all there, every single silver and gold coin we scrounged, including every piece of legacy jewelry and even the silverware. There was just enough room left for these two lockboxes, each with one of your names on it."

By now Xan knew what to expect and didn't react to the heavy weight when Tanner passed the box to him. He turned it so the lock was up, pressed his thumb against the pad, and it snapped with an electrical smell. He lifted the lid to reveal rows and rows of rolled silver dollars and four denominations of gold coins all stacked on end.

A waterproof leather pouch was stuffed into the lid with an attached aluminum tag etched in a series of dots and dashes. He gave his sister a nod as they closed their respective treasure safes to an electronic snap as the boxes automatically locked.

"It looks like we're all being steered into an alliance of mutual defense and being funded as we're recruited." He saw the look on Lilac and Stone's faces and wondered aloud, "We kept your cerapig but the wagon was too much to carry and wasn't needed with all the luggage room around the inside of the carrier. Have you gone through all the crates?"

"All but my toolbox," Stone said. "Didn't need to what with all that was going on. The doctor mounted it back in the same corner with the pig. It's the only thing he made inconvenient to get to."

"Of course he did," Tina muttered with a

smile. "Why don't you check your toolbox while we're all safe and snug in the middle of a packed public parking lot."

They weren't actually in the middle of the packed vehicles or even inside the seemingly solid security fence that was more for state of mind than protection. But it was a favored spot for early arrivals that didn't get a place along the inner curb.

With their defenses, they moved to the northern end of the fence on the grassway side, using the fence to protect their caravan from curious wanderers inside the rest stop. They also parked the turtles rear to rear with a gap wide enough to tie the horses and struthies out in the fresh air where there was a meager amount of grass growing along the fencerow.

Shuffling noises came from the back corner of the carrier bay, then there was silence for several minutes before Stone and Lilac came out carrying two metal boxes.

"Same thing," Lilac said. "Every single coin and valuable traded to get what we escaped with. Even the sword and long knife my brother brought back from Japan, the one he gave to *me*, but nobody would let me touch after he died. And I know it's mine because Simon let me carve my initials in the handles of both where nobody else would notice. And these boxes have your names on them."

Xan and Tina checked the boxes and found the same thing, rows of silver and gold coins and a pouch with a code stamped into a metal tag.

"Well, one thing for sure, we've each been given more than enough material support to get halfway across…" he stopped, and started chuckling. "We still have one more reservation confirmed and the message *mail package waiting* so maybe we'll find out what this is all about when we get there."

While the others got ready for sleep, Xan and Tina took their safe boxes to the small table in the front of Bear's carrier. They removed the four pouches and put the boxes full of coins on the floor at their feet.

Inspecting the metal tags first, they found the simple code they'd invented as children and spent several minutes deciphering the stamped message. When they were finished, they burned the papers they'd used to read the message with silently grim faces as Sesco looked up from his artwork at another table.

When Xan's turn at watch came, he made sure all the animals were fed and watered then pulled quills and reloaded the whacker poles. He was watching a small group of riders on unaltered horses when the first smells of breakfast wafted his way.

Being on watch, he was the first to be served and finished in record time while Bekka watched the riders. "Don't see many purebred animals nowadays."

"No, you don't," he mumbled almost to himself as she took his empty plate and returned to the carrier.

He watched the riders disappear in the distance as the camp awoke, ate, and the turtles were reloaded and ramps stowed. Within minutes they set out and the days passed as the kilometers flowed beneath their feet.

The sun was nearing the horizon when their strange convoy came to the village walls, then entered and found the stables and hotel they'd first stayed at. The turtles were too big to get through either gate so they stayed in the old parking lot next to the Smith Stables with two large vehicles.

One was a mobile kitchen and Xan and his sister found themselves inside sitting with Rick Shaw and his wife. "I was offered the spot as head cook and Amanda as head geek at more money per week than I thought was fair for a month. Guess it don't seem so bad now I see how many people we have to cook and geek for."

"All we were told was we were to cook three meals a day and drive the kitchen bus. There's enough armor to keep the most determined critter out and fold down arms with ground spikes to keep the bigger ones from tipping us over in a stampede. There are guns and stuff all over, two mechanical arms on separate rail pods, and we have enough food stores to feed an army for a month."

He looked cautiously left and right and leaned forward to whisper. "Has a safe chock full of gold and silver coins to buy whatever perishable supplies we might need."

He sat back up as he continued in a normal voice, "Amanda is in charge of cyber security and the cell station we carry. At your convenience, she'll synch all your phones to the bus's mini-server."

"What about the other bus?"

"Not with our group, Xan. It must be from the same people, though, because it's a duplicate of this one. They're going in a different direction as us from what their crew told me. Really nice couple of giants, Frederick and Francine. Said they were meeting with some others here after we leave then going south and west."

As Xan put his head in his hand and tried not to laugh aloud, Tina asked the next logical question, "So, you know the other bus is going south, then west. Does that mean you know which direction you're going?"

Rick shrugged. "Our map shows us going directly west on old I-80."

"The Black Hills," Xan and Tina said at the same time as the last clues snapped into place, then Xan continued, "He's building a refuge for the altered humans that are beginning to be persecuted all across the world as gene hacked monsters grow in number and living space for unaltered humanity diminishes."

[12] Lake Kraken.

"But what about our home?" Gar asked. "Are we just going to go off on some new adventure before we even get to see why my phone calls don't even go to voicemail and I can't get a return text from anybody?"

"It's on the way," Xan replied. "We'll take a boat to the island, check it out, then take a boat back to the mainland and head west to see what grampa is up to this time."

"You have a pretty good idea of what that is, don't you," Sesco stated instead of asking.

"Yes. His every act during this entire planned adventure, except for some of the monsters we ended up facing, was to offer sanctuary to people experiencing a growing fear-based intolerance as well as those who see some form of genetic augmentation as a necessary tool to survive a world changing too rapidly for natural adaptation."

"You say we're going to recruit an army of elves, giants, dwarves, were-folk, and people who want to be one of those? And all of us go west and form our own community? That doesn't sound like something I'd want to be part of," Tanner said. "Isolating ourselves would just create another group to label as *other* and the cycle starts all over."

"How many here are pureblood?" Sesco spoke from the side of the bus's expansive lounge. "Wasn't there a vaccination program a while back to get children immunized from disease while still in the womb? As far as I know that program is still active and is only one of several genetic alterations done to thousands of people every year as normal health care since the first woman President back in the twenties. Truth be known, there are only a few antivaxers in populated areas and isolated pockets of humanity that are actually pure of blood any longer."

"That's different," Bekka argued. "And it doesn't take anything away from Tanner's point just because we've chosen to make our children elves. Those vaccines cured defects. They didn't add new attributes. Using your rationale would mean that anyone who had invitro vaccinations would also be genetically altered."

"It's not always easy to detect augmentation," Sesco said softly. "And I'm willing to bet everyone here has had a gene hacker in their ancestry. I'm also aware it's being increasingly acceptable to demand to know what kind and how much of an Adnaq anyone has. The tendency is growing as the number of secure habitats is diminishing and people whose only apparent augmentation is a longer, healthier life."

"Tell a supposed pureblood people didn't use to live a hundred twenty years if they ate healthy and exercised, and they'll call you a liar. And they'll still insist the augmented are taking their jobs without realizing there *are no jobs*. The things that used to support the old ways aren't being made because genetic augmentation made them irrelevant."

"The turtle and this bus both show why. The

turtles are designed to grow a garden home made to feed the occupant. The turtle and carrier combined eliminate dozens of jobs a family owning it would need the products from to subsist the old way."

"This bus is another. Yes, it's a mechanical device that contains the most modern technology in existence, but it's also part plant. All the rail trays beneath the windows are a part of this bus's waste system, just like that of the turtles, and the windows are solar panels better than those made in the teens and twenties."

"The same people protesting augmented humans probably have the same modular system in their homes. They live longer, healthier lives, and their homes recycle all wastes into altered garden produce they eat before they go out to protest augmentation."

"More than ninety percent of everything society had jobs to produce we don't need any longer. People are so independent and self-sufficient, paper money hasn't been accepted my entire life. I've seen it and even have several samples to prove it used to be the major form of specie, but nobody uses it."

He smiled. "The last time gold and silver were the dominant form of money instead of barter was the last time this continent was wild and settlements were fortress homes."

"But I digress, we're all already augmented. I would be surprised if any pureblood actually *isn't* augmented in some way. Even if their parents didn't have a procedure doesn't mean *their* parents didn't in a time when gene corporations were getting government funding through special immunization programs."

"It's been going on for a long time. All voluntary but making grand claims for the unborn child." He shifted his gaze to Xan. "I'm more curious about what happens when the new variants start falling in love and mixing giant, dwarf, elven, and even werefolk genes."

Xan shrugged. "I don't know, but I suspect the results can be easily observed and added to all the other documented data since the variants first began showing up."

"Touché," Sesco laughed. "So, it looks like your grandfather is creating an enclave of safety for the augmented. Why the Black Hills?"

"The same reasoning as any persecuted group, there are fewer people to point out your differences when everybody is different. A geographically and ecologically isolated area where they can have time to heal and grow into their new *selves* while sharing that evolution with others like themselves."

"Grampa was always going on about how people divided themselves, color, religion, politics, he was amazed people would do that." Tina smiled at the memory.

"So, your grampa wants to start a magic mountain in the Black Hills just like he always complained about," Tanner said. "Why *there*?"

Xan traded a look with his sister before answering, "Again, we don't know but we can make a pretty good guess. Our family has documented Native American ancestry along all roots into the great-greats. We even learned some languages and histories from our ancestral tribes growing up."

"One of the places we used to go on two out of three vacations was the Black Hills. We've met distant relatives that are still on tribal residency rolls and Tina and I each own a hundred-acre patch on the side of grampa's mountain."

"Grampa is building his refuge from the final extinction of the un-augmented human species in the Black Hills because it's in the edge of the most dangerous place in the North American continent. Most of the only people left are descendants of the original occupants."

"And we're supposed to cross the Missip and the Monster Plains on foot?" Stone said with disbelief. "Have you seen the kinds of things that live between the Missip and the Rockies?"

"I have," Sesco said. "And I can tell you they are every bit as monstrous as the ones we've already faced in the past week. The thing is, and media dramatics gloss over this, the monsters have to eat and they're territorial. Almost every monster you see video of has had to kill a half-dozen *other* monsters growing up."

"There really aren't that many or they would all starve. We could cross the whole prairie and not see anything or we could be run over by stampede after stampede and see a new man-eating monster every day."

"We?" Tina smiled. "So, you're going with us?"

"Of course I am," he said with a theatrical pose. "A new civilization needs libraries and libraries need books. I *am* a Librarian, after all. How about the rest of you? Seems somebody has put considerable effort and funds to set something in motion that will be seen as a statement by the already fearful. A genetically created battle claw in the eye of the pureblood as we drive them to a final extinction. Do you want to be identified with the beginning of that statement, or the failed end?"

"Not much of a choice the way I see it," Lilac said as she looked at Bekka. "Some of us didn't just feel unwanted, we were *chased* out of our homes by family and friends because of how we want our children to be born. The monsters we'll face in the future can be no less horrible than the ones we leave behind."

With nods all around at that truth, the gathering broke up as they headed back to their landships, wagons, and hotel rooms and the next morning awoke to a massive outdoor buffet between the two buses.

"So, Frederick, do you know who's coming or is that secret?"

"Heh-heh," the stoic giant said with a tolerant smile as he gazed at the giant families around his bus. "The names of those joining us would mean nothing at this time. The two buses are electronically linked and reports will be exchanged when appropriate. When Francine and I leave tomorrow, your Amanda Shaw will post the video and lists of accumulating followers' identities at every stop."

"And again, I don't know why none of our communications are being accepted by the home compound. I'm tempted to go with you to find out but others have matched their schedule to ours at great cost and you will still be in contact."

"Grampa sure does trust the Orbitals a lot to let them run a private link."

Frederick, aka Frick, smiled again at his young friend. "The Orbitals owe much to your grandfather. It was he who found the cure to the plague Earth sent when the people of space decided to declare independence since most of them could no longer tolerate Earth gravity. He also developed three of the physiological variations the majority who did not have them gave their children."

"No, Xan, the Orbitals are constantly looking for ways to repay your grandfather for all he has done for them. Providing a secure communications link between designated locations is something many who can never set foot or tentacle on Earth are more than happy to do. And they will protect that privacy as much as they would their own."

"If they have such good communications then why doesn't he answer his phone?"

"That, my young friend, is something I hope you can answer when you get home. I will be the one speaking to Amanda Shaw every day as my Francine has no respect for my cooking. Now, you had better say good-bye to her or she will remember the next time we meet."

Xan and Tina did make one last stop before they had the convoy meeting and brought back three giant-sized pies that helped improve an already good mood.

In Huron, they discovered a larger ferry waiting for them and a captain who was already paid. "I've been contracted to bring your caravan to Kelly's so you can do what you need to do while we load cargo. We'll launch at midnight, take you and your vehicles to the west shore somewhere around Magee Marsh, set you ashore, and be well on our way to our next port before sunrise."

"Okay, Captain," Xan said. "We'll try not to disturb your schedule. It shouldn't take long."

After docking at Kelly's, he led his sister, best friend minus the pups, and the man his sister had taken a liking to off the ship and across the docks to the main street. They had spent most of their lives on this island and no one thought it strange when the three and a newcomer ran as fast as any of the few electric cars that traveled the streets. They were soon outside the large stone mansion that was their grandfather's private lab with housing for staff and his two orphaned grandchildren.

After a few minutes of staring at the house from the sidewalk alongside the maintained streets, Gar nudged Xan. "So, you think anybody's home?"

Tina moved first and when she tried her palm on the security plate the door easily unlocked. Xan felt her surge of emotion as she got her first look inside and couldn't help his own burst of anger when he saw the interior.

"This was done after it was evacuated," Tina said after they spent an hour going through as much as they needed. "Whoever did this, did it to what wasn't worth taking because they were late."

"What about the safe?" Gar gestured toward the back of the destroyed basement lab.

Xan led them into the back room and the obvious safe. He put his hand on the pad and there was a click, then another and another. He lifted his hand, then replaced it and tapped two fingers in a pattern. There was another trio of clicks and the door made a whooshing sound as its seal popped and the pressures equalized. Gar helped pull the door the rest of the way open and lights came on automatically to show an empty vault.

"Well that was melodramatic," Sesco deadpanned. "Now what?"

Xan smiled. "C'mon."

Tina shut the vault door from the inside and they heard six distinct snaps as it locked. As soon as the locks finished engaging, she put her hand on the security plate and tapped a pattern with two fingers. There was a series of clicks and the floor lowered one level to reveal a second vault with wider walls covered in empty shelves.

"Kind of cool, but not much better," Sesco said.

The three childhood friends moved to the single closed cabinet and opened the door.

"He didn't forget," Gar said as he reached in and pulled forth an impressive staff of composite materials made to look like wood interspersed with protruding tech buttons and plates. He moved back to test the swing and weight while the brother and sister looked to see what else was in the cabinet.

"Xan and I got another lockbox full of coins and there's a shoulder bag like Sesco's book bag with your name on it, Gar," Tina said with a smile. "It's pretty heavy."

Gar put the staff aside and pulled a large box out of the bag. He touched a thumb to the lock and opened the lid. "Oh look, I got my own allowance! There's enough here for me to take the pups to the Black Hills by first class air and still have a couple-three months' worth of party funds."

"What else?"

Gar put the large safety box full of rolls of coins back in the bag and pulled out an equally large book. He inspected it for several moments before speaking softly. "It's my mother's journal. There're pictures of her and pa and me before…"

He turned a few pages and smiled at some. "This is the greatest treasure your grandfather could have ever given me."

"Well, there's nothing else so we might as well get back to the boat," Tina said and turned to go.

Xan activated the lift and in seconds the floor was rising into the decoy vault as smoothly and silently as it had descended. Another coded signal over the palm pad and the door unlocked and pressure equalized as the seal popped. Xan and Tina pushed the door open then closed it again and waited till they heard all the locks click into place.

"Place like this has to have a library," Sesco said. "Maybe whoever trashed everything missed a book or two."

"Could be wrong," the young scholar said as they surveyed the damage a few minutes later.

"The two glassed-in shelves and all the

desks are missing," Xan said.

"And not near enough ashes in the fireplace for all the empty shelves," Tina said as she inspected the mantelpiece.

"Found one!" Sesco declared with a shout as he held up two half books. "Page numbers match up and both still have their spines. I can put a new cover on and it'll be good as new." He carefully put the two halves in his shoulder bag and resumed searching.

Several minutes later he inspected his haul. "Three old fiction novels I've never read before and all three written at the beginning of the twenty-first century when CRISPR was first developed. That was even before the first moon colony. To me these three books are a treasure beyond compare."

He scowled as he looked at the books shredded and pulled apart with so many thrown into the fireplace. "There are few things a person can do worse than destroying books. Not many, and those who would burn books are capable of doing all of them."

"We need to leave," Xan said. "Don't want to miss our boat."

"I found the front cover to the first book I made whole again," Sesco said as they left the mansion and walked toward the docks. "It has the binder's name inside the attaching sheet. Maybe he has done other ancient restoration work and knows where I can find other books from that era."

Xan and Tina smiled as their new friend gushed about books they had grown up ignoring for most of their life. They had read many of the books that filled the library's shelves growing up, but only a fraction.

"I've read the last one we made whole," Tina said as they neared the edge of the main village, waving to the few people they recognized. "It's about survival when the solar system goes through an ice cloud in space that floods most of the planet. You'll like it."

"There's some sort of commotion up ahead," Gar said as he let them catch up.

The disturbance turned out to be a wheeled car hitting and breaking the leg of one of the new walkers with mechanical limbs. They walked past the scene without incident or even notice by the crowd that came to witness a little excitement.

When they got to the dock, they saw the captain and her wife entering the nearby restaurant.

"Can't leave without their captain," Sesco observed. "If anyone's thirsty, I'm buying the first round."

Gar held the door for the rest and the first thing Xan saw was Bekka and Tanner sitting across from Lilac and Stone in one booth, and their son with Rick and Amanda Shaw in another. Several of the crew were scattered about at other tables and booths while the captain and her wife were being seated in the section furthest from the bar. Another officer and her husband shared a table with a married couple delivering a wheeled camper van with a double-barreled turret on the top somewhere up the coast.

Gar abandoned them when the waitress escorted them toward what looked to be the sober side, then saved Sesco by yelling loudly that he wanted his new friend to *meet somebody*.

The waitress hesitated and the captain waved and gestured toward the open half of her and her wife's table so they joined them for a leisurely meal with friendly conversation.

"Thank you, Tina, for recommending the surf and turf with bison and lake crab legs," the captain's wife said as they walked up the gangplank later. "It was one of the best meals I've had away from our ship's wonderful kitchen."

"You're welcome Stacie," she replied, Xan bringing up the rear as they went up to the bridge.

When they got inside Stacie took over the communications station while Rachel showed her guests her ship's fluid operation as the last of the crew and passengers were accounted for and the gangplank withdrawn.

The bridge crew worked quietly and efficiently with those on deck as the pilot took them away from the dock and through the heavy security gate to the artificially enclosed bay. A thick heavy fog enveloped the lights of the dock before the gate closed behind them.

The island disappeared behind as they did what only the largest ships could, travel the lake at night. But when you traveled in a ship the size of *Taylor's Dream* you didn't have to worry about any of the known aquatic lake monsters. All five lakes were certified safe for boats over fifty meters and each of *Taylor's Dream*'s two hulls were twenty meters longer than that.

Xan looked out over the arch of the wide

bridge as shapes appeared in the waves, some with huge eyes that stared back. Smaller shapes flew within the bow wave of the twin hulls, some eating smaller fliers then being eaten by larger wave fliers in their turn.

The large boat headed west through the fog and nearly two hours later they coasted up to a floating dock being towed by four compact tugs.

"Sorry son, this is where I was told to drop you off. Whoever that is will lock the other end of the dock to dry land then lift this end up to our cargo bay hatch and you'll drive or walk off. Once you're gone Stacie and I'll take the rest of our cargo north, collect more, and eventually come this way again when the contracts lead us back."

She pointed her chin at the four tugs maneuvering the floating bridge to dry land. "Once you're off that they'll pull out and we'll both be somewhere else at sunrise while you folks do what you have to do. Here, I was told to give you this after shaking hands good-bye."

Xan accepted the small padded envelope and followed his sister off the bridge and down to the cargo bay where the rest of the expedition waited. Not knowing what to expect, they had loaded all mounts onto the turtles to reduce congestion. He tucked the envelope into a vest pocket and kept Xanthos, Thoth, and Spot company while Tina and Sesco drove the turtle from the cargo hold to the floating bridge.

The unrehearsed departure was surprisingly smooth and Xan was watching out the back of the turtle's cargo bay when the big armored camper van with the heavy turret on top came out of the cargo bay. As they began their crossing he wondered if Gunny and Spider worked for his grandfather or the people that had trashed the already evacuated mansion.

The ship broke contact and was away quicker than he would have thought, the fog swallowing them in seconds. Moments later he felt the difference as Honey stepped from the floating dock bridge to solid ground with the heavy van halfway across.

Just then the bridge lurched and bucked as several tentacles lifted from the water and latched onto one of the tugs on the left end. The bridge shook and the van slid toward the edge and off the side of the floating dock, into the lake and began sinking.

[13] My, what big claws you have.

Sesco rushed by him just as the heavily armored van sank till it was half submerged before its wheels dug in and it began to drive out of the lake.

At the other end of the bridge the tentacled lake kraken had succumbed to the defenses of the tug and its electrocuted carcass was already being efficiently cut up and hauled aboard before scavengers arrived.

Sesco turned with a huge smile. "You people are just the greatest fun magnets I've ever had the pleasure of knowing. Gotta go," he added over his shoulder as he returned to his co-pilot saddle beside Tina.

The van slogged through the water and around the inner tug as the bridge dock began to move away from shore. The mobile dock bridge was out of sight in the fog before the van hauled itself out of the water dragging a smaller version of the lake kraken part of the way. The immature tentacled monster reluctantly relinquished its meal while it was still in water deep enough to swim away.

Keeping a hand on his weapons as he scanned for danger, Xan didn't allow himself to become relaxed just because they were off the water. They were now in an unfamiliar wilderness, at night and in the open.

"Lead unit reports a scouted refuge two

klicks from water's edge," Sesco called back to keep him informed.

Even with their slowest members they were inside a stone barn within an hour and gathered in the bus's kitchen lounge.

"First, let me apologize for not telling you all of our plans," Xan said to start. "And it doesn't matter that Tina and I don't know anything till the last minute either, we're used to grampa's games, you're not."

"We're going to head west on the I-80 grassway to Omaha, go north on I-29 up to intersect the I-90 grassway at Sioux Falls, then straight through west to the Black Hills."

"We're not *openly* recruiting but anyone who joins us moves at our pace and anyone who wishes to break away from our caravan is also welcome to do so and still retain whatever possessions or funding we have shared with you."

He hesitated long enough for everyone to digest that. "Another thing to remember, the kitchen bus is the lead vehicle at all times, our Command Central. All phones that haven't already been, need to be linked with the CC's cell tower. If you don't want your personal devices locked through CC, we have some old phones with the basic cameras, text, and media access to keep in contact with the rest of the caravan." He shifted his gaze to the youngest among them. "I suggest every group have at least one CC phone or know somebody who does."

"We leave at daylight. Each of you has to decide whether to spend this last couple hours with things you should've already done or get the sleep you didn't get on the boat ride."

The forward windows to the bus lit up with lightning through the open doors of the stone barn they had been directed to. Unable to all fit inside with the rest of the vehicles, the nose of the bus protruded into the open where they got a wide view of the storm while staying dry.

"Okay everybody, go do what you have to," Xan said as he stood and moved toward the front of the bus to watch the storm. "We leave when it gets light enough to see the trail. I want to be on the grassway early enough to get by the Toledo Wastes before dark."

The rain was still falling when the caravan of mixed vehicles pulled out of the barn and headed south. They caught the narrower grassway that used to be Rt163 through the ruins of Genoa and turned west when they got to the wider grassway that used to be the Ohio Turnpike and I-80. The rain got lighter just before midday but increased again as they slogged toward what was left of Toledo and most of the Maumee watershed and lake shoreline.

"Crappiest fracking weather forecasted for the next four days and it's through the worst gene-bombed territory we'll see this side of the Missip," Gar grumbled as he adjusted his waders and poncho so he could get to his weapons.

"We could take the I-75 grassway south and go around," Xan said as he made sure Xanthos was ready for a wet walk. "But that would take three days and the forecast is for continued rain the whole way south of us. Straight through gets us out of the rain in one day."

"And statistically, fewer chances of encountering the nastiest beasties," Sesco said, then explained before they could ask. "The worst the gene bomb could produce would need a large feeding territory. The Toledo Zone is longer than it is wide and mathematically the most we'll see is two of the worst and they'll have driven all the lesser monsters out or already eaten them. In fact, I'm kind of surprised we haven't seen something driven out of the Zone and looking for new territory already." He signaled and Spot squatted for him to mount.

"That's why we're riding," Xan said as he mounted Xanthos. "We need to get across before sunset and I want us to be out of the turtles where we can defend ourselves."

With Tanner riding Gar's Phobos, they formed two teams with Xan and Gar on the left flank with Fred. Tina, Sesco, and the detective covered the other side with Ginger while the armored van covered their rear.

The command bus led out with Honey next, followed by the Cloverfield cerawagon, then Bear as they headed toward one of the most dangerous stretches of grassway before they reached the Missip. With their cargo holds lighter, the two turtles were able to maintain a faster walk the cera could easily match. When they got to where I-75 crossed the turnpike grassway, the two mounted teams went wide around the ramps to the overpass to flush out any ambushers.

Xan had his carbine in hand as he scanned every shrub and dip in the ground with his empathic mind as the rain pounded, lightning flashed, and thunder rumbled. Xanthos flinched once and danced sideways a couple steps, but that was at a particularly close ground strike with a bone shaking thunderclap that sounded before the after-flash faded.

He brought his barrel up when Fred signaled on a particularly thick shrub but the hellhound only kept an eye on the offending plant as he led them around the ramp. When he was closest Xan probed the hiding place to detect a protective mother and her three young. He couldn't tell what they were other than small hunters not much larger than a housecat.

Ignoring them after that identification he peered through the downpour with senses greatly improved over the base human genome. His eyes cut through the gloom and his ears discriminated between the sounds of the storm and anything *other*, while his mind searched for the emotions that identified a patient ambush hunter.

Working quickly, they made it around the artificial hills of the overpass's on and off ramps without incident and reunited with the caravan on the other side.

"There was a wolf raptor nest in the center of the exit ramp on our side," Tina said. "They kept an eye on Ginger but didn't do much more than watch us."

"There weren't enough of them for the number of chicks," Sesco said as Spot pranced with pent-up energy. "I'm betting there's a hunting pack out there somewhere, maybe one big enough to take down a mount and rider."

"Mind your teammates' backs," Xan said. "Baker formation."

They split from their quick conversation, returning to their respective flanks but gathered more closely around the cerawagon as it was their weakest position. With the wagon flanked by riders and hellhounds, the caravan maintained a steady pace that quickly brought them to the Maumee River.

"Didn't expect the bridge to be standing," Bekka called out from her seat driving the cerawagon.

"They finished the new one just before the war," Xan replied. "It was one of the few times all the politicians worked together. Of course, that was because they were agitating to get tough with the Orbitals and showing how much they could do for the people."

The caravan went into a sprint across the bridge as it was one of the spots Sesco deemed a higher percentage of monster habitat. The guess was confirmed when a pair of tentacles reached up to try to snatch the last member of the prey crossing their owner's serving tray.

Gunny and Spider showed the folly of that attempt as they sprayed a steel rain through the driving storm, shredding the tentacles every time they came close. Stunned by its wounds, whatever was hiding within the girders above the central support pylon withdrew long enough for the van to join the rest of the caravan on the other side.

On the west side of the bridge they slowed

to a turtle trot that ate the kilometers at a steady pace despite the downpour. They were almost through the area hit by the gene bomb, the tower for the airport coming into view on their left, when the rain quickly diminished to a drizzle.

"We have movement around the airport tower," Xan said as the sky cleared enough to send several scattered shafts of light across the grassway and airport. "Looks like big birds."

They continued at the most enduring speed their slowest members could maintain as they passed the airport, keeping an eye on the mutant birds roosting on and around the tower.

Another extravagance in the lead-up to war, the tower was built to survive the end of the world when an impending apocalypse from space was a recurring theme. The tower had two disks above the ground floor, the one halfway up had been a fancy restaurant bar and gift shop, and the smaller air traffic control center at the top. From a distance, the tower showed the silhouette of a stylized pine tree.

"They're splitting up," Gar said as they came even with the distant tower.

"Pull in tight and stay alert," Xan called out. "We have incoming, possibly aerial so watch the sky too."

"Look kind of pretty," Gar said as he ushered Fred and Ginger inside their perimeter.

"A smaller version mixing bald eagle and parrots was a favorite attraction at the Toledo Zoo before the war," Sesco said from the right side of the cerawagon. "They're called roc. This gene bombed version is probably too heavy to fly very far or high."

"They look like running gliders," Xan said as the nearer group of roc began to circle the caravan.

Each massive bird took smooth flying leaps that covered a couple dozen meters between each step. With brightly colored plumage covering a body larger than Sesco's Spot, their spread wings gave them the appearance of being three times their actual size.

The sickle-like claws seemed to barely touch the grassy plains that had replaced the turnpike and airport as the roc silently glided around them. Beaks over a meter long could easily trisect a man.

They ignored the circling roc, maintaining a steady speed the iridescent hunters matched with their circle. After a couple of klicks, the birds began closing the distance in front of them.

"Got something coming in fast on the right," Tina called out.

Xan looked through the gap between the cerawagon and Bear, and between the circling roc. A line of five roc was coming at an intercept angle as the three riders on the right side pulled their mounts in tighter and raised weapons.

"Xan!" Gar yelled.

He felt the roc on his side break formation and was firing his carbine before he turned to look. Gar's heavier fifty caliber barked as the caravan defended itself on the run. The circle dissolved as birds fell to their death or had to avoid a cartwheeling body.

Xan changed magazines after his second

target fell then chanced a look at the oncoming line of roc.

"We lost *Recluse*," Tanner called out as he readied himself for the attacking line of roc.

"Getting trophies," Lilac yelled from Bear's driving saddle as they ran.

The line of roc coming at them from the right had lost the element of surprise the circle would have provided, but not their intent. The command bus engaged its heavy weapons seconds before *Recluse* added hers when the nearest bird was two hundred meters out. The riders added their fire when the attackers were one hundred meters from the convoy.

Two of the roc leaped higher than their normal ground effect glide. Their pounce took them fifty meters into the air and their spread wings made them look enormous as their massively clawed feet extended for the kill.

Bullets impacted both roc at the peak of their leap. One bird tumbled and fell short of the caravan while the other slammed into Bear, impaling itself on the turtle's spikes.

Bear swerved a little at the impact, then back again in response to the weight, doing the giant turtle version of fishtailing as they ran.

Two roc landed on the grassway in front of the bus, spread their wings wide to look bigger, and screamed a challenge. The command bus wasn't intimidated and only one of the roc was fast enough to jump out of the way. When Xan went by the slower one was trying to rise on a broken leg. A single shot from Gar's 50cal pistol ended the bird's suffering.

They continued running, one of the dead roc's wings dragging the ground beside Bear till Stone was able to get a line on it from inside the cargo bay. When he was finished tying it off, the wing partially covered the rear opening.

The roc were confused by the loss of so many with no food to show for it and milled around the bodies for a few moments.

"They're coming again!" Stone yelled from his rearguard position inside Bear's protected area.

They continued running, a little slower due to the weight of the impaled roc on Bear's back added to having run so far already, as the surviving roc resumed the chase. The hunt had been longer than the roc were used to, and they were tiring enough their gliding leaps weren't as long. But they still gained on their prey as their talons propelled them in gliding leaps.

Bringing up the rear, Gunny and Spider waited till the predators were coming in for the killing leap before they shot the two leaders. The tumbling bodies took out another and the roc again became uncertain and indecisive.

"Think they'll give up, Xan?" Gar asked over his shoulder as he ran.

"I don't think they know how. Doesn't matter though. They're big and scary and could bite a horse in half but they don't seem to be able to take much of a beating."

"Here they come again," Stone reported. "And now we're losing *Recluse* again."

Xan slowed Xanthos enough to look behind

as the van dropped back to engage the persistent mutant avians. He turned back to the caravan and caught up in a brief sprint to regain his position in the formation just as he felt a stalking mind choose him as a target.

He was already firing his carbine as he turned to see a roc fully extended with its claws as long as his forearms coming right at him from meters away. He emptied his magazine into the roc's chest before it hit, slamming him and Xanthos against the side of the Cloverfield cerawagon.

[14] Stampede!

When he came out of the black, Xanthos was thrashing against the heavy weight that pressed them against the ground. Noises from outside the surprisingly soft weight resolved into words and he yelled in response. "I'm okay, I'm okay! Get it off us!"

He sent calming thoughts to his frightened horse and Xanthos began to thrash less. "That's it buddy, relax and let our friends get us out from under this big bird."

The others quickly pulled the dead weight away, Xanthos surprisingly calm till he stood free, then he reared high and screamed his anger at the dead roc, kicking at its dead body with genetically altered hooves.

They hoisted the dead roc onto the back of the CC bus and set out again with their grisly trophies while the remaining roc hovered close, voicing their displeasure at their defeat while staying out of killing range. Snipers took out a few more as they ran.

"Hey Stone," Xan said later in the afternoon, "can you call Amanda and see if there's any place close by to stop for the night?"

Stone immediately got on his phone for a brief talk with the CC bus. "Their map shows a blue icon compound with a population of a couple hundred permanent and up to another couple hundred transient traders about eight or nine klicks ahead. She said she was going to let everybody know at five klicks when the screen finally settled down after that last attack."

The compound turned out to be an old water tower next to a large pond on the right side of the grassway, with three private towers connected by a ten-meter wall. The inside was decorated with dozens of roc heads mounted with glass eyes and feathers intact, or bare skulls with painted murals. Wings and feathers adorned walls or were bundled on short poles mounted around the landscaped plaza.

Within an hour they had their animals in newly freshened stalls while eager youngsters earned valuable coins taking care of the two turtles and cera. After caring for their mounts, Xan, Gar, and Sesco sat on a balcony of the central tower.

"So, do they call themselves a village, or three independent entities sharing a community wall?" Gar wondered aloud to no one in particular.

"Yes to the former, Oasis," Sesco replied then took a drink of his ale. "And yes again, according to their website they share the duties of wall security. Each tower is owned by a separate extended family. One, the gate tower, has the hotel and stables, one has the garden terraces inside the walls and the pond's fish, and the third controls all the infrastructure, the water tower, and wall maintenance."

"I was reading their home page," Sesco said, going into lecture mode as his new friends sampled finger foods. "This is a designed enclave made to protect against the coming gene-hacker apocalypse. They didn't expect the war with the Orbitals, but their design was perfect within the space they had when war came."

He took a swallow from his mug and nodded in admiration. "Like a lot of other folks, they saw what was coming, pooled their resources, and built an enclosed, self-sufficient enclave."

Their attention shifted as a reveler from further back in the tavern came smiling up to their table. "Hey, did you hear? Some crazy frackers went through roc territory and won. Killed dozens of the feathered bastards without losing a single person and even brought two intact bodies for proof."

The man waved his mug of ale. "Get regular traffic moving east again and we won't be throwing so much good food in the mulch pile cause even the livestock can't eat it fast enough."

Trading was greatly enhanced by the trophies they'd collected and they were surprised to see several large trucks and a couple of mounted groups around smaller trucks leave Oasis headed east. When they arose the next morning, there were several new trophies adorning the interior of the compound.

"The damned roc were breeding faster than we could handle," their server said as he brought their bill after they ate breakfast. "You folks killed enough of them we could go out and thin them some more without losing half our people."

His smile was genuine despite his words. "One guy lost an arm, but none dead and that's the best we've done in a long time. Some are saying we might even cut a safe path through the Toledo

Wastes. That would sure help sales so we don't have to keep throwing away good food."

"Kraken eggs are seasonal and about twice the cost of a room," Tina read from the hotel's website after the server left. "Says here they used to have roc egg omelets in the spring and roc roasts year-round."

"From what locals are saying," Xan said as he pushed away his cleaned plate, "they didn't cull the flock as much as normal two years ago and that's all it took to let the roc's numbers get ahead of them."

"Just like genetic monsters to take advantage," Gar said as he dragged a spicy meat roll through a bowl of ranch sauce and munched it happily.

"I talked to some people while we were moving things to the hotel rooms," Bekka said. "They were almost ready to cut back on staffing because so few people could get by the roc colony."

"We cut the bird numbers enough commerce just might start moving a little more reliably from here eastward. Thing is, they have to move fast while the roc are disrupted. Hit 'em hard now and collect more eggs next spring and they should be good to go."

"Roc omelets, yummy," Gar said.

They finished their meal and returned to their animals and were on the grassway by midmorning, the sky a cloud-free, solid blue from horizon to horizon.

The ride past Chicago was uneventful as the individual compounds grew so thick there was always one in sight. They stayed inside the walls of a dwarf home that night and a public stable in Joliet the next. Two uneventful days later they spent the night inside a shipyard warehouse waiting for a ferry across the Missip.

Along the way they had simply answered questions honestly, they were on their way to the Black Hills to settle where their genetic augmentation wasn't offensive. As a result, their numbers had grown more every day. The morning they assembled on the shore of the Missip they were surrounded by wagons, carts, mounted individuals with entire families, and groups of walkers pulling carts.

"Three trips to get them all," Xan told the ferryman. "The bus, cerawagon, mounted riders, and walkers the first trip, and a turtle and assorted wagons and carts the next. I'll be on the last trip with a turtle and our security van, and whatever doesn't fit on the first two trips."

It ended up taking four trips and Xan didn't disembark on the west side of the Missip till almost sunset. The compound they stayed in was just big enough to hold all but the bus, turtles, and security van inside tall walls. Luckily the weather was clear and warm and the lack of a roof mattered less.

With the added numbers of walkers, they moved all the animals out of the turtles and replaced them with the elderly, young, and injured or sick when they set out. They saw their first sign for Wall Drug before they'd gone a kilometer past the last compound on the west side of the Missip's clustered population.

It took four days to get to Des Moines, passing signs for Wall Drug every day, but five to get the shorter distance to where the old I-80 crossed I-29 going north. The delay was caused when they spent an entire day in a defensive circle while thousands of grazers streamed past in a mass following the track of a series of storms replenishing the grass of the newly wild plains.

"The computers in the command bus are sending us about seven klicks north of anything else anywhere near Omaha and that doesn't make you wonder?" Sesco probed as they rode north on I-29, passing a steel pole topped by a sign advertising Wall Drug once every travel day.

"Nope," Xan replied with a smile. "I stopped wondering what my grandfather was planning a long time ago. Now I just go with what path he has scripted and try not to be caught by the traps he sometimes sets."

Around them dozens of the varied designs called horse, several different kinds of struthy, as well as a few other base forms, walked along the grassway. The actual old interstate was still marked for convenience, but this far west the old signs of mankind had mostly disappeared between the cities.

As mankind's numbers dwindled and population centers condensed, the old prairie returned with a more varied type of resident. There were the expected gene altered bison, deer, and antelope, but others as well. Several kinds of dinosaur also inhabited the newly wild plains along with wolves made dire and a wolfish species of raptor.

"That looks like it," Xan said as a water tower rose from the skyline beside the grassway.

"Looks occupied already," Gar said. "You sure we have reservations?"

Xan looked at Sesco, who shrugged affirmatively. "That's it. Amanda has already confirmed it."

"Xan, I think we've seen that one bus before, and that armored camper van looks suspiciously familiar as well."

"Hey look," Gar called out. "That looks like Elly."

"Grampa!" he slumped in his saddle as the caravan entered the compound's gate.

"Don't be so down, boy," Rocky River said as they sat in the makeshift tavern a couple hours later. "Your grampa has been doing this sort of thing since before we were your age."

Xan couldn't even sulk because the old river rat was right. Instead he looked out at the raucous gathering inside the gated community with a growing fondness. A mixture of elf, dwarf, giant, were-folk, and a few kinds of human yet to be defined mixed in with those like Sesco that were augmented less obviously, they seemed to be more and more relaxed as they traveled. Even the more numerous were-folk, the wolfen and pantha, were getting along and their children playing with everyone else's. The only people missing were the merfolk, but they rarely traveled far from water.

The suspicious and fearful looks were absent as the growing number of people in the caravan relaxed inside the walls of their refuge. But now, for the rest of the journey they had enough to make their own wall and stand against anything the increasingly evolving world could throw at them.

"Gotta admit though," Rocky continued, "most critters know enough to be careful around a herd this big. I was glad to see *Recluse* when you rendezvoused with the rest of us."

"Glad to finally know whose side they're on," Xan muttered.

Rocky laughed. "Yeah, that's Gunny and Spider alright, always keeping it close to their vests. So, what do we do next?"

"You mean you don't already know?" Xan asked with a smile.

"Heh! It's your grampa, boy, you should know even his best friends don't get to know everything."

Xan grimaced. "Yeah, right. Okay, the last piece of information just said to make sure we had food and water crossing South Dakota."

"Yeah, we got real lucky so far," Rocky admitted. "The only thing our group faced other than the cannibals in the Ozarks was a pack of wolf raptors numbering over six hundred. Was fewer than a hundred fifty when they finally started eating their own instead of trying to get to us."

"Well, tomorrow is another long day so I'm for my bedroll. You might want to fuss less and get more rest yourself, Xan, you're no use to us if you're asleep on your horse."

He took the advice to heart and when he

was mounted and ready to ride the next day, he was wide awake and excited to continue. Standing in his stirrups, he looked across a line of tech vehicles and mutated creatures carrying everything from the few possessions of a walking family to self-sufficient mobile homes like their turtles and buses.

Their caravan now had two command buses and a second armed and armored van owned by a married couple with twin toddlers as crew. Other than their six official vehicles there were three heavy trucks with armored cabins and weapons turrets, more sauro- and cerawagons, and various smaller wagons and carts surrounded by mounted riders and walkers.

"Reminds me of the wagon trains that crossed the prairie back when the caucasians invaded this continent," Sesco said as Spot pranced next to Xanthos.

Xan looked behind their lead bus at the line of vehicles, some made of metal and ceramics, and others of meat and bone made in laboratories. Frick and Frack, Frederick and Francine, held the rear position with the larger landships scattered in a line between the two CC buses.

He spotted Elly as Rocky walked back to his position in line with more energy than a man his age should have. The oliphant was in a group of walking mounts that included two other oliphants, two longer legged cera that resembled an older Dancer, and something that looked like a wingless dragon accompanied by five miniature versions of itself with children and young adults as riders. The smaller versions were almost as large as his horse.

Smaller mounts like Xanthos and Spot outnumbered the larger specimens.

Behind Elly walked Bekka and Tanner's newly named Dancer for her moves getting away from the roc that had fallen on Xanthos and Xan. Behind Dancer was a team of something large and hairy that looked somewhat like elephant sized camels without humps. The team of six towed a two-story wagon with a wraparound balcony lined in children with hopeful faces.

Behind the orphan's wagon Honey and Bear held the middle of their caravan. Behind them came another random assortment of refugees riding mechanical and genetically constructed vehicles. Scattered around the larger conveyances, dozens of walkers paced a loaded wagon or carried all they owned.

Xan had tried to ensure those least able to walk the distances they needed to go each day could ride or at least space to stow their heavy backpacks, but was also sure some were missed. To catch any that might fall out he organized a group of riders and attending ambulances to ride up and down the caravan looking for people and animals in distress.

It took nearly an hour after sunrise before Frick and Frack pulled their bus out onto the grassway behind an immense, two-story, eight wheeled wagon towed by a team of eight triceratops. Xan waved to the two giants in the cabin of the bus then rode Xanthos forward along the line, Sesco riding beside him as giant children waved from the tower's upper windows and covered observation roof.

Ahead of the triceratops tower and its escort of six giants on megastangs, they passed a mixed group of cerapig carts and hadro, horse, and struthy mounts. He spotted two groups he knew wouldn't be able to keep up and had the ambulances deliver them to one of the heavier units, one pair of elders to Honey and a lost child to Dancer till his parents could be located.

By noon the child's frantic parents had been found and the family reunited, and a murderer had been put to trial, convicted, and banished to the wild. By the end of the first day they'd only made twenty-five kilometers. The second day was worse and they had to make camp in the open, but the third day the caravan made over fifty kilometers.

"I think we've found our rhythm," Xan said just before their planned lunch stop. "The second day out had me a bit nervous, but that was as much from sore muscles from the first hard day as it was a lack of organization."

"Took that long for you to admit everybody thinks you're in charge," Sesco said as they rode together.

They rode on for several minutes in companionable silence when Xan's phone vibrated and he read the text then put it back in his pocket just as Sesco finished reading his own alert. Without comment they did what their planning suggested, sweeping their mounts out from the double line of larger vehicles.

"All walkers report to your assigned wagons," he said calmly as he passed by each individual group. "All walkers report to your assigned wagons, there's a large number of grazers approaching from behind."

His phone vibrated and he was reading the message when the special alarm sounded from the rear bus. He didn't have to tell anyone what that meant and he tried to stay out of the way of those running for the nearest wagon.

The lead bus sounded another alarm signal and the larger vehicles began maneuvering into a closed formation with the smaller vehicles. Aiming for the highest point on a mostly flat landscape, they put the buses in a V formation with their armored rear ends almost touching and their tip-over spikes lowered and interlocked.

Honey and Bear took position in front of the buses with heavy trucks and larger sauro and cera wagons next and angled inward. The wagons with the least armor, mounted riders, and walkers filled the interior.

Gunny and Spider backed their van into the point of the 'V' with their back half embraced by the buses as the approaching herds grew closer. Gunners perched on the frames of the tip-over spikes while others climbed onto the roofs of the outer vehicles or lay on the ground between their wheels.

The ground began to shake, then a slow thunder built to the south. From their chosen high ground, they watched as dust rose in the distance with the rising thunder, then a moving line of immense bodies topped the hill south of theirs. Horns as long as Gar's staff waved above heads that stood four meters above the ground as the genetically augmented bison raced across the new prairie.

"That's not a fast migration," Xan yelled, "that's a stampede! All riders inside the wall!"

Horses, struthies, and a couple more unique designs ran around to the top of the 'V' and inside the protection of ceramic, steel, and horn. Just before he went in last, he watched the other security van race toward the oncoming monsters.

At the bottom of the hill the van spun a U-turn and began to race back up the hill to their defensive formation spraying flashbangs and smoke grenades behind them. They paced their speed to match that of the oncoming wall of horns and hooves as they laid down a line of chaos.

"They're not splitting," Sesco said as Spot pranced excitedly.

"Still have a half klick," Xan said as they watched the stampede approach. "They're slowing down, there, they just needed to get the flashbangs closer. The line is starting to split. Let's get inside."

They rode through the small gap between two cerawagons and walked their mounts to Honey's aft end. They gave the leads to their mounts to young hands eager to be of help and climbed up on the roof of the Shaw bus just as the security van raced around their formation and spun another U-turn to take position atop their enclosed formation.

Xan watched as genetically mutated bison streamed by on both sides, Gunny and Spider continuing to fire flashbangs into the oncoming horde. He was wondering how many of the explosives they had when the rate of fire diminished by half.

Looking back from their position, Xan still didn't see the back of the stampede. Scattered among the bison were several small herds of other denizens of the newly wild prairie states. Cera, hadro, sauro, oliphant, megastang, and several things he couldn't identify from their distance ran as fast as those around them.

The panicked animals flowed around their anchored position as the flashbangs from the point van reduced in number again. Then the turret hummed, focused, and spat a line of death into the oncoming bison.

Several of the massive beasts fell a mere body length from the front of the point of their formation. Two bison tried to climb the bodies and the van's turret fired a burst into each. First one then another tried to fill the empty space between the pile of carcasses and the point of their 'V', and added their meat mountain as shielding. The last bison's horns gouged the side of the van when its head crashed into the dirt.

Xan and Sesco ran to the back of the bus to add their weapons to their defense as the split began to narrow and the running bison closed in on them. Horns waved just above the roof of the bus but kept moving northward at a run. The bus shook as one of the bison rammed the side and the massive beast took a stagger-step as he ran.

The security van fired again as he reached the back end of the bus and the next bison trying to climb the growing mountain of dead bodies was close enough it fell atop the van, blocking the turret.

Then what had chased the last bison over the wall of flesh came over the top, stood nearly ten meters tall, and screamed a challenge. Before anyone could fire a second mega grizzly appeared and dashed toward the people standing on top of the bus.

Xan was fast, but the grizzly was faster and swatted at them as he emptied his weapon into the approaching paw. It still hit hard and flung him across the middle of their refuge and head first into the side of the Cloverfield wagon, to fall in a dazed heap on the ground. As he tried to clear his head and rise a massive foot stepped onto the ground beside him while screams and gunfire sounded all around the camp.

[15] Jinxed!

He'd lost his carbine and fumbled for his holstered pistol but couldn't get his hands to do what his brain said, then the foot and the tree sized leg it was attached to were gone.

"Easy there, easy," a strange voice said as strong hands held him steady.

He blinked and turned to gaze into a smiling face he had seen earlier riding a sleek panther almost as big as Xanthos. "Hi, what happened?"

"Baby grizzly batted you ten meters through the air and head first into the side of a cerawagon. I'm kind of surprised you didn't break your neck. Then you fell and the momma grizzly almost stepped on you on her way through."

"Momma and cub didn't stick around for snacks," she added, then her eyebrows creased. "They weren't chasing the stampede. They were running with it. Wonder what would make so many different kinds of animal stampede."

Xan's vision continued to clear and he blinked as his brain reconnected with his body. The young woman felt the change and released him to stand on his own.'

"Thank you…"

"Lilith Meadow. My friends call me Lily," she threw a thumb over her shoulder at the giant panther resting in bus shade. "That's Onyx. She's peaceful as long as I am."

Then Xan felt the emotions the young woman was probing with and she smiled when she felt him shield properly. "There you are, all back with us again. That really was a hard hit. I was kind of worried when you fell, especially when you shook your head when you first tried to stand. Lucky you didn't break your neck then snap it the rest of the way off shaking it so hard."

She smiled and he felt the sincere worry as he finished recovering. "Grampa put a lot into building my sister and me. In fact, I think there's some feline in there that might have helped me twist to roll with the impact even though it looked bad."

He closed his eyes and did an internal probe, then opened them to see a curious look on her face. "Sorry, another gift from grampa. Tina and I can do a sort of internal diagnostic through our NSI."

"Eneseye?"

"Heh, no. Nanocellus Sapien Immortallus, N-S-I, although Eneseye sounds good, too. It's an invention of my grandfather's, a sort of living machine the size of red and white blood cells. My sister and I have empathic augmentations and that allows us increased control over the Eneseye in our bodies. I have about twelve kilos of the stuff inside me."

"Thought you were a little denser than you looked, Lily said with a smile. "C'mon, the stampede is still flowing by and I want to watch."

He retrieved his carbine and she led him back up on the roof of the Shaw bus where several others watched the flow of animals around their huddled camp. The mechanical arms on the corners of the buses weren't very large, but there were four of them and they lifted the carcass off the van's turret.

"Thinning out," Gar said as he held his 50cal revolver in a relaxed manner.

"Not by much," Xan observed. "I'm more concerned with what would drive so many animals so fast."

"With predators mixed in with prey," Sesco said. "Either one of those grizzlies could have snatched up a people snack on their way through the middle of our camp. They didn't, why?"

"Still don't see an end to the herds," Lily said. "Any of you folks have one of those satellite links?"

Xan resisted the urge to empathically probe his new friend. Anybody who had accepted their command bus links knew both buses did. Then he felt her teasing mood when Sesco spoke up.

"Didn't you get one of the phones that connect to the buses? I'm sure there were still some left."

Her feelings of mirth increased. "Put it in a pocket out of the way in Onyx's saddlebags and wrapped tight. Every time I get it out there are a half-dozen messages, midday rest stop in x klicks, blah, blah, evening stop in y klicks, blah, blah, blah. So much talk just to walk north. Not used to it and didn't have any more to add, so didn't."

"Been on your own long?" Xan asked.

"That obvious?"

"No, just, you know," he said as he gestured toward his elven features she didn't share.

Her eyebrows creased. "Those Eneseye things are that good? Yeah, yeah, I know, you have pointy ears and perfect skin, but you have to know most people didn't want others knowing they turned their kids into freaks."

She nodded toward Sesco. "Ask him. Yeah, I had some secret ingredients added while I was in the oven. Mostly elf stuff but without the ears, just like that scholar. He got a more analytical mind with total recall and I got a link with animals. That's why I can ride a panther and keep her calm in the middle of all this food." She gestured toward the interior of their refuge in the middle of the stampede and Onyx displayed a wide yawn with jaws wide enough to bite a man in half.

"Told her we would get her all the red meat she could want." She gestured toward the beginnings of the butchering of the bison they had to kill to ensure their safety.

"We'll have that shortly," Xan said, missing the look Sesco and Tina shared.

"Look, there," Sesco pointed as the sun began to near the horizon. "Something in the sky, like a storm cloud."

They watched the shape, that resolved into dozens of floating masses, each the size of a small cloud.

"Heh, dirig clouds," Sesco named them. "Some people call them hindy. They were originally designed to harvest the oceans for hydrogen fuel. Then a couple of gene hackers decided to play with their makeup."

He gestured toward the floating apparitions. "That's what they ended up with, huge balloons that grow over the oceans, converting water to hydrogen to fill their bladders. Look kind of like a man-o-war cause that's where most of their genes came from."

"They fill up on hydrogen over water then get caught in wind currents and end up over land. Ground critters freak out when things fly overhead and dirig just float along but a lot lower than normal clouds. The root hairs are kind of like thinner strangler vines and they drag them along the ground."

"We need to spread tarps over the dead bison and livestock pretty quick," Xan suggested and people ran to get them.

The line of low floating dirig moved with the weather front as it came into view on the horizon, hundreds of grazers and predators fleeing ahead of the stinging clouds. The numbers increased again as the slowest began to crowd each other ahead of the hanging threads. As the dirig storm front approached they could see the occasional smaller animal being drawn upward into a dirig starved of fluids. They quickly threw tarps over the dead bison and livestock and staked them to the ground as the dirig floated closer with the weather front.

"Make sure all windows are closed and exposed skin on you and your animals covered!" Xan yelled as people hurried to prepare for the new threat. "Anybody that can't get inside crawl under any overhang on the downwind side and tie yourself to something heavy."

"Why don't we just laser the ones coming over us?" Bekka asked as she staked a tarp over Dancer.

"If we laser them, all the tentacles will burn up and set the bag on fire," the Librarian replied.

"Sounds okay to me," Stone laughed as he checked the ropes securing the tarp over his cera.

"We could, but then we'd lose the opportunity to get some valuable medicine and the people downwind would lose the medicine *and* the hydrogen fuel."

"Just make sure none of them touch your exposed skin, 'cause it'll sting. And be careful. Each individual tentacle may not be able to lift as much as a strangler vine, but there are more of them. Get a half dozen stuck on you, you'll be dirig food."

"Ready, buddy?" Xan asked his best friend as the line came directly at them.

"You bet!" Gar replied enthusiastically as he readied his sword.

The floating gasbags showed where the line of cold and warm air moved northward with the weather front as it swept up the heart of the country. The line of dirig stretched from horizon to horizon as it approached, the stinging tentacles dragging the ground in a silvery curtain that glistened with rainbow colors in the setting sun.

Xan stood ready, welcoming the first gusts of cooler air as he sweated inside his heavy clothes and he was soon swinging his sword. The tentacles were thick and more than once he or another of his friends was grabbed, but there was always someone there to sever the grasping ropes.

"Help! It's got me!"

Xan ran to the length of the rope he had tied

to a stake driven into the ground, jumped, and swung his sword to cut two of the tentacles that had latched onto Stone.

With his arm free and the rope connected to his cerawagon stretched tight, Stone was able to slash through the last three tentacles. He dropped to the ground, rolled, and ducked as another pair of tentacles swung by him.

Xan swung his sword and cut two silvery strands just as one began to curl around his waist. The tentacles were sticky and stayed wrapped around him as he slashed at a bundle of four that had snagged on the rope holding the tarp over Dancer.

As he rose and hacked at another bundle, he saw Gar swinging at a cluster that had picked up another man who was wrapped so securely he couldn't swing his own sword. The man fell back to the ground, then Gar stood over him while he fought to free his arms.

He heard screams coming from inside the nearest turtle as several tendrils gripped the wicker carrier and the dirig tried to lift it. It was far too heavy and the dirig only succeeded on stopping its flight with the wind.

Seconds later Tanner jumped up on the tarped turtle's head and hacked away at the clinging tentacles till the dirig was free of a weight it couldn't lift and floated away.

Gar ran over to him and they stood side by side and slashed at the tendrils dragging across the tarps covering the animals they couldn't get at. He could hear Lily trying to calm a snarling Onyx who wasn't at all happy about being covered while danger could be sensed. He moved to her side, projecting calm and slashed at another line of tendrils, Gar on the other side of the panther as they cut through the hanging tendrils.

All around them people hacked at the clinging tentacles until the ground around them was covered in silvery strands. People screamed as they were lifted into the air, but ropes secured to wagons, trucks, and stakes driven into the ground held them long enough for someone to cut them free of the sticky tendrils.

"Fun, hunh?" Gar said with a wide grin as he swung his sword at another bundle of tentacles, lopping off four-meter lengths.

Xan looked around at the glistening lines that hung down around them and swung his sword back and forth. "Having a blast, my friend."

Several tentacles latched onto Lily and lifted her into the air too far to cut and onyx let out a squall and fought the tarp covering him. Xan sent a calming projection to the panther's mind as Gar grabbed the rope tied to Lily's waist and pulled her back down where Xan could reach far enough to sever the grasping lines.

He couldn't see her face as everyone had their heads wrapped to keep the stinging tentacles from touching bare skin, but he could feel her mind as she laughed. "That was a rush! Thanks, boys!" Then she swung her sword over his head and another pair of tentacles dropped to the ground.

The last of the dirig finally flowed over the caravan and they could rest. There were three people whose security ropes were too long and it took another few minutes for several people to haul them down enough to cut loose. All three had wrapped themselves with enough clothing they didn't suffer any numbing stings.

The ground inside their defensive ring was covered in lengths of silvery tentacles two, three, and more meters long. They had to leave the animals covered as the cleanup started because the sticky tentacle tips would numb their feet.

"Don't worry about what's already drained out," Sesco said as they began collecting the tentacle tips and tying them into bundles. "Just get the cut end up and out of the dirt. Brush the end off and put the cut end down in whatever container you have. Leave it for about ten minutes for every meter in length. Seal that in something air tight and you have a strong sedative that will keep for years with a slow decrease in strength every time you open the bottle. Smaller bottles are best."

"After the tentacles are drained, you dry them and grind them up to a powder. Sprinkle a little in and around open wounds before bandaging to numb any pain and eliminate infection."

He smiled widely as he put another tentacle tip into a bucket and tucked the top into the ring holding the bundle upright. "Don't mistake the ground up tentacle shaker for the salt shaker, it's embarrassing."

It took almost an hour to collect all the tentacle tips they could find in the growing twilight and drain them into buckets, jars, and bottles.

Sesco had a big smile when he finally

declared it safe to let the animals up. "We've stirred the dirt up enough that what already drained onto the ground shouldn't affect the animals' feet if we move them now."

The process was soon finished and they resumed butchering the bison while the caravan reassembled away from their original position.

"We're going to be here a while finishing up butchering meat," Xan said after the camp settled down. "It's going to take the rest of the night and most of tomorrow. I don't see us leaving till the day after if we want to get as much of the meat processed as possible and get some rest. We'll have to jerk the rest on the move unless we spend a few more days in one spot."

"It's a good thing your grampa thought ahead there, too," the scholar said. "With both command buses designed to jerk or smoke an entire bison at a time, we can move by day after tomorrow."

"We should be able to spread the rest around the caravan and let people jerk their own while we move," Xan said.

"Gonna smell like a mobile snack bar," Gar laughed as they worked to process the unexpected bounty.

The security vans circled their repositioned camp, chasing off every animal that became curious while another group butchered the dead bison. They moved vehicles around to pull the piled bodies out across the grassway so they had room.

The command buses had a perimeter rail and two mobile tool platforms with a mechanical arm.

Each pod's arm could be attached to any of several modular tools and for butchering bison as large as an African bull elephant, one operator used the robotic arm and clawed hand while the other arm wielded the two-meter, electric butchering knife.

Other groups dragged the stripped hides away from the butchering area to be as quickly stretched and scraped as circumstances allowed. Quick-cure chemicals were applied and the skins left to air dry till later when they would be rolled and stored wherever there was room.

"This isn't that bad of a job, considering," Sesco said as they worked.

"Frederick and Francine do know their stuff," Xan said.

The vibrating knife whined as it sliced through the neck of the carcass while the other operator held the head up by one horn. Once clearance was ensured the bus moved around to place the head further away before moving where they could eviscerate the carcass.

They rolled out the freezer extension from between the wheels and leveled it just as the mechanical hand brought back one entire rear quarter. They got the door to the freezer opened and the operator lowered the trimmed rear quarter inside.

"Perfect fit," Sesco said as the mech pod returned to the front of the bus.

"Not surprising. Fred and Fran probably had as much to do with their design as anyone and had more practice with the mechs too. They know exactly how big each freezer is and are cutting the meat to fit. In fact, if I'm not mistaken the whole thing was designed around this specific breed of bison because they're the predominant species in and around the Black Hills."

Moments later the mech brought back a forward quarter and set it in place after they put a divider against the first one. They closed the section's door and rolled the extension inward. Half the ribs and huge neck filled the outer section and they rolled the filled freezer extension in and locked it. The other front and rear quarters, half of the ribs, and the tenderloin strips along each side of the backbone went in the freezer on the other side after being cut into half-meter lengths.

"Okay, now the cooker," Xan said as they started on the next carcass. "Same thing, unlock with the touch pad with the same code, and we roll the grill out. Now we switch it from grill to jerky cooker and fill it up."

They were just finishing preparing the first section when the first trays of sliced meat started arriving and they lay the strips on the spiced trays. As each tray filled, they stacked another, then another and another till the first section was full. The drying tray on the other side was quickly filled and by midday both Command buses had two bison completely processed.

"Amazing, simply amazing," Sesco said as they cleaned up. "He really did think of everything."

Horns and the occasional flashbang sounded in the distance as the security vans discouraged curious scavengers smelling death on the hillside as the others joined them, genetic tinkering allowing them to stay awake another day.

"We're running out of places to put the stuff," Gar said with a smile as Fred and Ginger gnawed on bison bones nearby. "I got all I need for the pups and my section of the fridge is full plus I have all the jerky I can store without throwing out clothes."

"No, please," Tina joked as they cleaned up, "don't do that, we need you to regularly change clothes."

"Har, har, har," the big man said theatrically as he dried freshly washed arms no longer bloody from hours of handling butchered meat. "If we don't fill our water tanks pretty soon, we'll all be a little ripe."

"We have more than enough to get us to Sioux Falls," Xan said as they finished cleaning up. "Our heavy use is over and the hydration vines are always sucking moisture out of the air."

"I'm worried more about the open drying racks so many wagons and carts are carrying," Sesco said as they headed for the kitchens where excess meat was being grilled. "It's not any different from any normal drying racks, but we have to guard a caravan in motion. A stationary jerking station can clear an area and keep it secure but one that moves is always entering a new predator or scavenger's territory."

"Till we get to Sioux Falls," Xan reminded his new friend as they got in line to eat. "We'll sell a lot of what we're harvesting and the more independent members of our entourage will probably do most of that commerce."

Xan's prediction came true when a large convoy came from the north before they moved out and they were able to sell or barter what they would have had to abandon.

"I want to check out the falls," Gar said as they entered the city gate two days later. "I read on their site where they have a nice park and the vendors have giant dogs with the works."

"You do know, *the works*," Xan made air quotes on the last two words, "is different everywhere we go, don't you?"

"Doesn't matter," Gar said. "The picture showed a bun baked around a mold that won't fall apart once juices soak in. Comes in three sizes, including one-pound giant size sausages. That's all it took to sell me so I want to go someplace that sells giant dogs in buns that don't fall apart. They can cover it in anything they want."

Their caravan was larger than most and they were directed to a large fenced area where they would be both contained and protected from casual intruders. Several captured dirig could be seen being slowly harvested nearby of their tentacles and hydrogen, and their skins turned into saddles and heavy clothing.

The next morning, they headed west with half the bison meat and twice the people they'd arrived with and passed the first of the ubiquitous Wall Drug advertisements just outside the west gate.

"Long stretch ahead across the wildest part,"

Sesco said as the Sioux Falls gate disappeared behind them, then looked around. "And we have more walkers, harder to protect."

Xan pursed his lips. "Yeah, can't be helped."

"At least we got some back-up," Gar said as he jogged beside their mounts.

In addition to their two security vans, three armored SUVs with heavy weapons and a half-dozen two-seat quads now ranged around their caravan keeping predators away and steering them around larger herds of grazers. Their speed was cut to no more than a walk, but it was a safe stroll across the grassway. Followers were still arriving as they set out after their brief lunch stop under a Wall Drug sign.

Their camp the first night took on the feel of a village celebration with several small herds of various kinds of grazer settling in nearby for herd safety despite the noise and smell of grilling meat. The security vans, large trucks, and quads formed a moving cordon around their central camp all night to keep predators away.

"I can't believe we've gone almost two whole days without something nobody's ever seen trying to kill us," Gar said the afternoon of the second day out of Sioux Falls.

"Way to go," Sesco said with a wave of his hand. "Now you've jinxed us."

They shared a laugh till the lead bus sounded an alarm and the caravan's lead vehicles moved to form a wall as the 'all stop' alarm sirens blared from the buses.

[16] Big dogs and Kraken.

"It's a prairie dog town," Sesco reported after riding forward to check while the rest looked at their phones. "Big ones, about a sixty, sixty-five kilos. Not a problem for a mount and rider, but walkers are small enough to challenge and these dogs are territorial. Either we'll have to carry all the walkers or form a double line of bigger vehicles to protect them."

"How wide is it?" Xan asked as he craned his head to see in front of the lead bus.

"Couple of kilometers with holes about every fifty meters. Scouts report two in the middle of our side of the grassway. Those are where we might have to act instead of *re*-act. I'd suggest letting the security vans block each hole as we pass over."

Xan checked his phone. "Looks like somebody else suggested the same thing to security. They're going to do what you just said."

Xan made the signal and a few minutes later the caravan began moving again as they changed positions to form up in two lines. Prairie dogs as big as a man paced them at a distance, chattering and darting in and out of holes hundreds of meters to either side of the grassway.

Gunny and Spider in *Recluse* covered the first hole in the westbound lane of the grassway with their van after pepper spraying the defenders.

"These fellas are going to close off this route if they're not thinned out," Sesco said as they approached the van. "Or else somebody is going to have to move the grassway, either up and over or around."

"Or simply have someone provide an escort service the dogs recognize," Xan said as the signals went out to split their formation. "Nonlethal training would let both coexist and not restrict travel."

The caravan split around the hole as the second security van raced ahead to the next hole in their side of the grassway. Xan kept an eye on the increasing numbers of prairie dogs as they paced the caravan through their underground town.

The two halves reunited on the other side of *Recluse*, the prairie dogs on either side of the caravan chattering and standing tall but keeping a safe distance from the intruders.

"With pelts like those," Xan nodded toward two youthful specimens on their right who approached closer than the older dogs, "I'm not sure this town will be here in another year or two."

The two adolescents barked at the intruders, standing almost as tall as Tina, and a couple of emboldened adults moved closer. Ready for any sign of aggression the bus on that side shot the two young prairie dog agitators with stinkballs. The gooey mess hit each in the chest with a sticky mass of adhesive soaked in a foul and putrid paste that smeared when wiped and dried as hard as stone.

"Ooh, that's not going to impress the girls," Xan laughed as dogs scattered.

The caravan approached the second van squatting atop a prairie dog hole and they split around it with growing confidence. Xan smiled and waved at the two in the forward seats, then reunited with Sesco on the other side as the two lines came back together. "Friendly pair."

"Heh-heh, yeah, friendly like a snake that isn't hungry."

Xan resisted the urge to probe his new friend, raising an eyebrow instead.

Sesco sighed. "Sounds dumb, even to me, but I just can't trust someone who doesn't name their gunship. And don't give me that frack about it's a working mobile home and they even have a six-month old baby."

"Well, if you've seen the inside you know it is the working home of a couple with a baby, two babies in fact, cute little twins with pointy ears and lavender eyes just like Tina's and mine. And they do have a name for their working home. It's Mobile Security and when they're not aboard their van they're MSM and MSD for mobile security mom and dad."

"But they didn't *name* their van," Sesco insisted as they approached the western edge of the prairie dog town. "When I can't figure something out it gnaws at me, and I can't figure them out."

Xan smiled at his new friend, then frowned at the actions of the man-sized mutant dogs that now numbered in the hundreds on either side of the grassway as they approached the edge of the prairie dog town. He could feel the pressure of their minds like a headache that almost made the sun too bright.

As they came closer the dogs began crowding their westbound lane. Xan made a signal and several people on the roofs of the buses raised rifles loaded with stinkballs

"Can we join the fun?" Tina asked as she came out of the interior of the formation on Thoth, Lilac and Stone following on their struthies.

"Got our stinkball shooters," Gar held his up.

He didn't need to display the staff strapped to his back with its more lethal add-ons. If their non-lethal defense didn't work, they wouldn't hesitate to kill the increasing numbers of gene-hacked prairie dogs.

"Getting a bit of a headache."

"Yeah, me too, sis. Says something about their intelligence level. Might be a way we can use that."

The numbers of dogs at the border of their claimed territory increased and they moved closer to the narrow lane the caravan would have to move through. When they were about fifty meters away the caravan stopped and Xan spoke on his phone a moment, then he and Tina rode ahead a few meters.

Dismounting, they each went to the edge of the wide lanes and shoulders of their lane and fired a stinkball into the ground and pointed toward the second hole in the middle of the grassway. The entire time they projected the strongest empathic cautions they'd ever attempted.

The number of dogs increased until they formed a solid mass on either side of the grassway, but none crossed the line in the grassway that was still visible despite the sod that had taken over the paved highway. Ahead of them several more dogs moved into the lane with the others already blocking their passage.

"Now what?" Gar asked as he looked skeptically at the five-shot stinkball air gun.

"We go to plan B, of course," Xan said, handing Xanthos' reins to his giant friend.

"Didn't know there was a plan A," Gar mumbled.

He signaled the people he'd phoned earlier and they brought out a large bag of their best turtle and horse feed and another of struthy sticks. Taking the ten kilo bags from the men, he and Tina moved forward toward the line of prairie dogs blocking their path and laid the two gifts on the grassway. Xan slit the top of the bag and pulled some of the large pellets out while Tina cut the bag of struthy sticks, then they both stepped back to their horses and waited.

After a few moments, a pair of dogs moved to inspect the offerings. First one then the other tasted the pellets and sticks and made whistle clicks to the others blocking their way. In seconds, the two kinds of food were surrounded by chattering prairie dogs for several minutes till they gathered up the gifts and separated to the edges of the line created by the old paved road and bordering shoulders.

Xan and Tina walked their horses at the edges of that line reaching out and touching paws with the line of man-sized prairie dogs while projecting a calm friendship. A trickle of humans of all shapes and sizes ventured out from between the four largest vehicles and touched paws with the lines of dogs, many of them presenting struthy sticks and other gifts to the genetically altered prairie town residents.

"I'm getting a better and better idea of what kind of person your grandfather is," Sesco said as they left the prairie dog town behind and headed for the Missouri River.

"How do you mean?" Xan asked as their team of riders scouted ahead of the caravan.

"The whole idea of offering food to the prairie dogs came from him."

"Didn't Amanda suggest that?" Lilac wondered as they trotted ahead of the caravan on horses and struthy mounts.

"Yes," Xan replied as they came over the hill to gaze at the slope where the Missouri cut through the prairie. "But not till the bus's computer made it one of the higher success options."

"So, you're saying your grandfather has expanded his devious genius mind to hacking computers too?" Gar wondered as Fred and Ginger stood on either side of him.

"No," Xan smiled as they stood at the top of the last hill down to the river. "But I'm betting I know who the computer tech is and it would follow grampa's pattern if he's been tinkering to uplift the dogs."

Tina pointed. "That looks like a good place to camp. We can put the turtles on the river side and protect our outer perimeter with the buses and vans on the land side."

"Uh, we might want to put the buses on the river side," Sesco said. "There's a reason that nice spot is empty. I'm betting they leveled it and had good intentions and gene hackers built something that makes it a deathtrap that close to the river."

"That's what I like about you," Tina laughed, "you're always so positive." She shrugged. "But you're also usually right."

Xan called the lead bus to let them know they'd arrived while they went down to the walled village on the east side of the river.

"Nice looking place," Gar said as he walked through the gate, Fred and Ginger beside him with their heads close to his hips. They tied their mounts to the hitching post outside the main building, gave them treats, and went inside.

"I'm sorry," a cowboy uniformed man came at them, "you will not be allowed…"

"That's okay, Malcolm," an authoritative voice cut in loudly. "I've been assured these particular hellhounds are well trained and are no danger to any patron."

The gaudily uniformed man backed off. "Of course, Sherriff. My mistake. I was already told but my instincts betrayed me. My apologies for any offense."

Gar nodded his head as Fred and Ginger lay down on the floor. "No offense taken. We didn't know this was a secure border before we entered."

"It isn't, actually," the elderly man said, then held out his hand. "Sherriff Mason Whitehorse. We've been watching you folks crossing the country. Oh, don't look like you don't know what I'm talking about. Ever since that kerfuffle at that bridge in Ohio, folks with an interest have been watching your progress."

"Heh-heh, got a little confusing when two

groups in different places kept being involved in interesting news. But then they merged and folks got interested in an even bigger story." He smiled and gestured toward the open compound. "Got room for a couple hundred riders and a couple dozen wheeled trucks and small carts inside our walls and enough folks to cater to that number every day. If you stay on the lower plaza you do so at your own risk. We haven't secured it yet and we're currently in the middle of river kraken spawning season."

"Thank you, Sheriff," Xan said. "We'll let our people know what's available."

"You folks have proven to be competent, so do whatever pleases you for camping as long as you accept the risks."

"Probably still jack up the price of the feed," Gar grumbled after the sheriff walked away.

"That happens everywhere we go," Tina reminded him as she looked over the wall at the arriving caravan.

On the other side of the grassway village that bordered the east side of the river the four larger vehicles pulled off the trail onto the leveled area closer to the riverbank. The buses, turtles, and security vans formed an arcing wall on the river side while the rest of the vehicles closed the arc on the grassway side with the smaller carts, single rider mounts, and walkers inside a protective wall.

"So, the kraken spawn upstream just like salmon," Xan said after they paid their camping fee and moved to a table where they could see their mounts tied up outside through the tall windows.

"And they lay a gazillion eggs like salmon and frogs and stuff," Tina said.

"Yes, and yes," the man at the next table confirmed. "When the sun sets your riverside vehicles are going to get some attention, but it's mostly for places to lay eggs. The tentacles can be a bit destructive, but if your seams are secure and you make a lot of noise or whack off a few tentacle tips, they'll stay back. It'll take an all-night watch but if you put out a few dozen buckets in pits along the riverbank you can collect a treasure in kraken roe."

Xan thanked the man and bought him another drink while Sesco called the information in to the command buses to those that could make quickest plans for securing the caravan and collecting a rare treat. They had a second drink and a large meal before walking their mounts from the higher compound down to the open plaza where the caravan assembled.

"We have the rail units on the buses loaded with stinger hands. That's pepper spray above the knuckles and shocker pads on the inside of the fingers," Tanner said, when they arrived. "We're as protected as we can be."

"We should have enough supplies to get across this last stretch," Xan said as he and his closest friends gathered at one section of the community campfire after tending their mounts. "From what our information confirms, we're coming into some good growth for grazing on the other side of the river. Hunting should be good, too, but so will the likelihood of encountering some big predators."

"Our plan is to cross the river tomorrow and travel till a late lunch and stop for an early overnight. We're cutting way back on our speed because we've collected so many walkers and we don't want to outrun them just because we can."

"At the rate they're following us, they'll still be coming in when we leave tomorrow," Bekka said. "Do you need somebody to stay back and keep order?"

Xan traded looks a moment with his sister before answering. "No, we're thinking we might need you more where we're going than where we've been. The way it looks, those numbers will just continue to grow. If you stayed it would be a fulltime job for you and your husband and most likely on opposite shifts."

"I withdraw the offer," she deadpanned then took a drink of ale while theatrically covering her eyes as if hiding.

"Hey Xan," Sesco called out, "you might want to check this out."

Xan left the fire to walk over to the gap between the two buses to see the first river kraken crawl out of the water under the gibbous moon to lay her eggs. Dozens of locals swarmed the riverbanks digging pits they buried large buckets or tubs in.

There was some commotion by Fred and Fran's bus and moments later both giants were hurrying to copy the locals. Xan and Sesco quickly joined them and within minutes were walking away from their second planted tub as a river kraken struggled onto dry land.

Considerably smaller than lake or ocean kraken, the river variety was still large with a body up to two meters long and arms that stretched half again that. They almost didn't back away fast enough as the territorial kraken slapped at them with her arms.

They dodged another energetic mother kraken before retrieving their first ten-liter tub of roe. They had a little more trouble collecting their second tub as the mother kraken objected to their presence, slapping at them with her tentacles and hissing wetly through a beaked mouth.

"Just let her guard it till she starts to dry out," the local advising them said. "Give it another half hour at the most and she'll bail."

"This is a nice setup you've built," Sesco said as he examined the local man's egg collector while they waited.

"Kraken prefer rocks to lay their eggs in and around," the gangly man explained. "But there aren't a lot of rocks in this stretch of the river so I built my own."

"With funnels and tubes between the rocks down to your collection tubs," Sesco observed with admiration.

"As long as I keep emptying the bottom tub, more females will use my rock pile till midnight when the mothers go back downstream to rest and feed in deeper water."

"I thought they went further upstream," Xan said as they helped the man fill his buckets from the collection tub after the trap's latest kraken headed back to the river.

"They do and a lot already have, but only the ones small enough to get through the shallower parts," the man said. "I'm actually kind of impressed with how big they're at this level this year. Bigger kraken means more eggs."

"Ours finally gave up," Sesco said and they recovered their second tub, then helped another local collect the bounty. "No, you can have our spot. We only had two tubs so you're welcome to use the hole."

"So, you've decided to go slow the last couple hundred klicks," Sesco said as they made their way up the riverbank and between the buses with their bounty.

"Yes," Xan replied as they gave their tubs of kraken roe to Rick and Amanda Shaw since Fred and Fran had several tubs of their own.

"And back to what you were asking," Xan said as they walked toward the main fire in the center of the camp's open interior. He spoke loud enough for all to hear after trading looks with his sister. "We intend to only travel half our normal distance every day as long as our supplies last to provide security for the walkers we're accumulating."

More people listened as he continued to speak loud enough everyone around the campfire could hear. "I'm not going to order anyone to do so, but I would like it if anyone with the extra space give rides to the slowest of those on foot. At least the elderly, children, and the injured and sick."

"And on a side-note I'd like to thank Rocky and Elly for going back after that family with the broken axle on their cart. For those who don't know what she did, Elly carried the back half of the cart almost ten klicks till they caught up and could fix the axle."

"Back to tomorrow, anybody who doesn't have the list of siren codes can get them from either of the two command buses. There are only a few that require sirens so they're easy to remember and we'll practice them just like we would have already if we hadn't needed to use them so often for real emergencies."

He smiled at several of the faces lit by the flickering flames. "I'd like to thank all those who reacted to everyone else's actions when they didn't know what was happening. And I'd especially like to thank those that helped the new people during our emergencies. Experience is a hard teacher and you saved lives by your willingness to risk danger to help others."

"Tomorrow we'll leave camp later than normal to make announcements and organize the arrangement of our numbers. Assignments of position will be determined by the quickest the caravan can be reduced to a compact defensive circle when danger presents itself."

"Be advised, we'll practice other things like fast-march and spread-out-to-scavenge at any time. One will be used to get to a favorable campsite ahead and the other for collecting firewood just before stopping or passing through an area with wood before the end of day."

"Pass all this down to every new group arriving," he gestured to the groups and individuals still coming into the outpost higher up on the eastern side of the Missouri. "Most of them will be with us when we leave tomorrow."

"Now, you all have things to do before tomorrow but there's no hurry, so relax. Our supplies are more than enough to get us the rest of the way as long as we work together."

His eyes went to another group that had joined them with their own command bus flanked by two mobile security trucks. "Those of you in established groups will be asked to make your group a part of the defensive circle when needed if you stay with us."

"For supplies, I encourage everyone to fill all your water containers, get what kraken eggs you can collect, and sharpen, clean, and load your weapons before we leave mid-morning. Direct all questions to the command buses, please, as that is where anyone else will have to go to get the answer to your questions, me included."

"And with that I am off duty," he said, raised the mug he held in salute, and took a long drink before walking away from the circle around the main campfire.

"That was smartly done," Sesco said as his friend joined him. "Basically, told them to leave you and your sister alone and direct all questions to the command buses."

He snorted a laugh. "Have you been following the news media? Your grampa has Orbitals casually mentioning a sanctuary for outcasts and the expected purist agitators are starting to say he's establishing a rebellion and a new country."

Xan sighed while trying to not project his true feelings. "Yeah, doesn't take long for conspiracies to be imagined when someone tries to protect themselves from something that doesn't exist."

The campfire grew quiet for a while as everyone nursed a relaxing drink. Xan was draining the last of his mug of ale before retiring when the alarms sounded just as an immense tentacle wrapped itself over the edge of the Shaw bus, then a second one, quickly followed by dozens of shouts and more than one shotgun blast.

"Looks like it's going to be another long night," Xan mumbled as people ran toward the newest intrusion of Kraken.

[17] "I call hex!"

"Satellite pictures look good," Sesco said as he put his sat-phone away. "Newest image shows clear prairie for the next day's travel."

Xan nodded as he looked at the crowded mass of people from atop Xanthos. "That'll make this a little easier."

"Heh, you're the one that wanted to wait till all the stragglers got ready," the scholar said as Spot pranced with excitement.

Xan looked at the large numbers of walkers gathered in wait. An equal number had anticipated being left behind and started out early to not be as far behind as others at the end of the day. The line of walkers stretched across the bridge and over the next ridgetop and contained several carts and wagons as well as mounted riders.

"You think your grandfather planned on this level of interest?" Tanner asked from atop his prancing struthy.

Xan pointed his chin at the river of people heading across the bridge. "According to the Library pictures, that's just a surge concentrated around our caravan."

"Aren't going to make twenty klicks a day at this rate," Gar grumbled as he walked beside a plodding Xanthos.

"Look on the bright side my friend, that'll give us at least a week to practice formations before we get to the Badlands."

"Oh joy. So, what does Sesco's *Library* say

we're going to face?"

"Ants the size of housecats. *Territorial* ants the size of *large* housecats with mandibles that can chop a child's arm off or bite ten-centimeter slices in exposed skin. They hunt in swarms, pick a target and attack, chop it up, and eat it alive."

"Just wonderful," Gar mumbled.

"Seems they found the mud cliffs of the Badlands a good place to dig a nest. Sesco says the nest is contained but every once in a while, there's a raid on the town when there hasn't been anything to eat on the grassway between Wall and the nest for a while."

"You're telling me the ants feed on the critters on the grassway *that we are traveling*?"

Xan failed at hiding a smile. "Yes, my friend, they feed on unprotected passersby. But again, the good thing is, we have over a week to practice defensive formations and make sure everybody knows what we're facing."

"Any idea how many there are?"

"Sesco is still researching, but he says several thousand. He also says only a fraction of those will be the hunters, maybe a few hundred in each foraging group. The rest are workers."

"So, that leaves more than enough hunters to take out a walker or three, or something bigger."

Xan shrugged. "One good thing is they don't come at you in organized formations. The first one to find you tests to see if you're viable prey, then signals with pheromones and waits for a second one to investigate. One will follow the target while the other goes for help, spreading the call till there are enough to start harassing the prey. Kill the scouts and the rest pass the extreme danger message instead of attacking one at a time."

"We need to have spotters and snipers targeting every big ant we see as soon as it's within kill range. Luckily it's all open plains from here to there so we'll have enough long shots to spread the danger message."

The day grew boring and they made more kilometers than they expected, passing more signs for Wall Drug every day since leaving Sioux Falls, and camping at a walled compound owned by a range rancher.

"So, you just wait for critters to come by, take your tractor out, kill something and butcher it on the spot, then deliver the meat to your daughter and son-in-law this side of Sioux Falls, and they sell it?"

"Yep," the gnarly old man said. "Me and the missus. I run the tractor's arms and do the butchering and filling the cooler bins while she snipes anything that gets too close. Sometimes we get a bonus monster head."

More than one set of eyes went to the dozens of skulls mounted around the compound's walls as the old man continued, "Every once in a while, we get lucky and get a pregnant cerapig or catch an orphan of something bigger. Live monsters sell for more and the younger the better."

"Sorry we don't have room for all your people," he said as he changed the subject, "but your walkers will have proven walls around them while they sleep."

"That's more than enough," Xan said as he handed the man the leather pouch full of coins.

After insuring the count was correct they shook hands and the old man returned to the compound, closing the door behind him.

"Pleasant fella," Lily commented.

"You could have stayed inside."

"That's nice, Xan, but Onyx and I prefer to not be trapped by walled-in people. Safer out here with the monsters."

"I'm not sure if you'll be safer out here," Sesco said as weapons fire sounded in the distance from one of the roving security quads, truck, or vans.

"Not for me and Onyx, safer for them," she threw a thumb over her shoulder at the compound packed with hundreds of walkers and several smaller carts. "We have a good spot between the Shaw bus and the compound wall. Nice and snug and private."

She gave Xan a smile. "Onyx is probably already asleep, something I should be doing too. See you tomorrow."

Xan watched her weave through the people who had chosen to stay with the larger animals and vehicles, then turned to see his friends looking at him and smiling. "What?"

"Gunny said he spotted two ants in the distance last night, but it looked like they were following a herd of hadro in the eastbound lane," Xan said as he walked beside Xanthos without holding the reins.

"That's three nights in a row," Lily said as Onyx walked beside her just as patiently.

"Sesco says it's just scouts so far, but once we're a couple days closer we'll start to get into their notice more. Murdo Station reports encounters daily but the ants stay away from the populated areas. We should be there this afternoon."

The day wore on and they encountered a herd of wild jackalope just past noon and waited for it to cross the grassway.

"Amazing what the hacker mind can come up with," Gar laughed as they watched the ridiculous looking animals.

"Actually," Sesco went into lecture mode, "jackalopes existed long before the first gene hacker put antlers on jackrabbits and made them bigger."

"They didn't exist *really*, but inventive people put antlers on stuffed jackrabbits and had fun convincing citified rubes with money they existed. Then CRISPR came along and tech advances made gene hacking basement-lab easy so now we have thirty kilo, wild jackalopes hopping across the prairie in herds of three and four hundred."

"A prairie also full of giant bison, oliphant, and dinosaurs, oh my," Lily laughed.

"That looks like the last of them," Xan said as he began walking again. "Murdo Station isn't far and I'd like to find a place for the stragglers when they catch up."

The friends all mounted and took off at a faster pace than the rest of the caravan. Two horses, three struthy, a panther, and three runners maintained a steady lope for an hour before the walls of the next village came into sight.

They split up and Xan found himself teamed with Lily. The new method of ensuring accommodations by an advanced group each day had developed over the three days since Sioux Falls and they were getting good at it.

He and Lily found two places on the east side of the walls that each agreed to take twenty walkers and allow as many vehicles as could fit, park beside their compound's outer wall. Coins changed hands, a sketch of the compound quickly made with the owner's signature, and one of the runners raced back to assign who best to spend the night there.

The next morning, the fourth since leaving Sioux Falls, Xan and Lily rode back to the east side of town to make sure the ones housed there got an early start.

"That went much better than expected," Tina said as she rode on the other side of Lily from Xan.

"Everybody had food, showers, and soft beds waiting for them while somebody else took care of any animals they have," Sesco said from the other side of Tina. "That little bit of extra time was more than enough, especially since somebody else paid for it all."

"Helped you had written checkout times and everybody knew what they were," Lily added. "Of course, more than half the people I saw were ready long before we showed up to make sure they were moving. I saw a good seventy or eighty walkers already on the march when we were riding back to the east side."

"They earned a safe relaxing night," Xan said. "What I thought would take five days took three. One more good stretch to Belvidere for one last night indoors and we'll be ready to make it to the edge of the Badlands."

"That'll be our biggest test, spending the night in the open on the edge of ant territory. Then it's a one-day race to Wall to be inside secure walls one more night."

"But first we have to get to Belvidere and there's a scattering of thunderstorms coming from the southwest," Sesco said. "It's clear blue sky as far as we can see now but by noon we'll have thunderstorm cells all around us. By the time we get to Belvidere we might be dodging tornados or herds of critters scared by thunder, lightning, and tornados."

"And why wasn't this in the morning briefing?" Xan couldn't help but be curious since Sesco had the best information source other than the buses.

"Just came through," he glanced at his phone's screen, "three minutes ago. And it's been half that since I told you. I would have told you sooner but I needed a half minute to study the data."

Tina snorted aloud. "Got you there. Hey Lily, did I ever tell you about the time my little brother left his history textbook at home because he already read the assignment. Teacher made him recite the first chapter aloud from memory then he did it exactly how it was written. Teacher gave him an 'F' for not correcting the five spelling, six punctuation, and three actual history mistakes in the chapter."

Xan scowled as the two women laughed while Sesco tried to stay out of it. He was just about to say something to divert attention away from him when both buses began sounding the sirens for extreme weather, then three firm blasts to signal three hours.

"Looks like you're not the only one to get the weather report," Lily said. "Or did you…"

Sesco held up his phone. "Sent them the file while we were talking, but they probably already saw it and were just double checking before giving the alert. Noon was about what I figured before we would see the storm. Good thing is it'll be a scattered front so the chances of one crossing the grassway at the same time as us is also less. Since it's coming from the west there won't be any dirig, so we might make it all the way to Belvidere without a windblown hair."

"Where I come from that's called a hex," Lily laughed. "So, if we get run over by a stampede running from a tornado, then get run over by the tornado, it'll be your fault."

"Considering the statistical chances of both happening, I'll accept your challenge."

The pace of the caravan picked up as people helped each other where they could. The security vans refused to stay back with the slowest, claiming that every time they did the walkers slowed even more, so the line began to stretch as the fastest and slowest spread out.

"Line is getting unwieldy," Lily said as she

trotted next to Onyx.

Xan had no trouble talking as he ran. "Might need to use that formation you suggested."

"Not as a drill, I hope. Could cause some anger after telling people we need to hurry."

"No, no drills the rest of the way," he laughed. "Only had the one anyway, all the rest were legitimate. We're too close to the end of the trail to waste time with drills when real emergencies are experience enough."

Before they could say more the lead bus sounded a new pattern, followed by another new series of sirens. In seconds, the caravan split into three individual formations with each one adjusting its speed to the slowest in their group.

There was some motion between the three for several minutes before the lead group began to move away. The middle group kept a steady pace that was better than they had been traveling while the third group fell behind by an ever-growing distance.

"Is it wise to send both buses with the lead group?" Gar asked as he ran beside his friends, all of them sparing their mounts from their weight.

"They're carrying the most infirm and youngest," Xan explained as they ran. "They'll get them housed then come back to get as many of the slowest as they can pack in."

"Last one before the run?"

Xan looked at the woman who had somehow become his partner in everything he did. "Shouldn't be too bad till we stop for camp tomorrow. That'll be in the open and with half again as many people as we left Sioux Falls with. Over a thousand at last count."

"Then, if we're not attacked by swarms of ants tomorrow night, we have a full day's run to the only sanctuary from said ants, so we can rest for another day's run. This is just practice for the next two days before things get serious."

"And finally get to see this Wall Drug thing that's been advertised along the grassway ever since we crossed the Missip," Lily laughed. "And here I thought billboards died with paved interstates."

They ran back to the central group led by their two turtles showing their stamina while carrying dozens of those less able to maintain a lengthy pace. Runners jumped on and off as they grew tired or rested, many of them grabbing onto turtle spines and bracing their feet above the ring of quills while they rested.

Xan and Lily trotted back till they reached the last group, consisting of those that insisted they weren't carrying too much or just couldn't leave family heirlooms, despite the fact they sometimes overfilled a wagon.

"Can't understand why they need so much *stuff*," Lily fumed after helping one family change tires on their old box truck converted into a patio-topped camper pulled by a team of gene-altered alpaca.

Xan looked at his newest friend, noting everything she owned was in saddlebags resting over Onyx's rump. "That big walnut table looked like it was a hundred years old and I don't think that mirrored chest of drawers was made in this millennium. Some things you don't leave behind."

"Besides, they've been weaving sweaters, cloaks, and blankets for years. They have enough finished product inside their camper to start their own shop when they get where they're going."

They helped others out of minor and major incidences through the day as clouds formed on the horizon and raced across the prairie. Almost all of them went wide and didn't drift above the caravan till early afternoon, but it barely left the grass wet before it was past. They continued on with the last group splitting into two as the majority moved ahead of the slowest.

"Here come the buses," Xan yelled as the wind picked up.

"Good thing, too," Lily said. "Slowest folk were starting to get nervous."

Xan looked over the group at the trailing end of the caravan. It couldn't be helped that someone would be last and they would most likely be the ones on the edge of their capabilities. Older and younger with nothing to carry got rides while those rescuing the last of several generations' worth of possessions usually had to push and pull those carts and wagons by hand.

"Okay people," he yelled as the wind swirled more with the approaching cloud, "bus is here to take you the rest of the way. Hey Rick, got room for this many?"

"We'll make room," the bus driver called out through the open window. "Can't take the carts though, just the people."

"Not a problem. Once all the riders are off,

the carts will move faster."

The walkers quickly boarded the bus, another group being loaded further ahead. When the last one could be stuffed aboard, the bus took off for the walled village of Belvidere.

They had just caught up to the trailing edge of the new last group when a siren sounded and their phones vibrated or sang.

"Hex! I call it!" Lily laughed as the smaller group began to draw into a more compact formation.

"Too soon," Sesco yelled back with a wide grin.

"Do we have enough to anchor?" Tanner wondered as he rode Gar's packhorse, Phobos.

Xan looked at Rocky River atop Elly and flanked by two other oliphants, one of them a male just coming into his prime. Behind them walked another team of giant alpaca. All four were draped in hanging cargo with a single rider except the one with the nursing mother. A triceratops with a single rider and several cargo bags trudged along at the rear with a ring of seven adult walkers of various ages.

"Hey Rocky, any of your riders want to transfer to a bus?"

"No thanks, Xan. All Elly's passengers have cargo they can't carry themselves or use to take up space for another person. Other two are about the same and the alpaca don't tolerate fleas hanging off their coat. We can handle our own if you want to get your mounts in a safer place."

"I'm thinking it's a little late for that," Xan

yelled into the growing wind. "You mind if we huddle with you if it gets worse?"

The old river rat laughed along with Elly as he rode the neck of his massive oliphant friend. "We'll hold you down if a funnel cloud tries to eat you, won't we Elly?"

The oliphant, as sentient as any human bugled her agreement as they hurried at the fastest pace they could as loaded as they were. The wind continued to bluster and blow as they trudged across the prairie toward the nominal safety of high walls. The rain started to fall and visibility grew less with a darkening sky as they followed the vaguely marked grassway toward Belvidere.

"I can see the village walls!" Xan called out as he rode Xanthos back to the compact group. "Another kilometer and we'll be safe!"

They struggled against winds that came from every direction enough to stagger an oliphant and just as they saw the high village walls in the driving rain a small herd of bison thundered into and around them. The oliphant were already in a compact formation with the alpaca and cera following close in and the bison flowed around them like water around rocks in a stream.

Lightning lit the sky and thunder rolled as frightened people and animals cried out at every flash and boom. One bolt struck so close hair stood on end and the thunderclap could be felt like a blow to the chest and would have knocked Xan from his saddle if he hadn't been already hanging on tight.

"There! There's the gate!" Xan yelled as they grew closer to the prairie village.

The gates were being shut behind them when the worst of the deluge poured down so hard Xan couldn't see Lily and Onyx only a few meters away. The gates were no sooner closed when the village began ringing its town hall bell in warning.

Lily pointed. "I call hex!"

The cloud above them began swirling and twisting and a funnel began to grow, aimed directly at them. People scattered in every direction as the twister emerged from the bottom of the black cloud, lightning shooting sideways in every direction.

With no place to run Xander and his friends looked up into the swirling tunnel as it reached for them.

The funnel twisted and wrenched sideways as it grew then flipped to the side and landed on the ground several hundred meters outside the wall before bouncing twice then dissolving as the parent cloud broke up.

"Ha!" Sesco exclaimed with a wide smile. "Missed by nearly a half klick so I didn't hex us. You owe me a mug of ale."

[18] Hunting rex.

"Wait, what?" Lily feigned indignation. "What makes you think you won? We got caught in a stampede and hit by a tornado, just like I said."

"Ptah!" Sesco scoffed with a relieved grin at their close call. "That wasn't a stampede, and the tornado missed by a half kilometer, so you weren't even close. You owe me a mug of ale."

The rain wasn't coming down as hard but it was falling steady and getting out of it and dry was more important than listening to his friends bicker. Xan led the rest toward where a figure stood in a wide, open door and into a large barn, his sister, Gar, Sesco, and Lily, following close behind, the last two still arguing good-naturedly.

He was removing Xanthos' saddle when three other riders came in followed by one of their caravan's slowest family carts towed by a pair of rain-drenched dwarves. Seven quad-cycles filled the barn with their supply van parked in front of the open door so the crowded barn could get fresh air while being somewhat protected.

"Sure hope this doesn't go on all night," Gar said as he brushed Fred and Ginger.

"Satellites show it ending about midnight," Sesco said, taking the hint for an update. "Tonight will be a little cooler, but the next two days are going to be about perfect for our run to Wall."

"What is this Wall Drug place, anyway?" Bekka wondered. "All I can find is it was a tourist trap back before the end of the world."

"That's about it," Sesco confirmed, then vacillated, "but it's also more than that. It was, still is in fact, a western marketplace that contains historical statues and plaques, and has restaurants and gift shops that probably sells the original versions of jackalope when they were still imaginary."

"It's only a small part of the village of Wall," he went into lecture mode as everyone smiled tolerantly. "There's even a bike shop that services and sells those things." He pointed his chin at the armed and armored quads.

"One of them told me they were supposed to meet up with another group in Wall," Lily said. "There's another group behind us. Our group is thinking of waiting for them if we leave before they get here since they're alone except for a supply van."

"That might work to our advantage," Tina said. "They could follow behind us after their friends catch up and maybe hang back with the stragglers for added security."

"That's what they were doing since they joined us in Murdo," Lily said. "I talked to a few of them the night we got there. They've just been riding up and down the line behind us harassing predators and watching for fall-outs."

A flash lit the windows and almost immediately a thunderclap revealed how close the lightning strike hit. Seconds later an alarm sounded and was echoed by two others from other directions.

Xan quickly found the stablemaster, then reported to his friends, "Fire alarm. Lightning hit an out building with bad grounding and started some hay on fire."

"Luckily, we already paid for our feed," Gar said with a smile.

"Heh, that's what the stablemaster said. And now, I know some of you will stay up late, but I'm going to find my bedroll. See you all tomorrow."

He brushed Xanthos and checked his gear before tossing his bedroll onto the shelf above the stall's feed bin and was asleep in seconds. His dreams ended with him covered in ants and he awoke to find himself twisted in his bedding.

After a quick trip to the toilet he went to the open door to see a starlit sky. Before he could return to Xanthos' stall the night watch began waking people so he readied his gear and saddled his horse. He was almost finished when the last of the sleepers rose and a wonderful smell came from the other side of the quad supply van.

"Looks like they made it last night," Lily said as he joined her in the line.

"It's a little bigger than the other group's supply van and that trailer has a freezer," he observed.

"Looks like they're serving real eggs, bacon, and hash browns," she said. "I could get used to this."

They found out the breakfast wasn't free when they had to stand in front of a camera, say their name, then give a short greeting that included where they were from and where they were headed. The line got backed up as Xan and his friends were asked extra questions.

The others were half finished when Sesco finally joined them. "One of the new group told me they're writing a travel documentary and doing stories on the most interesting people they meet. I might have gone into a bit more detail than necessary on a couple answers."

The others rolled their eyes and smiled but refrained from comment as they finished eating, delivered their plates and cutlery to the wash tubs, and went to ready their mounts.

"Our buses and fastest transport already left with the children and elderly," Tina said as they walked out of the barn to a brightening day. "There are two compounds there that have agreed to take them all in so the buses can return for another load. By the time they get to camp with the second load, Honey and Bear should be there to start our own defensive ring."

"Our job," Xan continued as they mounted, "is to protect the walkers till we can get them inside our wall."

They rode to the rendezvous area outside Belvidere's west gate and found a confused mess.

"Seems like we got some more additions last night," Tanner said from atop Phobos. "They just started gathering and most are too busy doing things they should've already done to listen to directions."

"A bunch of them took off after the buses before daybreak and another group had to be taken to the local hospital after they tried to climb on the turtles for a free ride. Seems when we took the skirts off the quills, they thought that was an invitation to ride and swarmed. Medics hauled away twenty-nine before the rest got the message."

Honey and Bear began moving through the crowd along with the security vans and the faster vehicles and people scattered out of their way.

"There were a lot of groups complaining they heard there were rides for those who didn't have them," Tanner continued. "We told them those spots were all taken by the time we left Sioux Falls and if they started now, they might make it to camp by dark."

"So instead of having three compact, easy to defend groups," Xan said, "we're going to have an almost solid line with a mix of people who've never traveled with us and don't seem to be listening to vital information."

"Yes, that pretty much sums it up," the detective reported. "On the plus side, there are several groups that *are* prepared and are seeking out our info. A few of those have linked to our buses and are spreading info to their members and beyond. One group with a half dozen quads and trucks and a family on a saurowagon have volunteered to form a core group."

"The buses have already updated the emergency site to show five distinct groups instead of the three we had earlier."

Xan and the others checked their phones to get the new updates and several minutes later began to scatter to their assigned positions.

"Is Onyx going to be able to run all day?"

Lily gave him the stinkeye as the panther in question growled. "She's panther in many ways but just like your Xanthos, she has genes from all over.

That includes legs built as much for endurance as stalking and a short burst of speed. She may not be able to last in a race with Xanthos, but then your horse wouldn't be able to last in a long-distance run with Sesco's Spot."

He smiled and sent an empathic apology for the implied insult and was pleased when Onyx's growl turned to a purr. "What we need to do, all the way to the next camp, is ride back and forth telling people the caravan rules and signals and answering the same questions over and over again."

"Oh, and rush in with guns blazing any time the caravan is attacked by monsters, no matter what they look like."

Lily looked around at the unorganized mass of people on foot, mounted riders, and small carts and wagons. "Looks like it'll be a long day."

"Let's get moving and maybe they'll follow." Xan said. He and Lily quickly became the point in a slow-moving group working its way out of the unorganized mass.

"Looks like those two giants on megastangs ahead on the left are moving to intercept," Xan commented as a cerapig fell in behind them, the cart it was towing covered in wolfen children. An elderly man with a beautifully embossed wolf on the front of his t-shirt sat atop piled supplies. Two adults with the beginnings of wolfen features pushing from behind was the only reason the cerapig could tow the heavy load.

It took several minutes to get to the edge of the crowded area where they could increase their speed. Xan looked back as the rest of their new retinue entered the open grassway. There were several mounted riders, including the dragon family and a saurowagon. A pair of quads flanking a small camper van came in from the side opposite the megastang and matched speed with them.

The driver of the camper stuck his head out of the window. "Linked our phones with the Command Base and gentleman by the name of Frederick said you were to lead us into the number three position, then fall back and organize the number four position."

"Thanks," Xan waved and moved around to begin watching the newly animated group settle in.

As soon as they were clear of the interfering bodies the wolfen children on the cart the cerapig was towing dropped off and folded down bars at each corner of the cart and began pushing. Relieved of the weight and helped by the additional muscle power, the cart was able to make a respectable pace.

A couple of walkers, one with a large backpack and the other carrying a toddler and an infant, talked with the two adults pushing the cart from behind as they walked. After a few minutes, they put the backpack and children on the cart and switched places with the youngest children while the old man entertained the toddler and infant.

An hour after leaving Belvidere, Xan approached the group after the couple on the megastangs took the wolfen group's two walking children and their campfire wood aboard their large mounts.

"We need somebody to act as lead for group four and you folks have set a steady pace that only a few are still passing."

"Uh, we're not actually together," the giant woman said as the child perched on a cargo sack behind her fidgeted.

"Yeah, we can see you're not," Lily laughed as she cooed at the baby while Onyx padded alongside the megastang. "You could take the parents and their backpack onboard and still move faster than this group. Instead of sticking with the faster bunch you started out with, you dropped back with this one and offered help to another team."

"Your group has come together to help each other and others have seen that and let you be their lead." Xan gestured toward the almost organized group behind them on the grassway. "You're already the group's four leaders, all you have to do is accept the phone link with the command buses to go with the position."

"Sid, give that to your grampa, please," the man pushing the cart said as they kept pace.

The older boy moved away from his pusher bar and accepted the phone with a polite 'thank you' and gave it to the elderly man riding the cart before resuming his position.

"Dad lost the bottom half of his legs in the attempt to clean up Cuba's raptor overpopulation," the woman said "He'll be out and about after we make camp, but his prosthetics won't carry him all day at the pace we need to go. He's more than able to act as our communications officer."

"Good, good, then all you have to do is turn it on and it automatically updates messages." The old man nodded as he followed Xan's directions.

"Icon on the upper right of the front page connects to the secure bus servers if you're in range or acts like any other cell phone out of caravan range by tapping the icon in the upper left."

When he was sure the old man was connected and following the tutorial confidently, he and Lily made a sweep around the group to answer a few questions and urge the ones falling behind to keep up. They fell back further to talk to those spread out between groups four and five, then moved back to see if they could make a cohesive group out of the strung-out line behind the last one.

"Good luck with that," Sesco said as he and Tina joined them. "We drew the short straw and have been back here the whole time trying to organize. It's not working, there are just too many individuals and families too scared to work with others."

"They're all looking for someplace where they'll be accepted, but too used to being used to open up with all those around them seeking the same thing. The old woman on the sauro is the worst, won't even answer simple questions. Ignores everybody and won't allow riders."

"Okay, thanks, Sesco." Xan looked at those they rode by as they backtracked along their path. Most were walkers or those with the smallest carts pulled by one or two people with a few riders mixed in and a couple of larger vehicles.

One area that was slightly bunched up centered on an elderly sauro covered in a wicker frame festooned with garden pots. Some contained vines covered in flowers while others were small trees or bushes. A tiny cabin not much more than a sleeping bag tent sat behind a high cushioned seat instead of a saddle at the base of the sauro's neck. A wrinkled elderly lady wearing a silk headscarf and a stern glare sat regally in the chair without a harness or reins to control her mount.

Xan didn't hesitate to match Xanthos' pace to the sauro and ride silently, ignoring Lily twice when she spoke. After nearly a half hour of being ignored she rode off in a huff. Several minutes later the old lady spoke softly, "Impatient one, that. You sure you want to hook up with her?"

"Heh, not really, but there seem to be more pluses than minuses so far."

"Don't read the numbers too quick, boy. Leads to heartache when the ratio flips if you've jumped too soon. Sometimes worse. You got something to say?"

Xan looked up at the luxurious seat perched in front of the tiny wicker cabin above a frame covered in growing food plants. The old lady was dark of skin but he couldn't tell if it was from genes or sun. Despite her glare, the wrinkles were as much from smiling as age as she returned his gaze with barely restrained humor while casually removing her headscarf to reveal pointed ears that sat as high as a cat's instead of lower like his own.

"We're trying to do some organizing and have marked five groups within our overall caravan we hope will act as autonomous defensive units in case of emergency if we get too spread out. There seem to be a few more people around you than any other focal point in this last group."

The old woman snorted, then smiled as she looked at him with impenetrable black eyes. "Just toss up one of those fancy phones, son. And don't bother telling me how to work it. I helped write the program to hack into the cell towers for 'Net connections and allow calls out but not in when in secure mode."

"Did you know we're making a biological one for our next generation babies? No, of course you didn't since I'm head of that project. Your grampa probably hasn't spoken my name since I left him for Rocky a lifetime ago. He went back to working with Rocky after that old river rat left me for some young lab tech werecat but didn't return my calls till he got stuck on a set of proteins in a strand I created. Ask him about me when you get a chance."

"Yes, I'll be your team five lead. Now go bother somebody else while I do something besides enjoy peace and quiet for a change."

"Uh, when I see grampa, who do I…"

"Ha! *That damned witch* ought to be enough." She gestured toward the potted plants in wicker racks covering the immense body of the sauro and smiled wickedly through perfectly white teeth too healthy to be in a face so old. "Didn't my herb garden give it away?"

"Okay then, I'll just go find Lily and patrol the perimeter."

The old witch, who only moments ago looked frail as she sat in the sun, swung out of the plush chair and slid down a rope to land gracefully next to an immense sauro leg. Ignoring him, she started approaching nearby walkers and speaking softly to each.

Xan nudged Xanthos away to find Lily talking with a couple riding a juvenile cera. It would grow beneath them but for now was only big enough to carry an all wicker, side-by-side seats with a storage bin behind.

Lily broke away from them before he could approach and met him in an open area. They turned their mounts through body language and plodded along at the same speed as the slowest group.

"At this speed, they'll still be on the road at sunset," she said. "If they can't do it today, they won't be able to do it tomorrow when they have ants coming at them. I'm not feeling a lot of confidence about our casualty rates."

"They're all armed and made it this far," he said as one of the quads raced off to the south. "When ants start getting close enough to spot, people are going to pick them off. Once the alarm goes out there'll be ten sets of eyes on every ant within a hundred meters. Once enough dead ants get associated with us the rest will stay away."

"Unless they come at you from holes like those prairie dogs."

He smiled as he felt her teasing intention. "We're still a day's ride before we get to the outer edge of their territory, and even further to where they have nest holes. This supposed *run*," he gestured toward the slow motion stretched out group, "is just practice. Tomorrow and the next day are when we do it where careless causes casualties."

Another quad and then a larger truck left the

moving border around the main line of traffic and both their phones vibrated.

Xan started to move toward the witch and sauro when he saw several smaller vehicles move inward with them at the core. Two cerapigs and a baby sauro with a single seat saddle moved closer to the larger beast. The witch trotted around the side of her sauro, saw him watching, and waved before directing a pair of riders on what looked like bears. The two werefolk looked remarkably similar to their mounts.

Alarms sounded in the distance then one of the SUVs pulling an overfilled cargo wagon began blaring its horn in the coded sequence for approaching carnivores.

"What is it?" a man wielding a professional shoulder camera and carrying a large shoulder bag on the other side asked as he moved toward the safety of the witch's sauro.

"Carnivore pack, chasing a herd of megastangs. If they're running that means the carnies are bigger than raptors, although raptor packs follow rex families."

"We need to get everybody in as tight a formation as we can in front of that sauro," he pointed as alarms continued coded cadences, "so she can have her tail free of obstruction."

"But they're still moving."

"Alarm says the danger is still a couple klicks away. We're trying to get to that ridge ahead," he pointed, "so we have the high ground of a bridge and the drainage ditch in the median to shield us. Present a big enough wall on either end of the ridge and the megastangs will go around."

"What about the carnies?"

"That's why large calibers were strongly suggested, instead of that popgun you're carrying," Lily said critically.

"Oh, my long rifle is with my wagon. Well, it's not mine, I paid for space in the bed big enough to lay my bedroll. Seven of us and the driver lined up like cordwood when we sleep, and on foot when we're on the move. Plenty of shoulder and headroom, the other giant feller with us even said so, and deep lockers underneath."

He craned his head all around. "Don't seem to see it close by. I fell behind a couple of times taking pictures and writing down what I was feeling. They're probably at the front of this group here and I just can't see them because there are so many people and other wagons in the way. It's a flat wagon with a canvas awning like a Conestoga, but they don't put it up unless it rains."

"Big flat wagon being towed by a team of what?"

"Oh, it's not big enough for a team, only got one critter pulling it. Ugly thing. Hump-backed like a bison and twice as big but with a different head. It would've had a single horn in the middle of its face if it wasn't cut off."

"A unitaur?" Lily said.

"Yes, that's what he called it, a unitaur. Big ugly critter hauling a flat wagon big enough to lay out eight giants side by side. Took every penny I had to fill my locker, well, except for enough coin to eat on. Lucky I got a share of the hunts or I might be getting hungry about now."

"They're at the front of the line," Lily said as she lowered her phone. "They were getting ready to make the move to go to the next group and sent two of their other passengers to find our friend here when the alarm went off. Whoa! Ugly as frack and one huge nose horn, or where one used to be. I faced wild unitaur once and cutting off the horn is a good idea if you want to not be turned into an impaled puppet corpse."

"You've faced a wild one of those with a full horn?" the man was shocked. "How many people did you lose?"

Lily made a sad face. "Actually, we lost two of our hunting party of twenty. Quad driver and his gunner got too close and rolled their quad when the unitaur shouldered them. It ignored the rest of us emptying our weapons into it while it crushed and gored the quad till it leaked bloody gore. Was still killing the quad five minutes after it was dead."

Xan looked at the unitaur pulling the flat wagon that looked like it was carrying eight giant caskets. "Sesco, Gar, and I got one half again that size to chase us several klicks before we lured it into running full speed over a gutting spike."

"Saw that on a news feed. That was you?" Lily's eyebrows rose as the man nearly left behind gaped.

"Yes, got pictures on my pad and phone. I'll show them to you next chance we get."

"There you are young fella," the giant driving the wagon called out. "Thought we'd lost you again. I'm thinking of tying one of those leashes on you some parents do to kids always wandering off. What did you do, take pictures or write poetry?"

"Uh, both," the embarrassed man admitted as another alarm sounded.

"Okay people, talk later, that was the ten-minute signal to a stampede of wild megastangs followed by two rex families being followed by a pack of raptors. You," his finger jabbed at the absent-minded man, "get that long rifle you said you had."

"You, back your wagon up in front of that sauro. What?"

"That's the damned witch that talked me into selling my girl's horn and it was just getting back long enough to have a point."

"Did you get a good price?" Lily tried to remain serious but her emotion leaked enough for Xan to have to clamp down on his own feelings to keep from causing a feedback that would have both of them rolling on the ground laughing in the middle of a stampede.

"Yes, an excellent price in fact, but Sarah has been despondent since I cut it off. We're usually in the front but she just can't get the enthusiasm for hauling weight she used to. Been thinking of getting her a prosthetic."

"Well you'll just have to suck it up big boy," Lily said as the absentminded man opened his locker and retrieved a fifty-caliber sniper's rifle with tripod and long scope. "And you're going to have to protect Sarah's face now she can't."

"Back her up in front of the sauro but leave

room for walkers and we'll pack as many heavier bodies around both of you as we can. Hurry, that was the five-minute alarm."

The confusion threatened to cause panic till Lily put her hand on his and said, "do it."

He felt her add her power to his and he *pushed* a feeling of calm confidence and attention outward as hard as he could.

In the ripple of stationary silence that spread from where they stood, he spoke loudly and firmly. "I want all large bodies on the outside ends of the ridge and all the walkers inside. We still have people hurrying to join us so it's going to get more crowded. Help them when they get here because they'll be more scared than we are now."

"Incoming Xan!"

He turned at Lily's yell and saw a beautiful horse that would have made two of Xanthos, and he was almost as large as a Clydesdale. With beefier legs and tri-hoofed feet like his mount, the wild megastang leaped into the opening where the arroyo cut through the land in times past. When mankind built the interstate system in bands across the landscape, they'd constructed ridges for more level roadways where the arroyo used to drain.

Once at the bottom, the stallion screamed his challenge as he found himself in a deep hole with the only way out being the way he'd come in. With him blocking the hole, other megastangs went around where the footing was more even.

The stallion let out another scream then surged out of the pit and directly into a rex about to snap the rump of a mare protecting her foal.

The two genetically created creatures lost their footing on the slope and tumbled into the pit that protected the caravan's southern edge, screaming and kicking and biting at each other all the way to the bottom.

The horse got lucky and came out on top and kicked with two powerful hind legs. The rex's leg snapped with a sound loud enough to echo off the ridge of the other lane of the grassway. The horse kicked again and the leg shattered to hang by a few tendons and muscle, then he surged up out of the arroyo pit and around to follow the rest of his herd.

The rex let out a fierce roar that started strong then turned into a pitiful yelp of pain as it tried to stand on a leg that was barely connected to the upper thigh any longer. Falling sideways and onto the broken leg, the crippled apex predator let loose with several squeals Xan had never heard from a rex before.

In the distance, an answering roar was followed by another from the other side. The wounded rex continued to squeal and within a minute an enormous female looked down at her mate screaming in mortal pain.

Then she looked up at the line of humans standing above her mate just as two of her adult young arrived to see what the screaming was about.

"Uh-oh," Xan said as all three rexes locked eyes on the snacks that weren't running as fast as the horses and immediately crouched in stalking postures.

[19] My, what big mandibles you have.

A loudly echoing 'crack' shattered the momentary silence and the large female jerked upright, then roared. The roar started strong, ended feeble and she tottered, then fell headlong into the pit with the male who screamed again when she landed on his shattered leg.

Xan turned to see the absentminded man look up from the tripod-mounted 50cal's smoking barrel. "Hunh! One shot kill spot is right where the simulations said it'd be. Guess all that money for VR practice does save ammo."

More shots sounded as other defenders realized the remaining two juvenile rexes were still on the hunt. Within seconds all four rexes were dead, but more of their family were responding to the original call. Soon after the sixth rex fell the first of the raptors arrived.

Crouched beside the still unnamed man with the 50cal and the deadly aim, Xan fired his slightly smaller carbine just as efficiently. He knew where the kill spots were as well and after a couple kills the larger rounds were making a mess of the smaller raptors and the man stopped helping.

After the rush of targets Xan helped the man collect the trophy teeth and claws that would fetch a good price cleaned or more with some craftwork or scrimshaw. Cleaning the killing claw of his last raptor, he almost missed the huge ant that was investigating the corpse he'd just stripped of valuable body parts.

"Everybody be on the alert," he said as he casually reached for the pistol at his side. Just as he put his hand on the grip a shot sounded behind him and the ant dropped onto the raptor carcass.

"There's another," Lily said as she shifted her aim and fired again.

Another volley of gunfire echoed across the plains as several more people saw, or thought they saw ants. Xan let others use up their ammo as he saw none close enough to concern him.

Before he could order it, the group seemed to know to begin moving almost as one. It took a few minutes for them to disassemble their emergency defensive huddle and get back in motion but when they finally got going, they moved faster than they had all day.

"You go ahead and keep them together," Xan said as the last of the group cleaned up their trophies and resumed their march. "Lily and I'll stay here and keep the stragglers from gawking or getting eaten by ants."

"If you're sure, little brother. Okay then, c'mon Sesco, let's get this last bunch moving so we can get to the next camp before sunset."

He watched them leave, then intercepted another small group that had set out late and hurried them along past after shooting another ant investigating all the fresh meat. During another gap in stragglers he and Lily collected more teeth and claws.

"I know you said you still have a lot of the

working capital your grandfather gave you, but what are you going to use for money once this little adventure is complete? You'll be in your new home in the mountains with ten times more people than available jobs. Then you'll have a choice. Find a job where there aren't any to spare or mooch off your grandfather like the descendants of so many rich folk still do."

"The teeth and claws of monsters is money to traveling folk like me. A rex canine like this can get you a room for a night and a shower, or a meal in a fancy restaurant. A lot more if you wrap the root in rex leather for a knife or polish the sides and etch the picture of a rex into it. A big raptor fang or killing claw can easily get you a decent mug of ale just about anywhere I've ever been."

They directed the next group to arrive to hurry, then helped another collect all the ant legs because they'd read they were as good as crab legs. When they'd waited as long as they could they packed up their collection of teeth and claws and warned the last group to come along they would have to move a lot faster to reach camp by nightfall.

"I hate to leave them on their own," Lily said as Onyx and Xanthos trotted at a steady, kilometer-eating pace.

"If we went back for every one of them, pretty soon we'd be going the wrong way. If they don't stop at all the dead bodies, they should be safe. Ants and other scavengers will focus their efforts there and it's concentrated in the arroyo gully between the main lanes, so that should make the rest of the grassway safer, even after dark."

They caught up to another small group and got them to move fast enough to catch the next to last collection of walkers. A few minutes later an SUV camper came up from behind with an escort of six mounted riders and rode with them instead of hurrying by.

"I have one phone left," Lily said. "What do you say we race back as soon as we foist this off to a worthy lackey to lead this group?"

"Sounds like the perfect end to an interesting day," he said, then put a hand on the bag that held his collection of raptor teeth and claws. "First round's on me."

They found a likely couple, normal humans in every appearance except for their golden eyes and the fact it was impossible to tell if they were male or female. Each wore a papoose style baby carrier complete with slobbering baby.

Each dragon mount carried four long barreled weapons in sheath-holsters in front of and behind their saddles, which sat astride the front shoulders. Behind the saddle a frame held a row of cargo panniers with a rolled tarp on top.

"Yes," the one that gave the name Alpha said, "Beta and I will act as lead for the newly designated team six and will do our best for the good of all."

"Thank you. Let me show you the activation sequence."

"Let's make one last run to those people just coming into view," Xan said to Lily after they finished showing the pair how to stay in contact with the buses. "Then we do the opposite of traveling backwards."

"No, nobody behind us as far as our rear guard rode back two klicks," the nominal leader of the last group said. "We've been scooping people up all the way and I think we were the last to leave Belvidere. Been trying to catch up to the rest and making good time till we got to the spot where somebody killed a lot of critters. It's all empty behind us."

"That's good," Xan said as Lily talked to a group of women. "If you catch up to a couple riding dragons, you'll be in the official group six team with a comm link to the command buses. They'll tell you what's coming your way and how to form a unified circle for defense."

"We have armed and armored vans, trucks, and quads roaming all up and down the line going where they're needed as fast as they can," Xan said. "If you see the ones ahead of you forming up into a circle you need to run as fast as you can to join them unless you have to go through monsters to do so. In that case find some high ground and form your own circle and hope for the best."

"You're leaving us?" a plaintive voice asked.

"We have other people to help," Lily came to his rescue when he froze looking at the young boy's frightened face staring down from a cerawagon. "But you have this strong cera to carry you faster and all these people to keep the bad away. And you know how you can help?" At the boy's towheaded headshake, she stage-whispered, "you can keep watch for anything the others miss.

And remember, there are quads and trucks out there protecting you, but if you see something dangerous you still need to report it."

As soon as he felt the child's confidence return, he nudged Xanthos. "Doing what you can for the team makes the team better. I'm sure you'll do well."

"I think Onyx is ready for a run."

"Maybe we should start out slow so it doesn't look like we're running *from* something."

She gave him a devious smile with Onyx flexing her muscles like she was ready to leap. "Might get them moving faster."

For answer he nudged Xanthos into a steady trot that was no faster than could be expected within a loosely packed group. Onyx made several dashes ahead to try and prod him into moving faster, then they slowed to talk to a couple on foot leading a pair of pack horses like their own, covered in supply bags and children.

"You'll be fine," he said to the adults. "The group ahead of you is the furthest back our caravan's protection can reach and you'll want to be with them if you haven't reached the main camp by sunset."

He nudged Xanthos ahead to catch up with Lily and she used the burst of speed to goad him faster till they were racing to the next group. They slowed and took a leisurely trot through, slowed even further to talk to a few people, then raced ahead again across the next gap. They reached the main base while the third group was just coming into sight over a distant ridge behind them.

"About time you got home," Sesco said as he threw Xan a sealed bottle.

"Pretty good timing," Tina said. "Hear you succeeded where Mr. I-got-this had a little set-back."

"Had a talk with this nice elderly lady on a walking greenhouse and she offered before I could ask."

Sesco snorted. "First off, you said *talk* and *nice* in the same sentence about said 'elderly lady', then you fell in some sort of fantasy rabbit hole."

"I actually understand that reference," he laughed at his new friend. "Still don't know her name, but you might get it out of Rocky if you're *really* careful."

He opened the seal on his ale and took a deep swallow. "Ah, the first drink is always the best. Anybody else hungry before the line gets too long."

Xan traded his empty for a full bottle when he went through the line and in moments the only sound was that of the contact between cutlery and plates, punctuated by satisfied grunts and sighs. Gar was the only one to go for seconds but he was still finished at the same time as the others when they took their empties to the galley.

"Sure am glad we don't have to do KP duty," the big man said as they went to check on their animals. "Having basics like that taken care of by someone else sure does make a crazy expedition a lot easier."

"Picked a good spot, too," Xan said, then mentally poked his friend. "As long as the bridge doesn't collapse."

"Won't work," Gar replied with a smile. "Already talked to Frederick and he said this stretch of bridge would hold three times our number and regularly did back in the day when folks drove all the way from one coast to see the other."

"That many people drove out here all at the same time?" Lilac was skeptical.

"Well, the way Frederick explained it there were big cargo trucks pulling trailers as long as the buses. Don't know how often, but he said the bridges were built to hold what was called a traffic jam. That's where trucks and buses and vans and even those little bitty cars no bigger than a quad people used to drive were jammed in nose to rear as far as the eye could see in each direction."

"Hard to imagine as many vehicles as we have now, much less packed that tight for near two kilometers or more, but that's what he said. Even showed me pictures of traffic jams eight lanes wide and backed up ten klicks. Line all our vehicles up and we'd barely fill one lane the full length of this bridge," He smirked his verbal victory over his best friend. "So, Mr. Glass Half Empty, we're safe from falling."

People kept arriving through the last of the evening and Xan joined his friends at the rail of their stretch of bridge and watched the sky change colors. With a bus, a turtle, a security van, and a dozen trucks and quads blocking each end, even those on foot could relax in comfortable safety.

The fifth group arrived just as the sun touched the horizon and the last group minutes after daylight fled before a starlit sky. The last riders confirmed there was no one behind them for at least three klicks. By the time of full dark, the scattered but safe interior camp began to relax like they hadn't expected to be able to.

"Beautiful sky," Lily said as she sat with her back to the low rail.

"There's Denver Station, or what's left of it," Sesco said, pointing to the southwest.

"Never could figure out why they bombed each other," Gar said. "Seemed kind of stupid."

"Stupid, yes," the Librarian agreed as he put away his sketchbook. "But so is openly creating an enclave for the genetically ostracized because it's bound to be taken wrong and lead to violence."

"We're taking our skills and possessions and going to a place we can call our own and many will fear that as an open establishment of concentrated power against the status quo. It's also directly on the only safe route through the Rockies around the Denver Wastes now that Texas is talking about declaring independence and seceding... again."

"Denver Station got its name because it was almost completely financed by bonds, private investments, and donations from the Denver area. They seriously overreacted to Denver Station's Declaration of Independence along with the other eleven geo stations. They took it personal and got goaded into trying to keep *their* station from breaking orbit to explore the solar system."

"Denver Station may have missed Detroit and Seattle when they retaliated for those regions' part in the destruction of their engineering section and the release of the gene plague, but they saturated Denver even after the core of their station was vaporized and five-sixths of their population killed. The Black Hills are barely outside the affected area and Rapid City is the last safe refuge on the grassway before Cheyanne and on west to California."

"In other words, you're openly claiming one of the most geographically vital areas connecting the east and west halves of the nation. A lot of people who've been watching us cross the country have seen our numbers grow and the video from inside shows all they've been told to fear by those that like to stir people up."

"What the people watching those videos see is their final extinction and the loss of what they've always had. It's the same as the social upheaval that happened at the turn of the millennium, the dominant social class being replaced by the next to come along and rebelling in fear because they want their old world back."

"There are always people who profit from other people's fears and they make more by stoking the flames of those fears than by helping people adjust to rapid change. The videos from within our caravan *do* show several different kinds of new people and getting along. But a certain segment of the world only sees the uneven ratio of *normal* humans and gene-muddied *other*, and their fear is being fed by those more concerned with the profit of fear."

"I've been researching the Hills and was surprised to discover the population is less than it was a century before the turn of the millennia," the Librarian said. "Between the Gene War hitting Denver so hard and evolutionary pressures from unregulated gene hacking, most of them high-tailed it to somewhere safer or were killed and eaten. In fact, Rapid City has half the total population of the Black Hills and the military base on the southwest corner of the Hills another eighth. The remaining three-eighths is owned and populated by the remains of several Native Tribes and a few true survivors."

"The majority of those traveling with us, and those that follow, will most likely stay in Rapid City to start with unless they make use of the information the buses are providing," Xan said. "I know of one entire group of three families that have confirmed jobs waiting for them in Hot Springs. Another small family is part owner in a general store in Deadwood and have a saurowagon full of tech, and woodworking, gardening, and farming tools."

"That second family is as pureblood as anyone nowadays and so are a considerable number of others in our caravan. It wasn't only those of us with the more obvious alterations in our genes that wanted a place away from hateful intolerance. No, the fear of a takeover will be easily shown false. That's why we encouraged people to record their traveling experiences and share those videos with distant friends and family."

"But, again, with just a little editing even those *normal*," he made air quotes, "folk can be shown to be anti-gene-muddied. There are others, and we all know who they are, who have no trouble sharing our table then going back to their isolated camps away from us and making their own videos to send to pureblood sites."

"Those are things we all know, but have no control over, Sesco," Xan interrupted his friend's lecture. "That's why we're here, to do something we *can* control. In two more days, all of us can find our separate ways to our respective destinations in the Hills. I'll consider my duty to my grandfather complete when the caravan begins scattering. I'll visit his new labs, report, then go to my own property and begin building while the rest of the country invents conspiracies."

Sesco nodded once, then turned his eyes on Tina. "I was wondering, your grampa had a pretty nice library back on that island in Ohio. Could you ask him if I could spend a few days reading some of what he saved?"

"I'm sure he would love to share some of the rare books he has collected," Tina said with a smile. "In fact, why don't you come with us when we give him our report. I'm sure there'll be room to keep Spot comfortable for a few days while you both rest from a stressful journey."

"She might even let you out long enough to have a drink or three with the rest of us," Gar deadpanned.

"Who says I'd want to," Sesco shot back.

"Then you can stay in the library while I go out and party," Tina said.

"Ha! I like this bunch!" Lily laughed then raised her bottle. "Here's to friendship and shared dangers survived."

Salutations made and drinks taken, they soon settled in with their bedrolls in the belief they were safe. Xan was just closing his eyes when a scream pierced the night.

Knowing enough to not get undressed when sleeping in the open, he threw the cover away as he stood. Around him lights that had been turned off or dimmed, brightened to show several shapes crawling up over the rails along the sides of the bridge.

He spun just as an ant crawled up over the rail beside him, its mandibles gnashing together with a sound like tight scissors. Drawing his pistol as fast as he could he knew he couldn't get it up in time as the nearest ant jumped.

[20] An empathic bond.

As he tried to bring the pistol up and block the ant with his closer hand Ginger crashed into it in mid leap and ripped its head off.

Weapons-fire competed with screams as people and animals feeling safe and secure came awake to find themselves under attack. Xan shot two ants in as many seconds then another one before he realized the shots around him were scattered and not continuous.

"They're coming up the support pylons," Sesco said after Xan shot another. "That's why you're the only one with close targets, you put your bedroll directly over the top of the pylon."

"Good thing we picketed the mounts in the center where they were out of the line of fire and less prone to panic," Gar said as he praised Ginger for saving Xan.

Xan kneeled down and gave the big hellhound a vigorous neck rub, then touched noses. "Thank you, my friend."

He stood as silence settled in again, then there was one shot from one end of the bridge and another from just across from them. "Maybe it was just a scouting party."

"Did some run to tell the hive or did they all climb up and get shot," Gar wondered as he swung his staff in an intricate pattern, then grounded it.

"We need to post a few more sentries, and go to sleep," Xan said as he retrieved his saddle, bags, and bedroll. "Anybody wants the pieces-parts of the ones I killed is welcome to them. I'm going to sleep with Xanthos."

Twice more during the night he was awakened by gunfire, but they were brief incidents. The next morning, he was one of the first in line at the kitchen and was brushing and feeding Xanthos when Lily found him.

"I was thinking we stay back with the cleanup crew and wait till the last are gone before we follow. We know how fast we can travel and for how long and we made it with dozens of side trips yesterday. Should be easy."

"Good idea," he replied as he groomed his horse, then pointed toward the eastbound lane's bridge further down the gully. "There they go."

The lights of the bus, turtle, and security van blocking their eastern end had taken a load of young and old across the median and bypassed the haphazardly camped caravan. Like the day before they would take their most vulnerable to Wall early and come back for more.

"And there goes the other end," Gar said as he looked over the heads of the others just as the lights came on and the Shaw bus, Honey, and *Recluse* set out before half the caravan was awake.

Heavy trucks and quads partially filled the space left by the three vehicles, ready to escort teams as they left on their run through ant territory. The first left just as the clouds began to color the horizon and the second group minutes after the sun was fully airborne.

As the two of them began working toward the back end of the extended camp, the remaining people were making the hard decision of what they felt they could risk their lives carrying any longer.

"I can't believe you talked me into this, Xan," Bekka grumbled as she drove the Cloverfield wagon up to him and the others gathered near the quad drivers that would be the caravan's rear guard.

Xan looked at Tanner, who returned an innocent gaze, so he didn't mention the fact Bekka had volunteered after seeing some of the things camps near their own were dumping from their wagons and carts.

"Hope it's worth your time and effort. I see you already got that huge oak and walnut dining table you were eyeballing. How did you?" He pointed toward the roof deck of their cerawagon.

"Elly put it up there for us after Rocky talked to Selene."

"Selene, who's Selene?"

"Who? You know, really nice elderly lady, rides an old sauro named Sweetness. Oh, you have to see her garden. Carries it with her on her sauro's back instead of a wagon full of useless stuff. Anyway, got all eight chairs, too. They're inside stacked with some quilts I can't believe I found in a fancy chest."

"Saw the widower dump it and a sitting table I now own, too. I was talking to him earlier and his wife died before they met with the rest of the caravan. They also lost two of their draft cerapigs on the journey so far and are so overloaded they barely made it yesterday after leaving earlier than anybody else."

"He said the table and chest were full of her

woman things and he wouldn't need them to raise his five boys. Told me I was welcome to it all no questions asked because he had all their important wealth in *his* chest and writing table."

She took on a smug look. "So, like I said, this was a good idea I had."

Lily snorted and Xan looked at Tanner. "Is she always like this?"

"Sometimes she's worse."

"So, what did this genius widower throw away because women don't have any sense of worth?" Lily wondered.

"Well," Tanner said as they gathered to wait for the rest of the caravan to thin out. "The sitting table is solid silver painted a gaudy lavender. Widower called it a damned useless *iron* monstrosity painted an ugly color and too heavy to lug a mile further. And yes, he said mile, not kilometer."

"Anyway, sitting table is solid silver and almost all the brushes and combs and things are solid silver and gold, and painted the most garishly ugly colors imaginable. Other than that, there's the normal assortment of fancy perfumes and makeups a wealthy woman would have plus a small store of garish paints to make sure the real treasure stayed camouflaged."

"The chest is bigger than most with four handles instead of two," Tanner continued as Bekka preened. "It was chock full of hand-stitched quilts, three luxurious gowns, and twelve fancy dresses. Oh, and dozens of silk underthings my lovely wife never thought she'd ever have enough money to waste on."

"And every single stitch fits like it was tailor made for me," Bekka said with a wide grin, then put her hands over her stomach. "For now, anyway, but each has room to let out for child-bearing or getting older. There was a separate box with necklaces, rings, and earrings I'm sure the widower never paid attention to if he ever saw them."

"You sure he didn't get her cheap imitations?" Lily wondered as Bekka showed Tina two of the rings and her earrings. "That sounds more like him."

"We've both made careers busting people stealing exactly the kinds of things in that table and chest. He's not the only man lost a wife and has to think of what memories he has to carry that's worth risking more lives. He won't be the last fool to throw away treasure he's too man-stubborn to see."

"Is it right to not tell him?" Sesco wondered.

"Got video of him giving it away free and clear at *his* insistence after Bekka hesitated when the chest still had the lock on it. He even volunteered the sitting table *after* insisting there was nothing in the chest he could ever have any use for and useless dead weight for the last two cerapigs to pull. Got him on video insisting we were doing him a favor by taking it off his hands and if we didn't, he was dumping it anyway. Ignored Bekka like she didn't exist and talked to me the whole time."

"Still didn't know its worth. Solid silver sitting table would buy a new wagon with electric motor backup, a team of bigger cera to pull it, *and* a new breeder herd of cerapigs."

"You go talk to Mr. Bannon for a while," Bekka said. "Get to know him between here and Wall, then tell me whether or not to return a treasure his wife was hiding from him on purpose."

"Oh, and you might want to look at this first." She handed him a large envelope. "There are two letters in there, one from the late Mrs. Bannon."

"Librarian Sesco Silverstone," Tanner intoned, "we give you our words of honor that we will abide by your decision. Say the word and we will return the chest and table and all of their original contents to the late Mrs. Bannon's husband when we get to Wall. If you haven't said anything by the time we leave Wall, please don't mention it again. Do you agree?"

Sesco nodded his head. "I agree." Without another word, he mounted Spot and left the group at a slow trot.

"Well, if I'd have known it was that easy to get rid of… *ow*!"

"Thanks, Lily, if I was close enough, I would have hit him too, but harder."

"Didn't want to hurt him, Tina, need him awake to take blame for what goes wrong. You okay?"

"Yeah, he has to do this," she said with a warm smile toward the departing Librarian. "It's one of the things I like about him. You going to tell us what's in those letters?"

"Yeah," Bekka said. "Found them in the locked chest. The first one was from a detective who was investigating a series of mysterious deaths to wealthy women married to the same man."

"The first Mrs. Bannon had a set of twin boys, then another boy nine months later. She and a baby girl died in childbirth nine months later and her husband was the only witness. The second Mrs. Bannon had a pair of boys seven months after a hurried wedding then her and a girl baby died in a cabin fire along with the midwife nine months later."

"The second letter was from the third Mrs. Bannon who managed to stay without child long enough to hide most of her personal wealth before her husband gambled it all away or lost it on shady business risks. It listed all her evidence her husband was going to kill her because she hadn't even gotten pregnant, much less given him a son. She never got a chance to send it. We gave Sesco copies but kept the originals."

"What about his five boys?" Tina wondered. "They're innocent in all this if he's been killing his wives. Do they deserve anything?"

"We'll have to think about that once Sesco decides what he's going to do," Bekka said. "Now, looks like just about everybody is gone except for that one wagon with those other people going through abandoned stuff."

"Oh, them," Xan said with a smile. "I met them yesterday. They always follow big caravans and claim all the stuff people finally decide is too heavy to carry another step. They load their wagon with discards, pretty it up, and sell it in the stores they run on both ends of the grassway between Sioux Falls and Rapid City."

"The man I talked to said he was thinking of

adding another wagon and collection team for the stretch west from Rapid City to Cheyanne. Anyway, he heard you talking about some of the things you'd like to get when you get settled and told me he knew of several people who were going to abandon just those things."

"When I was setting you up to be easier to convince, you suggested it before I could, then you had those two encounters before we even started." He pointed further up the bridge. "Almost at the end of the bridge will be a fancy glass case full of some of the finest dishware I've ever seen. Elly will be waiting there for us so nobody else claims it."

"Why are you doing this?" Bekka's face showed her confused surprise.

Tina smiled and patted her friend's arm. "We know how you ended up leaving your home and even though you had a fairly big cerawagon, it was full of survival supplies and not the things you needed for a home. You've shared every bit of those supplies with anyone in need and now you have empty space at the end of your voyage. These are things that should never have been brought out here the way they were. In fact, the China cabinet was destined for San Francisco and the people abandoning it will have no trouble replacing it when they get there, so it's not like you're benefitting from scavenging off your own."

"Lilac and Stone are also collecting what they can, plus we promised them a couple of Honey's eggs when she lays them."

"You're forgetting, not everybody is part of *our* caravan," Xan reminded them. "In the beginning, we joined a couple of larger groups for security or just because the grassway was crowded and we were going the same direction. I'd say only a little more than half our caravan, two-thirds at the most, are actually with *us*. The others simply made good use of a golden opportunity for security and companionship on a hard, dangerous journey."

"The ones thought they could cross the new American plains with more fancy furniture than food, bullets, and armor always drop what's less important somewhere along the way when reality sets in. There are people who make a living scavenging the stretches most likely to produce goods that will sell at a profit."

Tina smiled at her friend. "Now, let's mount up and collect more of your future home's furniture that you only have to carry the last couple of days."

"Books, I found books," Tina said with a smile as Elly lifted the China cabinet onto Dancer's wagon after they wrapped the dishware in dresses and lingerie. "About a hundred of them in a chest with big sheets of that paper Sesco gets excited about. Enough in cloth-wrapped packages to make eight or ten of those big books like the one he's been carrying around. Can you hide it on your wagon till we get to Wall, Bekka?"

"Sure, let's see if Elly will lift it up for us."

"Anybody see anything else they want to check out?" Xan asked when they reached the end of the bridge.

"Professional scavenger is already half a klick away," Gar said as he spun his staff in an intricate pattern. "I say we run a little to get the blood pumping. What do you say Fred, Ginger? Want to go for a run?"

Both pups let loose with happy yips. "Let's go." Before anyone could react the three of them were bounding away.

"Did he just leave us?" Bekka was shocked.

Xan chuckled. "No, he'll run ahead till just before he's out of sight then he'll turn around and come back. Like he said, just enough to get the blood pumping."

They passed the last group just before noon and Rocky moved Elly up next to Selene and Sweetness and waved them on. Even with the Cloverfield wagon newly loaded with heavy cargo they passed the second group just before it reached Wall.

"Killed a bunch of them on the bridge we camped on last night, but not a one the whole day's run from there to here," Xan said as he filled out the paperwork for stabling the horses and struthies.

"Damned strange if you ask me," the stablemaster said. "Can understand if they don't attack, but not even *seeing* any is damned strange, especially as well fed as they've been."

"How's that?" Xan kept the man talking as he pumped him for the best kind of information, meaningless and trivial casual conversation.

"Big herd of dinos got trapped by a flash flood down in the flats below the Badlands. When the water went down there were thousands of ants feeding for days. Usually after that they're all over the place thicker than, well, ants at a picnic."

"Folks around here enjoy a good barbeque

and a rack of ant legs is a favorite. Usually after they feed good there's an overabundance and they start coming across to the Wall side of the grassway. Then we sit on the wall and pick 'em off till their numbers fall back down to normal and they stop coming 'cept one or two a day. They've been eating better than usual for more than a month but the numbers seen haven't grown yet. I'm kind of anxious to add to the ant bones in my mulch pile 'cause they have such good minerals and now they go and change their habits. Damned strange."

"Okay son, your animals are paid for in full and I have my best people in to take care of you and your caravan. Well, those that stay with me, anyways. The hotel you asked about is one block toward the drugstore but you better hurry, rooms go quick when caravans show up and yours is a big one."

They trooped out of the stables and down the street to the hotel where they paid some of the last of their coin for what did prove to be the last of the available rooms.

"Did he say anything?" Tina asked Bekka when they met in the tavern after the last of their people made it inside the gate.

"No, but that's okay. Even if we have to give up every bit of what Bannon freely gave us, we're still further ahead than we could ever have imagined a few weeks ago. A wealth of friends is just a fraction of what we've gained. And in a couple days we can start building a new life with children that won't be treated as *other* just because they're different. No, the loss of a few baubles won't be missed."

"To friends and family," Tanner said as he raised his bottle.

"To friends and family," echoed from several lips before the toast was completed by a drink.

The celebration continued as the last of those following caught up and got inside Wall's wall where they were safe from the terrors of the apocalypse. Proof of the failure of the monsters were visible in the skulls and stuffed carcasses that decorated street corners, buildings inside and out, and lined the outside of the wall as spiked deterrents.

"So, Xan, Tina, we're almost there," Tanner said. "What next? Do we just split up and go our separate ways or do you have something else planned?"

"Like I said earlier, when we finish the last leg of this journey, I'm going to tell my grampa about the trip then go see my property and maybe start building right away. Might even be able to hire a few friends with particular skills to help get ready for winter."

He gestured toward Gunny and Spider, who joined them for once. "Some were hired to provide security to any like us who just happened to want the same thing and travel with us and will do as they see fit. Others," his eyes shifted to Rocky and Selene tending their massive companions, "are as mysterious as my grandfather and my sister and I will probably have to wait till they talk to him before he'll talk to us."

"They're here to take over if you and your sister fail," Sesco said softly. "That and rejoin an old friend and take this final extinction of normal humanity to the next level."

Everyone was silent for a while before Tina said, "You know, after seeing signs every day this side of the Missip, I was both disappointed and thrilled with Wall Drug. The former because it really is just a drug store with extras but thrilled because there is *so much* extra. There's no way I'll be able to explore all three floors before we leave."

"And there's so much more in the rest of the town," Bekka said. "The quad drivers are in heaven. There's a chapter in Rapid City that sent a hundred members to do the last leg with all our riders."

Just then the noise level from the parking lot beside the bike shop emphasized the party that continued to grow as more quads arrived.

"I found a nice saddle shop but just getting mine broke in," Stone said. "Did get a new hat, though, and got to watch the craftsman build it right in front of me after measuring my head and trying on a half-dozen kinds."

"I saw a dress I'd love to own," Bekka said with a sly smile the Librarian's way. "Would've traded three ugly ones out of my windfall if it was mine. Might wait till the last-minute tomorrow after everybody else leaves and make the trade."

"About that," Sesco said when every eye went to him. "I spent a couple of hours with a seriously disturbed fella on the last run to Wall. Fella I talked to was all worked up but wouldn't say why or about what."

"I left him to help some people and they had some equally disturbing things to say about the fella. Said he tried to get their virgin daughter to come into his wagon and he doesn't let *anybody* inside his wagon. Folks didn't even know he had five boys. Said they've only seen the three that help with the cera and he beats them more than the animals."

"Left them and rode with another fella who said our Mr. Bannon is going to Rapid City to join a group of purists massing to stop a bunch of freaks from invading their mountains."

Sesco hesitated a moment to let the surprise sink in. "Purebloods were trying to keep it quiet so they could spring their blockade when a certain celebrity freak show came to town. Bannon is late because he got held up with that little wife dying thing and got stuck riding *with* the freak show."

"I went back to talk with Mr. Bannon before we got to Wall and with a little prodding where I *might* have given the impression I sympathized with the purists, he admitted killing *all three* of his wives. He's really angry his latest dead wife made him think she had more money because he already spent the rest he did know about and was tapped out. His exact words were, 'if'n the barren slut warn't already dead I'd kill 'er agin, only slower and with more hurtful poison this time'."

"Being a registered Librarian, I was diligent in my duty to send a video recording my full interview with Mr. Bannon, including the unsolicited confession of multiple murders including the baby girls and midwife, to my superior with my report. The Sheriff will meet us on the grassway in Rapid City to detain Mr. Bannon for a trial."

He turned to Bekka with a smile. "It's the determination of the Library Council you may keep the items he willingly gave you. And now that I have passed on my information I'm going to our camp, give Spot a grooming and a snack and read some more of that book I found in your grampa's island library."

His good news and announcement was enough to send everyone to their bedrolls, wagons, and hotel rooms with satisfied hearts.

Xan was somewhat surprised to find Lily walking with him instead of heading to the stalls to sleep with Onyx.

"One more run and you're home," she said. "How does it feel?"

"Don't know yet. I didn't even know what I was doing till almost halfway through doing it. To answer your question with another. Am I home? Is it over or just phase one and I get another task to perform when I get *home*." He made air quotes on the last word. "What about you?"

"Won't know till tomorrow."

He raised an eyebrow.

"We're both empaths to a degree," she laughed as she took his arm. "After tonight we'll both know where I'll be."

[21] Ant War.

Xan jerked awake and looked around the room, then over at Lily and smiled, whatever had awakened him forgotten. She opened her eyes and smiled just as alarms began blaring all over the peacefully sleeping town.

Leaping from the bed at the same time they frantically got dressed as the caravan sirens signaled the code for ant attack inside the wall.

They were reaching for the door when Lily screamed and froze. "Onyx! Oh, my baby." Her face clouded and tears streamed as she threw the door open with one hand and stormed out of the room growling.

Xan was two steps behind her when he staggered at the feeling of terror and pain Xanthos felt as he died. His stumble was enough to break Lily from her imminent berserker rage as she returned to help him stand steady.

His lip curled as the death of his traveling companion echoed in his mind. "Let's purge a nest."

Her snarl mirrored his as she turned and ran for the lobby. They found a group of curious people looking through the bulletproof glass front of the building, but they cleared a path when they saw Xan and Lily's faces. Outside several people were running, all of them in different directions, with only a few carrying weapons. One couple grabbed the door and had to wait till the guard opened it before they could enter.

Xan led Lily toward the door and the guard held up his hand. "Sorry sir, the hotel recommends all guests remain inside for the duration of the emergency."

Xan's eyes bore into those of the guard as he growled. "*Move now*, please."

"Yes sir."

Stepping outside, they raised their shotguns and scanned the street for targets, then sprinted the block to the stables. Everybody they met was going the opposite direction.

Xan blasted the first ant he saw through the head, then a round through the neck of another that had a man by the leg. The man ran off with the ant's head still attached to his leg by the locked mandibles.

When they got to the stables they looked on in horror as ants covered all the stabled animals in a writhing mass. Smaller undulating piles of feeding ants covered the shapes of the stablehands and maybe some of their friends.

What was beneath those piles was beyond pain, so Xan and Lily didn't have to worry about where they aimed. They stood in the open door and blasted till they had to change magazines to continue killing ants. It took till their second pause to change mags before the ants realized they were dying and start to move toward the most likely source.

"Out of the way!" Sesco yelled from behind and they jumped to opposite sides as Spot stomped into the barn, crushing two and three ants with each clawed foot.

Tina followed and the three of them waded into the stables behind the struthy with weapons blazing at anything that crawled on six legs. "Hey little brother, Lily. Sorry about Onyx."

Lily picked off two ants climbing up toward the loft. "Yeah, me too, sorry about Thoth. We'll make them pay, and their little queen too." In a lull they switched mags, then headed for Onyx's stall, Xan a half step behind.

What was consuming what was left of Xanthos wasn't like a normal ant. The giant ants created by some deviant gene hacker had pincers like an ant but below that were feeding arms like those of a crab or lobster and a mouth that finished shredding what the mandibles sliced off.

Modern monster ants didn't cut off pieces and take them back to the hive. They ate their fill first, filled their community stomach for takeaway, *then* carried what they could back to the nest.

Xan didn't hesitate. Even if Xanthos were still alive he would have fired into the writhing mass feeding on the half-consumed body. In front of the stalls on either side Tina and Lily copied his actions as they exterminated the monsters that had killed their friends.

With the numbers of ants, they were each in danger every time they stopped to reload. It wasn't till they started to get more ants coming at them from the rear paddock they moved their efforts away from the ones consumed by their feeding frenzy.

"They're coming up through the bone midden!" Sesco yelled as Spot crushed two or three ants with every stomp. Ants that got a grip on the struthy's leather-clad legs were quickly dispatched by Sesco's shotgun rounds from above.

"I'm not sure we have enough ammo," Xan said as they tried to get to the stream of ants still coming out of a hole in the middle of the midden. "We're going to need some to get back out."

"Saddles!" Lily yelled. "Got plenty more there."

Nothing more needed to be said and they ran back to the stalls while Spot continued to dance around the paddock filled with ants. Using the last of their ammo except for their pistols, they cleared Onyx's stall first, then Xan and Tina cleared Thoth's stall while Lily rearmed.

"Okay, I'm ready," Lily said as Tina went to her saddle and the storage closet behind the feed trough.

Lily helped him clear the last of the ants from Xanthos' corpse, then ran behind Tina to return to the paddock to help Sesco.

He got inside the saddle closet and grabbed two bandoleers of drum magazines from the supply bag. Digging into another bag he retrieved a small ammo box on a shoulder strap and headed back to the open paddock blasting every ant that still moved.

Outside in the glare of the lights, dog-sized shapes covered the animals that still had meat and dozens more ran toward anything moving that wasn't another ant. Xan emptied his first barrel mag, tossed the empty away, retrieved another from a bandoleer pouch, and loaded it in two heartbeats.

Chambering a round and firing in another breath, he blew an ant in half that was leaping toward the only stablehand he'd seen alive. The young giant said 'thanks' as she retrieved the staff she'd dropped when she'd whacked an ant on a support pole.

Xan was already turning and pouring shotgun rounds into scurrying shapes as soon as they appeared. After a while he could feel their minds and found them unlike anything he would have imagined in a hive creature.

Emptying another drum, he placed it in the empty pouch, retrieved another, and spun two steps to the side as he clicked the mag home and chambered a round. The ant that had jumped at him from the pole it was climbing flew past and he slammed it in the side with the butt of his shotgun as it went by then kicked it in the head when it bounced back from the wall behind him.

Spinning again he dodged the end of the staff as the young stablehand again neglected to ensure her full reach was clear *in all directions* when she spun her weapon. He fired again at an ant with a firm grip on the youth's ankle, blowing its head off, then ducked as the staff whistled over his head again.

Two more spinning steps and three rounds from his shotgun and he was out of the giant's range and could concentrate on fewer dangers. When he changed out mags again, he did it on the run toward his friends still trying to stem the flow of ants coming up through the bone midden.

His extra weapon made the difference and

they advanced on the hole till they were killing ants still inside while Spot crushed the ones that tried to get at the fresh meat from behind. The ants had widened their hole since opening it so more than one could fit through at a time and it took dozens of rounds fired point blank to plug the tunnel below. After a few moments, the jumble of dead ants began to quiver and shake and Xan shone a shotgun-mounted light down the hole.

"They're pulling the bodies down and dragging them back through the tunnel." He raised his shotgun and shot into the hole, then opened the ammo box hanging from the shoulder strap. Pulling out two objects he closed the box again then plugged the cylinder into the palm control and tapped at the screen. He unplugged the cylinder and shoved it into the body cavity of one of the ants.

"Help me drag these bodies and throw them down the hole," he said just as the young giant stablehand ran up wielding two halves of her staff and swinging them to great effect.

At his smile, she shrugged. "Half of it kept getting in my way so I put both halves in front where I can see them. You want ants shoved back down where they came from?"

"Yes, please," he said as he threw the one he'd put the cylinder in down the hole.

The giant dropped both staff pieces and grabbed an ant in each hand and chucked them on the heads of the ones trying to dig their way out. She threw several more into the gaping hole and Xan shot a couple before he moved them away.

"Feel free to shoot anything that sticks its

head out while I make sure I do this right," Xan said as he studied the screen on the control pad. "Don't get too close, I don't know what's going to come back out because I don't know how far they carried the package."

"Just push the button already," Tina laughed as she shot the first ant to emerge after they'd stopped refilling the way out with dead bodies.

"Okay," he said as he made a theatrically exaggerated stab at the control unit.

The ground beneath them *thumped* and flames shot out of the mouth of the tunnel, the back half of an ant emerging from the pit disappearing into ash. Turning in the direction they felt the ground shake they could see a line of dust rising from the soft dirt of the paddock. The line pointed directly across the grassway toward the heart of the Badlands. Off in the distance over the fence around the stable property they could see another smoke plume like the one that rose above their own ant hole.

"Their plume is taller," Sesco observed. "That means the ants dragged your gift more than halfway, at least sixty, seventy meters."

Xan shot another ant coming at them from the other side of the paddock. "Let's go see where we can help. You, what's your name and where are the rest of the stablehands and the owner?"

"Feyona, my friends call me Fey. Ol' Ed saw the bone midden heaving and got the boss to show him while the rest of us tended the guests, that's what we called them. They were the first to get eaten. Foreman told me to run and give the alarm and no sooner I did than ants was crawling all over."

"I had to climb the outside of the building to get away and up to my bunk where I had my things. Ran out of bullets before you folks got here and was trying to find a way out that wasn't trying to eat me when you showed up."

"Everybody else is dead," she looked sadly at the stalls full of dead ants and half eaten occupants. "Even the poor horses and struthy and the most beautiful cat I ever saw in my life. All dead before I could give the alarm and get back to help."

"Okay, stay and do whatever or come with us. Let's go see if the rest of our friends are okay."

They were almost to the designated truck stop area where the largest vehicles were always parked when Fey caught up with them carrying a large duffel bag and wearing a larger backpack. "Had to get my things."

"We're not actually *going* anywhere, girl," Lily snapped. "Don't have a ride any longer."

Fey's face fell. "Killed as many as I could while they ate my two and four legged friends. Got here two months ago on the way to the Black Hills to pan for gold and only stayed after I got my first pay 'cause I liked the job and the people."

"No Ma'am, with things disrupted as much as they are and so many dead, some types of folk have been known to snoop where they think no one is watching any longer. It's all I own and it might look like a lot, but it's not that heavy."

She smiled as she wielded the two halves of

her staff, the duffel bag bouncing against her left hip. "Most of what's in the backpack is the thick fluffy quilt my gramma made for me for my eighteenth birthday just before I headed west. Looks big, don't weigh much. Hey, check out that big hunk of man there, ooh and he has puppies!"

"Hey Gar," Xan said as they met their friend near where the larger vehicles were parked. "Everybody okay?"

"Hey Xan, yeah, wasn't as bad here as other places. You okay?"

"Somewhat. Lost everything in the stables. All the animals and people except Fey."

The shorter than normal giant with the slightly pointed ears openly admired Gar as she spun her two staff halves. "Hey big fella."

"So, what happened?" Lily prodded as gunfire sounded again in the distance.

"Ants came up out of the ground and swarmed all over everything just when night was deepest and the fewest people were up and about. One good thing is most people were already indoors and the ants all came up in open areas, mostly through trash piles and bone middens."

"They came swarming up by the dozens every minute and just kept coming. By the time we got armed and ready they were thick everywhere."

The sound of multiple weapons sounded nearby for several seconds and they all spun into a defensive ring as Gar continued, "We'd been killing them as fast as we could reload for what seemed like a long time when some genius dropped a thermal charge into a hole somewhere and blew up one of their tunnels."

Xan raised his hand as several fingers pointed his way.

"Figured. Then somebody else poured some gas down another hole and set it on fire. Last I heard, that only plugged three of the five holes reported. Then I saw you folks coming down the street and here we are."

"On it," Sesco said and headed Spot in the direction of the Sheriff's office, Tina catching up in three strides and matching the struthy's speed.

"So, three out of five known holes plugged with fire but we don't know for how long. Gar, do you know if anybody is reloading empty mags?"

"Yes, both buses had people on it as soon as the gunfire became steady. They had full bandoleers ready as soon as people came looking for them. With this lull, they'll be ahead of any new surge if the ants clear the tunnels and come at us again."

Another series of shots sounded on the other side of town, then grew silent a moment before starting again and increasing steadily.

"That's a new spot," Gar said.

"I have three more thermal here and four fragment in the other box with my gear. Maybe if we take out the other two tunnels it'll cut off the new one."

"If they're connected like your first two were," Lily said. "I say nearest hole first."

"This way," Gar said and led them toward the quad shop. "They had a big leaky dumpster in the alley behind their place the ants dug under."

When they got there, shooting the

occasional ant along the way or smashing its head with a broken staff for a club, they found the quad riders having a party around the ant hole. Taking turns, they clubbed and chopped and kicked every ant that appeared, only having to wait while the ants pulled their dead down and out of the way so more could attack.

After a brief explanation about what they wanted to do, the bikers allowed Xan to plant one of his charges in the thorax of a dead ant and throw it into the hole the ants were trying to attack through.

"So, what do we do now?" one of the bikers asked.

"Just keep having fun for a little while longer so they have time to get it back along the tunnel. You have those pieces-parts ready? Okay, here goes. Step back."

The men and women circling the ant hole stepped away just as he and Lily stepped forward and sprayed the opening with shotgun blasts. They stepped back and several bikers threw in ant remains after they'd stripped them of their legs and the muscles along their sides.

"You know, that's probably what drew them," he said as they stood back and waited. "Every spot they came up through was either a bone midden or a mulch pile that was full of ant bones and what the cerapigs wouldn't eat." He pointed. "Or under a leaky dumpster. Okay, that's about the same time we waited before. Everybody stand back please."

They began moving away when the ant carcasses stuffed in the hole began twitching as they were dragged away from below. Xan didn't make as much of a show as he touched the screen.

The ground shook and another plume of fire shot skyward as a line of dust rose straight toward the grassway and the Badlands.

"Look!" A biker pointed to where another plume of fire like the one in front of them only much smaller lit the sky outside the city walls.

"That's in the middle of the grassway," a biker said. "That's a long way to burn ants. Nice job. If you make it in time tomorrow morning, we're going to grill up these ant legs before we ride. You're invited."

"No thanks," Xan said. "They seem to collect their dead and if they're focusing on something in their bones and guts then I don't want to smell like ant."

"You ate, like two whole racks before we went to bed," Lily said. "That's six legs *and* side ribs. That's probably why you used twice as much ammo as the rest of us, they were probably going to drag your smelly carcass back to whatever monster recycles their minerals and juices."

"You had some too," he replied, scowling at the laughing quad riders.

"One leg, no rib. It was good but I haven't had cerapig ribs in a while so went for that."

"Are you two through comparing recipes?" Fey wondered. "I'm all out of ant skulls to smash and I still got a lot of payback left in me for my friends. Can we go kill some bugs?"

"We need to find out where we're needed for my last two charges."

"Sesco went to the Sheriff's office," Lily said. "Knowing him he's probably running things by now."

Without a word, they ran to the Sheriff's office and found Spot being tended by a nervous Deputy just as Sesco and Tina exited the building with a man in a cowboy hat. They shook hands and the Sheriff returned to his duties while Sesco relayed what he'd learned.

"So that's it, once they realized what was happening, they got the civies and tourists safe while they mapped the attack points. Somebody mentioned middens and mulch piles, then a couple of somebody else-es recounted ant habits and everybody decided they were being drawn to where ant remains were the oldest and thickest."

"There are enough people about with weapons and experience in their use to keep the ants away from their own while the city officials enact their hasty plan. They're mapping every single bone midden, mulch pile, and dumpster in town and putting watches on them."

"That's first. Next is find a way to map the ground under the city so we can see where they've been digging, but that's going to take some time. In the meantime, I used my authority to contact some people and there're a couple of pump trucks and a CO_2 tanker leaving Rapid City as soon as the tanker is loaded."

"It seems there've been talks about how dangerous the ants have become and solutions talked about. The local university did some tests on live ones and found the safest way to kill them quick without ruining the meat is with CO2. The only reason they haven't done it yet is trying to decide who's going to pay and how to go about collecting the dead ants inside the nest before they go bad. Wall's city leaders voted an emergency fund about an hour ago."

He calmly pulled his pistol and shot an ant running in the shadows before continuing, "All we have to do is map the tunnels so they know which ones to put a hose into to get all the branches from Wall to the nest."

"That's all?" Fey laughed. "How're you going to map a maze three- or four-meters underground in a space a couple of kilometers on a side?"

Sesco smiled deviously as he looked at Xan and his sister. "I think I might know a way."

"Think it'll work?" Xan asked as he realized what his friend was suggesting.

"Still have a couple hours before we were going to leave. We can at least get started and give them something better to work from." He shrugged. "Might even nail it down so they can gas the entire hive in one shot and be heroes as we leave. You up for it, sis?"

She smiled, her emotions laced with a desire for revenge. "Get me one of those big posters like I saw in the drug store and I'll mark it up till I drop. Got more payback to get out of my system before I'll be ready to head west any further."

"How about an actual picture of Wall and the westbound lane of the grassway?" Fey said as she dug into her duffle bag and pulled out a rigid tube. "They sell them in the visitor's center. I have one here."

She unscrewed the top of the aluminum tube and turned it upside down. Several sheets of different kinds, all a meter on a side, fell out. Fey sorted through them till she found the one she wanted. "I had them laminate mine, but the ones they sell in the visitor's center aren't. The other posters are nice but they're artist's drawings and aren't to scale like a picture taken from directly above."

Gunfire from close by sounded and everyone put a hand to their nearest weapon. The sounds continued but moved away and they relaxed a little while still watching the shadows.

"So, we need to get some of those posters and something to mark the lines with. On it," Sesco said and dashed back to the Sheriff's office leaving Spot with Tina.

With nothing better to do than wait, Xan decided to start probing to see if he could detect ant tunnels four meters beneath his feet. Clearing his mind in a way that closed out everything around him he opened an emotional hole he'd learned to use to focus on a single person, only this time he opened it downward.

At first there was nothing any stronger than when he sat in the middle of a field and opened himself to the world. He pushed just a little and felt a ripple and focused on it, not pushing hard, but leaning into it. Without thinking he walked away from his friends until what drew him weakened.

Stopping, he looked up to see his friends

watching curiously. "Thought I'd test it while we waited for whatever he has in his book bag this time." He pointed down. "If I'm not mistaken there's a tunnel right here, going that way and that way."

He concentrated on the mental *feel* and walked several steps, then took a couple of steps to either side. "Yep! Ant tunnel directly below me."

They turned as Sesco came out of the building carrying several rolled tubes. "They had a bunch of them they use for monster spotting graphs and emergency planning. Better yet, they marked all the known holes on these two posters and I have red markers. Who gets one?"

Xan took one and laid it on the ground, turning it till it was lined up then he crouched and made a tiny mark in the middle of one of the streets. Picking the poster up he started in the line he felt was right. "Lily and Gar, you're with me. Tina, you get Sesco and Fey. Gar, have one of your pups go with them please."

"It's a big town, but not *that* big and the known holes are already marked. Just connect the dots and maybe in a couple hours we'll have something the gas team can use to their benefit. Good luck."

With that he turned and began walking along the line his senses dictated, stopping every now and then to make a mark on his poster. His path wasn't arrow straight but it didn't curve by much except where branches split, his first one taking him to the hole at the stables.

While they were there, they reloaded empty

magazines, refilled hydration bladders, and stuffed their pockets with food bars.

Xan gave the second ammo box with the fragmentation charges to Gar when they got back together. "You know how and when to use them as much as me."

An hour later they met face to face with Tina for the first time even though they had seen each other in the distance several times. One other time their efforts pointed to a busy tunnel and they were waiting when a new hole appeared and ants swarmed again.

"That should be enough to get an idea what they've built," Xan said after they sent a thermal charge down the new entrance. "Let's see what we have."

On hands and knees beside each other with their friends around them guarding, they filled in each other's poster with their own lines.

"Don't fill in the gaps through the buildings," Tina suggested. "There might be one of those large rooms and a line might make somebody complacent."

"Good idea. Looks like every single line meets up with these three on the south wall. I say we go out in the grassway and see if they come together further out."

"Are you sure you don't want to wait till daylight so you can see dog sized ankle biters in knee high grass?" Gar wondered. "Won't be that long."

"I'll go with you if he's afraid," Fey said, then ruffled Ginger's head. "Especially if I get to keep this beautiful lady."

"You do *not* get to keep her!" Gar insisted. "She stays with me."

"So, the only way to keep her is to keep you too? That's a tough choice there, Shorty."

"*Shorty*!" Gar squeaked, then made some other noises while the others laughed.

Without another word, a grumbling Gar led them to the nearest gate and out into the wild as Sesco put his phone back in his pocket. Moments later, the main gate opened and several quads and both security vans came out and began patrolling around them.

"There are three main tunnels, pretty wide ones, and this is the center one. The hole we saw flame from was a little further out," Xan said as they approached the edge of the westbound lane. "Hey quad driver, can you guys put lights on over in the median in front of me?"

The driver got on his radio and seconds later lights began appearing all over the edge of the westbound lane shining south.

"There! That's where the ground dips and they had a hole. Be careful Fey."

"It's okay, got my mother's eyes and ears. Whatever you put in those thermal charges collapsed the tunnel here and it looks like they didn't bother to reopen it."

"Okay, you can come on out of there now."

"Hey guys," Gar said. "I see the lights of the pump trucks and two tanker trucks, big ones. Got a bunch of security with them, too."

"Gar, could you go out and meet them

please? This is probably the best place to pump in both directions. Clear out the town and might even kill the nest. Fey, you can come out of there now so the trucks can get down."

"Hey driver, could you have your guys form a line over there and shine your lights down in that dip so I can direct the trucks in? Thanks."

"Okay, Fey," he said as he joined her in the low spot where the thermal charge had collapsed the tunnel, "you can stay down here with me while I direct the trucks in. What are you doing?"

"Lot of extra vibrating going on," she said as she put a hand to the ground. "Feels like more than wheeled trucks rolling closer."

On one side of the depression the quads were lining up on a high point and shining their lights down where the subterranean lines crossed the old median. On their other side, the two pump trucks and tankers were slowing and turning where Gar directed, their security fanning out and turning to watch outward from the chosen worksite.

Xan closed his eyes to block out the glare of the surrounding spotlights and sent his mind out and down. He didn't feel the senses of the normal ant and focused on the different mental signature. The mental image sharpened and lined up with three distinct points on one side of where he stood and his eyes flew open.

"Fey! Run! Warrior ants and they're digging holes from the nest side!" He grabbed her just as Ginger let out a battle howl, but before they could move shapes twice the size of normal ants erupted from the ground on the nest side and dozens more followed as they swarmed the three of them in the line of fire of the vehicles above.

[22] A skull-lined labyrinth.

Moving on instinct, Xan turned in the only direction he *felt* was open. "Ginger! Close guard! Fey, walk directly toward the big spotlights in front of you. Fast now, and club anything that comes in reach. I'll cover our rear. Fast now! *Move*!"

He didn't give her time to think and began walking backwards and into her. "Move now dammit, we're in their crossfire."

The quad drivers couldn't shoot because they were facing the three in the bottom of the depression and directly across from the pump and tanker trucks. The security for the trucks was mostly facing outward but two trucks had their weapons directed downslope and both sprayed death in front of and behind the three as they fled the swarming ants.

Ginger barely dodged pincers large enough to cut her head off in one bite but Fey smashed the skull with one powerful hit as Xan pumped shotgun shells into anything not directly in line with any headlights. He had to wait till the ants were closer on the uphill side of the slope because that's where truck security lined up but there were plenty of close targets.

Twice ants got near enough gore splattered back on him when heads exploded. In what seemed an eternity they were across the divide and the two truck security vehicles had a clear downrange. With the three of them out of the way, security had no crossfire hazards. Ants continued to stream out of the holes but after a few minutes they had to crawl through piles of their dead to get to open air.

As the three of them dodged between the pump and tanker trucks Gar rushed up to Fey. "Are you okay? Hey Ginger, you took care of her for me, good girl."

"Hey Gar, exciting night."

The big man looked up from the ones he was most worried about. "Hey Xan, you okay?"

"Yeah," he smiled at his best friend. "Ants got bigger, bodies almost as big as Ginger and serrated pincers easily big enough to cut legs off. This nest needs to be completely sterilized. If ants like this get established in a bigger territory, whole states could be lost."

"Supposed to be leaving soon after sunrise," Gar said as he glanced at the color coming to the eastern clouds with the end of night. "Got a long run with no horses through more ant territory and a bunch of purist yokels at the end."

Xan smiled wide. "What better reason to sit back a day."

"What about the rest of the caravan?"

"What about them? A bunch of them aren't even part of *our*," he made air quotes with the hand not holding his shotgun, "caravan. And we're just figurehead leaders anyway. Let Fred and Fran and the Shaws take them the rest of the way. The two security vans always were working for grampa and the rest are here to make their own way, so let them."

"Sometimes it's better to lead from behind, especially when you're doing it to clear a major danger to those coming after. The ants are here, not waiting to ambush the caravan. Let's go find the others and see who wants to stay and make sure nothing else dies like so many have tonight. The others will be okay the rest of the way without us."

"The protest…"

"Going to take a lot of angry protestors to block an entire grassway from a couple thousand travelers minding their own business, especially when so many are as pure of blood as any human nowadays. The Sheriff is going to be there to take Bannon into custody…"

"Ha, that's not happening," Gar laughed. "Seems he gorged on ant legs last night, got drunk and passed out, and got ate. Shame about his boys, though." The big man hung his head. "Bastard chained them up and drugged them asleep every night so they wouldn't wander and they got eaten too."

"Crazy world," Fey muttered as gunfire continued behind them. "So, what are we doing big fella? Whatever it is, I'm with you."

Gar looked at Xan, who decided. "We go find the others and see who wants to stay a day and take out an ant's nest."

The others found them first and he told them what he wanted to do then had to explain his plan a third time when they got to the buses, then again when Rocky and Selene came by their main camp.

"You quitting, boy?" Selene said with her hands on her hips.

"No Ma'am. Just delaying till after I make sure a vital task is completed properly. All the promised supplies are with the buses and turtles and the security vans aren't working for me and go where they're told by whoever pays them. If they stay, fine, if not, fine. At the end of the day every one of the thousands making this last leg will filter off at each exit or continue westward to the coast whether I ride with them or not."

"And not to sound rude or anything, Ma'am, but it seems you and Rocky have more to do with a lot of *all* this," he waved a hand around them, "than anybody but my grampa. It wouldn't surprise me if you two were always going to lead the buses and turtles to wherever the new main labs are."

"As for me, I have an important job to finish and I'm going to delay going home to my mountainside acres till after that job is completed to my satisfaction."

"Just like your grampa, always focusing on fixing somebody else's problems." She one-eyed him a moment. "Revenge against nature ain't a worthy cause, boy."

"These monsters aren't a part of nature."

"You don't think other bugs don't see normal ants as monsters? Lots of critters live together despite their size. For instance, if the good people of Wall found a spot at the edge of the grassway to discard all ant wastes, the ants might always leave the town alone."

"They only came up from their tunnels where they could recover the minerals that belonged to the nest. Of course, they found a lot of food running around and went for that too, but what they came for was theirs to take back by nature's rules."

"Ants," Xan said, "like people before the gene hacked took over, can become so overpopulated they destroy their ecology. Even ants have predators, and in this case, I'm taking on that task. Let the townies learn to live with any that survive my revenge for the loss of a friend and valued companion who trusted me with his wellbeing. And I can't help but remind you it was the craft you practice made Xanthos more than an animal and a true friend I failed. I will stay till I'm as sure as I can be that no one else has to endure what I'm going through now for that failure."

"Okay, son. I'll tell your grampa you passed. C'mon Rocky, let's get the rest of these pioneers going so we can get to the lab and test our newest theory."

Knowing they had to run the gauntlet of ants most of the way, and already up because of the ant invasion, the entire caravan was on the move within an hour of sunrise. Xan found a spot out of the way after they transferred their gear from the stables to the buses and waited.

When the last vehicle left for the front gate, he stood and faced the ones that stayed. "I talked with the gas team leader about not pumping toward the nest till after the main entrances could be guarded on the Badlands side. He said he'd already been told to wait."

"All the holes in town are being watched and they're getting some activity but the ones closer to the pumps are already showing elevated CO_2

levels. Another hour and all the ants in the tunnels under the town should be dead. Sesco, do you have anything?"

"Defenses on the Badlands side from the military report no ant activity. Looks like they were focused on the town. Tina's at the Sheriff's office right now getting us a ride in a military copter."

"I get to fly? Cool!" Fey ruffled Ginger's head and Fred came close for his share of attention.

"It's one of those big ones that carries four of the new four-man military Raptor Scouts. They're going to drop them off, then pick up a bunch of volunteer bikers and us before they go for a second load of Scouts. There are three main tunnel entrances out in the Badlands and they want to cover all three before they start pumping. Seems the concentrated surprise attack on the town combined with the bigger variety of warrior ant triggered something political and the threat went from a local nuisance level to national emergency once the videos of the attack went public."

"That's probably where the order to delay for the pumping came from. They wanted time to get military ordinance in place and go in full daylight. There's also a squad of drones for higher targets ready to lift as soon as the pumps start. Here comes our ride now."

Tina trotted up just as the large military transport landed in an open area. The four blades continued to spin as a couple of men in uniform ushered them and several quads inside.

"Boy! Can't wait for another ride like that!" Fey gushed after they were let off in front of a mudstone cliff. "What a view! Whoa! What the hell is that?"

"They're called cathedrals," Xan explained as the copter lifted and flew off to the west toward the military base on the southwest corner of the Black Hills.

They gathered together as they looked at one of the three main entrances to the Badlands ant nest. Around them military and volunteers from Wall got into position. Several shots rang out as scouting ants were killed and snipers targeted ants crawling around holes in the soft rock of the Badlands.

"I talked to the OIC," Sesco said. "She told me we're in the second wave inside after the CO_2 levels drop. Till then we're just another part of the picket line and kill anything in front of us."

"What are you going to do with Spot?" Gar wondered.

"Ride him. Colonel Sparks says drones show the first few hundred meters are tall and wide. It really is cathedral-like behind that," he pointed toward the impressive arched front of the ant's nest.

The sirens sounded and the chaos around them became more frenetic. "That's the signal, they're pumping gas from the grassway side. We're supposed to form up our people between those two quads and walk forward till they signal again."

The firing line was ragged at first then smoothed out as quad drivers adjusted their positions with the walkers. In a few minutes, they were an even line with about three meters between each person, then two meters when the siren sounded.

Their line arced in front of the wide cathedral carved into the face of the hard-packed mud cliff a little more than a hundred yards away from the high, arched, ground level entrance. Gunfire increased as ant sentries noticed the movement and moved out of the nest to investigate, exposing themselves to snipers.

Pheromones from the dead wafted into the nest to warn the interior of the danger and more sentries moved out from several higher holes to guard or prepare to defend. Another signal sounded and everybody stopped shooting as drones flew toward the higher entrances with heavier-than-air CO_2 spraying into upper tunnels.

They maintained their vigilance for several minutes and just when they started to relax ants poured out of several holes, then new holes appeared at higher levels and warrior ants swarmed out into daylight.

"Frack, sure hope somebody thought about evac," Fey said. "Hey boss, is there time to change my mind?"

Xan laughed as he lifted his shotgun. "Sure, you have about twenty seconds to start running."

"Ah well, might as well see how much I like this fancy shotgun Gar's Uncle Frederick gave me. Can always quit later."

Xan would have answered but they became busy as hundreds of hellhound sized ants rushed the defensive cordon. He dropped empty drums every few seconds as the line of friends and two pups killed everything that came into their area of responsibility. When their area was clear of targets, they shifted to help those on either side. An hour later a truck came by with freshly loaded magazine drums and they gathered up the empties and traded.

"Good timing," Xan said. "All I had left were the six drums in my two bandoleers and my pistol. There goes the first assault team. Air must be clear, they're going in. Let's assemble with team two."

They hurried the distance to where three squads of Marines were gathered and Sesco talked with the CO. "He's not happy about us going in with his troops, but he's been told to let us in. His people will go in first and we're supposed to stay in the front cathedral. Here we go."

The entrance consisted of three arches consisting of a ten-meter tall four-meter wide central door with flanking arches about two-thirds that. Spot led their charge behind the middle group of soldiers and they found themselves inside a single immense room bigger and more elaborate than some large churches. Holes scattered around the outer walls and ceiling let enough light in to illuminate the entire entrance theatre.

"They plastered the walls and ceiling with the skulls of their dead," Fey said in awe as they gaped at the inside of the nest's entry room.

"Not just their own," Sesco said from his higher viewpoint in Spot's saddle and pointed to a human skull among those of ants.

As their eyes adjusted to the lower light, they began to see larger skulls. On one side of the entrance cathedral the long horns of three triceratops skulls formed a ladder to a higher tunnel.

Soldiers with CO_2 canisters were nearing the black hole at the tunnel's mouth.

The soldiers split up and each checked another room with the third team coming in behind them and setting up communications gear with CO_2 fire extinguishers everywhere. Other soldiers dragged in fans and expandable tubes to bring fresh air into the tunnels.

"Hey Fey, Lieutenant Whatever-his-name-was said no further than the entrance," Sesco said as Spot pranced in the growingly crowded space despite its size.

"Pretty big entrance if you ask me," she replied ignoring Sesco's infallible memory. "Even big enough for you perched on the back of that big bird. I'd say we're doing exactly what he told us."

"Girl's got a point Brainiac," Gar said as he and the pups bounded after her when she went further inside the nest.

"Really should stay together," Xan said as he and Lily moved to catch up with the others. Don't go into any hole where you have to go low, CO_2 will still be thick nearest the floor of the tunnel."

With dead ants everywhere they went, they were able to explore several hundred meters of tunnels high enough for Spot to walk after Sesco dismounted. They guarded the entrances to smaller side tunnels the others explored and greeted the military and an increasing number of civilians roaming tunnels that continued toward Wall. Some of those higher tunnels might contain live ants barricaded against the poison gas that settled lower than normal air, so they kept their weapons ready as they explored where their lights took them.

"Why would they make tunnels so large," Fey wondered when they passed another group that said they came from the grassway side.

"Same reason we just experienced," Xan replied. "These big tunnels are the main passages with traffic going every which way and ants carrying things back and forth. The way the interior walls are shaped I bet a lot of the traffic climbed up and around the slower ones. With the wider walls needed to support two-way fast and slow traffic, sturdy arched ceilings high enough for a giant and a struthy to walk upright might be a lucky byproduct of ant architecture."

"Really should take Spot back out," Sesco said as he scratched his mount's neck. "Lamps are well and good and there are more people collecting fresh meat, but this is too cramped for a running beast. I can keep him calm but it distracts me from my surroundings."

"Which way?" Xan mused. "Have we gone far enough to head to town, get some supplies, and go on now that it looks like the nest is dead. Or do we go out the way we came in and see if we can get a ride into Rapid City."

"Still pretty early," Sesco said. "There's a chance that ride could set us down in time to watch the caravan reach the protest."

"Boy, wouldn't want to miss that!" Fey chuckled as she came out of a side tunnel. "Look what I found. They were piled around a bunch of wriggly things that looked like oversized grubs.

Stabbed them all with my knife so the military couldn't weaponize them, then collected these. Opals, big ones, too, not like all the little ones we've been kicking around in the dust since we got here. And check this out, an opal sabretooth fang."

"This is Park property," Sesco reminded them.

"Well maybe you should take your struthy back out where it won't get spooked and stomp on somebody and I'll just take my reward for helping save lives and go my own way."

"Wait, what?" Gar said nervously.

"Hang on there big fella, I ain't going anywhere, yet. Library man ain't gonna say nothing more than his reminder or he would have at every local and military man digging opals and other stuff out of the skull plastered walls. He scowls but doesn't speak. His words were just a reminder in case I want to think about what I'm gathering, or how much to gather."

Sesco nodded and pursed his lips. "I'll go outside and see if I can get us a lift a day's ride west."

"I'll go with you," Tina said.

Fey was showing the rest what she'd found before the others' lights split from theirs. "There's no way I could have taken them all. I filled my bags and that fang wasn't the only fossil opal I found."

She waved toward the smaller tunnel. "Egg crèche full of wriggly grubs and the ants lined the fracking thing with shiny rocks. You really gotta see it."

After checking out the crèche and another

hour of exploring, they found their way back to the front entrance and out in the open where Sesco updated them. "The locals have lain claim to the tunnels and the military thinks they'll make an awesome base on this side of the Hills, so political battle lines are being drawn."

"Somebody mentioned the opals and all the easy to harvest meat and both sides did an about face and are now openly arguing on the record for hands-off till the higher ups decide. Can't clear all the meat before it rots and have enough people watch for treasure collecting the conflicting government levels might claim."

"I recommended an amnesty lasting till ownership is determined and confirmed. And yes, we returned slow enough to seek out another egg room, although as a Librarian I collected only research samples that I'll send to the proper facilities."

"I'm not restricted by Library rules," Tina said. "I found a really nice fang, Fey, and a turquoise nugget as big as Gar's fist."

They spent the next few minutes showing each other their favorites, then collected their gear and reloaded magazine drums while they waited for a ride. When the copter landed off to the side of the grassway where the old Air Force base used to be, the core vehicles of their caravan were just coming over the furthest ridge.

Running around the cowlings to the rotors, they were met by Sheriff Timberwolf. "Welcome to the Hills, son. Hear you folks did a good job in Wall. I just got the message while you were in the air. They found three queens but only five attendants. There's evidence the sixth one left before the military had all the exits covered. We'll find her eventually and finish the job."

They walked toward the grassway as the rest of the caravan came into sight in the distance. "Wall Sheriff sent me all I needed to close out the Bannon file, so we're clear there as soon as I get copies of your documents."

When they got to the edge of the grassway, Sheriff Timberwolf introduced them to several of his deputies and a man with wolfen features.

"Was hired to carry whatever you got left after your ant war plus weapons and ammo I was told to purchase if you need them," Samuel Yelloweyes said as they shook hands.

"Saddles and other gear we're not carrying is with the buses," Xan said then touched his bandoleers. "Military reloaded our mags and our weapons are sufficient while afoot this last stretch but thank you."

"Good. Was also told to run you home tonight, no dawdling. You up for that?"

"Sorry, but we're not going anywhere till the caravan is safe. I thought there was supposed to be a big protest for racial purity? Don't see anything from here and if they were going to block the Hills, they should be here at the first exits for best results. Or are they going for the video crowd where they can get more spectators?"

"Neither," Yelloweyes said. "Seems they spent a lot of time building themselves up after they got outed to draw out the faithful they missed by trying to be sneaky. Agitators came in from all over. Trouble is, they had a few days to get ready for you and seemed to like to party and brag and do stupid things while working themselves into a frenzy."

"Most of 'em got thrown in jail for bar fights and some for things worse than fighting. Another bunch of 'em ended up in the hospital when they tried to enforce their opinions on local folk a little too violently."

"By the time the caravan of the corrupted they were here to stop showed up, there weren't that many of the truly faithful left to protest. Plus, the military from Ellsworth just happened to be doing something important down in Wall and had plenty of backup parked up and down the grassway in case they were needed in a hurry. All official like and everything."

"So, does that mean we don't have to wait any longer?" Gar asked.

"My missus is telling someone in the caravan you're going ahead. She'll catch up to us after we leave the grassway."

"That's okay, Samuel, we'll wait for our friends and stay in Rapid City a night before we go the rest of the way."

"Old man said you'd do that, but I could keep the full wage even if you came rushing through the night. Ain't no sense walking to them then turning around and coming back so we'll just wait here till the Sheriff's escort trucks move out if that's okay with you folks."

They followed the line of trucks with their emergency flashers along the grassway with crowds of people covering the few overpasses crossing the grassway. A mixture of anti and pro augmentation posters hung from the overpasses but the two groups seemed to be mingling without problems. A heavy military presence mixed with the overworked local law enforcement kept violence down to individual arguments between the overlapping borders of opposing sides.

"Looks more like a party than a protest," Fey said as she waved at a trio of dwarves on short stilts. One almost fell waving back.

"There's the main protest line, Xan," Sesco said. "You sure you don't want to get in among the wagons."

"Yeah, as a matter of fact I do want to hide among the wagons, but I can't. Besides, it's not like we're alone out here."

"There is that," Sesco said as they looked at the crowds on both sides of the grassway's westbound lane.

A huge banner across the overpass ahead had a large arrow pointing left followed by the words, BUSINESS EXIT HERE FOR HILLS. There were large orange barrels lined up to provide an open path up to and through the downtown area. Samuel and his wife, Margaret, calmly turned their massive horses to the left as the line of sheriff's SUVs continued toward the line of protestors.

"Guess this is where we're going," Fey said when there was a bit of confusion as those around them changed direction.

"Buses and turtles are following so it must be," Tina said. "Bunch of others are following

Johnny Law. Must be the ones going on to the coast."

"I thought this was your home," Fey said when they turned down a wide, paved street, her voice steady despite everyone jogging to keep up with their slowest wagons.

"We've never actually been here much," Tina said. "Most of the time we flew to the base on the southeast side of the Hills and when we went on the ground it was in an armed and armored camper bus with escort. I don't think we ever came this way."

"But there're the stables and the hotel I recognize from the reservation site on the 'Net. Don't know what it's like on the inside, only been to Rapid City twice and both times was for political functions with grampa."

"Looks like Samuel has everything under control," Xan said. "Shall we find out if we already have rooms."

The doorman directed them to the man Samuel had been talking to and he gave them each a separate key. "You can use any of the blue elevators and the hounds may ride *only* the blue elevators to the roof, which is all yours tonight. Sorry, but your hounds aren't allowed anywhere else in the hotel. I've been assured they've been well trained, but the safety fence is only two meters high and ten stories is a long way to fall, even for a hellhound. I would suggest no jumping games."

"Well, this whole day has just been one series of Whiskey Tango Foxtrot," Fey laughed. "Except for all the screaming and bleeding and dying, you folks sure are fun to be around. And I get my own room, so if I find me a lad with some extra energy, I have a private place to wear him out. I'm going to get gussied up, see y'all later."

Gar stood speechless for several seconds. "What just happened?"

"C'mon big fella," Xan said. "All six rooms are on the top floor and there are only two blue elevators and that's the only place they go. Let's get cleaned up and see if we can't find a restaurant with cloth napkins *and* a decent choice of ales. Maybe Fey will choose you."

His giant friend looked crestfallen for a moment, then smiled. "Yeah, maybe."

Xan slapped his friend on the shoulder. "C'mon buddy, we're going to party all night on somebody else's coin and tomorrow we're going to see what grampa has been up to all this time running us from one end of the country to the other."

[23] Centaur spiders.

"Do you want the job or not?" the old man said as he sat behind the desk with his hands steepled in front of him.

Xan sighed and looked at Tina. "He's doing it again, you know."

"Yeah. But at least we know a little more than we did the last time."

"Right into the middle of the Denver Wastes, on horses instead of armored scouts."

"Well, they're not really horses."

"What are they?" the siblings asked at the same time.

"Not really sure what to call them. Want to see? They're in the warehouse. Let's take a look while I tell you more about the mission."

When they arrived, their grandfather gestured. "Here we are. What do you think?"

"What is it?" they both said at the same time again.

"Centaur walkers. Half tech and half plant and animal."

"Centaurs have four legs and their torso is in front," Xan said.

"Okay, spider walkers, but spiders don't have muscular upper torsos with big beefy arms, centaurs do, so we're back to my choice for a name. Since I built and grew them, I win."

"Okay, we'll call them centaur walkers, grampa," Tina said to keep her brother from continuing. "How do they work?"

"I tried the torso in the front position but there was too much behind and I didn't like the feel of it. Had the same problem with the torso in the rear. Putting it in the center is the only one that felt comfortable the first time I tried it."

"With six legs for stability each operator's leg controls three legs equally. I got used to it pretty quick and can run at a sixty KPH average through the test track with jumps and hills. It's two klicks long and I did ten laps on three separate days to get the average."

"Just jump up on the lap and slide into the VR pod in front of the spine. Strap yourself in and all you have to do is walk and it walks with bigger steps. Verbal commands to the onboard A.I. program activate or disengage the arms to operate the control panel's keyboard."

"It runs on water and sunshine by hydration and solar vines, so there's nothing to feed. The chest is open right now but it has a door that will be installed before you leave."

"What about weapons?" Xan asked. "Big clawed hands are nice, but wouldn't much bother some of the things in the wastes."

"See the frames on the sides in front of the torso? They hold tools just like the rail units on the buses, pretty much the same concept."

"We're testing several designs and have more options than we have frames to hang them on. There are several kinds of slug throwers, energy weapons, swords, and saws as well as gloves with claws and knuckle studs."

"The VR pods are flexible enough to work

with operator heights of one point five meters up to three point two five, and they're designed to float with storage bins and magazines full."

"What about Fred and Ginger if Gar decides to join us?"

"Taking the hellhounds is not a wise option. If your friend goes with you, it would be best if the hounds stay here. But whether he goes or not or endangers the hellhounds by taking them with him is not up to me. My offer is for the two of you but there will be six walkers. If none of your friends volunteer to accompany you, the extra four walkers will be slaved to your two."

"When do you want us to leave?"

"As soon as I'm satisfied you're trained in their operation. Also, as in everything in the world, there is no guarantee the first monster you meet won't kill and eat you. So, will you accept my offer?"

"Maybe," Tina said then smiled at Xan.

He smiled back and turned to their grandfather. "There is this little matter of payment up front and over and above operating costs, but yeah, do that this time with a legal contract and we'll work the bugs out of your new centaur cyborgs."

"But I don't know what I did," Fey complained. "I was doing that jump and kick thing I've been practicing because you can't kick without using all three legs. I did the kick, took about two steps up the hill, and it just fell on its side."

"Nobody has ever broken one this way

before," the old man said with a scowl as he stroked his chin.

"You told us to work them as hard as we could," Gar came to Fey's defense as everybody else gathered around in their own centaur spiders.

"No, no," the old man waved a hand negligently. "That's actually a good thing. Every new way they fail gives us another deficiency to correct. It looks like the center left leg kicked into the base of the leg opposite and severely bruised that leg's muscle. The solution is simple. We limit the mobility of the legs inward so the walkers don't kick their own guts out. And we limit the extension of the outward kicking legs so they don't pop their own tendons and go lame."

"Probably add some verbal commands to the A.I. so only one leg kicks, or even some automatic, one-legged defensive kicks. Might even have the A.I. override so all three legs on one side kick."

"It'd be better to make the tendons stronger so I can kick like I do in real life. If I spend too much time being restrained in the walkers, I might do the same when I'm out of it. I don't want to ride one if it can't keep up with what I can do."

"So, what do we do now?" Sesco asked even though he already knew the answer.

"Ask your team leader, not me, the exercise has not ended," the old man said with a wave of a hand.

"I was," Sesco retorted.

"Strip the downed spider of anything we need and continue," Xan said. "Since it's a simulated exercise we won't tear Fey's spider apart for parts, just take the tools, modular tech trays, and battery packs. Fey can ride Gar's papoose seat and he'll take the center position."

They were finished within minutes and set off on the mountain trail again. As he ran, Xan marveled at the smooth gait of the huge spiders. Then he smiled at the minor victory over his grampa.

The remarkable machines with plant and animal hybrid muscles and organs wrapped around a carbon fiber skeleton had gone from centaur walkers, to centaur spiders, and then simply to spiders within the first hours of their training. His grampa and most of the techs and hackers still called them walkers, but those who rode them named them spiders.

The remaining spiders ran in a single file through the forest of their grampa's mountain. The trail was familiar because they had run it and three others several times in the last two weeks.

"Motion on the left," Lily said and a second later a rex burst out of the trees.

Tina and Sesco at the back of the line of spiders were closest and both grabbed at dummy weapons in their holsters inside the VR pods. The people-sized weapons weren't real but had the same relative weight.

Tina came up with a shotgun while Sesco brandished a six-barreled Gatling and the rex died ten meters short of his intended prey.

"Did your grampa stage that or was it real?" Gar wondered as they continued their run through the forest.

"Don't know," Xan replied, his voice relayed through the speakers and microphones inside his VR pod. "There's still a lot of wild space out here. Grampa has his own herds of bison and megastang that sometimes draw wild ones in and predators always follow."

"Doesn't mean grampa *didn't* catch and release that one," Tina said with a chuckle. "Anybody want to go back in those trees and see if there's a cage hidden just out of sight?"

"Pass," Fey said from her seat on the back of Gar's spider's torso, a 50cal carbine in her hands and a grenade launcher nearby.

Xan led the others on the trail through the forest at the fastest the spider could run on the path. Down hills and up the other side and over obstacles the training trail had been cut to run over so the spiders would be tested to their limits. Except for Fey in the half open papoose carrier, part of the test was not carrying a weapon but waiting till something happened and choosing the best tool for the situation as quickly as possible.

This last test before the final modifications were made was the hardest of the past three days. Several sections were a surprise when a sign showed up in the middle of the familiar trail and directed them to follow the arrows.

Xan was coming over a rocky outcrop and through a gap that was just wide enough for the spiders and he didn't slow as he burst out on the other side and into a tangle of strangler vines. He was a dozen meters into the tangle before he could grab two items, a laser with the left hand and a vibrating knife with the other.

It was too late to not be snared by the surprise trap but knowing the weaknesses of the grasping plant he immediately insured his spider's hands were free. He burned every vine surface he could reach till he freed his knife hand.

By this time his spider's left arm was caught but with his knife hand free he swung and two more vines separated. With a backhanded follow-up, he freed his right legs as he swung the laser to the left and burned through the vines holding his legs on that side.

He stumbled a little as he hit the ground, then spun around, swinging the three-meter long vibrating knife in an arc at the height of his spider's shoulders. He started to step forward to help Lily but she was standing from her own brief battle with the strangler vines.

He pointed the knife behind the bunched group. "Defend your rear!"

Sesco was already turning and bringing weapons to bear as he guarded behind them.

"Forward or back, boss?" Tina yelled from her position just inside the narrow stone cleft.

"Forward," he said as he chopped through another few vines and walked the last few meters.

Once he was free of the tangle, he started trotting then in three more steps was running at full speed again, the rest of his team pounding through the mountain forest behind him. They followed the arrows to another surprise and stood looking across a chasm.

"It's two meters further than the furthest any

one of us has ever jumped one of these things," Sesco said.

Lily frowned at the sign on their side. "Sign says go across here."

"Look for trees tall enough to reach all the way across," Xan said. "We'll make a bridge."

The spiders scattered and within minutes they were back at the sign and reported the trees they'd found and showed pictures.

"These three," Xan said. "We'll use the skinny one to level out the center. Gar, you get the one up on the hill above us. Sesco, you and Tina get the one a couple hundred meters back on the trail while Lily and I get the one below us."

Lily followed him down the side of the mountain to the tree they'd selected. Xan reached toward one of the small holsters inside his control pod and pulled out his choice and the massive cyborg arm reached into the holster on the spider's frame and pulled out the chainsaw. Looking up at the tree he swung the saw upward and lopped off every branch in reach.

In the distance, he could hear the other two teams cutting down their respective trees as Lily used her spider's cyborg strength to throw the branches he cut off to the side. When they got the lower section stripped, Lily moved uphill while he notched the trunk as low as he could reach on the downhill side. Moving again he cut into the back of the trunk opposite the notch.

When he heard the first crack he moved away and up the hill a couple of steps. Releasing the trigger on the electric chainsaw he reached out with the end and pushed at the back of the tree. The tree cracked as it leaned slowly at first, then crashed to the ground between the trees downslope.

Lily moved to the end of the trunk, picked it up, and began dragging it uphill while Xan lopped off the upper limbs. When the trunk was bare, he stowed the chainsaw and picked up his end and they carried it up to the trail.

Gar had no trouble getting his smaller tree down the hill by himself, Fey with her arms crossed and grumbling in the papoose carrier. Sesco and Tina brought the last tree along the trail from behind.

"These really are impressive machines, cyborgs, whatever," Sesco said as they arranged the trunks to plan their next move.

"Yeah," Gar laughed. "We probably won't start dying till the second day and a couple of us might even make it all the way through to wherever it is we're going."

"Getting cold feet, big fella?" Fey teased as they trimmed the trunks and lay them side by side to see how best to position them. "Don't worry, I got your back. But if you fall, I got dibs on the puppies."

Gar had long ago accepted Fey's brand of humor and adjusted accordingly. "You'll probably break another spider the first day then step in something and get turned into some sort of genetic goo monster."

"If you two are finished let's tie all this together and see if we can do what we think we can," Xan said with mock seriousness.

They fitted the three trimmed tree trunks together and pulled supplies out of the cargo beds behind the spiders' torsos and tied them into a bundle. After trimming and spiking together they used chainsaws to cut away the bark and projecting limb stumps to make as flat a surface as possible, then tightened the cables holding it together.

"Is that enough straps?" Gar wondered. "We have more cable and clamps."

"Spikes and quick-glue between the straps should be enough," Sesco said. "This little bridge will still be here in ten, maybe even twenty years."

"If we can chuck it across on the first try," Lily said.

"Okay people," Xan said, "take your positions."

They moved around to the sides of the platform made from three large trees and grabbed onto the ropes stapled into the trunks and signaled they were ready.

"Okay, we've practiced this with single logs so it shouldn't be any problem," Xan said. "Gar, you're the brake. Ready, lift on three, one, two, three."

With two to a side equally spaced the cyborg spiders lifted the massive weight nearly two meters off the ground.

"Four steps forward and throw on five," Xan said as team leader. "Begin on two… one, two," and they began moving faster with each step as Xan counted. "One, two, three, four and swing, five and throw!"

They heaved the three tree trunks strapped

together with heavy cable and threw it with all the strength in four, seven-meter tall cyborgs. The bundle of huge trees lofted another meter into the air and flew forward as they let go of the side ropes. When he reached a marked spot, Gar planted the feet of his spider and held the braking rope firm in his cyborg's grip.

The bridge flew the measured distance and the braking rope jerked it to a stop and it fell with a ground-shaking thump in the middle of the trail.

"Looks like it'll fit," Xan said. "Let's do it for real this time. "You ready, Fey?"

"Yeah, soon as I get my ride the rest of you can join me on the other side."

Sesco was already in position and pulled the proper tool from his forward holsters and shot a spike trailing a carbon fiber cable into a tree on the other side of the chasm. Leaning down so Fey could reach it and attach her pulley, he lifted the cable as high as he could and she rolled across to the other side trailing a second safety rope attached to the front of their bridge.

She disconnected from the cable and ran to a tree directly across from where they planned to set their bridge and tied the pulley to it. After running the cable through the pulley, she took out all the slack and hooked the cable to her safety rope and waved. "Okay, pull it over!"

They pulled the cable in till Xan could connect it to the winch on the front of his spider. "Okay, I'm hooked up. Everybody in position and let's do this."

This time when they threw the three-log

bridge it didn't hit solid ground its full length, but on the ends. The trunks were lashed together with carbon fiber cable and glued and spiked in a rough form of laminate, but they could still flex.

The two ends hit at almost the same time, flexed and bounced twice as Xan and Gar pulled from both ends and kept it centered. When the makeshift bridge finally settled down, they tied ropes to nearby trees to keep it from shifting.

Xan was the first to test the new bridge and he was quickly across with no problems and they secured the two ends so it would take a conscious effort to knock the structure into the chasm. As soon as they were finished, they took off again following the arrows and ended up at the western edge of the foothills of the Black Hills.

"He's joking, right?" Lily said as they read the last sign.

"Grampa hasn't told a joke in my presence in my entire life," Xan said. "Don't think he could get halfway through without explaining the set-up so long he'd forget the punchline."

"So, we run out into the wild, find six poles with flags on them, retrieve the flags, and be back to turn the spiders in to the techs by midnight." Tina smiled at them from inside her spider's control pod. "Piece of cake!"

"We don't have to stick together, do we?" Sesco's voice came through their pod speakers.

"No, we could split up to singles, but I don't want us to do that. Gar, you and Fey are at a disadvantage, don't take chances. If you don't think you can get your two with just one spider, call for help." He pointed out into the plains. "Let's go."

They had practiced several formations the past few days and spread out from the last arrow with its test instructions. They ran an overlapping grid pattern and an hour after dark silently assembled in a flood wash where they couldn't be seen as they discussed how to get the last flag.

"It's not like it's a unitaur," Gar said as he stood higher so the camera eyes atop the shoulders could see better.

"True," Sesco said. "Wild razorbacks are only two-thirds as big, but there are five of them and they're just as temperamental as unitaur."

"What I want to know is how the hell they planted that flag right in the middle of their wallow," Sesco said. "Now we know why the other five were so easy to get to once we found them."

"No way around it and we don't have time to waste," Xan said. "Gar, you have the passenger so you hold back, wait, where's Fey?"

"Right here, boss," the diminutive giant said as she sauntered into their group waving the flag. "Little piggies were snoozing so I tippy-toed past them and got this while you were staying quiet over here out of sight. Can we go home now?"

[24] Flying piranha.

"They were just standing around in those big goofy spider monster suits jabbering about what somebody should do," Fey said with a wave of her mug the next evening. "Still almost didn't make it back in time. Wouldn't have if I hadn't sneaked in and got the last flag so fast."

"The worst part was what happened when we *did* get back," Lily said with a laugh. "After all that we didn't even get to go to bed. Fracking old man made us work till sun-up hauling stone for some building he's putting up somewhere after we're gone."

"Sounds like loads of fun," Rick Shaw laughed. "So, when do you leave?"

"Day after tomorrow," Xan said. "That's why we asked you guys to meet us here tonight, so we could have a night out to celebrate graduation from CSU."

"CSU, what's that?" Amanda asked.

"Cyborg Spider University," Gar laughed. "Didn't get a diploma, but tomorrow we get to check out our upgraded spiders and take them for a run with a full load. Then one last night in a soft bed and off we go to Denver to deliver some sort of mysterious cargo to some goofball hermit living in the middle of the Wastes."

Spider laughed. "What I want to know is when I can get me one of these cyborg spiders. They really sound like a lot of fun to drive."

"They are," more than one of the spider

riders said, then they looked at each other and laughed.

"Are they more tech or bio and how does that work?"

"Haven't the faintest clue, Gunny," Xan said. "Well, that's not entirely true since I've been studying my ears off so I can do any maintenance we need on the way."

"In our defense," Tina interjected, "the people that built them don't completely know how they work either."

Their friends at the large table raised eyebrows as they waited for more of the story.

"They start with a skeleton of carbon fiber with some sort of biological Eneseye type goop inside that works like normal bones only lighter, stronger, and more flexible. The muscles and tendons are mostly plants and there are six or seven different kinds that work together and another dozen or so that live in symbiosis with the muscles. It's basically a living group of plants with a lot of animal genes that act like muscles, wrapped around a tech skeleton and the combination mimicking a normal body."

"Then, and this is the part where even the inventors get lost, they somehow grew this biological interface and connected it through a tech control panel to a computer with an artificial intelligence program."

"Wait," Gunny interrupted, "they built, grew, whatever, a plant brain?"

"Not actually a brain, per se," Xan replied. "It's more of a rudimentary nervous system linked with the muscles that a brain would be connected through. That's where the tech comes in and where they get all red-faced and argumentative when you ask them to explain something better."

"There's no head, just an armored sensor bar across the top of the shoulders. The actual onboard computer has a level three A.I. operating system with triple redundancy."

"That's what *Recluse* has now," Spider said. "We got upgraded from a level two last week. What kind of weapons do you carry?"

"All the same ones the buses carried and a few more. Gatlings, grenade launchers, cannon-sized shotguns, lasers, swords, and axes are just a few."

They have six legs and the VR control pod sits in the torso in the middle. The front cargo area is filled with holsters for all the tools and weapons, and the back has an open cargo bed like an oversized pickup truck."

"How are you going to sleep once you're in the Wastes?"

"That is the one downside," Lily cut in with a playful elbow into Xan's side. "There's a sleeve in the front between and under all the tools and weapons. Just disengage the VR pod and slide forward and you're inside a climate-controlled sleeping cubby. Only room for one, though. The legs disengage and the spider squats down till you slide back up into the VR pod."

"That's only if you're not linked to another spider," Xan said. "Any spider can follow the footsteps of another with the autonomous setting.

That way your teammate can sleep while you walk and the A.I. can wake you up if need be."

"What about the plant muscles?" Gunny wondered. "How reliable are they?"

"Pretty good, actually," Xan replied. "Plus, each spider carries spare muscles in sealed containers filled with nanite solutions. Pull a damaged muscle and replace it, then put it inside the storage tray and the nanites repair it. Takes about fifteen minutes to swap out the hardest to replace muscle sections and less than ten for the easiest."

"The techies did have to make some changes after Fey broke her spider," he continued. "The leg muscles are bulkier and they put more armor underneath where the third leg kicked and bruised the one underneath. In fact, all the muscles are a bit more robust and flexible, even around the upper arms and shoulders. By the time we leave they'll be a bit burlier looking."

"That's going to affect how they move," Gunny said.

"Yes," Xan agreed, "but we've been training with all cargo and supply bins and holsters both empty and overfilled and everything in between. It shouldn't be too hard to adjust. What about all of you. What's going on in your lives?"

"We got that A.I. upgrade on *Recluse*," Gunny said. "That and a drone rack behind the turret, then we're going to head to Sioux Falls with the mom and pop security team and escort a bunch of people across the prairie. Did you hear the people studying the prairie dogs say they have a language of about thirty words, well barks and whistles?"

The table was silent a moment then Amanda blurted. "We're having twins."

"That's our cue," Gar said as the women immediately converged on Amanda. "Anybody want to go check out the game room?"

Without answering Sesco and Xan bailed and got up from the large table. By the time they got to the door to the game room Fey was with them.

When Xan raised one eyebrow, she smiled and her eyes *almost* flicked to the side as she ignored him, muttering so low she didn't think he would hear. "Only one person I want to talk babies with."

"Hey Sesco, did you see that new game?" she called out boisterously. "It's us in the ant cathedral. Well, not us or they'd have to pay us and the ants haven't been gassed to death. C'mon, I'll play you for a mug of ale."

Xan smiled to himself as he followed his friends into the tavern's game room. Tech games and even a few old pinball machines lined the walls with a center table full of people wearing VR helmets. He cheered for Sesco when he won the first game and consoled Fey, then reversed the support when she won the second game.

They watched another pair of customers in front of a VR screen showing what they saw as they hunted raptors, then played an old pinball machine with pictures of a gene hacked bigfoot, a golden android, and a man with a plasma cutter all over the game.

When they went back to the restaurant side, they found their chairs occupied by more women, two of them with babes in arms.

"Don't see Tanner or Stone," Gar whispered theatrically as he put a restraining hand on Xan's shoulder. "Maybe they got away."

"Nope!" Fey said at a normal volume for a crowded, noisy restaurant. "Here they come. One with a tray of those kinds of drinks pregnant women and nursing mothers like and the other with a platter of healthy snacks. I say we go to the outdoor patio and get a refill."

"Works for me," Gar said and presented his arm. "Shall we, My Lady."

Xan caught the rosy glow of Fey's cheeks as she accepted the arm and the two walked through another door toward the patio. He looked at the Librarian and shrugged then followed them. They got drinks and went to the rail to watch the lights of scattered storms flowing eastward with the wind.

"Not like back in Ohio," Xan said after they'd settled in at the table next to the rail. "The horizon is so wide you can see individual storm clouds, almost like each one is alive and showing off to the others."

"Did you know there was once a tornado *season*?" Sesco asked. "Well there was, back when it used to snow over almost half the country at some time in the winter. A hurricane season, too."

"Yeah, yeah," Fey taunted. "Back in the *good old days* before half of Florida and Texas disappeared when most of the Greenland ice cap and half of Antarctica melted in a single decade and the North Passage opened up year-round. Blah, blah, blah. You need to get out of that damned library more when we're off duty, loosen up a little so you don't keep spouting useless information."

"C'mon, Gar and I will take you and boss man on in a game of VR Warrior. We'll be giant heroes and you can be cyclops or ogres."

Xan smiled all the way to the VR rental and allowed himself to be set up with a pre-gene hacker rex persona while Sesco chose an ogre with a tree for a club. Gar's VR avatar was dressed in leather armor with a sword longer than he was tall and an axe that would cut an ogre's leg off with one swing.

In their individual VR pods that reminded him of the controls to the spiders, Xan tested the motions of his avatar as he listened to the quick operations tutorial and for his game avatar. When the game activated, he was ready and walked out onto the arena.

Fey stayed hidden till almost the last second and as he and Sesco advanced she jumped out wearing one of the costumes of the fantasy artists of the kind collected by young adolescents.

"Hai!" she yelled as she leaped into the simulation at the last moment brandishing twin swords and wearing nothing more than knee boots and a tiny bikini. "You'll not get by me you dastardly evil creatures! My champion and I will..."

Sesco stepped forward and smashed the Gar avatar over the head as he gaped at the beautiful girl, then Xan leaned down, grabbed him up in massive jaws, flipped him head first, and gulped him down in one bite.

Fey had no trouble killing the two dastardly beasts because they were consumed by laughter that grew when the rex couldn't get his arms up far enough to high five the ogre. Gar took it well and bought the next round as the first to die, then they headed out to find the others.

"Baby gaggle is gone," Fey said as she led them back into the restaurant. "Anybody else hungry?"

They were soon continuing their celebration and the servers had cleared the latest round of finger foods and delivered fresh mugs when the lights flickered. A few seconds later they flickered again, then went out for several seconds before the emergency lights came on.

"There's starlight on the patio," Sesco said as he led them from the large table. "I'll clear the tab in here and meet you outside."

Xan followed the rest of their number through the milling restaurant guests, many of them just starting to eat, while Sesco peeled off to catch their server and settle up. When they got outside, they quickly found two tables, one next to the rail and the other next to a wall.

"Ptero flock knocked out the relay station," Sesco said as he joined them carrying two trays covered in mugs and finger foods. "Tavern has its own generator," he said just as the lights came back on inside. "And there you are."

"Nicer out here," Lily said as they gazed at the eastern horizon lit up by scattered storm clouds and an otherwise moonlit night. "I'm staying."

"What's that?" Bekka pointed. "It's not moving the same as the wind."

Xan could see the shape as it changed its

silhouette several times. "Kind of reminds me of video of thousands of birds flying in a compact swarm, a murmuration. I can't tell how far away it is. Looks close but I thought that a minute ago."

"It's getting bigger," Tina said.

Xan looked to see how close the nearest door was then back at the undulating cloud. Seeing a server, he casually asked what direction the transformer station that was damaged was and she pointed directly at the undulating cloud.

"Main transformer is about ten klicks that way. Talk in the kitchen is that it was the biggest flock of ptero piranha ever seen. They're nasty critters with a body as big as a large housecat. A big enough flock can strip a sauro in a minute. People call them pteranha."

"Miss," Xan pointed at the slightly larger cloud, "I'm going to guess that's the flock of pteranha and it looks like it's headed directly toward us."

The server stared at the cloud for a moment, then hurried to the nearest ordering podium and talked to someone inside. Moments later an alarm went off, then another in the buildings on either side of the one they were partying at. Within moments alarms started sounding all over the northeast corner of the city.

"Gave up our big window table to come out in the fresh air and get chased back inside by flying fracking piranha," Fey muttered as they moved slowly toward the door with the rest of the patrons on the wide patio. "Sure wish I had my swords."

"They're getting closer faster now," Sesco

said. "We're not going to make it inside before they get here."

Fey solved their dilemma by grabbing all the table knives she could reach in the table next to her. In seconds, they had scattered enough to each have at least one knife then Gar turned a table over and tore all four legs off, giving Fey two of the clubs after she gave her knives away.

The crowd around them realized how fast the danger was approaching and moved with more speed and shoving. Three other patrons, a giant and two wolfen, turned to face the threat and began selecting weapons.

The pteranha came on and Xan began to feel the swarm's mind. "You feeling that, sis?"

"Yeah, constant hunger. Must be a lot of them to feel this far away."

"Not that far," Gar said as he readied his giant-sized table legs.

The alarms continued to sound their warnings and below them they could see the people of the city caught out in the open enjoying the night. Vehicles and riding mounts raced for cover, their shadows flickering and jumping in the few emergency lights. The first screams came from a distance and the second and third each closer.

"Almost there!" Tanner yelled and he and Stone formed up behind them as they backed up.

The first pteranha crashed into one of the tall windows fronting the patio, then another and another. After enough years, almost every large window in any wealthy area was bulletproof and mostly monster proof. They held up without a crack or chip as extended claws and teeth impacted at speed.

Gar and Fey stepped forward before the wave hit, swinging their clubs in patterns that pulverized every pteranha that came close. The other giant joined their line at the front while the rest of them held chairs with the legs up, over the heads of the last of the patrons trying to get in the door.

Then the full force of the swarm hit just as Bekka and Amanda went through the door and the number of pteranha slammed into them like a wave, driving them backwards and into the glass around the door.

The chair Xan was holding was being shredded as the gnawing mouths tried to reach warm flesh. He knew what to do but the minds of the pteranha were driven to the point he began to feel such an overpowering ravenous need to feed he couldn't concentrate.

Staggering and falling backwards he fumbled with the remains of the chair and pteranha latched onto his arms as he was slammed against the glass, shocked faces looking out at him from the safety of the inside.

[25] You're on your own, goodbye.

"Up you go, Xan," Gar said as he grabbed Xan's arm. "We got a breather thanks to the floor staff."

He got his feet under him and followed his friend through the door as pteranha tried to get away as fast as they had come in only moments before. When they got inside, he could plainly see the bubble of open air around the patio as their server approached.

"Are you folks okay? Oh, you're bleeding." She motioned and another server ran to get a med kit. "You're the one saw the danger first. If it hadn't been for you, we'd be knee deep in casualties."

"Why didn't you turn on whatever it is earlier?" Tanner asked in his detective's voice.

She shrugged and smiled. "Can't. It covers the whole patio a couple meters away from the windows. Turn it on with all the tables full like they were, or even just that last of you almost getting eaten, would have driven you over the rail and it's a rough fall."

"What is it?" Storm asked.

"Some sort of radiation beam that makes it feel like your skin is on fire but isn't. There's a bunch of other stuff but it's expensive to use and makes a bloody mess. This way the only ones we have to clean up are the ones that dove face first into the glass."

"Do pteranha swarm the city often?" Bekka

wondered.

"Honey, the northern edge of the most gene bombed area in the whole country besides DC is only a little more than three hundred klicks from your grampa's mountain. The military base intercepts most of the monsters coming out of the Wastes but a lot still gets through."

She threw a thumb over her shoulder at the bubble of clear space over the empty patio. "Pteranha are one of the ones the burner works on. There are other gene bombed monsters that just get mad. Here's the medic. I was told to tell you you're being comped for saving us from being bankrupted by insurance claims with an open tab for meals and drinks till midnight."

"Could I get a real mug this time," Fey complained. "With them itty bitty ones I'm already half finished before you turn around."

"They're gone," someone in the crowd said. "They were there, then they were gone."

"Probably flew back off into the prairie," the server said. "Patio will remain closed, though, there are always a few hundred that don't stay with the rest. They're the smart ones, the ones that know food that got away from the swarm will be coming out of hiding. Get more casualties after a swarm than during every time."

"Well, I'm off duty and have a family to get to. You folks have a good night and thank you again for your quick thinking and actually telling somebody."

They spent the rest of the night, till midnight, sampling some of the choices on the menu they hadn't already tried and washing them down with different craft brews. Fey found a place that was open later and they moved their celebration and barely got back to their hotel in time to shower and check out.

The van that took them home after the hotel breakfast was a quiet ride as the last full meal combined with soft, luxurious cushions inside the armored limo's soundproofed cabin caught up with them. With their regimen of grampa's Eneseye serum they were all up and eager to go by noon when they met with the techs to go over last-minute updates and walkthroughs.

"We decided to go with full enclosure but the forward window rolls down," the lead tech explained. "The forward and side windows are connected to the sensors for HUD viewing."

"What are those things on the back of the cargo bed?" Fey asked.

The tech smiled. "Remember the hotel you stayed at last night, the skin burner ray? Those are projectors the operator can activate under battle conditions to give a little more protection. They look like sauro armor plates, but they have false burner projectors inside. They're each angled just a little bit different so they can cover a hundred-degree arc behind you. If you're behind another walker, you'll be shielded inside your spiders unless you have your forward window down."

"They were always going to be part of the final package. You just weren't supposed to train already knowing that. Same as the spiked gauntlets on the forearms and the shoulder missiles, something that was always going to be on the final model, but not something you needed for basic training."

"With the add-ons, there's been an increase in stripped down mass of a hundred seventeen kilos, so that's the amount you'll subtract from what you'll be authorized to carry when you leave here."

"You each know what you want, and how much you are authorized to carry, so," he gestured toward the supply warehouse with its many attendants. "Final inspection is at eighteen hundred and curfew for the Eneseye baths has been moved up from midnight to twenty-two hundred hours to compensate for the damage done to your bodies last night."

"What damage do you…" Fey started and Tina intercepted her.

"C'mon Fey, hey Lily, let's get one of those cool plasma swords before the boys figure out what they are."

"What plasma swords?" Gar wondered.

"Code for, let's go shopping and divert the boys with something that doesn't exist except in early millennium videos."

"Oh, you mean," he struck a pose and made sound effects with his mouth.

"Yeah, c'mon, let's go get the real plasma cutters. It's on the, *each spider is required to have one*, list."

"C'mon people," Xan said, "let's fill our Spiders' holsters."

The winnowing of choices down to what each could carry ran right up to the wire with Fey almost coming to blows with the giant tech that insisted two hundred twenty kilos over the allotted weight limit was *not* just a little.

They finally got things settled and Xan assured the lead tech there would be no changes and to ignore any attempts by *anyone* to do so. Fey took her anger out on the Eneseye tech who stoically endured her complaints with minimal eye rolls.

"You'll each receive an extra kilo of Eneseye specifically designed to combat the genetic agents most prevalent in the Wastes. I've been told you'll be given another immunization when you deliver the cargo. Now lie back and relax, the bath will put you to sleep and you'll be awakened when the treatment is complete."

Xan nodded, not having anything to say, and settled back into the Eneseye tub. Seconds later the grey goo that was nanocellus sapien immortallus began to fill the tub and climb up his body. Familiar with the process he relaxed and let the Eneseye seep into his pores and do its work as he drifted asleep.

"Okay sir," the tech said as he came awake, "you may join your friends in the ready room at your leisure."

Xan sat up in the tub with the renewed vigor he always felt after a full immersion session. Looking at the clock above the door as he stepped out of the tub, he didn't waste time getting dressed and joining the others.

"There you are," Gar said with a grin. "We were getting ready to leave without you."

"Did they say why they kept you in the tub an extra hour?"

His brows creased at the worry he felt in her mind. "No, sis, didn't say anything. In fact, the lead tech was the only one in the room and all he said was I could join the rest of you now. Usually he stays long enough to give me a rundown on my readings and there's at least one other tech finishing up. I did notice the hour's difference from the schedule, but there was no one to ask about it."

Sesco hummed the music from an old twentieth century sci-fi show.

"Hey!" Fey smiled and pointed at him. "I got that!"

"Well," Tina said, "you know what to do."

Xan pursed his mouth. "We don't have time."

"And that's what he's counting on you to think," she said then turned to finish preparing for their quest as the rest of them checked their spiders.

He snorted, then turned and headed for the main office, hitting the double doors a little harder than he meant to as he walked out of the ready room … and almost ran over his grandfather.

"Looks like that extra hour added some muscle," the old man said with a grin. "I was just coming to pass on some new data and wish you all a safe journey. Shall we join the others?"

Xan almost refused to take a step till he got an explanation but calmed himself quickly when he realized how he was acting. "By all means grandfather."

Every eye went to them as they entered the ready room and the old man started talking immediately.

"I thought it proper to see you off personally this morning to thank you for what you're doing and explain some things in more detail."

He ignored Fey's mumbled 'about time' as he continued. "First, I'm sure you all are wondering about the extended period Xan spent in the Eneseye bath. Oh, and I like that name and instead of the initials. I've stolen it for my newly named Eneseye Labs where we'll test and build the next generation centaur walkers you insist on calling cyborg spiders. You'll notice the logo all over your new walkers."

"But I digress," he said at Fey's mumbled 'get on with it'. "The reason for Xan's extended immersion was to imprint a new language you'll need with the individual you'll be meeting. The rest of you were given basics, but Xan's is designed to combine with his natural abilities to give him a deeper understanding."

He gave Lily an apologetic nod. "I would have given you the same but Xan got a more advanced version of my Eneseye in the womb than yours and has a higher empathic level."

"As for the newly upgraded walkers. They have improvements and additions to resolving the single instance of an operator revealing a design flaw that could have jeopardized the mission."

He turned and bowed toward Fey. "Thank you, Miss Stratus. Your efforts have made your mount worthy of your own exceptional abilities."

Xan and Tina smiled at the tactic as Fey stopped grumbling about everything and stood proud. "You're welcome, sir."

"There are other things you didn't train with

because we wanted you to learn with the bare minimum above the walkers themselves. You've already experienced the effectiveness of the false burner beam at your going away party. There are some other additions whose codes and operating parameters were given to you at the same time as the language basics. Opening those new icons on your screens will activate the memories as you perform the set-up sequences."

"Now, the purpose of your mission." He hesitated in a way the siblings were familiar with. "There's an individual within the mountains above Denver that is one of my oldest friends. He has dedicated years of his life to repairing the damage done by the Orbitals' gene bombs on the region, but it's time to go home while he is able."

"Your mission is simple. Go to the location marked on your walkers' maps, find my friend, and deliver the six cargo packages to him and assist in their installation. Once you've done that your mission will be completed and you'll be free to do as you please."

"As compensation for your efforts, upon completion of the mission, ownership of each of the walkers you use will automatically transfer to each of you. That was in the many papers you signed, finish the mission and you own your walker."

"What if we fail?" Sesco asked when the old man took another pause for effect.

"That's also in the papers you signed. If you fail, and live, you'll simply be required to return my property in person to receive the amount of monetary compensation your efforts accrue."

"You have special communications tech in your walkers which includes satellite links, but their use comes with more danger than benefit in some ways. For that reason, you'll *not* be in contact with this facility until after your mission is completed or failure is assured."

He smiled at his two grandchildren, then the others. "I would like to thank you again for taking on this quest and I hope I've done right by you in making sure you all live to see it finished. Your path is mapped to take you out into the prairie south of the city and around to the military base for a final shakedown run."

"There you'll meet the techs that have worked so hard to build and grow your walkers and they'll stand behind you and watch over your shoulders as you fix what the day's activities damaged. Don't worry about all the walkers you'll see while there, the military has ordered a hundred and already have more walking than your numbers and have been in training for a week. After you've repaired the damage done to your own walkers, you'll assist the techs as they work on the military's assets."

"That's all I have. Again, I thank you for taking on this mission and assure you it's of extreme importance to the world but must remain secret till its completion. At that point, success or fail, it will be made public."

"I took your preferences in mind in naming your walkers using the Native words. The resident A.I.s will introduce themselves when you activate them."

"Now, I'm sorry to have to rush you, but the sun is coming up and you have one day to break in your upgraded walkers, perform a last training and maintenance exercise, then begin the dangerous part of your mission. Again, thank you for what you are doing and good luck."

With that he simply turned and exited the ready room.

[26] "I got bitey-slashies on my back!"

"Sometimes he makes me so mad I could," Xan took a deep breath. "Well, like the man said, sun's coming up."

"I miss the puppies already," Fey said as they turned back to their cyborg mounts.

"Me too," Gar said, "but they would be dead by the second day at the most and there's no sense taking them if we have to lock them in a carrier the whole way."

They headed for their respective spiders, Xan admiring the new look of the cyborgs as he climbed into his. The solar leaves had changed to the color of the granite blocks that formed the walls of the large ready room, but there was enough of the woody color of the muscles to see the outline of each spider.

The black carbon fiber skeleton was hidden within the wrapping of planimal muscles and tendons with the thick layers of chameleon leaves forming a skin. From a distance and unmoving, they would almost be hidden from sight.

Xan grabbed the bar at the top of the open door, twisted, and slid backwards into the VR pod. He held his hand over the touch screen. "Hello Iktomi. Are you ready to go on a quest?"

"Hello, Xan. Yes. Enter your command password and we'll get started."

He tapped his initiation code into the control

panel and the VR pod's systems began to come online. Another tap and the onboard computer connected to its biological components and the spider stood.

He was across from Lily and she smiled at him as they closed their forward doors. As soon as his locked, Xan lowered the front window as he engaged the bottom half of the VR pod. Leaning back against the spine of the control pod he slid his hands into the arm sleeves and looked at the retinal reader above the two rows of video screens and gave his name and the activation code.

"Engage the arms, please, Iktomi," he said and the cyborg's arms moved to match the position of his. He looked to the sides, the viewpoint coming from the sensor bar above the shoulders showing on the screens as the side window HUDs activated.

Watching the screens, he lifted his arm and the spider lifted its hand, matched his motion as he extended a finger, and touched the button on the side of the large room. The armored door began to roll up and expose the open patio of the main campus of his grandfather's newly named Eneseye Labs. As they walked out of the ready room into the open, he saw several people smiling and looking proud of their accomplishment. Many of them waved, clapped, and cheered as Xan led his sister and four friends off the grounds at a trot toward the trail indicated by the map on his main panel.

Within moments he was jogging inside the grip of the cyborg's VR pod, his arms swinging exactly like they did when he jogged without the pod around him. He ran with a gait that was slow enough for the size of the trail he took, then he speeded up when they came out of the woods and into more open hillside.

"Doesn't feel any different," Gar's voice came through the speaker ring around the inside of the pod instead of from the screen with his friend's face.

The A.I., now named Iktomi after a mythical spider god, adjusted the volume to simulate the distance relatively. The spiders were much larger and the distance greater, but Iktomi made it sound like they were in formation without the walkers and physically closer.

"I can feel a little more resistance in my legs," Lily said, her voice much louder with her position next in line behind him. "Like when I haven't run in a while and my muscles are a little stiff."

"Same here," Fey called out from her number five position in front of Gar. "I thought it was because of the Eneseye bath and my legs were just tight. First time I ever had one of those and ain't never slept so good in all my life."

They weaved their way through the mountains and across the grassways that crisscrossed the region where roads used to lead to old tourist destinations. Although they barely trotted inside the pods, the spiders' longer legs covered greater distances with each step and a corresponding increase in speed.

Some of the trails they took were public and twice they were forced to walk where they passed another group of travelers going the other way.

When they were past the other group, they resumed their faster pace, but still slow enough to not run over other travelers.

They ran past a mountaintop carved with four heads, the left ear and cheek of one lying in pieces at the bottom of the cliff, a victim of a different kind of intolerance. Their path took them off the normal trails through the wooded hillsides then followed the grassway by another mountain sculpture of a Native atop a horse.

At various parts of their run they passed dozens of people on single rider mounts, dino carts and wagons, and armed and armored quads, trucks, and camper vans as they trotted their cyborg spiders along the grassways across the Hills and by Hot Springs.

"I hear that's where your grampa got some of the DNA to make Elly," Sesco said from his number four position behind Tina. "Used to be some sort of public excavation around an old sinkhole where they found all sorts of critters' bones."

Xan led them out of the Hills proper and into the edge of the repopulated territory, then past the last of the isolated compounds and into the wild prairie.

"So, we're supposed to go looking for a fight," Fey said as they spread out and began their sweep in a wide loop around south for several klicks before heading west toward the base.

"Not exactly *looking*," Xan laughed. "More like *instigating*, and the more belligerent our mark the better. What the techs want is for us to do the same kind of reckless stuff we've been pushed to do all through our training to see how much damage we can do."

"Then tonight when we get to the base, we get to service our own spiders while soldiers watch. After that we get to fix the ones the Army is tearing up for more practice and to help train them."

Once out in the open prairie they maintained a steady pace of 60kph as they continued their wide loop in a scattered formation of three teams. They were only a few degrees from heading due west when dark shapes appeared on the horizon.

"Bison ahead," Lily called out first. "A couple hundred and running this way."

The six, level three A.I.s examined the data from the shoulder-top sensor packs and put it on their main screens for the operators to see. Lines of identification readings appeared in front of the herd of approaching bison, including mass estimations of individual animals and the speed and diminishing time of intercept with the forward ranks.

"Two minutes people," Xan said as he scanned his screens. "Close windows, spread out in teams, and pick a fight."

"I have rex on the left side," Gar reported just as their screens linked with his sensors and updated information silhouettes where the rexes were driving the herd and looking for one of the bison to make a mistake.

Before Xan could give an order, Fey reported from their opposite flank. "Four rex dead ahead. Namid identifies them as dragon rex."

The data scrolled on Xan's screens as they

continued their run, then on his forward window HUD. "I read seven rex. One for each of us and a spare for whoever gets lucky. Pick your partner and let's dance."

He changed his angle to the side with Lily in Anansi as the others spread out to intercept the hunting rex on his left with his sister's team on the right.

"Are we supposed to kill them quick or let 'em get in a few licks first?" Fey asked as the distance closed quickly.

"Your choice as long as it's hand to hand, tooth, whatever," Xan said as he chose his opponent. "No long-range or power weapons, we're supposed to do a hard test so we have heavy damage to repair ourselves."

With Iktomi's IDing of the target, automatic systems cycled and the claws in the fingertips extended to the length that would do the worst damage to the enhanced armor of the gene hacked monster.

The rexes took the moves of the strange spiders as a challenge to their territorial rights, which for dragon rexes was wherever they wanted to be and abandoned their hunt of the bison. To them, the meat of a vanquished foe was just as nourishing as that of frightened food.

"We drew the lucky straw, Xan," Lily said as they ran at the armored monsters, "and got the odd man out."

"I read a large raptor pack coming in behind the rex," Gar reported from Misae. "Wait, refreshing. Twelve, now nineteen, now twenty-three confirmed allo and more coming from a southwest direction."

There was no time to reply as Xan ran the last few steps to the dragon rex he'd chosen and made fists with both hands. Controlled automatically by the A.I., the blades that were the claws at his fingertips retracted so they wouldn't puncture the cyborg's palms and short spikes extended from the knuckles.

He ran head on into the rex, the armored front of his spider impacting the monster's hip with a glancing blow when the rex spun with unexpected speed. His left-handed swing connected as he spun with the rex and left four puncture marks in the beast's side armor.

The two spun in a circle and the rex lunged and barely missed as he pulled his hand back. He finished the motion, cocking his arm back and extended his fingers while using his other hand to slap the beast on the snout.

When the rex snapped at his cyborg's distracting hand, he jammed the rigidly locked fingers of his left hand into the least protected part of the throat. Programmed to aid his operator, Iktomi spiked the fingertip claws to their full extension at the right time and the strength of the blow buried the cyborg's meter-long fingers up to the knuckles.

He hooked his fingers and yanked his arm back inside the control pod and the cyborg ripped half the dragon rex's throat out along with the carotid artery. Blood fountained as the rex gurgled a scream.

Doing the hop-kick he'd found worked best for him in close quarters, he could feel the impact as the nearside leg snapped in the weakest spot just above the rex's ankle. The rex gurgled another scream and fell toward him and into a solid right-handed punch to the side of the skull.

Continuing to do its job as a fighting partner, Iktomi activated the false burners in the rear when the third rex came after him from behind. He saw the sneak attack in his screens as the rex flinched and recoiled reflexively from the feeling of fire, but was still as busy with his first target as Lily was with hers several meters away.

"Got more fracking weapons than an attack copter," Fey's voice came through the surround sound speakers from her direction as she and Gar fought their targets.

He punched the rex twice more in as many seconds as the young giant continued ranting, "But no-o-o-o, don't kill gene hacked monsters the smart way from a distance he says." A fierce roar echoed through the speakers that turned into an equally loud cry of pain. "Hand to tooth combat to test cyborg limits he says. It'll be fun."

The rex he was hammering with his knuckle spikes finally fell, the side of its head crushed in by the jackhammer blows with spikes punching holes in the skull.

Spinning to face the last rex that had hesitated twice to rush into the unfamiliar pain of the false burners, Xan hopped and kicked just as the burning stopped when he turned and it rushed him. The spiders were big, with long legs and even though he didn't jump high in relation to his spider's height, that was still high enough to kick the rex in the chin as it lunged forward with its greatest weapon and tried to latch onto its prey with a mouth big enough to swallow Gar in a single bite.

Three of the five toes, with claws a half meter long, caught the rex under the lower jaw and buried themselves into soft flesh. He extended his leg as he came back down and the weight of the cyborg with its foot buried in the throat of the beast slammed it face first into the ground at his feet.

Xan drew his hand back to begin hammering at the rex as it fell but the neck snapped with a loud crack when it hit and the body almost flipped from its inertia.

Pushing the twitching carcass away, he spun his spider around to see where he was needed next as the others finished their battles and began to form a defensive ring. Around them the growing pack of allo converged on dead meat and the winners of the most recent evolutionary test.

"Wakanda is updating the ID again," Sesco said as Xan's HUD caught up to his friend's upgrade as the monsters approached. "It looks like we get to name a new allo species kids. Who wants to bet they didn't come out of the Wastes?"

"Hey boss," Fey called out as her spider's hands flexed above her favorite weapons, broadswords with blades three meters long. "Namid counts eighty-seven. We still on hand to hand?"

"Nope! We did our specified test with about the best adversaries we could face and got squat for damage. We'll practice maintenance on the damage done to the Army's spiders tonight."

"This pack would have worked its way around the base of the Hills to Rapid City by tonight or tomorrow. Armory is open. Let's thin them out to make it easier for the pest control people in the big city."

He spoke the code words and Iktomi unlocked his weapons and tools and the doors to the props arrayed around his control panel opened. He plunged his hands into two of the holsters in front of him to pull out the props for a grenade launcher with the left hand and a fifty-caliber pistol in the right.

There was a concentration of the new allo in front of him and he put two grenades in the middle of the group. When he'd loaded his magazines, he'd alternated between fragmentation and thermal grenades and his double shot put one of each in between five gene bombed monsters. When the fireball and smoke cleared only two of the mega raptors were dead.

"Thermal grenades have minimal effect, frag grenades moderate in a tight crowd," he reported aloud knowing Iktomi would share his voice over the community channel.

He raised the 50cal prop, aimed using his HUD, and pulled the trigger. The cyborg aimed the actual weapon and put three armor piercing rounds through the skulls of the allo that survived his first preemptive attack. Shifting his aim while he put the grenade launcher back in its holster, he put rounds through the skull or heart of four more allo.

Selecting targets in accordance to directions

from Iktome, he fired at the swift allo as they attacked, but there were too many. In seconds, he had three allo on him, biting and slashing with their razor-sharp hand and foot claws.

The spiders were built tough and had protections a normal living creature didn't, but yellow caution lights began to flicker as the allo damaged the cyborg body.

With his free left hand, he grabbed one allo and ripped it away from Iktomi's body and used it to beat another to a pulp. While bashing the two allo together he backhanded the third one with his gun hand, then shot it in the face when it jumped up to renew its attack.

The allo hadn't been idle and even though shedding himself of attackers only took a couple seconds, that was all it took for more of the vicious carnies to converge on their new prey. They couldn't know the giant deformed spiders were mostly metal, ceramics, and plants. All they knew was the spiders looked, and covered in rex blood, smelled like food.

The plant muscles and solar vine skin wasn't like other plants either. Modern genetic science had created a plant that had carbon fiber tendrils running through it like a layer of armor.

The skin and muscle vines were the strongest material that could be grown in a lab, but the allo were also beneficiaries of modern science. Xan swung with both hands, using the immense pistol as a club and shooting without hesitation the allo Iktomi highlighted in his HUD.

"Fracking false burner isn't working!" Fey

yelled. "I got bitey-slashies on my back!"

Xan didn't bother to answer as he swatted at and shot the allo he could reach, then shifted to cover his teammate on his right. Iktomi and Anansi linked and his targeting highlights shifted to add the area behind Lily. Three more allo died and he shoved the pistol in its holster when the *empty* icon appeared in his HUD. While the automatic re-loader fed a belt of ammo into the magazine box, he pulled the Gatling from its holster and sprayed the area around Anansi's cargo bed.

The Gatling rounds weren't as big as the 50cal, but there were a lot more being fired and they were all armor piercing.

Lily had been doing the same from her side and his screen showed pieces-parts of allo flying every which way as he pounded another monster to death with the one in Iktomi's left hand.

His Gatling flashed empty and he shoved it back in its holster and was reaching for the reloaded pistol when he realized there were no more flashing targets on his screen or the HUD.

"Well that was a fun party," Fey said and he turned to see her surrounded by dead allo, a three-meter sword in one hand and a Gatling in the other. "Do we have time to collect a few trophies before we head for the base and have a beer or three?"

[27] A rain of rocks.

Angostura Army Base's communications tower came into sight as they ran, their spiders covered in the blood and gore from rex and allo as well as the pteranha that swarmed them as they came into sight of the base.

"Told you," Fey laughed as she swung her sword and chopped three pteranha in half when they came at her from the front.

"Doesn't matter, girlfriend," Lily laughed back as she bisected another of the swarming aerial carnies, adding in a theatrical voice. "Teeth and claws are money in the bank when you're out of silver and when it gives itself to me, I takes it."

Xan sliced at his own attackers as they ran for the base's wall with its ring of false burner cannon. He watched the three red signals on his panel closely but their damage didn't seem to be affecting Iktomi's performance.

"Birds are starting to peel away," Gar said as they came closer to the base's three-kilometer long South Wall and the guards targeted the higher portion of the swarm.

Xan killed two more before the attackers lifted and shifted en masse away from the burning sensation. When they reached the gate, they waited patiently as the guards inspected their credentials while another team washed most of the blood off them and their trophies.

"Don't appreciate you bringing that swarm down on us," the base commander grumbled. "Then you insist on bringing your trophies inside where fracking gene bombed monsters from the Wastes are sure to smell them."

"Getting worse, isn't it?" Xan said as he ignored the complaint. Everyone knew the teeth and claws of the worst monsters were almost as valuable as silver by weight in the new world.

"Seems like every day there's something new and they don't get any easier to kill. Lots more of them, too. Almost like they're breeding faster than they should and spreading out into new territory. If what we have to deal with are the losers, you folks are in for a rough hike."

Xan pursed his lips and nodded in agreement. "Or they're the next generation expanding to new territory, but these cyborg spiders are an equalizer."

"Seem kind of fragile to me," the general said. "Lot of maintenance costs. Not as much as an old jet or even the new attack copters, but quite a bit and funds are scarce even though the Wastes are a bigger threat than other countries."

"It'll get better now the first week of your training is over," Xan confided. "At least it did with the six of us. Parts that rebuild themselves only cost once instead of over and over, and the nanite repair solution is easy to refresh from everyday ingredients."

"Speaking of which I have to get to Iktomi and swap out a few muscles and restock ammo."

The general waved him on and went back to his own duties of running the military presence closest to the gene bombed wasteland that surrounded the Denver metropolis, south to the Air Force Academy, and deep into the mountains.

Minutes later he was using the tools taken from the storage bins in the spider's body and replacing one of the calf muscle vines on Iktomi's right rear leg.

"Okay," he said to the training inspector looking over his shoulder, "you push the root hairs of the other muscles out of the way by tugging them loose close to their contact point, they'll reconnect around the new vine when you're finished. Now you brush away all the stuff stuck to the bone, even the tops of the tendons and nutrient vines. They're tough, they can take it and it'll give the new muscle a clean surface to attach its gripper roots onto."

"Blow the dust out and shove the end of the new muscle in with the root hairs into that shaped depression and hold it down for a few seconds … nine, ten, okay, that should be enough."

He reached for a special tool as he continued performing for the inspector and a couple of soldiers. "Move the spreader down the length of the calf and press the line of hairs to the bone, clean the lower end, and press the end pad into its depression, press and hold, count to ten… and you're done."

"Pull the spreader out and put the damaged muscle vine in the nutrient solution you took the replacement out of, top it off with fresh goop, and stow it in your parts bin. That one wasn't too bad. It will be fully integrated almost immediately. This next one is worse but the replacement will integrate just as quickly while the two ends of the damaged part will grow back together in the repair tube within hours."

When they were finished changing out their damaged parts the base gave them new parts for their damaged ones and refreshed their nutrient goop bags. The rest of the day they spent working with the military on their spiders while sharing their own training experiences.

"You actually broke one?" one of the corporals asked once they'd finished servicing their spiders. "How did you manage that?"

"Remember," Sesco answered before the preening young giant could, "that was before the bone pads covering the muscles underneath were thickened and the expanders put in the leg muscle and tendon vines."

"Besides that, the A.I. was reprogrammed," Xan said. "Before, when you kicked with one leg, all three corresponding legs on the spider kicked. Now the A.I. follows your eyes and recognizes what leg you intend to kick with and only kicks that one. It can also kick with two specific legs or all three on one side as determined by the threat. It can also kick autonomously when an attacker comes at the spider from a direction the operator isn't looking. There are other programs that give the A.I. temporary control under certain emergency conditions."

"What do you like best, energy weapons or slug throwers?" another asked.

"Swords!" Fey replied before anyone else could. "You can *feel* the battle through your spider's VR pod's sensors and they don't run out of energy or ammo. Plasma swords are next, but the blades are shorter."

"How in the frack does that work, anyway?" yet another soldier asked to get all the intel they could from the people with the most experience with their new special forces mounts.

Fey shrugged. "Same way as any tech-based VR pod. And while wearing decent clothes instead of those body suit things that are worse than being nekkid," she added with a laugh. "I mean, what's the point in that kind of teasing? If you're going to get nekkid, then get nekkid."

The party lasted till midnight when the special forces commander made a noisy show of going to bed and the next morning they were all again in the large maintenance hangar after a large breakfast when the sun cracked the horizon.

"Okay, saddle up!" Xan yelled.

He checked a last few cargo bins then stepped up onto Iktomi's forward section, grabbed the bar above the forward hatch, and pulled himself inside. Startup took seconds and he was standing and moving around to settle into the VR pod as the A.I. ran through a systems check.

Around him all the other spiders did the same little shakeout dance as the cyborgs copied their operators' moves. He smiled as he remembered one of the soldiers showing him a video clip of the dance put to music.

Xan led them out of the hangar, Lily at his side and within moments they were running at 60kph long before the three klicks long South Wall of Angostura Army Base was out of sight. Cutting a little west of due south, they ran up and down the low hills of the prairie and around large herds of dinos for an hour till they caught the old state Rt20 grassway where the running surface was smoother.

Picking up their pace to seventy, they ran another few klicks, then left the grassway at Van Tassell and went cross-country again, cutting their speed for the rougher terrain. An hour later they reduced their speed again when they came to the corrugated landscape southeast of Glendo Reservoir and across Middle Bear Creek.

When they walked their spiders onto the old I-25 grassway, they turned left and headed south toward Cheyanne at a steady 60kph because they were in no hurry.

"Hope they have a decent night life," Fey said as they entered Cheyanne's outer burbs. "I got one more night before things get serious and I ain't wasting it."

"We might want to be careful," Tina said. "I'm getting more hostile vibes than not."

"We have reservations in the Little America Resort next to the grassway south of the airport," Xan said. "They have a good rep and screen the gate for known troublemakers."

They found the place easily and were soon inside and getting ready for the night long before sunset.

"Initiate shut down protocols with Class Five Security, please, Iktomi."

"Acknowledged, Xan, shut down with C5S commencing."

He shut down his VR pod, climbed up and out, and hopped down to the ground as Iktomi shut the forward hatch and settled into a ready standby mode.

"Nice view," Lily said as she looked at the mountains rising to the west and south as the sun neared their peaks. Then she smiled at him. "I get the shower first."

"As long as you don't use all the hot water," Xan said as he pulled out his overnight bag and followed her into the building.

A five-story tower with four suites on each floor, it was one of a row of ten lining the eastern shore of the resort's flood pond. After a large meal and a leisurely walk through the complex, he was sitting with Lily, Tina, and Sesco on the rooftop patio with a cooler full of ale when they saw Gar and Fey heading toward the main buildings and the resort's entertainment areas.

"Sure hope they don't leave the complex," Xan said. "I haven't felt that much animosity directed toward us at any time since Bridgetown."

"They'll be fine," Tina said. "I haven't felt anything close to that since we got on this side of town. I think that's why grampa made reservations for us here, most of the staff is augmented."

"Good morning, Iktomi," he said as he looked directly at the spider logo above the hatch. "Open the hatch, please."

Iktomi's A.I. verified his retinal signature, three frequencies of face recognition, and voice patterns and the door popped and rose slowly. "Good morning, Xan. Welcome aboard."

In seconds, he was in his VR pod and the hatch was closing as he activated his cyborg's systems. "Okay people, when we get out on the grassway let's take it up to 100kph once we're on the grassway. We have a lot of distance to travel and I want to get to our rendezvous as quick as possible."

There were a couple of mumbled replies and one raspberry as the others settled into their control pods and followed him toward Little America's East Gate. The attendant checked their accounts, then let them out and in moments they were headed south toward the most dangerous wasteland in America west of the Missip. It didn't take long before they were coming up to where the open prairie turned into city.

Just before the Gene Wars, when Denver and Denver Station were still getting along, the entire Denver region benefitted from continued prosperity and expansion. The Denver Megalopolis was one of the richest places on Earth and began to build up as a way of showing that wealth.

The outer layers were just getting started when the world ended, first with the release of many of the initial gene-hacked dinos, then with the Orbitals declaring Independence and the first interplanetary war.

As they ran closer Xan could see the line where buildings suddenly appeared. Much of the grasslands in front of that line were covered in the many kinds of animals that covered the rest of the American Plains, with obvious differences.

Few of the tall buildings on the edge of the Wastes were finished, many of them nothing more than steel and molded carbon fiber skeletons. Each block inward was another level of completion as if the resident oligarchs were in denial their age of prosperity was over and they were expanding at their normal rate regardless of the facts around them.

When the gene bombs fell, everything stopped and the dying began. But one of the benefits of the new orbital technology and fabrication was the almost indestructible construction materials they had access to. Add that to the fact gene bombs didn't destroy infrastructure, and the buildings were mostly undamaged.

The cityscape they approached was still intact, just infested with monsters continuously evolving at an accelerated rate. Many of those monsters used to be human.

"Reduce speed to 60kph, close windows, and arm yourselves, people," Xan said as he drew a Gatling with his right hand and a bladed plasma cutter with the other.

Construction on the expanding megalopolis had continued all the way up to the first exchanges of hostilities and a wide swath of the prairie north of Denver had already been cleared for the next block of buildings. The creatures that had taken over continued to graze the flattened area and kept it and the wide streets between the buildings mostly clear of trees, giving them an unobstructed view in almost every direction.

"Reduce speed to 50kph and activate false burners and sonics," Xan said when they got within five hundred meters of the edge of the largest gathering of grazers at the boundary of the border grasslands.

In seconds, they were within range of the forward sonic projectors and some of the animals in front of them moved out of their way. Some slower than others because their particular genetic augmentation wasn't affected by sonics. Those moved only because the animals around them did, but they did move by the time the six cyborg spiders got to the edge of the grass border around the city.

"We have roc circling above us," Sesco informed them as they ran between the skeletons of buildings only started when the end of the world came.

"Don't look anything like the ones we faced in Toledo," Gar said.

"Roc is just a name for all the different giant birds," the Librarian informed them. "Like raptor or rex, there are different kinds of roc. The ones in Toledo were a combination of eagles and parrots. These look more like bat-winged vultures."

A large rock impacted the ground close to Xan, then another and another along their double line before one smashed into the cargo container on Tina's spider.

"Frackers are bombing us!" Fey said indignantly as she raised her fifty-caliber pistol and began shooting.

The vulture roc were well above the tops of the building skeletons around them and hard to hit, but she did get one and it spiraled downward. The attack from above faltered a moment, then another round of large stones fell around and on them, several hitting their cyborgs.

One particularly large boulder smashed into the left shoulder of Xan's cyborg and several amber and red lights flashed on his panel.

"Their aim is getting better," Tina said.

"Evade, evade!" Xan said at the same time.

They abandoned their compact formation and spread out with each of them jinking left and right and running faster.

"Status report, Iktomi."

"Minimal damage to main sensors, two cameras on the left shoulder inoperative. Redundant systems are able to cover the areas affected for all but the upward lenses. Spares are in the supply trays and will require a stop to change out."

"Look out, Sesco!" Gar yelled just as a massive grizzly almost as large as their cyborgs surged out of the building to his right.

Focused on the vultures and their evasive running they had missed the gaping hole where windows used to be in the building and hadn't noticed the gene mutated bear. It clamped jaws longer than a giant is tall on the cyborg's forearm and tore it off at the elbow. In a motion seemingly too fast for a creature that size, it swung a huge right paw and smashed it into the window of the forward hatch and the armored glass cracked.

[28] "I see you little morsels."

Fey didn't hesitate to blast away with her fifty-caliber pistol as she had the best angle, but the rounds didn't seem to affect the enraged animal.

Lily spun a hundred eighty and plunged the plasma cutter in Anansi's right hand into the grizzly's arm as it drew back for another swing. The hot plasma created a tunnel of exploding air, meat, and bodily fluids instantly turned to steam. A flick of her wrist separated the bear's arm in the same place as the cyborg arm in its mouth.

The grizzly dropped the cyborg's forearm when it screamed in pain and rage. Both forearms fell on the front of Sesco's spider as he walked Wakanda backwards, beating on the bear's head with the stump of the cyborg's right arm. One spider step back and he had the angle to add the Gatling in his left hand to the firepower now pouring into the grizzly. The gene bombs had done their job of accelerated evolution well and the thick fur absorbed every bullet that hit.

Lily's plasma cutter did more damage than the slug throwers as she stabbed the bear repeatedly. The smell of burnt hair and meat being transferred inside the VR pod by her A.I., Anansi, let her know the strikes were making it through the thick fur armor.

More boulders fell around them as the vultures continued their own attack on the intruders into their territory. With them not moving erratically, more of the dropped stones found their target.

Lily finally got her opening as the bear turned to flee and swung downward with all the strength of her cyborg. The plasma cutter encountered a little resistance when it connected with so much of the thick fur, but she continued to bear down on the blade. The head leapt free of the body, propelled by the force of the meat and fluids being instantly turned to steam.

Dozens of heavy boulders began to rain down around them as the vultures increased their attack.

"Inside the building!" Xan said as he raised his Gatling toward the sky and held the trigger down.

The mutated grizzly was almost as large as their cyborgs and they had no trouble getting through the maw of the shattered windows fronting the main lobby.

Xan continued to fire upwards as the others went through one at a time. Since the vultures were still too high for the false burner to reach, he pulled his heavy laser and waved it overhead as he holstered his empty Gatling and pulled the 50cal. The others were also spraying death upwards and vultures began to fall as the rain of stones diminished.

Stepping through the frame of the street-side wall, Xan admired the opulence of the immense lobby. The almost indestructible sign above the front desk identified this as a luxury hotel before the end of the world. A wide curved staircase wrapped around the side with a large landing in front of the second-floor level before continuing up to the wide balcony on the third floor.

Elevator doors lined both sides of the two hallways flanking the main desk below the hotel name. The third-floor balcony rail was as enduring as anything else imported from space and showed little decay to the etched glass wall that allowed guests to see the lobby and still be safe from falling.

Peeking through the glass of the rail, Xan counted three cubs watching the intruders just as his sister said, "We're not alone."

"Vultures are landing," Gar said. "You're closest to their only way in, Xan."

"On it," he said as he turned a one eighty, drawing a plasma cutter and shotgun as he stepped forward enough his shoulder mounted sensor bar was outside the window frame.

The vultures knew the smell of death and were beginning to land around the headless carcass of the grizzly. Mutated by the gene bombs, the roc were as large as anything could be and fly.

Where the grizzly had developed a fur so thick and tough it stopped armor piercing rounds, the vultures had lost feathers to shed weight. The wings were bare and looked more like those of a bat, or a mythical dragon. The head was huge with a beak over half a meter long. Despite the toughness of the bear's fur, the vultures didn't have any trouble burrowing through to start shredding the skin where Lily's plasma blade had cut to get at the tender meat.

The window frame was recessed enough none of the still airborne vultures could drop rocks on him but two couldn't resist hopping his direction. The sound of his shotgun made several of the nearest vultures scatter a few steps away then return to their prize. Several others didn't hesitate to begin feeding on the easier to get to bodies of their kin.

"We're not going to get out this way for a while unless we want to use up a lot of ammo," he said as he shot another overly curious vulture.

"What are we going to do about the cubs?" Fey asked through their common link. "They'll grow up to be as dangerous as momma bear."

"You're not suggesting we kill babies, are you?" Tina said behind him as he shot another vulture.

"Yes, I am," Fey replied without hesitation. "They may be babies now, but they're baby *monsters*. You saw what momma did to Sesco's Wakanda. Imagine what three could do to some citizen's armored bus or an outlying family compound."

"I hate to say it, but she's right," Sesco said. "There's been an exodus of monsters out of the Wastes lately. This little family is close enough to the edge it's likely the cubs would have moved out within a year to seek new territory."

Xan shot two more vultures. "Might not have to. If we can get out of here the vultures might take care of the problem for us."

"Looks like the bear made a back door this way," Lily said. "I see another hole in the wall across the room. Might be a different path momma bear opened for hunting."

"Well, if it doesn't, we can always blow something up," Gar said. "Who goes first?"

"Sis, you take the lead since you're the better empath and can detect any ambush. I'll take the rear after I draw the vultures in."

He ran out of the window frame he was protecting, chasing several vultures away from the closest two he'd killed as he holstered his weapons. Grabbing the dead vultures, he dragged them back to the window and dropped one on the edge so it was visible from the street. Stepping inside the building he threw the other into the middle of the lobby floor before running through the bear escape route.

The next room wasn't as large as the lobby, only two stories high, with the shattered remains of tables and chairs scattered about. There was noise behind him as he went through the second bear widened door, wondering if he'd done the right thing.

The death the cubs faced was more terrible than a plasma cutter beheading, but there was a chance they would survive. If any of the three cubs survived, they might leave the Wastes and kill humans in the future. If that happened, it would be his fault.

He couldn't take back his choice to let monsters deal with monsters, then wondered where he sat in that equation. When he went through the fourth door, he found the rest of the team gathered inside another building's lobby facing a different street.

"Hey boss, can we stop long enough for me to get the claws and teeth out of our trophy?"

"What the hell, Fey," Xan laughed. "You took the time to collect *trophies*?"

"Didn't take any time at all," the young giant replied from inside Namid's protection. "The arm fell in Sesco's lap and the head was between me and the window."

"Give me a few more minutes and I can throw most of this away." The cyborg, Namid gestured toward the head and arm on its forward lap.

"What about my window?" Sesco asked. "The missing arm I can deal with, but an open window is a little more than I like."

"We have three replacement windows," Xan said. "Tina, you and Lily did the quickest team change-out when we practiced it. Find a corner and get it done while Fey does her thing. The rest of us are on guard."

He turned to face their back trail with a shotgun in one of Iktomi's hands and a plasma sword in the other. "Iktomi, could you give me a new plot, please?"

"Of course, Xan," the A.I. replied as it displayed a map of the area on his forward window's HUD. "Our best projected time of arrival is being delayed by the length of our stop." The TOA timeclock icon flashed as the A.I. continued, "Four blocks from our current position will take us back to our original route. Or we can parallel it for seven or eight blocks. The parallel route is different only in street width but the buildings are shorter."

Xan studied the map for a few moments. "What about the collapsed building at the four-block junction?"

"That building was undermined from within," Iktomi said. "Satellite pictures show a species of ant or termite inhabiting the ruins. They seem to be more active at night so our daytime passage should be safe."

"Should be?"

"The hive does send scouts out a block or two in every direction, but migrating and grazing animals don't seem to be bothered. The scouts are frequently seen in close proximity to other animals without the reactions normally seen between prey and predator."

"Uh, hey boss," Fey interrupted. "What do I do?"

Xan turned his sensors her way as he watched their back trail for danger... and saw a wounded grizzly bear cub sniffing at the remains of its mother. Before he could think of anything to say, the giant inside the spider leaned Namid down and scooped up the injured animal in gentle cyborg hands. "Oh, poor baby, you're all bloody."

She set the injured bear cub onto Namid's lap, where the arm and head had rested earlier while she cut out the claws and teeth. The cub sniffed, cried a little, then settled down and almost immediately fell asleep.

"Oh shit, boss! *Now* what do I do?"

Xan froze. What *did* she do? What did *he* do? "Uh, Gar knows how to train hellhounds.

Maybe he has some ideas."

"Thanks, buddy! And unless you've forgotten, most of the training comes from those Eneseye critters your grandfather grows. Cute cuddly monster grizzly baby there doesn't have any lab grown domesticators."

"Wait a minute, Gar. What about the special med kits we all have in our supply cabinets? Iktomi, can any of the nanite injection packets be altered to domesticate the specimen currently sleeping on Namid's forward hips?"

"Yes. There is a special injection administered in conjunction with a class five nanite infusion. The procedure can be adjusted to make the cub imprint on Namid as a surrogate mother with Fey as a smaller sibling."

"You can do that?" Fey sounded indignant.

"You love Fred and Ginger, don't you?" Gar said. "It's the same stuff they got."

"Fred and Ginger got theirs in the womb," Xan reminded his friend. "Namid can monitor the brain scans of the cub as it grows and better adjust the training parameters with subsequent injections."

He turned Iktomi to face Namid. "You have two choices. Adopt this Waste mutated monster, train her, and be responsible for her actions as an adult in your care… or kill her now."

He watched the screen linked to her cyborg's VR pod as several emotions washed across her face. "Gods, Boss! What kind of choice is that? Who but a monster would hurt a sweet little baby like this one?"

Xan tried to not be surprised by the scene

through his forward window as Namid's massive steel, carbon fiber, and biologically muscled arms and hands made a gentle gesture of protection around the sleeping cub in the cyborg's lap.

He smiled as Gar's Misae hovered over the pair, wielding a vibro-broadsword in one hand and a shotgun in the right hand. "Sesco, how're the repairs coming along?"

"Another five minutes to finish replacing the hatch window. The arm is down till we can get to a machine shop. What we can do with a few extra minutes is bolt a sword, plasma cutter, or laser on the stub. At least then it won't be a handicap."

"Good idea," he said as he glanced at Iktomi's time-line on his window HUD. "Take the time to do it right. Can you hook up a fuel feed so a plasma cutter has more operating time?"

"Might take a couple more minutes with another set of hands. Can you watch the doors?"

Xan snorted a laugh. "Gar, you and Fey help him with the arm, please. Do your best with five minutes."

"On it," the giant said as his hatch popped open and Fey moved forward to assist from within her spider.

Minutes later the four of them finished swapping out the shattered front hatch window and bolting a plasma cutter onto the stub of the severed right arm. The sleeping cub didn't stir when they set out through the broken window of the building.

"Looks peaceful," Lily said from her lead position. "Don't see an ant or termite anywhere. No wait, there are a whole bunch of little ones crawling around those furry plants."

"Farmer ants," Sesco said as his Wakanda held its weapons upward away from the ant garden. "Look at the side of the ruins."

Xan focused on a nearby spot of color and zoomed in to see a balcony covered in the same multicolored plants. As Iktomi's connections with the other cyborgs examined the data, a file on the new species grew.

"Looks like they're growing and harvesting those three different plants," Xan said.

"They're a lot smaller than the ones in Wall, too," Gar said. "I wonder what their leg racks taste like."

"Do *not* kill one of them!" Sesco said loud enough to get everybody's attention. "They couldn't have a nest this big if they didn't defend it when they need to. They're peaceful now, but we don't want to test their defensive tolerances."

They made their way past the collapsed building without incident while getting video of the many tiny garden plots that dotted the rubble pile. Within a few minutes they were back on track and only an hour behind their best projected time.

"What was so important you had to get those trophies, Fey?" Tina wondered as they ran between the monster infested skyscrapers.

"I'm going to make a battle necklace for Wakanda. He deserves it. Strap it on his sensor bar and across his shoulders. It'll look good."

"Looks like we might get to add to that," Xan said as he scanned his rear camera view. Knowing the scene was being relayed to his teammates, he planted his feet in a practiced stop and reverse as he pulled the trigger on the shotgun in Iktomi's right hand.

The lead razorback's face disappeared in a bloody mess but it kept on coming. Engaging the plasma cutter, he stepped to the side as the blinded mutant pig ran by him. Swinging the cutter as it went past, he cut the leg off at the halfway point as he traded his shotgun for the 50cal pistol.

The elephantine razorback collapsed and rolled and he just had time to see his sister stab it through the skull with her plasma cutter before he had to face the next one. Luckily for him, the second razorback was more to the side and going after Lily. The hog wasn't as lucky as she put three well placed fifty caliber armor piercing rounds into its skull as he brought his cutter back into a defensive angle.

With seconds to spare he holstered the pistol and drew the fifteen-millimeter twin barrel rail gun. Even the prop the VR pod used felt heavy as he aimed at the next attacker and pulled the trigger. The heavy rounds cracked as they broke the sound barrier leaving the barrel and the nearest razorback's head disappeared.

He shifted his aim and emptied the rest of the magazine into another hog to his right, then holstered the RG and drew his grenade launcher. Laying a line of mixed shrapnel and thermal rounds in front of the next nearest monster, he remembered something he'd read in the papers his grandfather had given him.

"Let's move people! Razorbacks in these

numbers can only mean Ogres!"

Nobody argued as they turned and ran as fast as their cyborgs could move, although Fey grumbled about lost trophies.

Xan's HUD lit up with a flashing icon at the next crossing. "Take the left street!"

They were almost to the next crossing when the trained razorbacks spotted them. He emptied the grenade launcher more as a diversion than to hit anything at that distance. Smoke and fire from Lily and Gar gave them enough time to choose a direction without being seen.

"There!" Xan pointed toward a building with the window shattered and open.

They were all inside in seconds and as he went through, Xan reached up as high as he could and stuck a spy-cam on the arch over the entrance. Once inside they found a wide stairway and quickly climbed up from the two-story lobby. Safely out of sight and quiet, they watched through the spy-cam as razorbacks milled around the crossing. One dashed away in every direction and the one coming their way ran past without hesitating.

The spy-cam picked up the sound of a horn, then the responding squeals of the enormous hogs. Moments later the scout that had run by their building ran back the other way and several more gathered at the crossing.

"Uh-oh," Fey whispered as a pair of ogres came into view. "Might have to look for a back door."

The two hogs split up with one taking the opposite street and the other coming toward their hiding place. Their refuge was out of sight of the lobby and only had one access route, that could be defended as long as their ammo and power supplies lasted.

The ogre was in no hurry as it, *he*, ambled along, swinging his massive head from side to side. Standing over four meters high, the mouth sported twin tusks from the lower jaw. The tusks were anchored far enough back to not interfere with the bite of the slightly lengthened muzzle.

The body was heavily muscled with a thick skin covered in bony nodules bordered by a mat of fibrous hair. Obviously male, the ogre that approached their building carried a polished, dual-bladed sword with the base anchored at the wrist and forearm. The three-meter blades extended two meters from the fist grip and spikes adorned the base at the wrist. He wore no clothes but did have a huge leather shoulder bag hanging opposite the sword hand.

The massive mutated human walked purposefully down the street, examining everything on the ground as a pair of razorbacks flanked him. The ogre walked past their building with his eyes almost even with their camera as he looked down for signs of passage.

Xan heard more than one sigh of relief as the ogre moved slowly on. The spy-cams were made to blend into the surface of their anchor and should have looked like no more than a lump on the side of the building.

He was just about to relax in the belief they had eluded discovery when the ogre searching their street spun on a heel and lurched toward the spy-cam.

An immense eyeball filled the screen as the ogre growled like stone boulders being rubbed together. "I see you little morsels."

[29] The Race of Death.

"He didn't just say that," Fey grumbled as she put a protective cyborg hand over the still sleeping grizzly cub. "I ought to add his tusks to Namid's battle necklace since I didn't have time to collect the razorback tusks."

"Are you inside this old building, quivering in fear little morsels," the ogre's laugh was more garbled than his voice.

The massive man-monster backed away from the spy-cam and lifted a horn and blew three times, then he lowered it and peered at the camera.

"I am perplexed," the ogre's voice was like gravel grinding together. "The smell is food human mixed with a hint of grizzly, but the footprints are something I have never seen. There is also a garden scent that does not match local plant life."

"Do not hide little morsels. Come forth and play the game of life. We promise to play fair."

"What the hell kind of game are they playing?" Fey grumbled. "Hey boss, let's just kill them and finish delivering this special cargo."

Xan tapped at his screen to open the speaker on the spy-cam. "What kind of game do you suggest?"

"Depends on where you're headed," the ogre smiled at being spoken to, "whether you're just passing through or coming to loot our city."

"We're not looters, but we're not passing through either. Got cargo to deliver."

"Ah, going to see old Fourhands. That run

might make a good game. We'll do that."

"We haven't agreed to your game yet," Xan said through the tiny speaker.

"You don't get a choice little morsel," the ogre laughed as a female with another pair of razorbacks joined him. "This is my mate, Voice Of Wind, and I am Eye Of Eagle. When you are ready, we will give you one minute to run then we will chase you."

"What is the prize in this game?"

"If you win you live. If you lose, we eat you."

"What's to stop us from just blasting you into lumpy meat sacks, ya big overgrown…" Fey stopped when she remembered only Xan had a link to the spy-cam's speakers. "Tell him what I said, Boss!"

"I'll do that," Xan laughed. "You saw what we did to your pets. What if we decide to do the same to you instead of playing your game?"

The massive human mutant stroked his chin in thought. "You could do that, but I do not see the fun in that path. Ah, look, here come my children. The taller one is Dances With Thunder and the younger one is Reader Of Books. They will also run with us."

"Xan, look at the map," Sesco said. "It's only thirty-five klicks. With a one-minute lead there's no way they can catch us before we get to the rendezvous coordinates."

"As long as there are no surprises along the way," he said. "They've had plenty of time to set an ambush since they've figured out where we're going. No matter what, we have to go, and the longer we wait the better prepared they'll be."

"Okay, Eye Of Eagle, we're coming down. Any sign of breaking truce and people will start dying."

"I would expect no less in meeting my own in-laws," the gargled laugh was accompanied by a sincere feeling of humor tinged with respect.

"Okay, people, choose your weapons wisely. We'll be on the move as soon as possible with full knowledge we'll be attacked before we get where we're going. Fey, take care of your friend. Let's do this."

He drew his plasma cutter and sword combination with Iktomi's left hand and the 15mm rail gun in the other as he led the way down to the lobby. In a further sign of truce, he lowered his forward window as he reached the floor of the lobby. The ogres and their hunting razorbacks were arrayed in an arc in the street in front of the building.

"Ah, there you are!" Eye Of Eagle boomed, then turned to the others. "Look, my family, our morsels are each in their own package with extra prizes inside and there are enough for each of us to have our own with additional half servings to share."

Eye Of Eagle reached up and tore the spy-cam off the side of the building, crushed it in a huge fist, and threw the remains into the lobby. "You may have this back now that we can talk face to face like civilized people."

"Civilized!" Fey spat through Namid's

exterior speakers. "You intend to *eat* us! That's not very civilized."

"Ah, yes, that," the ogre said with a negligent wave of the three-meter sword in his left hand. "You see, we know who you are and who sent you. To be honest, the Eneseye in your bodies would be an impressive addition to our diet. My daughter told us that's what it's called, Eneseye, and it makes one age slower, heal faster, and even overcome fatal wounds."

"No offense to any of you, but I would rather have this wondrous elixir pulsing through my body than yours. But think of it this way, we honor you by choosing your essences to live on through us."

He smiled and Xan could feel the sincerity of the comment as the ogre continued, "Now step out into the street so we can begin. I give you my word none under my foot will move from this spot for the agreed minute."

"Oh look, father, that one has an appetizer. Can I have that one?"

"Yes, Dances With Thunder, but you must catch it on your own."

The open area in front of the building forced them to come close enough the grizzly cub stood on her back legs and gave a weak roar of defiance.

"How cute," Voice Of Wind said in as sweet a tone as grinding gravel could. "Look, Dances With Thunder, it's almost like it's saying 'eat me first'."

The cub backed up and jumped when Fey lowered her forward window, then rushed into her arms. Fey quickly stuffed the cub into the sleeping niche to the laughter of the four ogres and squealing of their pet monster pigs.

"Okay, time to run. Reader of Books has proven adept with correctly pacing numbers and will count to sixty. Begin now, please daughter."

The youngest ogre began counting as Eye Of Eagle continued, "I feel it necessary to warn you many of my in-laws and other Families do not agree with my attempts at fairness. If you encounter them before we catch you, feel free to wake them from the Dream Of Life".

"Didn't think we could trust you," Fey snapped as Reader Of Books continued counting.

"You may trust me to keep *my* word, young morsel. But I only speak for we four and our four-legged friends. Other families have their own Speaker. You have forty seconds now."

"What? But you kept talking!"

"Again yes, but I also told you when the sixty seconds started, thirty seconds ago."

Xan bowed from inside his spider and Iktomi copied the motion. "I thank you for the courtesy. Let's get moving people."

The others didn't waste any time as they bolted toward the open street, with him trailing. "How's your passenger, Fey?"

"Got a little whiney there to start because she went in head first, but once she got turned around enough to see me, she calmed down. The protein bars helped."

"Good. Go to Battle Red everybody. We're thirty-five klicks from the rendezvous point and ambush is a certainty. Iktomi, sensors to max."

His forward window rose and the internal HUD lit up with the immediate data feed as they ran at the fastest their cyborgs could move through the ruins. The street they ended up on used to be the style known as boulevard and the central strip contained large trees. Instead of staying on one side or the other, they used the trees in the center for cover with three of them on either side.

A horn sounded behind them when Eye Of Eagle's family began their chase.

"Delayed our start long enough they're going to catch us," Sesco said.

"Not right away," he replied. "We'll probably meet some of their kin long before then."

"Got something two hundred yards ahead on our left flank," Gar said from his lead spot.

"More of the same on the right," Fey said from the opposite side of the tree line to her teammate.

"Hold your fire on this first group unless they attack," Xan said. "Let's give them a chance to change their minds or take sides."

Surprisingly, the two groups didn't attack, but did converge in the street and battle *each other* after the cyborgs passed. After a couple of shapes fell, they split up with half chasing the spiders and half facing the other way in a battle line.

"No way to tell who is for whom," Xan said. "All I could get was feelings of restrained anticipation."

"The ones trailing us are keeping a steady gap behind," Lily said. "I have Anansi ready with fire and forget mini-missiles and targeting pictures loaded."

"I have mini missiles targeted, too," Xan reported from his left rear position.

"Movement on rooftops after the next corner," Tina said.

"Followers are moving up," Lily said. "Launch decision is now Anansi's."

"They're spreading out instead of coming at us," Xan said. "They're checking out every ambush spot at street level, protecting themselves instead of looking for attack options on us."

"Still doesn't put them on our side," Fey made her thoughts known.

"They're staying out of the way of whatever's waiting for us at the next corner," Xan said. "Their caution is defensive. I'm switching my targeting from the escort and putting them on fire and forget seeker ahead of us."

"I'm putting mine on forward target seeker as well," Lily said as their HUDs and screens flickered with added data constantly shared and updated by the six A.I.s.

Their escort of five ogres ran ahead to the corner on their side of the intersection, then watched them closely as they approached.

"Go to high alert in the crossing!" Sesco warned them.

"Who would have guessed, Brainiac!" Fey taunted as she and Gar led the squad across the crossing roads.

The crossing wasn't a boulevard and the scant cover of a line of old growth trees vanished.

Gar and Fey were almost across and their middle pair already in the killing field when the stones began to rain down on them.

"Launching missiles," Xan said as he tried to pick out targets with his twin, fifteens.

Three mini-missiles streaked upward and their targeting cameras showed only sky till they were well above the fifteen and twenty story buildings. When they turned to dive back down Xan saw the rooftops covered in ogres with slings holding stones as large as his head. The ogres twirled and twirled their missiles, then stepped forward, aimed and released all in one second.

With Iktomi compiling the data, a targeting triangle flashed and he aimed his rail gun and pulled the trigger just as an ogre stepped forward. The short burst shredded the top half of the man as the three missiles *chose* other targets and their screens went blank.

A stone crashed into Iktomi's shoulder and one of his remaining missile tubes flashed red. He re-targeted the remaining two and launched.

Others of his team had launched their own missiles and the view changed as each found a target while their own targeting algorithms allowed them to shoot just before an ogre leaned over the edge of the roof to launch a missile.

A well-aimed stone smashed into his right middle leg and red lights flashed as he began to feel the jarring of the leg as it continued to run as best it could. He was halfway across the intersection when their escort made their break to the next corner.

"Escort is safe on this side," Lily reported as

he and his teammate finished the crossing.

"Ditto this side," he reported as he took out the last rooftop ogre just before the last missile took out its target.

He plunged the empty twin-RG15 into its holster and Iktomi cycled a reload in three seconds. Pulling the heavy weapon from the holster he sprayed ten-round bursts wherever the A.I.s predicted enemy ogres *might* still be as two more missiles streaked skyward.

When they flipped to fall downward the scene showed the last of the ogres fleeing toward the doors to lower floors. One caught an ogre too slow to run and the other chased the last through the door to explode inside.

"Don't take to time to gloat people," Xan said as he picked his up pace. "Damage reports by team."

"Lead team," Gar said as they regained their top speed. "I have two missile tubes red-lighted but empty and a broken left forearm but still operable at sixty percent."

"Lead team," Fey was next as they ran. "My entire right-side missile battery is red-lighted and two tubes loaded. Right forward leg is flashing amber and my shotgun holster is crushed. I'll have to tear it off to get to the shotgun and I don't know if it is damaged."

"Team two," Tina said. "My sleeping niche is bent out of shape and two empty missile tubes flashing amber. Nothing else other than some missing foliage."

"Team two," Sesco spoke next. "Left front

leg's hip joint is alternating between amber and red, there's a huge dent in the left front corner of my bed, and that entire section is missing foliage."

By the time he and Lily finished the damage report, everybody knew everybody else's new handicaps and limitations. They continued at the fastest they could safely move and scan the buildings ahead, soon enough to act instead of *re*-act.

Setting their pace to match their slowest, they ran on with sensors probing every meter ahead they could reach. They were at the halfway mark when they heard three distinct long notes from a familiar horn.

"Park a half klick ahead," Gar reported.

"That'll be the next ambush spot," Sesco said.

"Watch your spacing," Xan reminded them. "Stones are going to come from between the trees and we don't want to be in rows."

Xan heard it just before his HUD identified the first target. The sound of the sling with the head-sized stone inside began to whistle as the ogre spun it up to launching speed. He matched another whistle to the trees it hid and fired before the HUD flashed and instead of a clean kill, he only blew off the sling arm of the targeted ogre.

"Maiming without killing is a useful tactic to divert enemy resources," Iktomi generously offered.

"I'm glad we switched sides," Lily said as she scanned the overgrown park on her side. "I know we're supposed to go outside our comfort zones, but I say *be comfortable* when circumstances warrant and I'm a lefty."

"Ditto," the rest of them replied at almost the same time.

Every dozen, ten-round bursts with his best ogre gun, Xan slid the cyborg-sized forearm pistol back into the holster. In three seconds, Iktomi refilled the internal, hundred twenty round magazine and recharged the power cells.

Even with their advanced technology and durable construction, the cyborg spiders still accumulated damage. Xan took a direct hit to his forward window that sent a spider web of cracks outward from the dead center impact point. The HUD continued to work, but it flickered and jumped between the branching spokes of cracks as the combined sensors tried to identify hidden ambushers and show it on his cracked window.

One ogre triggered the strangler vine he was using for cover and his friends took time out from hunting the six cyborgs to laugh at their friend before he freed himself. The ambushers they didn't kill ran out behind them and added their numbers to those chasing the running spiders.

"Where's our escort?" Lily wondered.

"Lost in the rest of our new chasers," Xan laughed. "I count thirty-seven and all of them are trying to look like they get along while glaring at anybody that comes close."

"Every once in a while, two of the groups following us get into a spat," Sesco informed them. "I've seen at least three fatal confrontations and twice that many with various degrees of wounds.

Our followers are of different loyalties and there's no way to know which ones are less than aggressive to us."

"Yeah," Fey laughed, "hard to decide when even your best ogre friends consider it an honor to eat you."

Their pace slowed again as three more legs fell victim to sling-fired boulders.

"Ten more klicks," Sesco informed them.

Xan glanced at his shattered HUD window to see their speed at 32kph as they left the old growth park and reentered the canyons between buildings.

Xan did a quick ammo scan and realized he was low on reloads for his favorite weapon. They had all gotten in the habit of an energy weapon in one hand and a slug thrower in the other and he decided to shift. Holstering his plasma sword, he drew the grenade launcher with the thermal and shrapnel alternating drum magazine. Both would be effective against ogres while being only moderately damaging to the spiders at close range.

Behind them the familiar horn sounded again and those following behind began to drive the middle to each side. Xan zoomed the rear camera to see Eye Of Eagle and his family, Voice Of Wind with Reader Of Books thrown over her shoulder in a fireman's carry. Blood soaked her shoulder and back.

The occasional ogre tried to block their path ahead but they were no match for the cyborgs' weapons. Fey and Gar closed the front of their formation as the ogres began to rush them for hand to hand fighting.

"Three more klicks!" Sesco called out as he exchanged his RG15 for a steel clawed glove with wrist spikes for close quarters fighting. "There's an Honor thing going here folks. Lose the slug throwers and go to swords and battle gloves."

"Do it!" Xan said as team leader and switched to a broadsword just as Eye Of Eagle came pounding up from behind. The ogre laughed as he easily deflected Xan's first swing.

"You will have to do better than that little morsel. I was almost thinking of letting you live after catching you, but my daughter has been grievously injured." The ogre had no trouble talking as he ran with only a little more gravel on rock sounds as he fended off Xan's harassing swings. "One of you has to die to give her the Eneseye she needs to survive."

Xan smiled and swatted again at the ogre as Iktomi adjusted his speakers to a whisper. "Do you see that supply cabinet door that just popped its lock? That cabinet holds one of my two main emergency med-kits."

"An enterprising man might tear that cabinet door off and pull out a supply crate with directions how to apply medical Eneseye *specifically designed* for battlefield injuries."

Eye Of Eagle slashed at the door then grabbed the edge, ripped it off, and began pounding Iktomi's right rear hip with it where the armor was strongest.

"If I fall away before you reach Fourhands' territory the others will be free to attack without hindrance," Eye Of Eagle said as he used the cabinet door to fend off Xan's ineffective sword swings, slung it into Iktomi's side window, grabbed the med kit and pulled it free.

"Save your daughter, we'll be fine," he said as he slapped the large crate in the ogre's hands with the flat of his sword.

Eye Of Eagle looked surprised for a moment, then smiled as he fell headlong on the ground over the med kit.

As if the fall were a signal, dozens of ogres let out battle screams that echoed within the canyons of the city. With increased intensity, the ogres rushed the six cyborg spiders en masse in a berserker rage.

"Hand to hand Honor is over," Xan yelled as he slashed the arm from an opponent. "Go to full battle weapons!"

The ogre numbers were so great their formation was stopped dead in its tracks two hundred meters from the cross street that was their rendezvous safe line.

[30] Fourhands.

"Circle formation!" Xan yelled as he swung around to back into his position and switched his broadsword for a plasma sword. "Gar take point! Everybody link your A.I.s to Misae and sound off. Iktomi is engaged in Circle."

The others quickly followed suit as they swung swords and slashed with plasma cutters, pieces of ogre flying in every direction. Gar's HUD told him when the last spider was linked to his and he started walking toward the rendezvous line less than two hundred meters away.

As Iktomi walked backwards Xan zoomed in on Eye Of Eagle and his family gathered around their prize and being ignored by the ogres trying to get at him and his friends. Several others circled the four but faced outward to protect them. He was busy for a few moments and when the line cleared again, he saw Voice Of Wind help her daughter stand.

The numbers attacking his position in the circle increased again and he took a blow to the sensor bar over his right shoulder that resulted in three more red lights. The wild-eyed ogre that landed the blow died before he could strike again.

"Can't you go any faster, babe," Fey asked. "Grizzy has to pee."

"I'm running inside here like when we trained, but Misae tells me this is as fast as we can go with our combined damage and maintain Circle. A hundred meters to go."

Xan concentrated on keeping his section clear, with heads and arms falling with every swing of his plasma cutter and his Battle Glove allowing him to throw bodies and body parts back into the crowd. The battle glove's gauntlet extended far enough back and over his forearm he could use it to block a club or sword without damaging the cyborg's arm.

He caught one sword on the downswing in the armor-clawed glove, snapped it with a twist of the wrist, and stabbed the former owner through the eye with the broken blade. As one ogre fell away, he stabbed another with his plasma cutter, then slashed another across the belly spilling blood and ropes of intestines onto Iktomi's forward hips.

They were almost to the street the ogres supposedly wouldn't cross when two wounded ogres being walked over surged up in the only weak spot in their circle formation. The weakness had been studied and a solution designed through programming and as soon as the danger was identified the linked A.I.s took control of certain arms and stabbed and slashed behind them till the two were in multiple parts and the attack neutralized.

Finished clearing the danger using sensors to avoid hitting their own cyborg bodies or the cargo containers, the hands returned to the position of the operators just in time for Xan to bring the plasma cutter down through the head and chest of an enraged ogre.

"I thought this street was neutral," Lily said as she stabbed an ogre Xan had by the throat in his battle glove. "Why are they still attacking?"

"I don't see the intelligence in their eyes Eye Of Eagle and his family had," Sesco said as the attacks began to slack off.

Xan cut the head and left shoulder and arm off an ogre wielding a tree with the remains of the root ball wrapped in chain link fencing. In front of him, what was the rear of their circle formation, only a few more screaming ogres lumbered toward them.

"Hey everybody, there's a line of ogres right at the center of the crossing street just watching our fight. I'm going to bet we're weeding out the lower end of the local gene pool. I'm calling it. Cancel Circle Formation Iktomi."

He immediately felt the change as his spider moved a couple of steps to adjust to the position of his legs, then he stepped forward to meet the next charging ogre.

As the others spread out from their circle and began to draw their own attackers. The ogres unable to refrain from a mindless bloodlust charged them in a steady stream, then only one or two at a time as the less cognitive ogres were killed.

When no others attacked for a full minute, Xan walked through steaming ogre body parts toward the obvious border.

"Ha, little morsel!" Eye Of Eagle boomed as he held up the medical crate. "If not for the interference of the mindless ones, I would have gotten more than this treasure!"

"Bah!" Xan responded with a wave of a gauntleted cyborg hand. "You got an old one past its expiration date."

Eye Of Eagle's laugh echoed inside the canyons of buildings as he motioned behind him. Reader Of Books walked out of the crowd, a little unsteady, but under her own power. "My daughter tells me the packaging date on the treasure is only a month ago. Anything less than a year from packing date is almost unheard of."

"No, little morsel, despite your cheating during an honest race and using the mindless ones to block me, I still bested you! Admit it for all to witness." He gestured grandly and the surrounding ogres cheered him, one of them slapping him on the back loud enough to echo between the deserted buildings.

Eye Of Eagle didn't flinch at the blow as he gloated with the medical pouch raised high.

Xan had already lowered his forward window so the ogres could see his face inside his spider. He scowled and made faces like he was trying to get around Eye Of Eagle's logic. Going on the emotions he could feel around him, he threw his hands up in frustration. "Okay! You win the *obvious* treasure of a fresh batch of Eneseye medical serum *instead* of getting to eat one of us."

"Ha! I knew it! Agreed, wait, oh you devious morsel. You tricked me into agreeing to not eat one of you in recompense for using the mindless ones to block me in the Honorable Race." He shook the medical kit in Xan's direction. "Okay, little morsel, I confirm my mistake in agreeing to your outlandish terms to conclude our verbal contract."

Eye Of Eagle gave a short bow that Xan

copied inside his spider. When both stood erect again the line of ogres cheered and the six cyborgs returned the celebratory posturing.

"Uh, now what, Boss?" Fey was the first to throw cold water on the mood... again.

Eye Of Eagle stepped forward as she spoke to Xan through their internal comm link. "You have made it across the agreed upon border of he we call Fourhands. He has waited for the usual negotiations to be completed before coming out to meet his guests."

The ogre gestured toward the building that covered an entire city block and was the only neutral spot in the entire area known locally as Ogre Mountains. Xan turned by reflex to see a two-legged cyborg stride out of a door constructed to that size. The cyborg walked on what were arms and hands in place of legs and feet.

"A fracking *Orbital*," Fey sneered as she raised her plasma cutter. "We're delivering cargo to a fracking Orbital. Xan, Tina, I've come to love you both the last few weeks, but, a *fracking Orbital*?"

"I would have thought all the ogres calling him Fourhands might have been a pretty good hint, *babe*," Gar laughed.

If Namid would have had a proper head instead of a thick sensor bar and missile tubes on the shoulders, Gar would have gotten a laser-like glare from his girlfriend. He wisely avoided looking at her screen inside his pod.

The four-handed cyborg stood as tall as their spiders, with arms and hands out of proportion to the VR pod that occupied the torso. Just like the gene-altered, orbital humans, the cyborg's arms and fingers were longer, but were considerably more muscular.

"Welcome, welcome," the Orbital said with a friendly emotional projection that almost overwhelmed Xan with its sincerity. "Thank you so much Eye Of Eagle and those other Mountain Families that supported logic and reason. I hereby Honor my Promise upon safe delivery of the six cargo containers. In seventy-two hours, total ownership of the Fourhands Block will become your legal property."

"For those delivering my cargo, now that you are here, we must hurry. Please follow me." The oddly shaped cyborg turned and hand-walked toward the door large enough for their spiders.

"Go ahead, little morsels," Eye Of Eagle's laugh was like boulders of granite being slowly crushed. "I have found it best to just do what he says and discuss the results with my family afterwards. Sometimes the only thing we disagree on is how he would taste."

Since their A.I.s confirmed the cargo successfully delivered they followed the oddly shaped cyborg into a building that took up the entire city block.

"First off, my name isn't Fourhands. That's just what my ogre friends call me. My real name is Neil. Uh, Neil Armstrong, a direct descendent of the original Orbital Armstrongs. And yes, I know, Neil A. is alien backwards. I've heard it my entire life and it quit being funny by the time I was six."

"Like I said, we don't have a lot of time now

you're here. Clock is a tickin' so to speak. Please follow me to the roof. Well, you won't follow me actually. Each of these elevators is able to hold one of you. Please step inside so you can complete your contracts."

"You're kidding me, right?" Fey hesitated. "Come all this way then step inside a box inside an Orbital fortress? Did I mention earlier that Grizzy has to pee?"

"Any accidents can be easily cleaned Miss Stratus, and special Eneseyes injected to ensure a level of controlled domestication rivaling that of Gar's hellhounds," Neil said as he led them into the heart of the ground floor of his chosen fortress.

"Like I said, time is short now you have arrived and secrecy is in jeopardy of being compromised. Please hurry, all our lives depend on it."

Xan didn't hesitate and chose one of the open doors. "Going up."

The ride was just like that of any elevator but when the doors opened, he faced a wide patio that held an odd framework with six legs and an egg-shaped environmental pod atop a large cargo doughnut. The pod was as oversized as Neil's cyborg was to its operator.

As each of them came out on the rooftop patio, their A.I.s took control of their cyborg bodies and backed their spiders up against the framework holding the oversized Orbital environmental pod.

Drones of all sizes swarmed them before they could do anything and all their weapons red-lined. There were more than a few curses and complaints, most of them from Frey, before all six cargo pods were offloaded, repositioned, and connected to the cyborg-sized Orbital launch vehicle.

"And that's all it was," Neil explained after the first successful test of the six launch pods. "I could build everything but the pusher-puller doo-hickies to get me into orbit without a huge smoke trail exhaust. My best friend with feet was the only one who could. Luckily, he also had a team recently trained in dealing with extreme adversity to deliver that means to me."

Tina calmed Fey as Xan spoke. "We've completed our contract, but our spiders are damaged to the point a return home could be defined as *problematical* at best."

"Oh, that is no problem," the Orbital waved a cyborg hand in dismissal. "I have the facilities to repair all six of your cyborgs, or there are other options. One is to construct two into copies of my two-legged cyborgs and carry a few additional spare parts strapped to your frames of the remainder of your spiders."

"There are sufficient materials to completely replace almost every part of your cyborgs, but the ogres take possession in just under three days. You would have to renegotiate with Eye Of Eagle after that."

"You can repair the spiders you have or claim and repurpose the two, two-legged backup units I constructed and use the two spiders for replacement parts.

"You mean just a walking junkyard of

parts?" Tina chuckled. "Won't that show a lack of any fashion conscience of a respectable level."

"Like rows of holstered death instruments is a fashion statement," Lily laughed. "So, what else do these two-legged cyborgs have to offer over our six-legged versions?"

"Well, for one, they feel more natural. I may be walking on my hands, but I would do that in microgravity too. And that's something else *dirtbags* get wrong, and, yes, that's what we call you. *You people* think we float around all the time. No, we don't, we exist in *micro and mini gravity* environments where we actually do walk around on our lower arms and hands, especially on the Moon, Mars, and Ceres. Those are our *power* limbs, arms and hands that are *stronger* than our upper pair, but just as dexterous when we need them to be."

"The bipedal model just feels right, it moves just like I do and there aren't things sticking out fore and aft like your spiders. Less stable, yes, and only a fraction of the cargo space, but it feels comfortably natural. I've done overnights in the field and slept soundly and safely in the current model." His massive cyborg suit gestured toward itself.

"So, what's next?" Fey pressed.

"As soon as I turn the operation codes to my building over to you, you will decide what you have time to do before leaving while I return to orbit to announce my success in war reparations."

"Well, doesn't that sound nice," Gar growled. "Exactly what reparations are you talking about?"

"The sentient ogres would be one," Neil replied with a sincerity Xan could feel through his empathic ability. "I have been able to inject a strain of cognitive advancements that counteract the mindless berserker mentality that was becoming dominant because of the gene bombs. Your culling of the excessive population of regressive specimens has been a positive addition to that corrective exercise."

Xan tried not to react to being used in such a manner as he spoke. "You've tampered with their genes."

Neil laughed. "Oh yes, long ago, that's the only reason there were some able to talk to you. Their lines were regressing at a rapid rate till I intervened genetically. In fact, before I upgraded their children in the womb, Eye Of Eagle's parents were nearing the same intellectual level as the ones that attacked you at the end of your most recent combat exercise. His children received the final adjustment along with several other unrelated second-generation ogre families."

"I enlisted enough ogres worried about their devolution to submit to an Eneseye bath that there's a sufficient base number to maintain a viable sentient population. The sentient strain may or may not cull the rest, but they will be as sentient as you or I. Now, if you don't mind, I would really like to go home."

"What else have you done?" Xan asked as they hooked up the cables and tubes to stock the launch vehicle with air and water.

"There's a hive nearby you may have

noticed was showing signs of a higher level of cognition. You passed it on your way here. I was able to send a drone into the queen's chambers and collect samples. About ten years ago the first of the uplifted attendants were born. Seems the queens aren't the smart ones, the male and female attendants are, six of each. The drones I've sent in the last four years have shown the twelve attendants starting to create art and the newest *supervisor* variant have begun to use some of the wheeled artifacts abandoned in the ruins. They're a new breed that can direct both workers and defense warriors. The only reason I didn't exterminate them was because they were nonaggressive farmer vegans."

"There are also several other species I have uplifted to sentience. Three simian species, a squirrel population, and one racoon family have been the most successful, but only time will tell if the latter two have sufficient numbers to survive considering their neighboring obstacles."

"In addition, I have inserted sterilizing formulas into the worst of the majority of the other gene-bombed species. Most of them will soon die out or revert to a more benign state, while the remainder will stabilize at their current evolution. In another couple generations, the Denver Wastes will be cleared of the worst aftereffects of our war."

"Now, let us go to my workshop and I'll transfer all my entry codes so you can choose how to make repairs to your vehicles."

"Wow, nice toy store," Fey stage whispered when they walked their cyborgs out of the row of elevators and into Neil's machine shop.

"There're only two Eneseye vats, and they're ogre sized because they had to be to save them from bestiality, so that's how big I made them," Neil explained. "There's time for each of you to get a full treatment if you wish."

Transferring the codes took only a few minutes and a quick tutorial later they returned to the roof to watch Neil's return to orbit.

The Orbital checked all the water tanks and the connections and fittings between the main cabin and the six propulsion pods, then the seals on all the cargo hatches in the launch vehicle's base. When he was satisfied everything checked out, he walked his four-handed cyborg over to Iktomi and opened the hatch. Even with arms for legs he was as tall as Xan when they stood face to face.

Xan and the others met him in front of their spiders and he shook hands with and thanked each of them and gave each a container of thick gray liquid. "That is my final gift to the Homeworld. The one flaw in your grandfather's wonderful Eneseye was that it wasn't self-replicating."

He pointed to the vial in Xan's hand. "The new nanites in those containers solve that problem. I know because I was fifty-nine when the gene bombs fell and over a hundred when I finally came up with a version for human testing. That was several years ago and I have not needed an Eneseye booster since."

"You look pretty good for a hundred and whatever," Fey said as she one-eyed the vial. "My legs and feet won't change into arms and hands, will they?"

"Heh-heh, no. The new nanites don't actually do anything more than construct a cyberneural interface with you and repair and replace the Eneseye that actually does the work of keeping you young and healthy."

"Wait," Xan said, "what cyberneural interface?"

"Drink the entire contents," Neil said, then tapped the side of his head. "About three or four hours after ingestion a three-note tone will sound and a voice will say, *neural interface on line,* and from there it's just like any voice activated computer. You tell it what to do and it does it using the Eneseye in your bodies."

"I've used mine to construct a HUD inside my eyes and extra sensors in the edges of my ears," he said as he ran a finger along one. "I didn't have the benefit of elven augmentation in the womb, but I now have a larger range through miniature tech implants constructed by my Eneseye."

"All my research has been loaded into the main computer and you'll be able to access that data to gain as much of my experience with the new process as possible before you leave. After you drink the contents, give the empty vials to my old friend and he and his genius friends will be able to make as much more as they wish."

"Oh, and each neural implant contains its own data files so you'll each be able to replicate my research with the proper lab equipment. Now, I don't wish to appear rudely abrupt, but I must leave you and return home."

Sesco spoke up as Neil turned to climb back into his four-handed cyborg. "Hey, won't people notice your takeoff and blow this building to rubble when they realize an Orbital lived in the heart of the Denver Wastes?"

Neil turned toward them as he clung halfway up the front of his cyborg. "No. They get their planetary data from my people and we have always replaced this flat launch pad with the original peaked roof and communications tower. They will delete the launch data as well and when you leave the ogres will occupy the building. A few months afterward the video of my original rebuilding of the rooftop with ogre laborers two years ago will be played and from then on the feed will be unaltered as the ogre tribes evolve."

"And now I must go," he said and finished crawling up the front of his cyborg. "You may take as much time as you wish to resupply, but remember, I have promised the ogres they can have the building when I leave. I would appreciate it if you stay long enough to teach them the basics of building care, but in less than three days they own this building and everything in it not claimed by you. Goodbye and thank you for bringing me the means to return home."

With that he shut the hatch and walked the four-handed cyborg around to the ramp up to the launch vehicle while they remounted their spiders. Once inside the upper dome lowered and sealed him inside. It took several minutes for him to run his preflight tests and his cyborg to give them a thumbs-up gesture through the window of the environmental pod.

The six propulsion pods began to hum and their sensors recorded the increase in energy as the pods pushed harder and harder at the gravity holding them down. The ship lifted slowly at first as Neil fed more energy to the gravity pods, then moved faster and faster. In less than a minute there was nothing more than a black spot in the sky, then only their strongest cameras could see him, then nothing.

"Well, that was anti-climactic," Xan muttered. "Okay people, let's get moving. The workshop isn't any different from any others we've been using since we got cyborgs, so we shouldn't take long to finish our rapidly fleeing benefactor's quickest conversion scenario. Then some basic training for whatever ogres want it and all our responsibilities are completed and we own what we wear out of here."

[31] Endgame death race.

"I like this body better than the spider," Xan said as he walked it around the shop two days later. "How about you Iktomi?"

"It has both pros and cons," the transferred A.I. replied diplomatically. "The head is a plus, the lessened stability a minus."

"Yeah, got that right. One of the cons being me not getting one, but this'll do," Fey said as she admired the cabin where the cargo pod used to be. Tall enough on the inside for Gar to stand up in, each cabin could *almost* comfortably house two giants.

The other three spiders also sported actual heads as well as new cabins, each with kitchenette, comfort closet, and giant-sized double recliner chair/bed. Spare arms and legs hung from the newly refurbished solar and camo vines and the upper decks were piled high with supplies.

"Well sis, what do you think?"

"I like this better, too. It moves more like me. The spiders were easy to learn, but six legs just never felt *natural*, especially when trying to kick with the corner legs. I felt more like I was driving instead of… you know."

"Yeah, same here. Even the few times when we sparred it felt just as natural as could be. Helps to have some of the weapons mounted permanent, too, even though our weapons choice and ammo supply is smaller."

He admired the single barrel, RG15

mounted on each forearm. Two holsters on each hip gave him four more weapons choices and sword sheaths behind his shoulders on either side of the rear hatch held twin bladed plasma cutters. Two-meter knives in calf sheaths, a forehead laser, and shoulder mounted mini missiles and grenade launchers rounded out his more limited arsenal.

"Good thing you figured out how to tweak the fabrication shop, sis."

"Heh-heh, had to once you kept adding new toys, little brother. Had to make everything bulkier to carry it all and still function. I'm just glad Neil's lab was up to the task in the time we had to work with."

"Well, I like my new arms better," Sesco said as he admired his own new replacements.

Xan shrugged and his new two-legged cyborg copied the move. "Figured since we were bulking up the ogre models, might as well upgrade the others too."

"Won't grampa be pissed?" Fey wondered as she inspected the upgrades on her spider's forearms.

"Don't care," Xan replied. "Part of the contract was that we get full ownership of our own spiders upon successful delivery of the cargo. Then Neil gave us full use of all the neat stuff in his workshop to do whatever we needed to do before we turn the building over to the new tenants. Done and done, right Eye Of Eagle?"

"Yes, little morsel," the ogre said with his hands clasped behind him to keep from breaking something else. "Reader Of Books says she and her brother and two cousins have passed the test the building A.I. gave them. The building says the other two students will be finished before the end of the day. That will be the six building caretakers needed to release you from your last duty."

"We'll do the changeover with the first light of day tomorrow," Xan said and bowed to the man that, at four-plus meters tall, was only slightly smaller than the five-plus meter, ogre class cyborg.

"Agreed, then we can have a race to see if you and your *cyborg* bodies are worthy of the name, Ogre."

"Wait, what?" Fey was indignant. "We already did that win-a-race-or-get-eaten thing. Why do we have to do it again?"

"You will be running through ogre territory, little morsel. *Everyone* passing through ogre territory either runs till they are out of our lands, or fights to the death. One good thing for you this time is the number of poor fighters has been considerably reduced. That means you will only be facing our strongest and smartest so your testing can be the best possible."

"And we have to do this every time we go through ogre territory?" Lily wondered.

"No, once in and once out makes you one of us, even cheating by wearing skins of power. If you live to the edge of our lands you will be given a proper name you will invoke whenever meeting one of my kind."

He looked into the window of the ogre cyborg and tilted his head. "I would not chance travelling outside your power skins, even with your proper name. Now I must inform the others to be ready to do a proper naming race for tomorrow. I will see you on the street at sunrise."

"Did that really just happen?" Lily said as they watched the huge man enter an elevator and head down to the lobby.

"Pretty sure it did," Xan snorted a laugh. "Well, we have till tomorrow to get ready. Has everybody got everything they want to pile on your cyborg? There's plenty of stuff left and once we leave, everything we don't carry out belongs to the ogres."

"Xan," Iktomi said in private mode, "the building A.I. has just informed me the final two students have passed their sentience level test. I have also been given access to the second basement level and told to take you all there now. The others are being informed by their A.I.s."

"Another suspicious secret," Fey muttered loudly as they moved to the elevators. "This Orbital is almost as annoying as your grampa, Xan."

They walked their cyborgs into the elevators again and when the doors opened Xan found himself in a long hallway lined with heavy steel doors. The hall was large enough to walk their cyborgs single file, but the doors to the side rooms were barely large enough for Gar to walk through without ducking.

Inside the first four vaults they found shelves and shelves of treasures looted from homes and museums. Paintings and sculptures lined the walls and covered the shelves. The next two contained trays of rolled silver, gold, and platinum coins of every denomination and from every country. One of the last pair held the nearly indestructible coins minted by the Orbitals while the one with the 'Open Me Last' note on the outside held six, cargo cyborgs. There was another note taped to the inside of the door.

"Well, that was nice of him," Xan said after scanning the message. "What it says is he sometimes got bored over the last few decades after the gene bombs fell and went exploring while he tested his cyborgs. After a while he collected stuff and already loaded his favorites into his launch vehicle, so we can have whatever we think won't cause us to lose the race out of here."

"How do these things work?" Gar examined the nearest cargo cyborg, each twice the size of a hellhound.

"Same as our spiders almost," Sesco said, then pointed. "The control collar is a voice actuated link to the cyborg with a level one A.I. operating system. Each one has its own control collar and their onboard computer can learn a couple hundred commands with up to ten syllables each."

"This model's teeth has knockout venom, and can carry five hundred kilograms of cargo inside the body cavity plus twenty liters of drinking water refilled by the early version of hydro vines. It can run 75kph when fully loaded and keep its partner's head and shoulders above water swimming across a river. In the last ground action before the Orbital War every infantryman that didn't rate the first-generation wearable cyborg suit had his own dire wolf class, cyborg partner."

"So, what do we do, Boss?" Fey asked as she eyed one of the dire wolf cyborgs.

"Just like the note says," he said as he waved it. "We take what we think won't weigh us down when we run from our friends who consider it an honor to eat us if they win."

When they gathered in the lobby the next morning, Eye Of Eagle was there with Voice Of Wind and Dances With Thunder. Reader Of Books stood off to the side with the newly named bear cub, Young Of Spirit.

The youngest ogre stepped forward and the cub stepped with her. "I thank you Fey, for the gift of this young one to join the clans of mountain ogres. The building A.I. assures me the domestication Eneseye injections will ensure she gives birth to a smaller and more restrained generation that will be valued members of our clan and tribe."

Xan could see Fey's lips moving through her closed forward window, but thankfully the sound was muted as the cyborg's torso with its new turret head bowed in response.

"I wish you both well," she said through her speakers in what sounded like she meant it as she rose from the bow.

"There are six of you and three from my Family declaring First Challenge rights. The additional challengers are my cousin Killer Of Griffin and our clan friends, Thrower Of Stones and Sword Of Death. It is still two minutes till first light. Do you wish to pray to your gods for a swift death?"

"Shove it up your momma's butthole you vulture's fecal stain!" Fey growled through Namid's speakers. "Just be glad this wimp Sword Of Dirt chose me to race so he could lose quick, or I'd teach you some manners!"

"I will strip you of dignity before I recycle your meat, wench!" Sword Of Death yelled as he waved a three-meter broadsword in one hand.

Xan shook his head in wonder at the spectacle. "One minute from the start you may begin your chase."

"One-minute lead time! Outrageous!" Eye Of Eagle boomed. "That was before Fourhands gifted you with newly improved skinsuits!"

He stamped a massive foot as Xan's countdown clock hit one minute to sunrise. "Thirty seconds lead time."

"No," Xan argued. "The same full minute we got on the way in. Our pledge to not use tech weapons negates your endurance and speed abilities. We will be in hand to hand long before we reach the border."

"Poor little whiney morsels!" Thrower Of Stones taunted. "What's the matter little morsel, got greedy and can't outrun a mean ol' ogre two years younger than you?"

Xan ignored the continuing argument as he mock-bickered with Eye Of Eagle. "The full minute is only fair considering the supplies we are carrying."

"Ha!" Eye Of Eagle gloated. "Your greed proves you are unworthy of consumption. When I win, I will probably feed your carcass to my garden. Maybe you will be better food for what our food eats than warriors."

Xan was still trying to come up with a better insult than that when the ten second signal came. Xan had time to realize it was a full minute when Fey started arguing with Sword Of Death and all the other ogres rushed over to watch and cheer as the sun cracked the horizon and Reader Of Books began her countdown.

There were, 'out of the way furry butt' and 'tick-tock little morsels' thrown about as they tried to get their cyborgs out of the lobby to even start to run as their minute counted down.

"Think we gave them enough delay time?" Gar wondered on a secure channel as they ran ahead of the chase team.

"It's pretty much the same half minute as the first time," Sesco said as they ran. "The only difference is the ambushers and the number of berserkers crawling over us while we run and we can only use swords and battle gloved fists."

"Actually, sounds like a lot more fun," Fey said as she turned and her spider cyborg gave Sword Of Death a double, one-fingered salute.

Gar's chuckle sounded in all their VR ears. "That's my girl."

They ran as fast as their upgraded cyborgs could move as overloaded with supply bags as they were and it was, predictably, not near enough. Eye Of Eagle was the first to catch up to them and begin taunting Xan.

"That's mine, you can't have it!" Xan

boomed through Iktomi's speakers as he swatted at Eye Of Eagle's hand a second too late.

The chasers plucked supply bags from the nets covering each spider and the two ogre cyborgs. All six were not just covered in more spare legs and arms than they could damage on the return trip to the Black Hills, but individual bags filled with plundered treasure, including vials of pure Eneseye specifically programmed to upgrade the recipient ogre.

The first six challengers fell away to be replaced with more. Holding to their pledge they only used swords and battle gloved fists to engage and slow their next new current challenger. Xan and the others taunted the ogres that chased them or cursed them when they plucked away one of the many treasure bags conveniently hanging about their cyborg bodies.

The last defensive move for Xan was when his dire wolf cyborg blocked Eye Of Eagle only ten meters from the end of the race on the designated border of ogre territory. The ogre snatched up a special gift from the dire wolf's back before missing a swipe at the cyborg.

After they crossed the line, Xan railed about Eye Of Eagle's cheating and Eye Of Eagle taunted him about losing so many of his treasure bags before his cyborg wolf escaped to join them across the finish line.

Once the race ended, the two groups met again on the outer boundary of ogre territory so Xan and his team could receive their ogre clan names.

"Beware of the hive people," Eye Of Eagle

said as they made their final goodbyes.

Off to one side Fey was out of her spider and wrestling with the arm of a female she'd befriended by race combat while Sesco was showing his newest drawings to another pair of ogres. In another group Tina and Gar showed their new friends how to administer the Eneseye they'd won by competition.

"Some*thing* or some*one* has made them angry," Eye Of Eagle said. "They have expanded the area their warriors prowl and become less tolerant of even non-aggressive intruders into their new borders."

Xan wasn't sure if a thank you would be insulting, even if they *had* been accepted into the ogre clans and everybody seemed to be getting along, so he simply nodded while keeping his eyes on the big man. Without another word, he climbed into his newly proven ogre class cyborg and they turned away from their new friends to go home.

"Hey Boss, that was brilliant hanging all those bags and crates all over us full of plunder from that four-handed critter's building. What made you think of it?"

"Heh-heh, Fey, it was a little bit of devious inside information," he replied as they trotted away from the ogre territory and headed for the hive nest inside the ruins of a collapsed skyscraper. "I was at one of the Library consoles and Reader Of Books asked me to read two sections of the book she's writing to see which sounded best."

He shook his head at the memory and his bipedal cyborg copied the motion as they loped along still adorned with dozens of *booty bags*, and more inside the cargo cabinets inside their cyborgs and hounds.

"She had these two descriptions of ogre social rules and they both thoroughly explained the unwritten laws of the race we had to run twice, just with different words. They both explained that all ogres make such a run into and out of all bordering neighboring Families' territories at adulthood to prove their worthiness. If they don't carry booty bags to offer as prizes for individual combat exchanges during the run, then each do battle for the entire run."

"The adulthood test is done one or two neighbors at a time while those crossing from one side to the other can be *attended to* by all Families. But regardless of the distance traveled through ogre territory, if you don't provide a prize for a running friendly fight with verbal insults, then the race really *is* for life itself."

"Wow, that's actually kind of awesome," Fey said. "Hey what name did everybody get? I'm Sharp Tongued Fighter."

"I got, Librarian Knowledge Speaker," Sesco said with pride that leaked through his sister to Xan.

"I'm, Strong Mind Talker," Tina said.

"Fierce Clan Mother, here," Lily identified her new Clan name as she smiled at Xan through the video link.

"I'm Fierce Short Warrior," Gar said with a laugh. "Only one other person ever called me short and didn't lose teeth before. Seems we got different kinds of names than the ogres. Hey buddy, Ol' Eagle Eye spent some extra time whispering to you, so you must be our Clan Head, Speaker, or whatever they call it. What Family are we?"

Xan was glad the ogre class cyborg didn't have actual facial expressions in its head as he scowled, but the individual cameras did show his response to his friends inside their VR pods.

"Our Family name is," he hesitated and blew in frustration through his nose, "Swift Running Morsels."

When he didn't add his own name, there were several obvious throat clearing sounds from his speakers. "Okay, okay, I am now known as, Cunning Tasty Morsel."

He ignored the noises coming through his communal speakers as he continued, "Okay, we're wasting time! Let's go see who or what is messing with our friends at the hive before we go home."

...End

From the author: Thank you for taking the time to read *Final Extinction.* If you enjoyed my Sci-Fi adventure, please consider telling a friend or posting a short review, as word of mouth is an author's best friend and greatly appreciated.

Thank you,
Rick A. Mullins

ABOUT THE AUTHOR

Rick A. Mullins

 When I was twelve, my older brother, Randall, turned me on to his copy of the Hobbit, then his Edgar Rice Burroughs' Pellucidar series, and thought… 'I can do that'… and I've been writing ever since.

After high school, I served four years in the Air Force, a year at Ohio University, two years of working travel, four years in the Navy, then another couple years of working travel before I finally returned to northern Ohio to become a factory drone. I retired in July of 2015, and now get to devote my full attention to my two favorite passions: writing my own sci-fi and fantasy adventures, and reading those from other authors.

I hope you, the reader, will enjoy the many worlds I have visited in my dreams and converted to sci-fi and fantasy adventures as I allow my imagination to entertain me at night, and you on these pages.

~Rick A. Mullins

BOOKS BY THIS AUTHOR

Godstone Mage

The Civil War is over. Slavery has ended, Changelings can no longer be skinned alive with impunity, and the non-magical can patent magic spells.

Two magical families, united in tragedy at the hands of black magic, seek justice western style against war profiteers in the age of steam.

Circle of Magic

Magic has come to a four-hundred-mile circle centered over northern Ohio.

Confrontation is inevitable as old ideas clash with new powers.

Is the Circle of Magic a gateway to hell… or an alien invasion?

BOOKS BY THIS AUTHOR

Mustang Riders

An alien invasion has begun!

Super genius, flying aliens have opened portals between Earth and thousands of parallel worlds in the multiverse.

Ravenous flying predators have followed them to our skies, and their hunger is insatiable.

Zombie Labyrinth

IS-42 made everyone immortal. The only problem was, it killed nine out of ten people first, and the dead ate half the survivors before things settled down.

Three years after the end of the world, a team of salvagers has discovered a mountain Labyrinth full of military equipment… and hungry zombies. Is an almost unlimited treasure worth the risk of being eaten alive?

Also by Rick A. Mullins

http://www.dreamquestbooks.com

WORLDHOLE SERIES

DRAGONHOME
MAGI
FLOATSTONE PIRATE
CRYSTALLINE DREAMS

T.F.T.M. BUNDLES SERIES

TALES FROM THE MULTIVERSE: VOLUME 1
TALES FROM THE MULTIVERSE: VOLUME 2
TALES FROM THE MULTIVERSE: VOLUME 3

TEMPORAL ZOO SERIES

TEMPORAL ZOO
TEMPORAL ZOO 2: ALPHA CENTAURI

NON-SERIES

CHANGELING MOON
CIRCLE OF MAGIC
CREATACEOUS ANOMALY
FINAL EXTINCTION
GODSTONE MAGE
MUSTANG RIDERS
ZOMBIE LABYRINTH